The Whale Isles
Lef
North Enwas
South Enwas
Bereswek
The North Reach
Ferrins
The Andrades
Sea
The North Teeth
The Jaws
The S. Teeth
Andrad
Orandrad
Perregal
Gont
Armouth
Gont Port
Kameber
South Port
Spevy
Oranéa
Gar-rilrion
Ea
Ebéa
Ea
Barnisk
Torheven
Reynian Mts
Mt Onn
Eskel
Great Port
The Toríkles
Kembermouth
Eskel
Way
Shelieth
Felkway
Waymarsh
Straits
O tokne
Ilien
Vissti
Leng
Perilane
Outer Innran
Kamery
Ported
The Closed Sea
Bars of Uny
Uny
Sowl
Namíen
Misk
Set
Dunnel
Wasny
The Great South Shoals
Isle of the Ear
The Kargad Lands
Hur-at-Hur
Mesreth
Atnini
Awabath
Tombs
Atuan
Karego-At
The Hands
Sattins
Vemish
Mishport
Yor
Venway
The East Reach
Ismay
Iffish
Sneg
Far Toly
Koppish
Tok
Insmer
Korp
Holp
Kopp
Apso
The Sellets
Rolameny
Soders
Gale
Pelimer
Gosk
Kornay
Astowell
Ursula K. Le Guin

Tales From Earthsea
&
The Other Wind

Books by Ursula K. Le Guin

The Books of Earthsea
A Wizard of Earthsea
The Tombs of Atuan
The Farthest Shore
Tehanu
Tales from Earthsea
The Other Wind

Other Novels
The Lathe of Heaven
Very Far Away from Anywhere Else
The Eye of the Heron
The Beginning Place
Threshold
Always Coming Home

Orisinia
Orisinian Tales
Malafrena

The Hainish Novels
Rocannon's World
Planet of Exile
City of Illusions
The Left Hand of Darkness
The Word for World Is Forest
The Dispossessed
The Telling

Story Collections
The Wind's Twelve Quarters
The Compass Rose
Buffalo Gals and Other Animal Presences
Searoad: The Chronicles of Klatsand
A Fisherman of the Inland Sea
Four Ways to Forgiveness
Unlocking the Air and Other Stories

Nonfiction
The Language of the Night
Dancing at the End of the World

Tales From Earthsea
&
The Other Wind

Ursula K. Le Guin

SF BC
FANTASY

Originally published in hardcover by Harcourt, Inc. May 2001

Originally published in hardcover by Harcourt, Inc. September 2001

First SFBC Science Fiction Printing: October 2001

Published by arrangement with:
Harcourt, Inc.
15 East 26th Street
New York, NY 10010

Visit the SFBC online at http://www.sfbc.com
Visit Harcourt's website at http://www.harcourtbooks.com/

ISBN: 0-7394-2123-9

PRINTED IN THE UNITED STATES OF AMERICA

CONTENTS

Tales From Earthsea

Contents

The Inner Lands of the Archipelago

An eighth-century map from the Isle of Ark

This is a teaching map, not a sailing chart, as the proportions of the islands are exaggerated, though their relative positions and distances are fairly accurate. There is no writing of any kind on the map. The lost island of Soléa is shown by a spiral.

Foreword

AT THE END OF the fourth book of Earthsea, *Tehanu,* the story had arrived at what I felt to be *now.* And, just as in the now of the so-called real world, I didn't know what would happen next. I could guess, foretell, fear, hope, but I didn't know.

Unable to continue Tehanu's story (because it hadn't happened yet) and foolishly assuming that the story of Ged and Tenar had reached its happily-ever-after, I gave the book a subtitle: "The Last Book of Earthsea."

O foolish writer. *Now* moves. Even in storytime, dreamtime, once-upon-a-time, *now* isn't *then.*

Seven or eight years after *Tehanu* was published, I was asked to write a story set in Earthsea. A mere glimpse at the place told me that things had been happening there while I wasn't looking. It was high time to go back and find out what was going on *now.*

I also wanted information on various things that had happened back *then,* before Ged and Tenar were born. A good deal about Earthsea, about wizards, about Roke Island, about dragons, had begun to puzzle me. In order to understand current events, I needed to do some historical research, to spend some time in the Archives of the Archipelago.

The way one does research into nonexistent history is to tell the story and find out what happened. I believe this isn't very different from what historians of the so-called real world do. Even if we are present at some historic event, do we comprehend it—can we even remember it—until we can tell it as a story? And for events in times or places outside our own experience, we have nothing to go on but the stories other people tell us. Past events exist, after all, only in memory, which is a form of imagination. The event is real *now,* but once it's *then,* its continuing reality is entirely up to us, dependent on our energy and honesty. If we let it drop from memory, only imagination can restore the least glimmer of it. If we lie about the past, forcing it to tell a story we want it to tell, to mean what we want it to mean, it loses its reality, becomes a fake. To bring the past along with us through time in the hold-alls of myth and history is a heavy undertaking; but as Lao Tzu says, wise people march along with the baggage wagons.

When you construct or reconstruct a world that never existed, a wholly fictional history, the research is of a somewhat different order, but the basic impulse and techniques are much the same. You look at what happens and try to see why it happens, you listen to what the people there tell you and watch what they do, you think about it seriously, and you try to tell it honestly, so that the story will have weight and make sense.

The five tales in this book explore or extend the world established by the first four Earthsea novels. Each is a story in its own right, but they will profit by being read after, not before, the novels.

"The Finder" takes place about three hundred years before the time of the novels, in a dark and troubled time; its story casts light on how some of the customs and institutions of the Archipelago came to be. "The Bones of the Earth" is about the wizards who taught the wizard who first taught Ged, and shows that it takes more than one mage to stop an earthquake. "Darkrose and Diamond" might take place at any time during the last couple of hundred years in Earthsea; after all, a love story can happen at any time, anywhere. "On the High Marsh" is a story from the brief but eventful six years that Ged was Archmage of Earthsea. And the last story, "Dragonfly," which takes place a few years after the end of *Tehanu,* is the bridge between that book and the next one, *The Other Wind* (to be published soon). A dragon bridge.

So that my mind could move about among the years and centuries wihout getting things all out of order, and to keep contradictions and discrepancies at a minimum while I was writing these stories, I became (somewhat) more systematic and methodical, and put my knowledge of the peoples and their history together into "A Description of Earthsea." Its function is like that of the first big map I drew of all the Archipelago and the Reaches, when I began to work on *A Wizard of Earthsea* over thirty years ago: I needed to know where things are, and how to get from here to there—in time as well as in space.

Because this kind of fictional fact, like maps of imaginary realms, is of real interest to some readers, I include the description after the stories. I also redrew the geographical maps for this book, and while doing so, happily discovered a very old one in the Archives in Havnor.

In the years since I began to write about Earthsea I've changed, of course, and so have the people who read the books. All times are changing times, but ours is one of massive, rapid moral and mental transformation. Archetypes turn into millstones, large simplicities get complicated, chaos becomes elegant, and what everybody knows is true turns out to be what some people used to think.

It's unsettling. For all our delight in the impermanent, the entrancing flicker of electronics, we also long for the unalterable. We cherish the old stories for their changelessness. Arthur dreams eternally in Avalon. Bilbo can go "there and back again," and "there" is always the beloved familiar Shire. Don Quixote sets out forever to kill a windmill . . . So people turn to the realms of fantasy for stability, ancient truths, immutable simplicities.

And the mills of capitalism provide them. Supply meets demand. Fantasy becomes a commodity, an industry.

Commodified fantasy takes no risks: it invents nothing, but imitates and trivialises. It proceeds by depriving the old stories of their intellectual and ethical complexity, turning their action to violence, their actors to dolls, and their truth-telling to sentimental platitude. Heroes brandish their swords, lasers, wands, as mechanically as combine harvesters, reaping profits. Profoundly disturbing moral choices are sanitized, made cute, made safe. The passionately conceived ideas of the great storytellers are copied, stereotyped, reduced to toys, molded in bright-colored plastic, advertised, sold, broken, junked, replaceable, interchangeable.

What the commodifiers of fantasy count on and exploit is the insuperable imagination of the reader, child or adult, which gives even these dead things life—of a sort, for a while.

Imagination like all living things lives *now,* and it lives with, from, on true change. Like all we do and have, it can be co-opted and degraded; but it survives commercial and didactic exploitation. The land outlasts the empires. The conquerors may leave desert where there was forest and meadow, but the rain will fall, the rivers will run to the sea. The unstable, mutable, untruthful realms of Once-upon-a-time are as much a part of human history and thought as the nations in our kaleidoscopic atlases, and some are more enduring.

We have inhabited both the actual and the imaginary realms for a long time. But we don't live in either place the way our parents or ancestors did. Enchantment alters with age, and with the age.

We know a dozen different Arthurs now, all of them true. The Shire changed irrevocably even in Bilbo's lifetime. Don Quixote went riding out to Argentina and met Jorge Luis Borges there. *Plus c'est la même chose, plus ça change.*

It's been a joy to me to go back to Earthsea and find it still there, entirely familiar, and yet changed and still changing. What I thought was going to happen isn't what's happening, people aren't who—or what—I thought they were, and I lose my way on islands I thought I knew by heart.

So these are reports of my explorations and discoveries: tales from Earthsea for those who have liked or think they might like the place, and who are willing to accept these hypotheses:

things change:

authors and wizards are not always to be trusted:

nobody can explain a dragon.

The Finder

I. In the Dark Time

THIS IS THE FIRST PAGE of the *Book of the Dark,* written some six hundred years ago in Berila, on Enlad:

> "After Elfarran and Morred perished and the Isle of Soléa sank beneath the sea, the Council of the Wise governed for the child Serriadh until he took the throne. His reign was bright but brief. The kings who followed him in Enlad were seven, and their realm increased in peace and wealth. Then the dragons came to raid among the western lands, and wizards went out in vain against them. King Akambar moved the court from Berila in Enlad to the City of Havnor, whence he sent out his fleet against invaders from the Kargad Lands and drove them back into the East. But still they sent raiding ships even as far as the Inmost Sea. Of the fourteen Kings of Havnor the last was Maharion, who made peace both with the dragons and the Kargs, but at great cost. And after the Ring of the Runes was broken, and Erreth-Akbe died with the great dragon, and Maharion the Brave was killed by treachery, it seemed that no good thing happened in the Archipelago.
>
> "Many claimed Maharion's throne, but none could keep it, and the quarrels of the claimants divided all loyalties. No commonwealth was left and no justice, only the will of the wealthy. Men of noble houses, merchants, and pirates, any who could hire soldiers and wizards called himself a lord,

claiming lands and cities as his property. The warlords made those they conquered slaves, and those they hired were in truth slaves, having only their masters to safeguard them from rival warlords seizing the lands, and sea-pirates raiding the ports, and bands and hordes of lawless, miserable men dispossessed of their living, driven by hunger to raid and rob."

The *Book of the Dark,* written late in the time it tells of, is a compilation of self-contradictory histories, partial biographies, and garbled legends. But it's the best of the records that survived the dark years. Wanting praise, not history, the warlords burnt the books in which the poor and powerless might learn what power is.

But when the lore-books of a wizard came into a warlord's hands he was likely to treat them with caution, locking them away to keep them harmless or giving them to a wizard in his hire to do with as he wished. In the margins of the spells and word lists and in the endpapers of these books of lore a wizard or his prentice might record a plague, a famine, a raid, a change of masters, along with the spells worked in such events and their success or unsuccess. Such random records reveal a clear moment here and there, though all between those moments is darkness. They are like glimpses of a lighted ship far out at sea, in darkness, in the rain.

And there are songs, old lays and ballads from small islands and from the quiet uplands of Havnor, that tell the story of those years.

Havnor Great Port is the city at the heart of the world, white-towered above its bay; on the tallest tower the sword of Erreth-Akbe catches the first and last of daylight. Through that city passes all the trade and commerce and learning and craft of Earthsea, a wealth not hoarded. There the King sits, having returned after the healing of the Ring, in sign of healing. And in that city, in these latter days, men and women of the islands speak with dragons, in sign of change.

But Havnor is also the Great Isle, a broad, rich land; and in the villages inland from the port, the farmlands of the slopes of Mount Onn, nothing ever changes much. There a song worth singing is likely to be sung again. There old men at the tavern talk of Morred as if they had known him when they too were young and heroes. There girls walking out to fetch the cows home tell stories of the women of the Hand, who are forgotten everywhere else in the world, even on Roke, but remembered among those silent, sunlit roads and fields and in the kitchens by the hearths where housewives work and talk.

In the time of the kings, mages gathered in the court of Enlad and later in the court of Havnor to counsel the king and take counsel together, using their arts to pursue goals they agreed were good. But in the dark years, wizards sold their skills to the highest bidder, pitting their powers one against the other in duels and combats of sorcery, careless of the evils they did, or worse than careless. Plagues and famines, the failure of springs of water, summers with no rain and years with no summer, the birth of sickly and monstrous young to sheep and cattle, the birth of sickly and monstrous children to the people of the isles—all these things were charged to the practices of wizards and witches, and all too often rightly so.

So it became dangerous to practice sorcery, except under the protection of a strong warlord; and even then, if a wizard met up with one whose powers were greater than his own, he might be destroyed. And if a wizard let down his guard among the common folk, they too might destroy him if they could, seeing him as the source of the worst evils they suffered, a malign being. In those years, in the minds of most people, all magic was black.

It was then that village sorcery, and above all women's witchery, came into the ill repute that has clung to it since. Witches paid dearly for practicing the arts they thought of as their own. The care of pregnant beasts and women, birthing, teaching the songs and rites, the fertility and order of field and garden, the building and care of the house and its furniture, the mining of ores and metals—these great things had always been in the charge of women. A rich lore of spells and charms to ensure the good outcome of such undertakings was shared among the witches. But when things went wrong at the birth, or in the field, that would be the witches' fault. And things went wrong more often than right, with the wizards warring, using poisons and curses recklessly to gain immediate advantage without thought for what followed after. They brought drought and storm, blights and fires and sicknesses across the land, and the village witch was punished for them. She didn't know why her charm of healing caused the wound to gangrene, why the child she brought into the world was imbecile, why her blessing seemed to burn the seed in the furrows and blight the apple on the tree. But for these ills, somebody had to be to blame: and the witch or sorcerer was there, right there in the village or the town, not off in the warlord's castle or fort, not protected by armed men and spells of defense. Sorcerers and witches were drowned in the poisoned wells, burned in the withered fields, buried alive to make the dead earth rich again.

So the practice of their lore and the teaching of it had become perilous. Those who undertook it were often those already outcast, crippled, deranged, without family, old—women and men who had little to lose. The wise man and wise woman, trusted and held in reverence, gave way to the stock figures of the shuffling, impotent village sorcerer with his trickeries, the hag-witch with her potions used in aid of lust, jealousy, and malice. And a child's gift for magic became a thing to dread and hide.

This is a tale of those times. Some of it is taken from the *Book of the Dark,* and some comes from Havnor, from the upland farms of Onn and the woodlands of Faliern. A story may be pieced together from such scraps and fragments, and though it will be an airy quilt, half made of hearsay and half of guesswork, yet it may be true enough. It's a tale of the Founding of Roke, and if the Masters of Roke say it didn't happen so, let them tell us how it happened otherwise. For a cloud hangs over the time when Roke first became the Isle of the Wise, and it may be that the wise men put it there.

II. Otter

There was an otter in our brook
That every mortal semblance took,
Could any spell of magic make,
And speak the tongues of man and drake.
So runs the water away, away,
So runs the water away.

OTTER WAS THE SON of a boatwright who worked in the shipyards of Havnor Great Port. His mother gave him his country name; she was a farm woman from Endlane village, around northwest of Mount Onn. She had come to the city seeking work, as many came. Decent folk in a decent trade in troubled times, the boatwright and his family were anxious not to come to notice lest they come to grief. And so, when it became clear that the boy had a gift of magery, his father tried to beat it out of him.

"You might as well beat a cloud for raining," said Otter's mother.

"Take care you don't beat evil into him," said his aunt.

"Take care he doesn't turn your belt on you with a spell!" said his uncle.

But the boy played no tricks against his father. He took his beatings in silence and learned to hide his gift.

It didn't seem to him to amount to much. It was such an easy matter to him to make a silvery light shine in a dark room, or find a lost pin by thinking about it, or true up a warped joint by running his hands over the wood and talking to it, that he couldn't see why they made a fuss over such things. But his father raged at him for his "shortcuts," even struck him once on the mouth when he was talking to the work, and insisted that he do his carpentry with tools, in silence.

His mother tried to explain. "It's as if you'd found some great jewel," she said, "and what's one of us to do with a diamond but hide it? Anybody rich enough to buy it from you is strong enough to kill you for it. Keep it hid. And keep away from great people and their crafty men!"

"Crafty men" is what they called wizards in those days.

One of the gifts of power is to know power. Wizard knows wizard, unless the concealment is very skillful. And the boy had no skills at all except in boat-building, of which he was a promising scholar by the age of twelve. About that time the midwife who had helped his mother at his birth came by and said to his parents, "Let Otter come to me in the evenings after work. He should learn the songs and be prepared for his naming day."

That was all right, for she had done the same for Otter's elder sister, and so his parents sent him to her in the evenings. But she taught Otter more than the song of the Creation. She knew his gift. She and some men and women like her, people of no fame and some of questionable reputation, had all in some degree that gift; and they shared, in secret, what lore and craft they had. "A gift untaught is a ship unguided," they said to Otter, and they taught him all they knew. It wasn't much, but there were some beginnings of the great arts in it; and though he felt uneasy at deceiving his parents, he couldn't resist this knowledge, and the kindness and praise of his poor teachers. "It will do you no harm if you never use it for harm," they told him, and that was easy for him to promise them.

At the stream Serrenen, where it runs within the north wall of the city, the midwife gave Otter his true name, by which he is remembered in islands far from Havnor.

Among these people was an old man whom they called, among themselves, the Changer. He showed Otter a few spells of illusion; and when the boy was fifteen or so, the old man took him out into the fields by Serrenen to show him the one spell of true change he knew. "First let's see you turn that bush into the seeming of a tree," he said, and promptly Otter did so. Illusion came so easy to the boy that the old man took alarm. Otter had to beg and wheedle him for any further teaching and finally to promise him, swearing on his own true and secret name, that if he learned the Changer's great spell he would never use it but to save a life, his own or another's.

Then the old man taught it to him. But it wasn't much use, Otter thought, since he had to hide it.

What he learned working with his father and uncle in the shipyard he could use, at least; and he was becoming a good craftsman, even his father would admit that.

Losen, a sea-pirate who called himself King of the Inmost Sea, was then the chief warlord in the city and all the east and south of Havnor. Exacting tribute from that rich domain, he spent it to increase his soldiery and the fleets he sent out to take slaves and plunder from other lands. As Otter's uncle said, he kept the shipwrights busy. They were grateful to have work in a time when men seeking work found only beggary, and rats ran in the courts of Maharion. They did an honest job, Otter's father said, and what the work was used for was none of their concern.

But the other learning he had been given had made Otter touchy in these matters, delicate of conscience. The big galley they were building now would be rowed to war by Losen's slaves and would bring back slaves as cargo. It galled him to think of the good ship in that vicious usage. "Why can't we build fishing boats, the way we used to?" he asked, and his father said, "Because the fishermen can't pay us."

"Can't pay us as well as Losen does. But we could live," Otter argued.

"You think I can turn the King's order down? You want to see me sent to row with the slaves in the galley we're building? Use your head, boy!"

So Otter worked along with them with a clear head and an angry heart. They were in a trap. What's the use of a gift of power, he thought, if not to get out of a trap?

His conscience as a craftsman would not let him fault the carpentry of the ship in any way; but his conscience as a wizard told him he could put a hex on her, a curse woven right into her beams and hull. Surely that was using the secret art to a good end? For harm, yes, but only to harm the harmful. He did not talk to his teachers about it. If he was doing wrong, it was none of their fault and they would know nothing about it. He thought about it for a long time, working out how to do it, making the spell very carefully. It was the reversal of a finding charm: a losing charm, he called it to himself. The ship would float, and handle well, and steer, but she would never steer quite true.

It was the best he could do in protest against the misuse of good work and a good ship. He was pleased with himself. When the ship was launched (and all seemed well with her, for her fault would not show up until she was out on the open sea) he could not keep from his teachers what he had done, the little circle of old men and midwives, the young hunchback who could speak with the dead, the blind girl who knew the names of things. He told them his trick, and the blind girl laughed, but the old people said, "Look out. Take care. Keep hidden."

In Losen's service was a man who called himself Hound, because, as he said, he had a nose for witchery. His employment was to sniff Losen's food and drink and garments and women, anything that might be used by enemy wizards against him; and also to inspect his warships. A ship is a fragile thing in a dangerous element, vulnerable to spells and hexes. As soon as Hound came aboard the new galley he scented something. "Well, well," he said, "who's this?" He walked to the helm and put his hand on it. "This is clever," he said. "But who is it? A newcomer, I think." He sniffed appreciatively. "Very clever," he said.

They came to the house in Boatwright Street after dark. They kicked the door in, and Hound, standing among the armed and armored men, said, "Him. Let the others be." And to Otter he said, "Don't move," in a low, amicable voice. He sensed great power in the young man, enough that he was a little afraid of him. But Otter's distress was too great and his training too slight for him to think of using magic to free himself or stop the men's brutality. He flung himself at them and fought them like an animal till they knocked him on the head. They broke Otter's father's jaw and beat his aunt and mother senseless to teach them not to bring up crafty men. Then they carried Otter away.

Not a door opened in the narrow street. Nobody looked out to see what the noise was. Not till long after the men were gone did some neighbors creep out to comfort Otter's people as best they could. "Oh, it's a curse, a curse, this wizardry!" they said.

Hound told his master that they had the hexer in a safe place, and Losen said, "Who was he working for?"

"He worked in your shipyard, your highness." Losen liked to be called by kingly titles.

"Who hired him to hex the ship, fool?"

"It seems it was his own idea, your majesty."

"Why? What was he going to get out of it?"

Hound shrugged. He didn't choose to tell Losen that people hated him disinterestedly.

"He's crafty, you say. Can you use him?"

"I can try, your highness."

"Tame him or bury him," said Losen, and turned to more important matters.

Otter's humble teachers had taught him pride. They had trained into him a deep contempt for wizards who worked for such men as Losen, letting fear or greed pervert magic to evil ends. Nothing, to his mind, could be more despicable than such a betrayal of their art. So it troubled him that he couldn't despise Hound.

He had been stowed in a storeroom of one of the old palaces that Losen had appropriated. It had no window, its door was cross-grained oak barred with iron, and spells had been laid on that door that would have kept a far more experienced wizard captive. There were men of great skill and power in Losen's pay.

Hound did not consider himself to be one of them. "All I have is a nose," he said. He came daily to see that Otter was recovering from his concussion and dislocated shoulder, and to talk with him. He was, as far as Otter could see, well-meaning and honest. "If you won't work for us they'll kill you," he said. "Losen can't have fellows like you on the loose. You'd better hire on while he'll take you."

"I can't."

Otter stated it as an unfortunate fact, not as a moral assertion. Hound looked at him with appreciation. Living with the pirate king, he was sick of boasts and threats, of boasters and threateners.

"What are you strongest in?"

Otter was reluctant to answer. He had to like Hound, but didn't have to trust him. "Shape-changing," he mumbled at last.

"Shape-taking?"

"No. Just tricks. Turn a leaf to a gold piece. Seemingly."

In those days they had no fixed names for the various kinds and arts of magic, nor were the connections among those arts clear. There was—as the wise men of Roke would say later—no science in what they knew. But Hound knew pretty surely that his prisoner was concealing his talents.

"Can't change your own form, even seemingly?"

Otter shrugged.

It was hard for him to lie. He thought he was awkward at it because he had no practice. Hound knew better. He knew that magic itself resists untruth. Conjuring, sleight of hand, and false commerce with the dead are counterfeits of magic, glass to the diamond, brass to the gold. They are fraud, and lies flourish in that soil. But the art of magic, though it may be used for false ends, deals with what is real, and the words it works with are the true words. So true wizards find it hard to lie about their art. In their heart they know that their lie, spoken, may change the world.

Hound was sorry for him. "You know, if it was Gelluk questioning you, he'd have everything you know out of you just with a word or two, and your wits with it. I've seen what old Whiteface leaves behind when he asks questions. Listen, can you work with the wind at all?"

Otter hesitated and said, "Yes."

"D'you have a bag?"

Weatherworkers used to carry a leather sack in which they said they kept the winds, untying it to let a fair wind loose or to capture a contrary one. Maybe it was only for show, but every weatherworker had a bag, a great long sack or a little pouch.

"At home," Otter said. It wasn't a lie. He did have a pouch at home. He kept his fine-work tools and his bubble level in it. And he wasn't altogether lying about the wind. Several times he had managed to bring a bit of magewind into the sail of a boat, though he had no idea how to combat or control a storm, as a ship's weatherworker must do. But he thought he'd rather drown in a gale than be murdered in this hole.

"But you wouldn't be willing to use that skill in the King's service?"

"There is no king in Earthsea," the young man said, stern and righteous.

"In my master's service, then," Hound amended, patient.

"No," Otter said, and hesitated. He felt he owed this man an explanation. "See, it's not so much won't as can't. I thought of making plugs in the planking of that galley, near the keel—you know what I mean by plugs? They'd work out as the timbers work when she gets in a heavy sea." Hound nodded. "But I couldn't do it. I'm a shipbuilder. I can't build a ship to sink. With the men aboard her. My hands wouldn't do it. So I did what I could. I made her go her own way. Not his way."

Hound smiled. "They haven't undone what you did yet, either," he said. "Old Whiteface was crawling all over her yesterday, growling and muttering. Ordered the helm replaced." He meant Losen's chief mage, a pale man from the North named Gelluk, who was much feared in Havnor.

"That won't do it."

"Could you undo the spell you put on her?"

A flicker of complacency showed in Otter's tired, battered young face. "No," he said. "I don't think anybody can."

"Too bad. You might have used that to bargain with."

Otter said nothing.

"A nose, now, is a useful thing, a salable thing," Hound went on. "Not that I'm looking for competition. But a finder can always find work, as they say . . . You ever been in a mine?"

The guesswork of a wizard is close to knowledge, though he may not know what it is he knows. The first sign of Otter's gift, when he was two or three years old, was his ability to go straight to anything lost, a dropped nail, a mislaid tool, as soon as he understood the word for it. And as a boy one of his dearest pleasures had been to go alone out into the countryside and wander along the lanes or over the hills, feeling through the soles of his bare feet and throughout his body the veins of water underground, the lodes and knots of ore, the lay and interfolding of the kinds of rock and earth. It was as if he walked in a great building, seeing its passages and rooms, the descents to airy caverns, the glimmer of branched silver in the walls; and as he went on, it was as if his body became the body of earth, and he knew its arteries and organs and muscles as his own. This power had been a delight to him as a boy. He had never sought any use for it. It had been his secret.

He did not answer Hound's question.

"What's below us?" Hound pointed to the floor, paved with rough slate flags.

Otter was silent a while. Then he said in a low voice, "Clay, and gravel, and under that the rock that bears garnets. All under this part of the city is that rock. I don't know the names."

"You can learn 'em."

"I know how to build boats, how to sail boats."

"You'll do better away from the ships, all the fighting and raiding. The King's working the old mines at Samory, round the mountain. There you'd be out of his way. Work for him you must, if you want to stay alive. I'll see that you're sent there. If you'll go."

After a little silence Otter said, "Thanks." And he looked up at Hound, one brief, questioning, judging glance.

Hound had taken him, had stood and seen his people beaten senseless, had not stopped the beating. Yet he spoke as a friend. Why? said Otter's look. Hound answered it.

"Crafty men need to stick together," he said. "Men who have no art at all, nothing but wealth—they pit us one against the other, for their gain not ours. We sell 'em our power. Why do we? If we went our own way together, we'd do better, maybe."

Hound meant well in sending the young man to Samory, but he did not understand the quality of Otter's will. Nor did Otter himself. He was too used to obeying others to see that in fact he had always followed his own bent, and too young to believe that anything he did could kill him.

He planned, as soon as they took him out of his cell, to use the old Changer's spell of self-transformation and so escape. Surely his life was in danger, and it would be all right to use the spell? Only he couldn't decide what to turn himself into—a bird, or a wisp of smoke, what would be safest? But while he was thinking about it, Losen's men, used to wizard's tricks, drugged his food and he ceased to think of anything at all. They dumped him into a mule-cart like a sack of oats. When he showed signs of reviving during the journey, one of them bashed him on the head, remarking that he wanted to make sure he got his rest.

When he came to himself, sick and weak from the poison and with an aching skull, he was in a room with brick walls and bricked-up windows. The door had no bars and no visible lock. But when he tried to get to his feet he felt bonds of sorcery holding his body and mind, resilient, clinging, tightening as he moved. He could stand, but could not take a step towards the door. He could not even reach his hand out. It was a horrible sensation, as if his muscles were not his own. He sat down again and tried to hold still. The spellbonds around his chest kept him from breathing deeply, and his mind felt stifled too, as if his thoughts were crowded into a space too small for them.

After a long time the door opened and several men came in. He could do nothing against them as they gagged him and bound his arms behind him. "Now you won't weave charms nor speak spells, young 'un," said a broad, strong man with a furrowed face, "but you can nod your head well enough, right? They sent you here as a dowser. If you're a good dowser you'll feed well and sleep easy. Cinnabar, that's what you're to nod for. The King's wizard says it's still here somewhere about these old mines. And he wants it. So it's best for us that we find it. Now I'll walk you out. It's like I'm the water finder and you're my wand, see? You lead on. And if you want to go this way or that way you dip your head, so. And when you know there's ore underfoot, you stamp on the place, so. Now that's the bargain, right? And if you play fair I will."

He waited for Otter to nod, but Otter stood motionless. "Sulk away," the man said. "If you don't like this work, there's always the roaster."

The man, whom the others called Licky, led him out into a hot, bright morning that dazzled his eyes. Leaving his cell he had felt the spellbonds loosen and fall away, but there were other spells woven about other buildings of the place, especially around a tall stone tower, filling the air with sticky lines of resistance and repulsion. If he tried to push forward into them his face and belly stung with jabs of agony, so that he looked at his body in horror for the wound; but there was no wound. Gagged and bound, without his voice and hands to work magic, he could do nothing against these spells. Licky had tied one end of a braided leather cord around his neck and held the other end, following him. He let Otter walk into a couple of the spells, and after that Otter avoided them. Where they were was plain enough: the dusty pathways bent to miss them.

Leashed like a dog, he walked along, sullen and shivering with sickness and rage. He stared around him, seeing the stone tower, stacks of wood by its wide doorway, rusty wheels and machines by a pit, great heaps of gravel and clay. Turning his sore head made him dizzy.

"If you're a dowser, better dowse," said Licky, coming up alongside him and looking sidelong into his face. "And if you're not, you'd better dowse all the same. That way you'll stay above ground longer."

A man came out of the stone tower. He passed them, walking hurriedly with a queer shambling gait, staring straight ahead. His chin shone and his chest was wet with spittle leaking from his lips.

"That's the roaster tower," said Licky. "Where they cook the cinnabar to get the metal from it. Roasters die in a year or two. Where to, dowser?"

After a bit Otter nodded left, away from the grey stone tower. They walked on towards a long, treeless valley, past grass-grown dumps and tailings.

"All under here's worked out long since," Licky said. And Otter had begun to be aware of the strange country under his feet: empty shafts and rooms of dark air in the dark earth, a vertical labyrinth, the deepest pits filled with unmoving water. "Never was much silver, and the watermetal's long gone. Listen, young 'un, do you even know what cinnabar is?"

Otter shook his head.

"I'll show you some. That's what Gelluk's after. The ore of watermetal. Watermetal eats all the other metals, even gold, see. So he calls it the King. If you find him his King, he'll treat you well. He's often here. Come on, I'll show you. Dog can't track till he's had the scent."

Licky took him down into the mines to show him the gangues, the kinds of earth the ore was likely to occur in. A few miners were working at the end of a long level.

Because they were smaller than men and could move more easily in narrow places, or because they were at home with the earth, or most likely because it was the custom, women had always worked the mines of Earthsea. These miners were free women, not slaves like the workers in the roaster tower. Gelluk had made him foreman over the miners, Licky said, but he did no work in the mine; the miners forbade it, earnestly believing it was the worst of bad luck for a man to pick up a shovel or shore a timber. "Suits me," Licky said.

A shock-haired, bright-eyed woman with a candle bound to her forehead set down her pick to show Otter a little cinnabar in a bucket, brownish red clots and crumbs. Shadows leapt across the earth face at which the miners worked. Old timbers creaked, dirt sifted down. Though the air ran cool through the darkness, the drifts and levels were so low and narrow the miners had to stoop and squeeze their way. In places the ceilings had collapsed. Ladders were shaky. The mine was a terrifying place; yet Otter felt a sense of shelter in it. He was half sorry to go back up into the burning day.

Licky did not take him into the roaster tower, but back to the barracks. From a locked room he brought out a small, soft, thick, leather bag that weighed heavy in his hands. He opened it to show Otter the little pool of dusty brilliance lying in it. When he closed the bag the metal moved in it, bulging, pressing, like an animal trying to get free.

"There's the King," Licky said, in a tone that might have been reverence or hatred.

Though not a sorcerer, Licky was a much more formidable man than Hound. Yet like Hound he was brutal not cruel. He demanded obedience, but nothing else. Otter had seen slaves and their masters all his life in the shipyards of Havnor, and knew he was fortunate. At least in daylight, when Licky was his master.

He could eat only in the cell, where they took his gag off. Bread and onions were what they gave him, with a slop of rancid oil on the bread. Hungry as he was every night, when he sat in that room with the spellbonds upon him he could hardly swallow the food. It tasted of metal, of ash. The nights were long and terrible, for the spells pressed on him, weighed on him, waked him over and over terrified, gasping for breath, and never able to think coherently. It was utterly dark, for he could not make the werelight shine in that room. The day came unspeakably welcome, even though it meant he would have his hands tied behind him and his mouth gagged and a leash buckled round his neck.

Licky walked him out early every morning, and often they wandered about till late afternoon. Licky was silent and patient. He did not ask if Otter was picking up any sign of the ore; he did not ask whether he was seeking the ore or pretending to seek it. Otter himself could not have answered the question. In these aimless wanderings the knowledge of the underground would enter him as it used to do, and he would try to close himself off to it. "I will not work in the service of evil!" he told himself. Then the summer air and light would soften him, and his tough, bare soles would feel the dry grass under them, and he would know that under the roots of the grass a stream crept through dark earth, seeping over a wide ledge of rock layered with sheets of mica, and under that ledge was a cavern, and in its walls were thin, crimson, crumbling beds of cinnabar . . . He made no sign. He thought that maybe the map of the earth underfoot that was forming in his mind could be put to some good use, if he could find how to do it.

But after ten days or so, Licky said, "Master Gelluk's coming here. If there's no ore for him, he'll likely find another dowser."

Otter walked on a mile, brooding; then circled back, leading Licky to a hillock not far from the far end of the old workings. There he nodded downward and stamped his foot.

Back in the cell room, when Licky had unleashed him and untied his gag, he said, "There's some ore there. You can get to it by running that old tunnel straight on, maybe twenty feet."

"A good bit of it?"

Otter shrugged.

"Just enough to keep going on, eh?"

Otter said nothing.

"Suits me," said Licky.

Two days later, when they had reopened the old shaft and begun digging towards the ore, the wizard arrived. Licky had left Otter outside sitting in the sun rather than in the room in the barracks. Otter was grateful to him. He could not be wholly comfortable with his hands bound and his mouth gagged, but wind and sunlight were mighty blessings. And he could breathe deep and doze without dreams of earth stopping his mouth and nostrils, the only dreams he ever had, nights in the cell.

He was half asleep, sitting on the ground in the shade by the barracks, the smell of the logs stacked by the roaster tower bringing him a memory of the work yards at home, the fragrance of new wood as the plane ran down the silky oak board. Some noise or movement roused him. He looked up and saw the wizard standing before him, looming above him.

Gelluk wore fantastic clothes, as many of his kind did in those days. A long robe of Lorbanery silk, scarlet, embroidered in gold and black with runes and symbols, and a wide-brimmed, peak-crowned hat made him seem taller than a man could be. Otter did not need to see his clothes to know him. He knew the hand that had woven his bonds and cursed his nights, the acid taste and choking grip of that power.

"I think I've found my little finder," said Gelluk. His voice was deep and soft, like the notes of a viol. "Sleeping in the sunshine, like one whose work has been well done. So you've sent them digging for the Red Mother, have you? Did you know the Red Mother before you came here? Are you a courtier of the King? Here, now, there's no need for ropes and knots." Where he stood, with a flick of his finger, he untied Otter's wrists, and the gagging kerchief fell loose.

"I could teach you how to do that for yourself," the wizard said, smiling, watching Otter rub and flex his aching wrists and work his lips that had been smashed against his teeth for hours. "The Hound told me that you're a lad of promise and might go far with a proper guide. If you'd like to visit the Court of the King, I can take you there. But maybe you don't know the King I'm talking of?"

Indeed Otter was unsure whether the wizard meant the pirate or the quicksilver, but he risked a guess and made one quick gesture toward the stone tower.

The wizard's eyes narrowed and his smile broadened.

"Do you know his name?"

"The watermetal," Otter said.

"So the vulgar call it, or quicksilver, or the water of weight. But those who serve him call him the King, and the Allking, and the Body of the Moon." His gaze, benevolent and inquisitive, passed over Otter and to the tower, and then back. His face was large and long, whiter than any face Otter had seen, with bluish eyes. Grey and black hairs curled here and there on his chin and cheeks. His calm, open smile showed small teeth, several of them missing. "Those who have learned to see truly can see him as he is, the lord of all substances. The root of power lies in him. Do you know what we call him in the secrecy of his palace?"

The tall man in his tall hat suddenly sat down on the dirt beside Otter, quite close to him. His breath smelled earthy. His light eyes gazed directly into Otter's eyes. "Would you like to know? You can know anything you like. I need have no secrets from you. Nor you from me," and he laughed, not threateningly, but with pleasure. He gazed at Otter again, his large, white face smooth and thoughtful. "Powers you have, yes, all kinds of little traits and tricks. A clever lad. But not too clever; that's good. Not too clever to learn, like some . . . I'll teach you, if you like. Do you like learning? Do you like knowledge? Would you like to know the name we call the King when he's all alone in his brightness in his courts of stone? His name is Turres. Do you know that name? It's a word in the language of the Allking. His own name in his own language. In our base tongue we would say Semen." He smiled again and patted Otter's hand. "For he is the seed and fructifier. The seed and source of might and right. You'll see. You'll see. Come along! Come along! Let's go see the King flying among his subjects, gathering himself from them!" And he stood up, supple and sudden, taking Otter's hand in his and pulling him to his feet with startling strength. He was laughing with excitement.

Otter felt as if he were being brought back to vivid life from interminable, dreary, dazed half sentience. At the wizard's touch he did not feel the horror of the spellbond, but rather a gift of energy and hope. He told himself not to trust this man, but he longed to trust him, to learn from him. Gelluk was powerful, masterful, strange, yet he had set him free. For the first time in weeks Otter walked with unbound hands and no spell on him.

"This way, this way," Gelluk murmured. "No harm will come to you." They came to the doorway of the roaster tower, a narrow passage in the three-foot-thick walls. He took Otter's arm, for the young man hesitated.

Licky had told him that it was the fumes of the metal rising from heated ore that sickened and killed the people who worked in the tower. Otter had never entered it nor seen Licky enter it. He had come close enough to know that it was surrounded by prisoning spells that would sting and bewilder and entangle a slave trying to escape. Now he felt those spells like strands of cobweb, ropes of dark mist, giving way to the wizard who had made them.

"Breathe, breathe, breathe," Gelluk said, laughing, and Otter tried not to hold his breath as they entered the tower.

The roasting pit took up the center of a huge domed chamber. Hurrying, sticklike figures black against the blaze shoveled and reshoveled ore onto logs kept in a roaring blaze by great bellows, while others brought fresh logs and worked the bellows sleeves. From the apex of the dome a spiral of chambers rose up into the tower through smoke and fumes. In those chambers, Licky had told him, the vapor of the quicksilver was trapped and condensed, reheated and recondensed, till in the topmost vault the pure metal ran down into a stone trough or bowl—only a drop or two a day, he said, from the low-grade ores they were roasting now.

"Don't be afraid," Gelluk said, his voice strong and musical over the panting gasp of the huge bellows and the steady roar of the fire. "Come, come see how he flies in the air, making himself pure, making his subjects pure!" He drew Otter to the edge of the roasting pit. His eyes shone in the flare and dazzle of the flames. "Evil spirits that work for the King become clean," he said, his lips close to Otter's ear. "As they slaver, the dross and stains flow out of them. Illness and impurities fester and run free from their sores. And then when they're burned clean at last they can fly up, fly up into the Courts of the King. Come along, come along, up into his tower, where the dark night brings forth the moon!"

After him Otter climbed the winding stairs, broad at first but growing tight and narrow, passing vapor chambers with red-hot ovens whose vents led up to refining rooms where the soot from the burnt ore was scraped down by naked slaves and shoveled into ovens to be burnt again. They came to the topmost room. Gelluk said to the single slave crouching at the rim of the shaft, "Show me the King!"

The slave, short and thin, hairless, with running sores on his hands and arms, uncapped a stone cup by the rim of the condensing shaft. Gelluk peered in, eager as a child. "So tiny," he murmured. "So young. The tiny Prince, the baby Lord, Lord Turres. Seed of the world! Soul-jewel!"

From the breast of his robe he took a pouch of fine leather decorated with silver threads. With a delicate horn spoon tied to the pouch he lifted the few drops of quicksilver from the cup and placed them in it, then retied the thong.

The slave stood by, motionless. All the people who worked in the heat and fumes of the roaster tower were naked or wore only breechclout and moccasins. Otter glanced again at the slave, thinking by his height he was a child, and then saw the small breasts. It was a woman. She was bald. Her joints were swollen knobs in her bone-thin limbs. She looked up once at Otter, moving her eyes only. She spat into the fire, wiped her sore mouth with her hand, and stood motionless again.

"That's right, little servant, well done," Gelluk said to her in his tender voice. "Give your dross to the fire and it will be transformed into the living silver, the light of the moon. Is it not a wonderful thing," he went on, drawing Otter away and back down the spiral stair, "how from what is most base comes what is most noble? That is a great principle of the art! From the vile Red Mother is born the Allking. From the spittle of a dying slave is made the silver Seed of Power."

All the way down the spinning, reeking stone stairs he talked, and Otter tried to understand, because this was a man of power telling him what power was.

But when they came out into the daylight again his head kept on spinning in the dark, and after a few steps he doubled over and vomited on the ground.

Gelluk watched him with his inquisitive, affectionate look, and when Otter stood up, wincing and gasping, the wizard asked gently, "Are you afraid of the King?"

Otter nodded.

"If you share his power he won't harm you. To fear a power, to fight a power, is very dangerous. To love power and to share it is the royal way. Look. Watch what I do." Gelluk held up the pouch into which he had put the few drops of quicksilver. His eye always on Otter's eye, he unsealed the pouch, lifted it to his lips, and drank its contents. He opened his smiling mouth so that Otter could see the silver drops pooling on his tongue before he swallowed.

"Now the King is in my body, the noble guest of my house. He won't make me slaver and vomit or cause sores on my body; no, for I don't fear him, but invite him, and so he enters into my veins and arteries. No harm comes to me. My blood runs silver. I see things unknown to other men. I share the secrets of the King. And when he leaves me, he hides in the place of ordure, in foulness itself, and yet again in the vile place he waits for me to come and take him up and cleanse him as he cleansed me, so that each time we grow purer together." The wizard took Otter's arm and walked along with him. He said, smiling and confidential, "I am one who shits moonlight. You will not know another such. And more than that, more than that, the King enters into my seed. He is my semen. I am Turres and he is me . . ."

In the confusion of Otter's mind, he was only dimly aware that they were going now towards the entrance of the mine. They went underground. The passages of the mine were a dark maze like the wizard's words. Otter stumbled on, trying to understand. He saw the slave in the tower, the woman who had looked at him. He saw her eyes.

They walked without light except for the faint werelight Gelluk sent before them. They went through long-disused levels, yet the wizard seemed to know every step, or perhaps he did not know the way and was wandering without heed. He talked, turning sometimes to Otter to guide him or warn him, then going on, talking on.

They came to where the miners were extending the old tunnel. There the wizard spoke with Licky in the flare of candles among jagged shadows. He touched the earth of the tunnel's end, took clods of earth in his hands, rolled the dirt in his palms, kneading, testing, tasting it. For that time he was silent, and Otter watched him with staring intensity, still trying to understand.

Licky came back to the barracks with them. Gelluk bade Otter goodnight in his soft voice. Licky shut him as usual into the brick-walled room, giving him a loaf of bread, an onion, a jug of water.

Otter crouched as always in the uneasy oppression of the spell-bond. He drank thirstily. The sharp earthy taste of the onion was good, and he ate it all.

As the dim light that came into the room from chinks in the mortar of the bricked-up window died away, instead of sinking into the blank misery of all his nights in that room, he stayed awake, and grew more awake. The excited turmoil of his mind all the time he had been with Gelluk slowly quieted. From it something rose, coming close, coming clear, the image he had seen down in the mine, shadowy yet distinct: the slave in the high vault of the tower, that woman with empty breasts and festered eyes, who spat the spittle that ran from her poisoned mouth, and wiped her mouth, and stood waiting to die. She had looked at him.

He saw her now more clearly than he had seen her in the tower. He saw her more clearly than he had ever seen anyone. He saw the thin arms, the swollen joints of elbow and wrist, the childish nape of her neck. It was as if she was with him in the room. It was as if she was in him, as if she was him. She looked at him. He saw her look at him. He saw himself through her eyes.

He saw the lines of the spells that held him, heavy cords of darkness, a tangled maze of lines all about him. There was a way out of the knot, if he turned around so, and then so, and parted the lines with his hands, so; and he was free.

He could not see the woman any more. He was alone in the room, standing free.

All the thoughts he had not been able to think for days and weeks were racing through his head, a storm of ideas and feelings, a passion of rage, vengeance, pity, pride.

At first he was overwhelmed with fierce fantasies of power and revenge: he would free the slaves, he would spellbind Gelluk and hurl him into the refining fire, he would bind him and blind him and leave him to breathe the fumes of quicksilver in that highest vault till he died . . . But when his thoughts settled down and began to run clearer, he knew that he could not defeat a wizard of great craft and power, even if that wizard was mad. If he had any hope it was to play on his madness, and lead the wizard to defeat himself.

He pondered. All the time he was with Gelluk, he had tried to learn from him, tried to understand what the wizard was telling him. Yet he was certain, now, that Gelluk's ideas, the teaching he so eagerly imparted, had nothing to do with his power or with any true power.

Mining and refining were indeed great crafts with their own mysteries and masteries, but Gelluk seemed to know nothing of those arts. His talk of the Allking and the Red Mother was mere words. And not the right words. But how did Otter know that?

In all his flood of talk the only word Gelluk had spoken in the Old Tongue, the language of which wizards' spells were made, was the word *turres.* He had said it meant semen. Otter's own gift of magery had recognised that meaning as the true one. Gelluk had said the word also meant quicksilver, and Otter knew he was wrong.

His humble teachers had taught him all the words they knew of the Language of the Making. Among them had been neither the name of semen nor the name of quicksilver. But his lips parted, his tongue moved. *"Ayezur,"* he said.

His voice was the voice of the slave in the stone tower. It was she who knew the true name of quicksilver and spoke it through him.

Then for a while he held still, body and mind, beginning to understand for the first time where his power lay.

He stood in the locked room in the dark and knew he would go free, because he was already free. A storm of praise ran through him.

After a while, deliberately, he re-entered the trap of spellbonds, went back to his old place, sat down on the pallet, and went on thinking. The prisoning spell was still there, yet it had no power over him now. He could walk into it and out of it as if it were mere lines painted on the floor. Gratitude for this freedom beat in him as steady as his heartbeat.

He thought what he must do, and how he must do it. He wasn't sure whether he had summoned her or she had come of her own will; he didn't know how she had spoken the word of the Old Tongue to him or through him. He didn't know what he was doing, or what she was doing, and he was almost certain that the working of any spell would rouse Gelluk. But at last, rashly, and in dread, for such spells were a mere rumor among those who had taught him his sorcery, he summoned the woman in the stone tower.

He brought her into his mind and saw her as he had seen her, there, in that room, and called out to her; and she came.

Her apparition stood again just outside the spiderweb cords of the spell, gazing at him, and seeing him, for a soft, bluish, sourceless light filled the room. Her sore, raw lips quivered but she did not speak.

He spoke, giving her his true name: "I am Medra."

"I am Anieb," she whispered.

"How can we get free?"

"His name."

"Even if I knew it . . . When I'm with him I can't speak."

"If I was with you, I could use it."

"I can't call you."

"But I can come," she said.

She looked round, and he looked up. Both knew that Gelluk had sensed something, had wakened. Otter felt the bonds close and tighten, and the old shadow fall.

"I will come, Medra," she said. She held out her thin hand in a fist, then opened it palm up as if offering him something. Then she was gone.

The light went with her. He was alone in the dark. The cold grip of the spells took him by the throat and choked him, bound his hands, pressed on his lungs. He crouched, gasping. He could not think; he could not remember. "Stay with me," he said, and did not know who he spoke to. He was frightened, and did not know what he was frightened of. The wizard, the power, the spell . . . It was all darkness. But in his body, not in his mind, burned a knowledge he could not name any more, a certainty that was like a tiny lamp held in his hands in a maze of caverns underground. He kept his eyes on that seed of light.

Weary, evil dreams of suffocation came to him, but took no hold on him. He breathed deep. He slept at last. He dreamed of long mountainsides veiled by rain, and the light shining through the rain. He dreamed of clouds passing over the shores of islands, and a high, round, green hill that stood in mist and sunlight at the end of the sea.

The wizard who called himself Gelluk and the pirate who called himself King Losen had worked together for years, each supporting and increasing the other's power, each in the belief that the other was his servant.

Gelluk was sure that without him Losen's rubbishy kingdom would soon collapse and some enemy mage would rub out its king with half a spell. But he let Losen act the master. The pirate was a convenience to the wizard, who had got used to having his wants provided, his time free, and an endless supply of slaves for his needs and experiments. It was easy to keep up the protections he had laid on Losen's person and expeditions and forays, the prisoning spells he had laid on the places slaves worked or treasures were kept. Making those spells had been a different matter, a long hard work. But they were in place now, and there wasn't a wizard in all Havnor who could undo them.

Gelluk had never met a man he feared. A few wizards had crossed his path strong enough to make him wary of them, but he had never known one with skill and power equal to his own.

Of late, entering always deeper into the mysteries of a certain lore-book brought back from the Isle of Way by one of Losen's raiders, Gelluk had become indifferent to most of the arts he had learned or had discovered for himself. The book convinced him that all of them were only shadows or hints of a greater mastery. As one true element controlled all substances, one true knowledge contained all others. Approaching ever closer to that mastery, he understood that the crafts of wizards were as crude and false as Losen's title and rule. When he was one with the true element, he would be the one true king. Alone among men he would speak the words of making and unmaking. He would have dragons for his dogs.

In the young dowser he recognised a power, untaught and inept, which he could use. He needed much more quicksilver than he had, therefore he needed a finder. Finding was a base skill. Gelluk had never practiced it, but he could see that the young fellow had the gift. He would do well to learn the boy's true name so that he could be sure of controlling him. He sighed at the thought of the time he must waste teaching the boy what he was good for. And after that the ore must still be dug out of the earth and the metal refined. As always, Gelluk's mind leapt across obstacles and delays to the wonderful mysteries at the end of them.

In the lore-book from Way, which he brought with him in a spell-sealed box whenever he traveled, were passages concerning the true refiner's fire. Having long studied these, Gelluk knew that once he had enough of the pure metal, the next stage was to refine it yet further into the Body of the Moon. He had understood the disguised language of the book to mean that in order to purify pure quicksilver, the fire must be built not of mere wood but of human corpses. Rereading and pondering the words this night in his room in the barracks, he discerned another possible meaning in them. There was always another meaning in the words of this lore. Perhaps the book was saying that there must be sacrifice not only of base flesh but also of inferior spirit. The great fire in the tower should burn not dead bodies but living ones. Living and conscious. Purity from foulness: bliss from pain. It was all part of the great principle, perfectly clear once seen. He was sure he was right, had at last understood the technique. But he must not hurry, he must be patient, must make certain. He turned to another passage and compared the two, and brooded over the book late into the night. Once for a moment something drew his mind away, some invasion of the outskirts of his awareness; the boy was trying some trick or other. Gelluk spoke a single word impatiently, and returned to the marvels of the

Allking's realm. He never noticed that his prisoner's dreams had escaped him.

Next day he had Licky send him the boy. He looked forward to seeing him, to being kind to him, teaching him, petting him a bit as he had done yesterday. He sat down with him in the sun. Gelluk was fond of children and animals. He liked all beautiful things. It was pleasant to have a young creature about. Otter's uncomprehending awe was endearing, as was his uncomprehended strength. Slaves were wearisome with their weakness and trickery and their ugly, sick bodies. Of course Otter was his slave, but the boy need not know it. They could be teacher and prentice. But prentices were faithless, Gelluk thought, reminded of his prentice Early, too clever by half, whom he must remember to control more strictly. Father and son, that's what he and Otter could be. He would have the boy call him Father. He recalled that he had intended to find out his true name. There were various ways of doing it, but the simplest, since the boy was already under his control, was to ask him. "What is your name?" he said, watching Otter intently.

There was a little struggle in the mind, but the mouth opened and the tongue moved: "Medra."

"Very good, very good, Medra," said the wizard. "You may call me Father."

"You must find the Red Mother," he said, the day after that. They were sitting side by side again outside the barracks. The autumn sun was warm. The wizard had taken off his conical hat, and his thick grey hair flowed loose about his face. "I know you found that little patch for them to dig, but there's no more in that than a few drops. It's scarcely worth burning for so little. If you are to help me, and if I am to teach you, you must try a little harder. I think you know how." He smiled at Otter. "Don't you?"

Otter nodded.

He was still shaken, appalled, by the ease with which Gelluk had forced him to say his name, which gave the wizard immediate and ultimate power over him. Now he had no hope of resisting Gelluk in any way. That night he had been in utter despair. But then Anieb had come into his mind: come of her own will, by her own means. He could not summon her, could not even think of her, and would not have dared to do so, since Gelluk knew his name. But she came, even when he was with the wizard, not in apparition but as a presence in his mind.

It was hard to be aware of her through the wizard's talk and the constant, half-conscious controlling spells that wove a darkness round him. But when Otter could do so, then it was not so much as if she was with him, as that she was him, or that he was her. He saw through her eyes. Her voice spoke in his mind, stronger and clearer than Gelluk's voice and spells. Through her eyes and mind he could see, and think. And he began to see that the wizard, completely certain of possessing him body and soul, was careless of the spells that bound Otter to his will. A bond is a connection. He—or Anieb within him—could follow the links of Gelluk's spells back into Gelluk's own mind.

Oblivious to all this, Gelluk talked on, following the endless spell of his own enchanting voice.

"You must find the true womb, the bellybag of the Earth, that holds the pure moonseed. Did you know that the Moon is the Earth's father? Yes, yes; and he lay with her, as is the father's right. He quickened her base clay with the true seed. But she will not give birth to the King. She is strong in her fear and wilful in her vileness. She holds him back and hides him deep, fearing to give birth to her master. That is why, to give him birth, she must be burned alive."

Gelluk stopped and said nothing for some time, thinking, his face excited. Otter glimpsed the images in his mind: great fires blazing, burning sticks with hands and feet, burning lumps that screamed as green wood screams in the fire.

"Yes," Gelluk said, his deep voice soft and dreamy, "she must be burned alive. And then, only then, he will spring forth, shining! Oh, it's time, and past time. We must deliver the King. We must find the great lode. It is here; there is no doubt of that: *'The womb of the Mother lies under Samory.'*"

Again he paused. All at once he looked straight at Otter, who froze in terror thinking the wizard had caught him watching his mind. Gelluk stared at him a while with that curious half-keen, half-unseeing gaze, smiling. "Little Medra!" he said, as if just discovering he was there. He patted Otter's shoulder. "I know you have the gift of finding what's hidden. Quite a great gift, were it suitably trained. Have no fear, my son. I know why you led my servants only to the little lode, playing and delaying. But now that I've come, you serve me, and have nothing to be afraid of. And there's no use trying to conceal anything from me, is there? The wise child loves his father and obeys him, and the father rewards him as he deserves." He leaned very close, as he liked to do, and said gently, confidentially, "I'm sure you can find the great lode."

"I know where it is," Anieb said.

Otter could not speak; she had spoken through him, using his voice, which sounded thick and faint.

Very few people ever spoke to Gelluk unless he compelled them to. The spells by which he silenced, weakened, and controlled all who approached him were so habitual to him that he gave them no thought. He was used to being listened to, not to listening. Serene in his strength and obsessed with his ideas, he had no thought beyond them. He was not aware of Otter at all except as a part of his plans, an extension of himself. "Yes, yes, you will," he said, and smiled again.

But Otter was intensely aware of Gelluk, both physically and as a presence of immense controlling power; and it seemed to him that Anieb's speaking had taken away that much of Gelluk's power over him, gaining him a place to stand, a foothold. Even with Gelluk so close to him, fearfully close, he managed to speak.

"I will take you there," he said, stiffly, laboriously.

Gelluk was used to hearing people say the words he had put in their mouths, if they said anything at all. These were words he wanted but had not expected to hear. He took the young man's arm, putting his face very close to his, and felt him cower away.

"How clever you are," he said. "Have you found better ore than that patch you found first? Worth the digging and the roasting?"

"It is the lode," the young man said.

The slow stiff words carried great weight.

"The great lode?" Gelluk looked straight at him, their faces not a hand's breadth apart. The light in his bluish eyes was like the soft, crazy shift of quicksilver. "The womb?"

"Only the Master can go there."

"What Master?"

"The Master of the House. The King."

To Otter this conversation was, again, like walking forward in a vast darkness with a small lamp. Anieb's understanding was that lamp. Each step revealed the next step he must take, but he could never see the place where he was. He did not know what was coming next, and did not understand what he saw. But he saw it, and went forward, word by word.

"How do you know of that House?"

"I saw it."

"Where? Near here?"

Otter nodded.

"Is it in the earth?"

Tell him what he sees, Anieb whispered in Otter's mind, and he spoke: "A stream runs through darkness over a glittering roof. Under the roof is the House of the King. The roof stands high above the floor, on high pillars. The floor is red. All the pillars are red. On them are shining runes."

Gelluk caught his breath. Presently he said, very softly, "Can you read the runes?"

"I cannot read them." Otter's voice was toneless. "I cannot go there. No one can enter there in the body but only the King. Only he can read what is written."

Gelluk's white face had gone whiter; his jaw trembled a little. He stood up, suddenly, as he always did. "Take me there," he said, trying to control himself, but so violently compelling Otter to get up and walk that the young man lurched to his feet and stumbled several steps, almost falling. Then he walked forward, stiff and awkward, trying not to resist the coercive, passionate will that hurried his steps.

Gelluk pressed close beside him, often taking his arm. "This way," he said several times. "Yes, yes! This is the way." Yet he was following Otter. His touch and his spells pushed him, rushed him, but in the direction Otter chose to go.

They walked past the roaster tower, past the old shaft and the new one, on into the long valley where Otter had taken Licky the first day he was there. It was late autumn now. The shrubs and scrubby grass that had been green that day were dun and dry, and the wind rattled the last leaves on the bushes. To their left a little stream ran low among willow thickets. Mild sunlight and long shadows streaked the hillsides.

Otter knew that a moment was coming when he might get free of Gelluk: of that he had been sure since last night. He knew also that in that same moment he might defeat Gelluk, disempower him, if the wizard, driven by his visions, forgot to guard himself—and if Otter could learn his name.

The wizard's spells still bound their minds together. Otter pressed rashly forward into Gelluk's mind, seeking his true name. But he did not know where to look or how to look. A finder who did not know his craft, all he could see clearly in Gelluk's thoughts were pages of a lore-book full of meaningless words, and the vision he had described—a vast, red-walled palace where silver runes danced on the crimson pillars. But Otter could not read the book or the runes. He had never learned to read.

All this time he and Gelluk were going on farther from the tower, away from Anieb, whose presence sometimes weakened and faded. Otter dared not try to summon her.

Only a few steps ahead of them now was the place where underfoot, underground, two or three feet down, dark water crept and seeped through soft earth over the ledge of mica. Under that opened the hollow cavern and the lode of cinnabar.

Gelluk was almost wholly absorbed in his own vision, but since

Otter's mind and his were connected, he saw something of what Otter saw. He stopped, gripping Otter's arm. His hand shook with eagerness.

Otter pointed at the low slope that rose before them. "The King's House is there," he said. Gelluk's attention turned entirely away from him then, fixed on the hillside and the vision he saw within it. Then Otter could call to Anieb. At once she came into his mind and being, and was there with him.

Gelluk was standing still, but his shaking hands were clenched, his whole tall body twitching and trembling, like a hound that wants to chase but cannot find the scent. He was at a loss. There was the hillside with its grass and bushes in the last of the sunlight, but there was no entrance. Grass growing out of gravelly dirt; the seamless earth.

Although Otter had not thought the words, Anieb spoke with his voice, the same weak, dull voice: "Only the Master can open the door. Only the King has the key."

"The key," Gelluk said.

Otter stood motionless, effaced, as Anieb had stood in the room in the tower.

"The key," Gelluk repeated, urgent.

"The key is the King's name."

That was a leap in the darkness. Which of them had said it?

Gelluk stood tense and trembling, still at a loss. "Turres," he said, after a time, almost in a whisper.

The wind blew in the dry grass.

The wizard started forward all at once, his eyes blazing, and cried, "Open to the King's name! I am Tinaral!" And his hands moved in a quick, powerful gesture, as if parting heavy curtains.

The hillside in front of him trembled, writhed, and opened. A gash in it deepened, widened. Water sprang up out of it and ran across the wizard's feet.

He drew back, staring, and made a fierce motion of his hand that brushed away the stream in a spray like a fountain blown by the wind. The gash in the earth grew deeper, revealing the ledge of mica. With a sharp rending crack the glittering stone split apart. Under it was darkness.

The wizard stepped forward. "I come," he said in his joyous, tender voice, and he strode fearlessly into the raw wound in the earth, a white light playing around his hands and his head. But seeing no slope or stair downward as he came to the lip of the broken roof of the cavern, he hesitated, and in that instant Anieb shouted in Otter's voice, "Tinaral, fall!"

Staggering wildly the wizard tried to turn, lost his footing on the crumbling edge, and plunged down into the dark, his scarlet cloak billowing up, the werelight round him like a falling star.

"Close!" Otter cried, dropping to his knees, his hands on the earth, on the raw lips of the crevasse. "Close, Mother! Be healed, be whole!" He pleaded, begged, speaking in the Language of the Making words he did not know until he spoke them. "Mother, be whole!" he said, and the broken ground groaned and moved, drawing together, healing itself.

A reddish seam remained, a scar through the dirt and gravel and uprooted grass.

The wind rattled the dry leaves on the scrub-oak bushes. The sun was behind the hill, and clouds were coming over in a low, grey mass.

Otter crouched there at the foot of the hillslope, alone.

The clouds darkened. Rain passed through the little valley, falling on the dirt and the grass. Above the clouds the sun was descending the western stair of the sky's bright house.

Otter sat up at last. He was wet, cold, bewildered. Why was he here?

He had lost something and had to find it. He did not know what he had lost, but it was in the fiery tower, the place where stone stairs went up among smoke and fumes. He had to go there. He got to his feet and shuffled, lame and unsteady, back down the valley.

He had no thought of hiding or protecting himself. Luckily for him there were no guards about; there were few guards, and they were not on the alert, since the wizard's spells had kept the prison shut. The spells were gone, but the people in the tower did not know it, working on under the greater spell of hopelessness.

Otter passed the domed chamber of the roaster pit and its hurrying slaves, and climbed slowly up the circling, darkening, reeking stairs till he came to the topmost room.

She was there, the sick woman who could heal him, the poor woman who held the treasure, the stranger who was himself.

He stood silent in the doorway. She sat on the stone floor near the crucible, her thin body greyish and dark like the stones. Her chin and breasts were shiny with the spittle that ran from her mouth. He thought of the spring of water that had run from the broken earth.

"Medra," she said. Her sore mouth could not speak clearly. He knelt down and took her hands, looking into her face.

"Anieb," he whispered, "come with me."

"I want to go home," she said.

He helped her stand. He made no spell to protect or hide them. His strength had been used up. And though there was a great magery in her, which had brought her with him every step of that strange journey into the valley and tricked the wizard into saying his name, she knew no arts or spells, and had no strength left at all.

Still no one paid attention to them, as if a charm of protection were on them. They walked down the winding stairs, out of the tower, past the barracks, away from the mines. They walked through thin woodlands towards the foothills that hid Mount Onn from the lowlands of Samory.

Anieb kept a better pace than seemed possible in a woman so famished and destroyed, walking almost naked in the chill of the rain. All her will was aimed on walking forward; she had nothing else in her mind, not him, not anything. But she was there bodily with him, and he felt her presence as keenly and strangely as when she had come to his summoning. The rain ran down her naked head and body. He made her stop to put on his shirt. He was ashamed of it, for it was filthy, he having worn it all these weeks. She let him pull it over her head and then walked right on. She could not go quickly, but she went steadily, her eyes fixed on the faint cart track they followed, till the night came early under the rain clouds, and they could not see where to set their feet.

"Make the light," she said. Her voice was a whimper, plaintive. "Can't you make the light?"

"I don't know," he said, but he tried to bring the werelight round them, and after a while the ground glimmered faintly before their feet.

"We should find shelter and rest," he said.

"I can't stop," she said, and started to walk again.

"You can't walk all night."

"If I lie down I won't get up. I want to see the Mountain."

Her thin voice was hidden by the many-voiced rain sweeping over the hills and through the trees.

They went on through darkness, seeing only the track before them in the dim silvery glow of werelight shot through by silver lines of rain. When she stumbled he caught her arm. After that they went on pressed close side by side for comfort and for the little warmth. They walked slower, and yet slower, but they walked on. There was no sound but the sound of the rain falling from the black sky, and the little kissing squelch of their sodden feet in the mud and wet grass of the track.

"Look," she said, halting. "Medra, look."

He had been walking almost asleep. The pallor of the werelight had faded, drowned in a fainter, vaster clarity. Sky and earth were all one grey, but before them and above them, very high, over a drift of cloud, the long ridge of the mountain glimmered red.

"There," Anieb said. She pointed at the mountain and smiled. She looked at her companion, then slowly down at the ground. She sank down kneeling. He knelt with her, tried to support her, but she slid down in his arms. He tried to keep her head at least from the mud of the track. Her limbs and face twitched, her teeth chattered. He held her close against him, trying to warm her.

"The women," she whispered, "the hand. Ask them. In the village. I did see the Mountain."

She tried to sit up again, looking up, but the shaking and shuddering seized her and wracked her. She began to gasp for breath. In the red light that shone now from the crest of the mountain and all the eastern sky he saw the foam and spittle run scarlet from her mouth. Sometimes she clutched at him, but she did not speak again. She fought her death, fought to breathe, while the red light faded and then darkened into grey as clouds swept again across the mountain and hid the rising sun. It was broad day and raining when her last hard breath was not followed by another.

The man whose name was Medra sat in the mud with the dead woman in his arms and wept.

A carter walking at his mule's head with a load of oakwood came upon them and took them both to Woodedge. He could not make the young man let go of the dead woman. Weak and shaky as he was, he would not set his burden down on the load, but clambered into the cart holding her, and held her all the miles to Woodedge. All he said was "She saved me," and the carter asked no questions.

"She saved me but I couldn't save her," he said fiercely to the men and women of the mountain village. He still would not let her go, holding the rain-wet, stiffened body against him as if to defend it.

Very slowly they made him understand that one of the women was Anieb's mother, and that he should give Anieb to her to hold. He did so at last, watching to see if she was gentle with his friend and would protect her. Then he followed another woman meekly enough. He put on dry clothing she gave him to put on, and ate a little food she gave him to eat, and lay down on the pallet she led him to, and sobbed in weariness, and slept.

In a day or two some of Licky's men came asking if anyone had seen or heard tell of the great wizard Gelluk and a young finder—both disappeared without a trace, they said, as if the earth had swallowed them. Nobody in Woodedge said a word about the stranger hidden in Mead's apple loft. They kept him safe. Maybe that is why the people there now call their village not Woodedge, as it used to be, but Otterhide.

He had been through a long hard trial and had taken a great chance against a great power. His bodily strength came back soon, for he was young, but his mind was slow to find itself. He had lost something, lost it forever, lost it as he found it.

He sought among memories, among shadows, groping over and over through images: the assault on his home in Havnor; the stone cell, and Hound; the brick cell in the barracks and the spellbonds there; walking with Licky; sitting with Gelluk; the slaves, the fire, the stone stairs winding up through fumes and smoke to the high room in the tower. He had to regain it all, to go through it all, searching. Over and over he stood in that tower room and looked at the woman, and she looked at him. Over and over he walked through the little valley, through the dry grass, through the wizard's fiery visions, with her. Over and over he saw the wizard fall, saw the earth close. He saw the red ridge of the mountain in the dawn. Anieb died while he held her, her ruined face against his arm. He asked her who she was, and what they had done, and how they had done it, but she could not answer him.

Her mother Ayo and her mother's sister Mead were wise women. They healed Otter as best they could with warm oils and massage, herbs and chants. They talked to him and listened when he talked. Neither of them had any doubt but that he was a man of great power. He denied this. "I could have done nothing without your daughter," he said.

"What did she do?" Ayo asked, softly.

He told her, as well as he could. "We were strangers. Yet she gave me her name," he said. "And I gave her mine." He spoke haltingly, with long pauses. "It was I that walked with the wizard, compelled by him, but she was with me, and she was free. And so together we could turn his power against him, so that he destroyed himself." He thought for a long time, and said, "She gave me her power."

"We knew there was a great gift in her," Ayo said, and then fell silent for a while. "We didn't know how to teach her. There are no teachers left on the mountain. King Losen's wizards destroy the sorcerers and witches. There's no one to turn to."

"Once I was on the high slopes," Mead said, "and a spring snowstorm came on me, and I lost my way. She came there. She came to me, not in the body, and guided me to the track. She was only twelve then."

"She walked with the dead, sometimes," Ayo said very low. "In the forest, down towards Faliern. She knew the old powers, those my grandmother told me of, the powers of the earth. They were strong there, she said."

"But she was only a girl like the others, too," Mead said, and hid her face. "A good girl," she whispered.

After a while Ayo said, "She went down to Firn with some of the young folk. To buy fleece from the shepherds there. A year ago last spring. That wizard they spoke of came there, casting spells. Taking slaves."

Then they were all silent.

Ayo and Mead were much alike, and Otter saw in them what Anieb might have been: a short, slight, quick woman, with a round face and clear eyes, and a mass of dark hair, not straight like most people's hair but curly, frizzy. Many people in the west of Havnor had hair like that.

But Anieb had been bald, like all the slaves in the roaster tower.

Her use-name had been Flag, the blue iris of the springs. Her mother and aunt called her Flag when they spoke of her.

"Whatever I am, whatever I can do, it's not enough," he said.

"It's never enough," Mead said. "And what can anyone do alone?"

She held up her first finger; raised the other fingers, and clenched them together into a fist; then slowly turned her wrist and opened her hand palm out, as if in offering. He had seen Anieb make that gesture. It was not a spell, he thought, watching intently, but a sign. Ayo was watching him.

"It is a secret," she said.

"Can I know the secret?" he asked after a while.

"You already know it. You gave it to Flag. She gave it to you. Trust."

"Trust," the young man said. "Yes. But against— Against them?— Gelluk's gone. Maybe Losen will fall now. Will it make any difference? Will the slaves go free? Will beggars eat? Will justice be done? I think there's an evil in us, in humankind. Trust denies it. Leaps across it. Leaps the chasm. But it's there. And everything we do finally serves evil, because that's what we are. Greed and cruelty. I look at the world, at the forests and the mountain here, the sky, and it's all right, as it should be. But we aren't. People aren't. We're wrong. We do wrong. No animal does wrong. How could they? But we can, and we do. And we never stop."

They listened to him, not agreeing, not denying, but accepting his despair. His words went into their listening silence, and rested there for days, and came back to him changed.

"We can't do anything without each other," he said. "But it's the greedy ones, the cruel ones who hold together and strengthen each other. And those who won't join them stand each alone." The image of Anieb as he had first seen her, a dying woman standing alone in the tower room, was always with him. "Real power goes to waste. Every wizard uses his arts against the others, serving the men of greed. What good can any art be used that way? It's wasted. It goes wrong, or it's thrown away. Like slaves' lives. Nobody can be free alone. Not even a mage. All of them working their magic in prison cells, to gain nothing. There's no way to use power for good."

Ayo closed her hand and opened it palm up, a fleeting sketch of a gesture, of a sign.

A man came up the mountain to Woodedge, a charcoal burner from Firn. "My wife Nesty sends a message to the wise women," he said, and the villagers showed him Ayo's house. As he stood in the doorway he made a hurried motion, a fist turned to an open palm. "Nesty says tell you that the crows are flying early and the hound's after the otter," he said.

Otter, sitting by the fire shelling walnuts, held still. Mead thanked the messenger and brought him in for a cup of water and a handful of shelled nuts. She and Ayo chatted with him about his wife. When he had gone she turned to Otter.

"The Hound serves Losen," he said. "I'll go today."

Mead looked at her sister. "Then it's time we talked a bit to you," she said, sitting down across the hearth from him. Ayo stood by the table, silent. A good fire burned in the hearth. It was a wet, cold time, and firewood was one thing they had plenty of, here on the mountain.

"There's people all over these parts, and maybe beyond, who think, as you said, that nobody can be wise alone. So these people try to hold to each other. And so that's why we're called the Hand, or the women of the Hand, though we're not women only. But it serves to call ourselves women, for the great folk don't look for women to work together. Or to have thoughts about such things as rule or misrule. Or to have any powers."

"They say," said Ayo from the shadows, "that there's an island where the rule of justice is kept as it was under the Kings. Morred's Isle, they call it. But it's not Enlad of the Kings, nor Éa. It's south, not north of Havnor, they say. There they say the women of the Hand have kept the old arts. And they teach them, not keeping them secret each to himself, as the wizards do."

"Maybe with such teaching you could teach the wizards a lesson," Mead said.

"Maybe you can find that island," said Ayo.

Otter looked from one to the other. Clearly they had told him their own greatest secret and their hope.

"Morred's Isle," he said.

"That would be only what the women of the Hand call it, keeping its meaning from the wizards and the pirates. To them no doubt it would bear some other name."

"It would be a terrible long way," said Mead.

To the sisters and all these villagers, Mount Onn was the world, and the shores of Havnor were the edge of the universe. Beyond that was only rumor and dream.

"You'll come to the sea, going south, they say," said Ayo.

"He knows that, sister," Mead told her. "Didn't he tell us he was a ship carpenter? But it's a terrible long way down to the sea, surely. With this wizard on your scent, how are you to go there?"

"By the grace of water, that carries no scent," Otter said, standing up. A litter of walnut shells fell from his lap, and he took the hearth broom and swept them into the ashes. "I'd better go."

"There's bread," Ayo said, and Mead hurried to pack hard bread and hard cheese and walnuts into a pouch made of a sheep's stomach. They were very poor people. They gave him what they had. So Anieb had done.

"My mother was born in Endlane, round by Faliern Forest," Otter said. "Do you know that town? She's called Rose, Rowan's daughter."

"The carters go down to Endlane, summers."

"If somebody could talk to her people there, they'd get word to her. Her brother, Littleash, used to come to the city every year or two."

They nodded.

"If she knew I was alive," he said.

Anieb's mother nodded. "She'll hear it."

"Go on now," said Mead.

"Go with the water," said Ayo.

He embraced them, and they him, and he left the house.

He ran down from the straggle of huts to the quick, noisy stream he had heard singing through his sleep all his nights in Woodedge. He prayed to it. "Take me and save me," he asked it. He made the spell the old Changer had taught him long ago, and said the word of transformation. Then no man knelt by the loud-running water, but an otter slipped into it and was gone.

III. Tern

There was a wise man on our hill
Who found his way to work his will.
He changed his shape, he changed his name,
But ever the other will be the same.
So runs the water away, away,
So runs the water away.

One winter afternoon on the shore of the Onneva River where it fingers out into the north bight of the Great Bay of Havnor, a man stood up on the muddy sand: a man poorly dressed and poorly shod, a thin brown man with dark eyes and hair so fine and thick it shed the rain. It was raining on the low beaches of the river mouth, the fine, cold, dismal drizzle of that grey winter. His clothes were soaked. He hunched his shoulders, turned about, and set off towards a wisp of chimney smoke he saw far down the shore. Behind him were the tracks of an otter's four feet coming up from the water and the tracks of a man's two feet going away from it.

Where he went then, the songs don't tell. They say only that he wandered, "he wandered long from land to land." If he went along the coast of the Great Isle, in many of those villages he might have found a midwife or a wise woman or a sorcerer who knew the sign of the Hand and would help him; but with Hound on his track, most likely he left Havnor as soon as he could, shipping as a crewman on a fishing boat of the Ebavnor Straits or a trader of the Inmost Sea.

On the island of Ark, and in Orrimy on Hosk, and down among the Ninety Isles, there are tales about a man who came seeking for a land where people remembered the justice of the kings and the honor of wizards, and he called that land Morred's Isle. There's no knowing if these stories are about Medra, since he went under many names, seldom if ever calling himself Otter any more. Gelluk's fall had not brought Losen down. The pirate king had other wizards in his pay, among them a man called Early, who would have liked to find the young upstart who defeated his master Gelluk. And Early had a good chance of tracing him. Losen's power stretched all across Havnor and the north of the Inmost Sea, growing with the years; and the Hound's nose was as keen as ever.

Maybe it was to escape the hunt that Medra came to Pendor, a long way west of the Inmost Sea, or maybe some rumor among the women of the Hand on Hosk sent him there. Pendor was a rich island, then, before the dragon Yevaud despoiled it. Wherever Medra had gone until then, he had found the lands like Havnor or worse, sunk in warfare, raids, and piracy, the fields full of weeds, the towns full of thieves. Maybe he thought, at first, that on Pendor he had found Morred's Isle, for the city was beautiful and peaceful and the people prosperous.

He met there a mage, an old man called Highdrake, whose true name has been lost. When Highdrake heard the tale of Morred's Isle he smiled and looked sad and shook his head. "Not here," he said. "Not this. The Lords of Pendor are good men. They remember the kings. They don't seek war or plunder. But they send their sons west dragon hunting. In sport. As if the dragons of the West Reach were ducks or geese for the killing! No good will come of that."

Highdrake took Medra as his student, gratefully. "I was taught my art by a mage who gave me freely all he knew, but I never found anybody to give that knowledge to, until you came," he told Medra. "The young men come to me and they say, 'What good is it? Can you find gold?' they say. 'Can you teach me how to make stones into diamonds? Can you give me a sword that will kill a dragon? What's the use of talking about the balance of things? There's no profit in it,' they say. No profit!" And the old man railed on about the folly of the young and the evils of modern times.

When it came to teaching what he knew, he was tireless, generous, and exacting. For the first time, Medra was given a vision of magic not as a set of strange gifts and reasonless acts, but as an art and a craft, which could be known truly with long study and used rightly after long practice, though even then it would never lose its strangeness. Highdrake's mastery of spells and sorcery was not much greater than his pupil's, but he had clear in his mind the idea of something very much greater, the wholeness of knowledge. And that made him a mage.

Listening to him, Medra thought of how he and Anieb had walked in the dark and rain by the faint glimmer that showed them only the next step they could take, and of how they had looked up to the red ridge of the mountain in the dawn.

"Every spell depends on every other spell," said Highdrake. "Every motion of a single leaf moves every leaf of every tree on every isle of Earthsea! There is a pattern. That's what you must look for and look to. Nothing goes right but as part of the pattern. Only in it is freedom."

Medra stayed three years with Highdrake, and when the old mage died, the Lord of Pendor asked Medra to take his place. Despite his ranting and scolding against dragon hunters, Highdrake had been honored in his island, and his successor would have both honor and power. Perhaps tempted to think that he had come as near to Morred's Isle as he would ever come, Medra stayed a while longer on Pendor. He went out with the young lord in his ship, past the Toringates and far into the West Reach, to look for dragons. There was a great longing in his heart to see a dragon. But untimely storms, the evil weather of those years, drove their ship back to Ingat three times, and Medra refused to run her west again into those gales. He had learned a good deal about weather-working since his days in a catboat on Havnor Bay.

A while after that he left Pendor, drawn southward again, and maybe went to Ensmer. In one guise or another he came at last to Geath in the Ninety Isles.

There they fished for whales, as they still do. That was a trade he wanted no part of. Their ships stank and their town stank. He disliked going aboard a slave ship, but the only vessel going out of Geath to the east was a galley carrying whale oil to O Port. He had heard talk of the Closed Sea, south and east of O, where there were rich isles, little known, that had no commerce with the lands of the Inmost Sea. What he sought might be there. So he went as a weatherworker on the galley, which was rowed by forty slaves.

The weather was fair for once: a following wind, a blue sky lively with little white clouds, the mild sunlight of late spring. They made good way from Geath. Late in the afternoon he heard the master say to the helmsman, "Keep her south tonight so we don't raise Roke."

He had not heard of that island, and asked, "What's there?"

"Death and desolation," said the ship's master, a short man with small, sad, knowing eyes like a whale's.

"War?"

"Years back. Plague, black sorcery. The waters all round it are cursed."

"Worms," said the helmsman, the master's brother. "Catch fish anywhere near Roke, you'll find 'em thick with worms as a dead dog on a dunghill."

"Do people still live there?" Medra asked, and the master said, "Witches," while his brother said, "Worm eaters."

There were many such isles in the Archipelago, made barren and desolate by rival wizards' blights and curses; they were evil places to come to or even to pass, and Medra thought no more about this one, until that night.

Sleeping out on deck with the starlight on his face, he had a simple, vivid dream: it was daylight, clouds racing across a bright sky, and across the sea he saw the sunlit curve of a high green hill. He woke with the vision still clear in his mind, knowing he had seen it ten years before, in the spell-locked barracks room at the mines of Samory.

He sat up. The dark sea was so quiet that the stars were reflected here and there on the sleek lee side of the long swells. Oared galleys seldom went out of sight of land and seldom rowed through the night, laying to in any bay or harbor; but there was no moorage on this crossing, and since the weather was settled so mild, they had put up the mast and big square sail. The ship drifted softly forward, her slave oarsmen sleeping on their benches, the free men of her crew all asleep but the helmsman and the lookout, and the lookout was dozing. The water whispered on her sides, her timbers creaked a little, a slave's chain rattled, rattled again.

"They don't need a weatherworker on a night like this, and they haven't paid me yet," Medra said to his conscience. He had waked from his dream with the name Roke in his mind. Why had he never heard of the isle or seen it on a chart? It might be accursed and deserted as they said, but wouldn't it be set down on the charts?

"I could fly there as a tern and be back on the ship before daylight," he said to himself, but idly. He was bound for O Port. Ruined lands were all too common. No need to fly to seek them. He made himself comfortable in his coil of cable and watched the stars. Looking west, he saw the four bright stars of the Forge, low over the sea. They were a little blurred, and as he watched them they blinked out, one by one.

The faintest little sighing tremor ran over the slow, smooth swells.

"Master," Medra said, afoot, "wake up."

"What now?"

"A witchwind coming. Following. Get the sail down."

No wind stirred. The air was soft, the big sail hung slack. Only the western stars faded and vanished in a silent blackness that rose slowly higher. The master looked at that. "Witchwind, you say?" he asked, reluctant.

Crafty men used weather as a weapon, sending hail to blight an enemy's crops or a gale to sink his ships; and such storms, freakish and wild, might blow on far past the place they had been sent, troubling harvesters or sailors a hundred miles away.

"Get the sail down," Medra said, peremptory. The master yawned and cursed and began to shout commands. The crewmen got up slowly and slowly began to take the awkward sail in, and the oarmaster, after asking several questions of the master and Medra, began to roar at the slaves and stride among them rousing them right and left with his knotted rope. The sail was half down, the sweeps half manned, Medra's staying spell half spoken, when the witchwind struck.

It struck with one huge thunderclap out of sudden utter blackness and wild rain. The ship pitched like a horse rearing and then rolled so hard and far that the mast broke loose from its footing, though the stays held. The sail struck the water, filled, and pulled the galley right over, the great sweeps sliding in their oarlocks, the chained slaves struggling and shouting on their benches, barrels of oil breaking loose and thundering over one another—pulled her over and held her over, the deck vertical to the sea, till a huge storm wave struck and swamped her and she sank. All the shouting and screaming of men's voices was suddenly silent. There was no noise but the roar of the rain on the sea, lessening as the freak wind passed on eastward. Through it one white seabird beat its wings up from the black water and flew, frail and desperate, to the north.

Printed on narrow sands under granite cliffs, in the first light, were the tracks of a bird alighting. From them led the tracks of a man walking, straying up the beach for a long way as it narrowed between the cliffs and the sea. Then the tracks ceased.

Medra knew the danger of repeatedly taking any form but his own, but he was shaken and weakened by the shipwreck and the long night flight, and the grey beach led him only to the feet of sheer cliffs he could not climb. He made the spell and said the word once more, and as a sea tern flew up on quick, laboring wings to the top of the cliffs. Then, possessed by flight, he flew on over a shadowy sunrise land. Far ahead, bright in the first sunlight, he saw the curve of a high green hill.

To it he flew, and on it landed, and as he touched the earth he was a man again.

He stood there for a while, bewildered. It seemed to him that it was not by his own act or decision that he had taken his own form, but that in touching this ground, this hill, he had become himself. A magic greater than his own prevailed here.

He looked about, curious and wary. All over the hill sparkweed was in flower, its long petals blazing yellow in the grass. Children on Havnor knew that flower. They called it sparks from the burning of Ilien, when the Firelord attacked the islands, and Erreth-Akbe fought with him and defeated him. Tales and songs of the heroes rose up in Medra's memory as he stood there: Erreth-Akbe and the heroes before him, the Eagle Queen, Heru, Akambar who drove the Kargs into the east, and Serriadh the peacemaker, and Elfarran of Soléa, and Morred, the White Enchanter, the beloved king. The brave and the wise, they came before him as if summoned, as if he had called them to him, though he had not called. He saw them. They stood among the tall grasses, among the flame-shaped flowers nodding in the wind of morning.

Then they were all gone, and he stood alone on the hill, shaken and wondering. "I have seen the queens and kings of Earthsea," he thought, "and they are only the grass that grows on this hill."

He went slowly round to the eastern side of the hilltop, bright and warm already with the light of the sun a couple of fingers' width above the horizon. Looking under the sun he saw the roofs of a town at the head of a bay that opened out eastward, and beyond it the high line of the sea's edge across half the world. Turning west he saw fields and pastures and roads. To the north were long green hills. In a fold of land southward a grove of tall trees drew his gaze and held it. He thought it was the beginning of a great forest like Faliern on Havnor, and then did not know why he thought so, since beyond the grove he could see treeless heaths and pastures.

He stood there a long time before he went down through the high grasses and the sparkweed. At the foot of the hill he came into a lane. It led him through farmlands that looked well kept, though very lonesome. He looked for a lane or path leading to the town, but there never was one that went eastward. Not a soul was in the fields, some of which were newly ploughed. No dog barked as he went by. Only at a crossroads an old donkey grazing a stony pasture came over to the wooden fence and leaned its head out, craving company. Medra stopped to stroke the grey-brown, bony face. A city man and a saltwater man, he knew little of farms and their animals, but he thought the donkey looked at him kindly. "Where am I, donkey?" he said to it. "How do I get to the town I saw?"

The donkey leaned its head hard against his hand so that he would go on scratching the place just above its eyes and below its ears. When he did so, it flicked its long right ear. So when he parted from the donkey he took the right hand of the crossroad, though it looked as if it would lead back to the hill; and soon enough he came among houses, and then onto a street that brought him down at last into the town at the head of the bay.

It was as strangely quiet as the farmlands. Not a voice, not a face. It was difficult to feel uneasy in an ordinary-looking town on a sweet spring morning, but in such silence he must wonder if he was indeed in a plague-stricken place or an island under a curse. He went on. Between a house and an old plum tree was a wash line, the clothes pinned on it flapping in the sunny breeze. A cat came round the corner of a garden, no abandoned starveling but a white-pawed, well-whiskered, prosperous cat. And at last, coming down the steep little street, which here was cobbled, he heard voices.

He stopped to listen, and heard nothing.

He went on to the the foot of the street. It opened into a small market square. People were gathered there, not many of them. They were not buying or selling. There were no booths or stalls set up. They were waiting for him.

Ever since he had walked on the green hill above the town and had seen the bright shadows in the grass, his heart had been easy. He was expectant, full of a sense of great strangeness, but not frightened. He stood still and looked at the people who came to meet him.

Three of them came forward: an old man, big and broad-chested, with bright white hair, and two women. Wizard knows wizard, and Medra knew they were women of power.

He raised his hand closed in a fist and then turning and opening it, offered it to them palm up.

"Ah," said one of the women, the taller of the two, and she laughed. But she did not answer the gesture.

"Tell us who you are," the white-haired man said, courteously enough, but without greeting or welcome. "Tell us how you came here."

"I was born in Havnor and trained as a shipwright and a sorcerer. I was on a ship bound from Geath to O Port. I was spared alone from drowning, last night, when a witchwind struck." He was silent then. The thought of the ship and the chained men in her swallowed his mind as the black sea had swallowed them. He gasped, as if coming up from drowning.

"How did you come here?"

"As . . . as a bird, a tern. Is this Roke Island?"

"You changed yourself?"

He nodded.

"Whom do you serve?" asked the shorter and younger of the women, speaking for the first time. She had a keen, hard face, with long black brows.

"I have no master."

"What was your errand in O Port?"

"In Havnor, years ago, I was in servitude. Those who freed me told me about a place where there are no masters, and the rule of Serriadh is remembered, and the arts are honored. I have been looking for that place, that island, seven years."

"Who told you about it?"

"Women of the Hand."

"Anyone can make a fist and show a palm," said the tall woman, pleasantly. "But not everyone can fly to Roke. Or swim, or sail, or come in any way at all. So we must ask what brought you here."

Medra did not answer at once. "Chance," he said at last, "favoring long desire. Not art. Not knowledge. I think I've come to the place I sought, but I don't know. I think you may be the people they told me of, but I don't know. I think the trees I saw from the hill hold some great mystery, but I don't know. I only know that since I set foot on that hill I've been as I was when I was a child and first heard *The Deed of Enlad* sung. I am lost among wonders."

The white-haired man looked at the two women. Other people had come forward, and there was some quiet talk among them.

"If you stayed here, what would you do?" the black-browed woman asked him.

"I can build boats, or mend them, and sail them. I can find, above and under ground. I can work weather, if you have any need of that. And I'll learn the art from any who will teach me."

"What do you want to learn?" asked the taller woman in her mild voice.

Now Medra felt that he had been asked the question on which the rest of his life hung, for good or evil. Again he stood silent a while. He started to speak, and didn't speak, and finally spoke. "I could not save one, not one, not the one who saved me," he said. "Nothing I know could have set her free. I know nothing. If you know how to be free, I beg you, teach me!"

"Free!" said the tall woman, and her voice cracked like a whip. Then she looked at her companions, and after a while she smiled a little. Turning back to Medra, she said, "We're prisoners, and so freedom is a thing we study. You came here through the walls of our prison. Seeking freedom, you say. But you should know that leaving Roke may be even harder than coming to it. Prison within prison, and some of it we have built ourselves." She looked at the others. "What do you say?" she asked them.

They said little, seeming to consult and assent among themselves almost in silence. At last the shorter woman looked with her fierce eyes at Medra. "Stay if you will," she said.

"I will."

"What will you have us call you?"

"Tern," he said; and so he was called.

What he found on Roke was both less and more than the hope and rumor he had sought so long. Roke Island was, they told him, the heart of Earthsea. The first land Segoy raised from the waters in the beginning of time was bright Éa of the northern sea, and the second was Roke. That green hill, Roke Knoll, was founded deeper than all the islands. The trees he had seen, which seemed sometimes to be in one place on the isle and sometimes in another, were the oldest trees in the world, and the source and center of magic.

"If the Grove were cut, all wizardry would fail. The roots of those trees are the roots of knowledge. The patterns the shadows of their leaves make in the sunlight write the words Segoy spoke in the Making."

So said Ember, his fierce, black-browed teacher.

All the teachers of the art magic on Roke were women. There were no men of power, few men at all, on the island.

Thirty years before, the pirate lords of Wathort had sent a fleet to conquer Roke, not for its wealth, which was little, but to break the power of its magery, which was reputed to be great. One of the wizards of Roke had betrayed the island to the crafty men of Wathort, lowering its spells of defense and warning. Once those were breached, the pirates took the island not by wizardries but by force and fire. Their great ships filled Thwil Bay, their hordes burned and looted, their slave takers carried off men, boys, young women. Little children and the old they slaughtered. They fired every house and field they came to. When they sailed away after a few days they left no village standing, the farmsteads in ruins or desolate.

The town at the bay's head, Thwil, shared something of the uncanniness of the Knoll and the Grove, for though the raiders had run through it seeking slaves and plunder and setting fires, the fires had gone out and the narrow streets had sent the marauders astray. Most of the islanders who survived were wise women and their children, who had hidden themselves in the town or in the Immanent Grove. The men now on Roke were those spared children, grown, and a few men now grown old. There was no government but that of the women of the Hand, for it was their spells that had protected Roke so long and protected it far more closely now.

They had little trust in men. A man had betrayed them. Men had attacked them. It was men's ambitions, they said, that had perverted all the arts to ends of gain. "We do not deal with their governments," said tall Veil in her mild voice.

And yet Ember said to Medra, "We were our own undoing."

Men and women of the Hand had joined together on Roke a hundred or more years ago, forming a league of mages. Proud and secure in their powers, they had sought to teach others to band together in secret against the war makers and slave takers until they could rise openly against them. Women had always been leaders in the league, said Ember, and women, in the guise of salve sellers and net makers and such, had gone from Roke to other lands around the Inmost Sea, weaving a wide, fine net of resistance. Even now there were strands and knots of that net left. Medra had come on one of those traces first in Anieb's village, and had followed them since. But they had not led him here. Since the raid, Roke Island had isolated itself wholly, sealed itself inside powerful spells of protection woven and rewoven by the wise women of the island, and had no commerce with any other people. "We can't save them," Ember said. "We couldn't save ourselves."

Veil, with her gentle voice and smile, was implacable. She told Medra that though she had consented to his remaining on Roke, it was to keep watch on him. "You broke through our defenses once," she said. "All that you say of yourself may be true, and may not. What can you tell me that would make me trust you?"

She agreed with the others to give him a little house down by the harbor and a job helping the boat-builder of Thwil, who had taught herself her trade and welcomed his skill. Veil put no difficulties in his path and always greeted him kindly. But she had said, "What can you tell me that would make me trust you?" and he had no answer for her.

Ember usually scowled when he greeted her. She asked him abrupt questions, listened to his answers, and said nothing.

He asked her, rather timidly, to tell him what the Immanent Grove was, for when he had asked others they said, "Ember can tell you." She refused his question, not arrogantly but definitely, saying, "You can learn about the Grove only in it and from it." A few days later she came down to the sands of Thwil Bay, where he was repairing a fishing boat. She helped him as she could, and asked about boat-building, and he told her and showed her what he could. It was a peaceful afternoon, but after it she went off in her abrupt way. He felt some awe of her; she was incalculable. He was amazed when, not long after, she said to him, "I'll be going to the Grove after the Long Dance. Come if you like."

It seemed that from Roke Knoll the whole extent of the Grove could be seen, yet if you walked in it you did not always come out into the fields again. You walked on under the trees. In the inner Grove they were all of one kind, which grew nowhere else, yet had no name in Hardic but "tree." In the Old Speech, Ember said, each of those trees had its own name. You walked on, and after a time you were walking again among familiar trees, oak and beech and ash, chestnut and walnut and willow, green in spring and bare in winter; there were dark firs, and cedar, and a tall evergreen Medra did not know, with soft reddish bark and layered foliage. You walked on, and the way through the trees was never twice the same. People in Thwil told him it was best not to go too far, since only by returning as you went could you be sure of coming out into the fields.

"How far does the forest go?" Medra asked, and Ember said, "As far as the mind goes."

The leaves of the trees spoke, she said, and the shadows could be read. "I am learning to read them," she said.

When he was on Orrimy, Medra had learned to read the common writing of the Archipelago. Later, Highdrake of Pendor had taught him some of the runes of power. That was known lore. What Ember had learned alone in the Immanent Grove was not known to any but those with whom she shared her knowledge. She lived all summer under the eaves of the Grove, having no more than a box to keep the mice and wood rats from her small store of food, a shelter of branches, and a cook fire near a stream that came out of the woods to join the little river running down to the bay.

Medra camped nearby. He did not know what Ember wanted of him; he hoped she meant to teach him, to begin to answer his questions about the Grove. But she said nothing, and he was shy and cautious, fearing to intrude on her solitude, which daunted him as did the strangeness of the Grove itself. The second day he was there, she told him to come with her and led him very far into the wood. They walked for hours in silence. In the summer midday the woods were silent. No bird sang. The leaves did not stir. The aisles of the trees were endlessly different and all the same. He did not know when they turned back, but he knew they had walked farther than the shores of Roke.

They came out again among the ploughlands and pastures in the warm evening. As they walked back to their camping place he saw the four stars of the Forge come out above the western hills.

Ember parted from him with only a "Good night."

The next day she said, "I'm going to sit under the trees." Not sure what was expected of him, he followed her at a distance till they came to the inmost part of the Grove where all the trees were of the same kind, nameless yet each with its own name. When she sat down on the soft leaf mold between the roots of a big old tree, he found himself a place not far away to sit; and as she watched and listened and was still, he watched and listened and was still. So they did for several days. Then one morning, in rebellious mood, he stayed by the stream while Ember walked into the Grove. She did not look back.

Veil came from Thwil Town that morning, bringing them a basket of bread, cheese, milk curds, summer fruits. "What have you learned?" she asked Medra in her cool, gentle way, and he answered, "That I'm a fool."

"Why so, Tern?"

"A fool could sit under the trees forever and grow no wiser."

The tall woman smiled a little. "My sister has never taught a man before," she said. She glanced at him, and gazed away, over the summery fields. "She's never looked at a man before," she said.

Medra stood silent. His face felt hot. He looked down. "I thought," he said, and stopped.

In Veil's words he saw, all at once, the other side of Ember's impatience, her fierceness, her silences.

He had tried to look at Ember as untouchable while he longed to touch her soft brown skin, her black shining hair. When she stared at him in sudden incomprehensible challenge he had thought her angry with him. He feared to insult, to offend her. What did she fear? His desire? Her own?— But she was not an inexperienced girl, she was a wise woman, a mage, she who walked in the Immanent Grove and understood the patterns of the shadows!

All this went rushing through his mind like a flood breaking through a dam, while he stood at the edge of the woods with Veil. "I thought mages kept themselves apart," he said at last. "Highdrake said that to make love is to unmake power."

"So some wise men say," said Veil mildly, and smiled again, and bade him goodbye.

He spent the whole afternoon in confusion, angry. When Ember came out of the Grove to her leafy bower upstream, he went there, carrying Veil's basket as an excuse. "May I talk to you?" he said.

She nodded shortly, frowning her black brows.

He said nothing. She squatted down to find out what was in the basket. "Peaches!" she said, and smiled.

"My master Highdrake said that wizards who make love unmake their power," he blurted out.

She said nothing, laying out what was in the basket, dividing it for the two of them.

"Do you think that's true?" he asked.

She shrugged. "No," she said.

He stood tongue-tied. After a while she looked up at him. "No," she said in a soft, quiet voice, "I don't think it's true. I think all the true powers, all the old powers, at root are one."

He still stood there, and she said, "Look at the peaches! They're all ripe. We'll have to eat them right away."

"If I told you my name," he said, "my true name—"

"I'd tell you mine," she said. "If that . . . if that's how we should begin."

They began, however, with the peaches.

They were both shy. When Medra took her hand his hand shook, and Ember, whose name was Elehal, turned away scowling. Then she touched his hand very lightly. When he stroked the sleek black flow of her hair she seemed only to endure his touch, and he stopped. When he tried to embrace her she was stiff, rejecting him. Then she turned and, fierce, hasty, awkward, seized him in her arms. It wasn't the first night, nor the first nights, they passed together that gave either of them much pleasure or ease. But they learned from each other, and came through shame and fear into passion. Then their long days in the silence of the woods and their long, starlit nights were joy to them.

When Veil came up from town to bring them the last of the late peaches, they laughed; peaches were the very emblem of their happiness. They tried to make her stay and eat supper with them, but she wouldn't. "Stay here while you can," she said.

The summer ended too soon that year. Rain came early; snow fell in autumn even as far south as Roke. Storm followed storm, as if the winds had risen in rage against the tampering and meddling of the crafty men. Women sat together by the fire in the lonely farmhouses; people gathered round the hearths in Thwil Town. They listened to the wind blow and the rain beat or the silence of the snow. Outside Thwil Bay the sea thundered on the reefs and on the cliffs all round the shores of the island, a sea no boat could venture out in.

What they had they shared. In that it was indeed Morred's Isle. Nobody on Roke starved or went unhoused, though nobody had much more than they needed. Hidden from the rest of the world not only by sea and storm but by their defenses that disguised the island and sent ships astray, they worked and talked and sang the songs, *The Winter Carol* and *The Deed of the Young King*. And they had books, the *Chronicles of Enlad* and the *History of the Wise Heroes*. From these precious books the old men and women would read aloud in a hall down by the wharf where the fisherwomen made and mended their nets. There was a hearth there, and they would light the fire. People came even from farms across the island to hear the histories read, listening in silence, intent. "Our souls are hungry," Ember said.

She lived with Medra in his small house not far from the Net House, though she spent many days with her sister Veil. Ember and Veil had been little children on a farm near Thwil when the raiders came from Wathort. Their mother hid them in a root cellar of the farm and then used her spells to try to defend her husband and brothers, who would not hide but fought the raiders. They were butchered with their cattle. The house and barns were burnt. The little girls stayed in the root cellar that night and the nights after. Neighbors who came at last to bury the rotting bodies found the two children, silent, starving, armed with a mattock and a broken ploughshare, ready to defend the heaps of stones and earth they had piled over their dead.

Medra knew only a hint of this story from Ember. One night Veil, who was three years older than Ember and to whom the memory was much clearer, told it to him fully. Ember sat with them, listening in silence.

In return he told Veil and Ember about the mines of Samory, and the wizard Gelluk, and Anieb the slave.

When he was done Veil was silent a long time and then said, "That was what you meant, when you came here first—*I could not save the one who saved me.*"

"And you asked me, *What can you tell me that could make me trust you?*"

"You have told me," Veil said.

Medra took her hand and put his forehead against it. Telling his story he had kept back tears. He could not do so now.

"She gave me freedom," he said. "And I still feel that all I do is done through her and for her. No, not for her. We can do nothing for the dead. But for . . ."

"For us," said Ember. "For us who live, in hiding, neither killed nor killing. The dead are dead. The great and mighty go their way unchecked. All the hope left in the world is in the people of no account."

"Must we hide forever?"

"Spoken like a man," said Veil with her gentle, wounded smile.

"Yes," said Ember. "We must hide, and forever if need be. Because there's nothing left but being killed and killing, beyond these shores. You say it, and I believe it."

"But you can't hide true power," Medra said. "Not for long. It dies in hiding, unshared."

"Magic won't die on Roke," said Veil. "*On Roke all spells are strong.* So said Ath himself. And you have walked under the trees . . . Our job must be to keep that strength. Hide it, yes. Hoard it, as a young dragon hoards up its fire. And share it. But only here. Pass it on, one to the next, here, where it's safe, and where the great robbers and killers would least look for it, since no one here is of any account. And one day the dragon will come into its strength. If it takes a thousand years . . ."

"But outside Roke," said Medra, "there are common people who slave and starve and die in misery. Must they do so for a thousand years with no hope?"

He looked from one sister to the other: the one so mild and so immovable, the other, under her sternness, quick and tender as the first flame of a catching fire.

"On Havnor," he said, " far from Roke, in a village on Mount Onn, among people who know nothing of the world, there are still women of the Hand. That net hasn't broken after so many years. How was it woven?"

"Craftily," said Ember.

"And cast wide!" He looked from one to the other again. "I wasn't well taught, in the City of Havnor," he said. "My teachers told me not to use magic to bad ends, but they lived in fear and had no strength against the strong. They gave me all they had to give, but it was little. It was by mere luck I didn't go wrong. And by Anieb's gift of strength to me. But for her I'd be Gelluk's servant now. Yet she herself was untaught, and so enslaved. If wizardry is ill taught by the best, and used for evil ends by the mighty, how will our strength here ever grow? What will the young dragon feed on?"

"This is the center," said Veil. "We must keep to the center. And wait."

"We must give what we have to give," said Medra. "If all but us are slaves, what's our freedom worth?"

"The true art prevails over the false. The pattern will hold," Ember said, frowning. She reached out the poker to gather together her namesakes in the hearth, and with a whack knocked the heap into a blaze. "That I know. But our lives are short, and the pattern's very long. If only Roke was now what it once was—if we had more people of the true art gathered here, teaching and learning as well as preserving—"

"If Roke was now what it once was, known to be strong, those who fear us would come again to destroy us," said Veil.

"The solution lies in secrecy," said Medra. "But so does the problem."

"Our problem is with men," Veil said, "if you'll forgive me, dear brother. Men are of more account to other men than women and children are. We might have fifty witches here and they'll pay little heed. But if they knew we had five men of power, they'd seek to destroy us again."

"So though there were men among us we were the *women* of the Hand," said Ember.

"You still are," Medra said. "Anieb was one of you. She and you and all of us live in the same prison."

"What can we do?" said Veil.

"Learn our strength!" said Medra.

"A school," Ember said. "Where the wise might come to learn from one another, to study the pattern . . . The Grove would shelter us."

"The lords of war despise scholars and schoolmasters," said Medra.

"I think they fear them too," said Veil.

So they talked, that long winter, and others talked with them. Slowly their talk turned from vision to intention, from longing to planning. Veil was always cautious, warning of dangers. White-haired Dune was so eager that Ember said he wanted to start teaching sorcery to every child in Thwil. Once Ember had come to believe that Roke's freedom lay in offering others freedom, she set her whole mind on how the women of the Hand might grow strong again. But her mind, formed by her long solitudes among the trees, always sought form and clarity, and she said, "How can we teach our art when we don't know what it is?"

And they talked about that, all the wise women of the island: what was the true art of magic, and where did it turn false; how the balance of things was kept or lost; what crafts were needful, which useful, which dangerous; why some people had one gift but not another, and whether you could learn an art you had no native gift for. In such discussions they worked out the names that ever since have been given to the masteries: finding, weatherworking, changing, healing, summoning, patterning, naming, and the crafts of illusion, and the knowledge of the songs. Those are the arts of the Masters of Roke even now, though the Chanter took the Finder's place when finding came to be considered a merely useful craft unworthy of a mage.

And it was in these discussions that the school on Roke began.

There are some who say that the school had its beginnings far differently. They say that Roke used to be ruled by a woman called the Dark Woman, who was in league with the Old Powers of the earth. They say she lived in a cave under Roke Knoll, never coming into the daylight, but weaving vast spells over land and sea that compelled men to her evil will, until the first Archmage came to Roke, unsealed and entered the cave, defeated the Dark Woman, and took her place.

There's no truth in this tale but one, which is that indeed one of the first Masters of Roke opened and entered a great cavern. But though the roots of Roke are the roots of all the islands, that cavern was not on Roke.

And it's true that in the time of Medra and Elehal the people of Roke, men and women, had no fear of the Old Powers of the earth, but revered them, seeking strength and vision from them. That changed with the years.

Spring came late again that year, cold and stormy. Medra set to boat-building. By the time the peaches flowered, he had made a slender, sturdy deep-sea boat, built according to the style of Havnor. He called her *Hopeful.* Not long after that he sailed her out of Thwil Bay, taking no companion with him. "Look for me at the end of summer," he said to Ember.

"I'll be in the Grove," she said. "And my heart with you, my dark otter, my white tern, my love, Medra."

"And mine with you, my ember of fire, my flowering tree, my love, Elehal."

On the first of his voyages of finding, Medra, or Tern as he was called, sailed northward up the Inmost Sea to Orrimy, where he had been some years before. There were people of the Hand there whom he trusted. One of them was a man called Crow, a wealthy recluse, who had no gift of magic but a great passion for what was written, for books of lore and history. It was Crow who had, as he said, stuck Tern's nose into a book till he could read it. "Illiterate wizards are the curse of Earthsea!" he cried. "Ignorant power is a bane!" Crow was a strange man, wilful, arrogant, obstinate, and, in defense of his passion, brave. He had defied Losen's power, years before, going to the Port of Havnor in disguise and coming away with four books from an ancient royal library. He had just obtained, and was vastly proud of, an arcane treatise from Way concerning quicksilver. "Got that from under Losen's nose too," he said to Tern. "Come have a look at it! It belonged to a famous wizard."

"Tinaral," said Tern. "I knew him."

"Book's trash, is it?" said Crow, who was quick to pick up signals if they had to do with books.

"I don't know. I'm after bigger prey."

Crow cocked his head.

"The Book of Names."

"Lost with Ath when he went into the west," Crow said.

"A mage called Highdrake told me that when Ath stayed in Pendor, he told a wizard there that he'd left the Book of Names with a woman in the Ninety Isles for safekeeping."

"A woman! For safekeeping! In the Ninety Isles! Was he mad?"

Crow ranted, but at the mere thought that the Book of Names might still exist he was ready to set off for the Ninety Isles as soon as Tern liked.

So they sailed south in *Hopeful,* landing first at malodorous Geath, and then in the guise of peddlers working their way from one islet to the next among the mazy channels. Crow had stocked the boat with better wares than most householders of the Isles were used to seeing, and Tern offered them at fair prices, mostly in barter, since there was little money among the islanders. Their popularity ran ahead of them. It was known that they would trade for books, if the books were old and uncanny. But in the Isles all books were old and all uncanny, what there was of them.

Crow was delighted to get a water-stained bestiary from the time of Akambar in return for five silver buttons, a pearl-hilted knife, and a square of Lorbanery silk. He sat in *Hopeful* and crooned over the antique descriptions of harikki and otak and icebear. But Tern went ashore on every isle, showing his wares in the kitchens of the housewives and the sleepy taverns where the old men sat. Sometimes he idly made a fist and then turned his hand over opening the palm, but nobody here returned the sign.

"Books?" said a rush plaiter on North Sudidi. "Like that there?" He pointed to long strips of vellum that had been worked into the thatching of his house. "They good for something else?" Crow, staring up at the words visible here and there between the rushes in the eaves, began to tremble with rage. Tern hurried him back to the boat before he exploded.

"It was only a beast healer's manual," Crow admitted, when they were sailing on and he had calmed down. "'Spavined,' I saw, and something about ewes' udders. But the ignorance! the brute ignorance! To roof his house with it!"

"And it was useful knowledge," Tern said. "How can people be anything but ignorant when knowledge isn't saved, isn't taught? If books could be brought together in one place . . ."

"Like the Library of the Kings," said Crow, dreaming of lost glories.

"Or your library," said Tern, who had become a subtler man than he used to be.

"Fragments," Crow said, dismissing his life's work. "Remnants!"

"Beginnings," said Tern.

Crow only sighed.

"I think we might go south again," Tern said, steering for the open channel. "Towards Pody."

"You have a gift for the business," Crow said. "You know where to look. Went straight to that bestiary in the barn loft . . . But there's nothing much to look for here. Nothing of importance. Ath wouldn't have left the greatest of all the lore-books among boors who'd make thatch of it! Take us to Pody if you like. And then back to Orrimy. I've had about enough."

"And we're out of buttons," Tern said. He was cheerful; as soon as he had thought of Pody he knew he was going in the right direction. "Perhaps I can find some along the way," he said. "It's my gift, you know."

Neither of them had been on Pody. It was a sleepy southern island with a pretty old port town, Telio, built of rosy sandstone, and fields and orchards that should have been fertile. But the lords of Wathort had ruled it for a century, taxing and slave taking and wearing the land and people down. The sunny streets of Telio were sad and dirty. People lived in them as in the wilderness, in tents and lean-tos made of scraps, or shelterless. "Oh, this won't do," Crow said, disgusted, avoiding a pile of human excrement. "These creatures don't have books, Tern!"

"Wait, wait," his companion said. "Give me a day."

"It's dangerous," Crow said, "it's pointless," but he made no further objection. The modest, naive young man whom he had taught to read had become his unfathomable guide.

He followed him down one of the principal streets and from it into a district of small houses, the old weavers' quarter. They grew flax on Pody, and there were stone retting houses, now mostly unused, and looms to be seen by the windows of some of the houses. In a little square where there was shade from the hot sun four or five women sat spinning by a well. Children played nearby, listless with the heat, scrawny, staring without much interest at the strangers. Tern had walked there unhesitating, as if he knew where he was going. Now he stopped and greeted the women.

"Oh, pretty man," said one of them with a smile, "don't even show us what you have in your pack there, for I haven't a penny of copper or ivory, nor seen one for a month."

"You might have a bit of linen, though, mistress? woven, or thread? Linen of Pody is the best—so I've heard as far as Havnor. And I can tell the quality of what you're spinning. A beautiful thread it is." Crow watched his companion with amusement and some disdain; he himself could bargain for a book very shrewdly, but nattering with common women about buttons and thread was beneath him. "Let me just open this up," Tern was saying as he spread his pack out on the cobbles, and the women and the dirty, timid children drew closer to see the wonders he would show them. "Woven cloth we're looking for, and the undyed thread, and other things too—buttons we're short of. If you had any of horn or bone, maybe? I'd trade one of these little velvet caps here for three or four buttons. Or one of these rolls of ribbon; look at the color of it. Beautiful with your hair, mistress! Or paper, or books. Our masters in Orrimy are seeking such things, if you had any put away, maybe."

"Oh, you are a pretty man," said the woman who had spoken first, laughing, as he held the red ribbon up to her black braid. "And I wish I had something for you!"

"I won't be so bold as to ask for a kiss," said Medra, "but an open hand, maybe?"

He made the sign; she looked at him for a moment. "That's easy," she said softly, and made the sign in return, "but not always safe, among strangers."

He went on showing his wares and joking with the women and children. Nobody bought anything. They gazed at the trinkets as if they were treasures. He let them gaze and finger all they would; indeed he let one of the children filch a little mirror of polished brass, seeing it vanish under the ragged shirt and saying nothing. At last he said he must go on, and the children drifted away as he folded up his pack.

"I have a neighbor," said the black-braided woman, "who might have some paper, if you're after that."

"Written on?" said Crow, who had been sitting on the well coping, bored. "Marks on it?"

She looked him up and down. "Marks on it, sir," she said. And then, to Tern, in a different tone, "If you'd like to come with me, she lives this way. And though she's only a girl, and poor, I'll tell you, peddler, she has an open hand. Though perhaps not all of us do."

"Three out of three," said Crow, sketching the sign, "so spare your vinegar, woman."

"Oh, it's you who have it to spare, sir. We're poor folk here. And ignorant," she said, with a flash of her eyes, and led on.

She brought them to a house at the end of a lane. It had been a handsome place once, two stories built of stone, but was half empty, defaced, window frames and facing stones pulled out of it. They crossed a courtyard with a well in it. She knocked at a side door, and a girl opened it.

"Ach, it's a witch's den," Crow said, at the whiff of herbs and aromatic smoke, and he stepped back.

"Healers," their guide said. "Is she ill again, Dory?"

The girl nodded, looking at Tern, then at Crow. She was thirteen or fourteen, heavyset though thin, with a sullen, steady gaze.

"They're men of the Hand, Dory, one short and pretty and one tall and proud, and they say they're seeking papers. I know you had some once, though you may not now. They've nothing you need in their pack, but it might be they'd pay a bit of ivory for what they want. Is it so?" She turned her bright eyes on Tern, and he nodded.

"She's very sick, Rush," the girl said. She looked again at Tern. "You're not a healer?" It was an accusation.

"No."

"She is," said Rush. "Like her mother and her mother's mother. Let us in, Dory, or me at least, to speak to her." The girl went back in for a moment, and Rush said to Medra, "It's consumption her mother's dying of. No healer could cure her. But she could heal the scrofula, and touch for pain. A wonder she was, and Dory bade fair to follow her."

The girl motioned them to come in. Crow chose to wait outside. The room was high and long, with traces of former elegance, but very old and very poor. Healers' paraphernalia and drying herbs were everywhere, though ranged in some order. Near the fine stone fireplace, where a tiny wisp of sweet herbs burned, was a bedstead. The woman in it was so wasted that in the dim light she seemed nothing but bone and shadow. As Tern came close she tried to sit up and to speak. Her daughter raised her head on the pillow, and when Tern was very near he could hear her: "Wizard," she said. "Not by chance."

A woman of power, she knew what he was. Had she called him there?

"I'm a finder," he said. "And a seeker."

"Can you teach her?"

"I can take her to those who can."

"Do it."

"I will."

She laid her head back and closed her eyes.

Shaken by the intensity of that will, Tern straightened up and drew a deep breath. He looked round at the girl, Dory. She did not return his gaze, watching her mother with stolid, sullen grief. Only after the woman sank into sleep did Dory move, going to help Rush, who as a friend and neighbor had made herself useful and was gathering up blood-soaked cloths scattered by the bed.

"She bled again just now, and I couldn't stop it," Dory said. Tears ran out of her eyes and down her cheeks. Her face hardly changed.

"Oh child, oh lamb," said Rush, taking her into her embrace; but though she hugged Rush, Dory did not bend.

"She's going there, to the wall, and I can't go with her," she said. "She's going alone and I can't go with her— Can't you go there?" She broke away from Rush, looking again at Tern. "You can go there!"

"No," he said. "I don't know the way."

Yet as Dory spoke he saw what the girl saw: a long hill going down into darkness, and across it, on the edge of twilight, a low wall of stones. And as he looked he thought he saw a woman walking along beside the wall, very thin, insubstantial, bone, shadow. But she was not the dying woman in the bed. She was Anieb.

Then that was gone and he stood facing the witch-girl. Her look of accusation slowly changed. She put her face in her hands.

"We have to let them go," he said.

She said, "I know."

Rush glanced from one to the other with her keen, bright eyes. "Not only a handy man," she said, "but a crafty man. Well, you're not the first."

He looked his question.

"This is called Ath's House," she said.

"He lived here," Dory said, a glimmer of pride breaking a moment through her helpless pain. "The Mage Ath. Long ago. Before he went into the west. All my foremothers were wise women. He stayed here. With them."

"Give me a basin," Rush said. "I'll get water to soak these."

"I'll get the water," Tern said. He took the basin and went out to the courtyard, to the well. Just as before, Crow was sitting on the coping, bored and restless.

"Why are we wasting time here?" he demanded, as Tern let the bucket down into the well. "Are you fetching and carrying for witches now?"

"Yes," Tern said, "and I will till she dies. And then I'll take her daughter to Roke. And if you want to read the Book of Names, you can come with us."

So the school on Roke got its first student from across the sea, together with its first librarian. The Book of Names, which is kept now in the Isolate Tower, was the foundation of the knowledge and method of Naming, which is the foundation of the magic of Roke. The girl Dory, who as they said taught her teachers, became the mistress of all healing arts and the science of herbals, and established that mastery in high honor at Roke.

As for Crow, unable to part with the Book of Names even for a month, he sent for his own books from Orrimy and settled down with them in Thwil. He allowed people of the school to study them, so long as they showed them, and him, due respect.

So the pattern of the years was set for Tern. In the late spring he would go out in *Hopeful,* seeking and finding people for the school on

Roke—children and young people, mostly, who had a gift of magic, and sometimes grown men or women. Most of the children were poor, and though he took none against their will, their parents or masters seldom knew the truth: Tern was a fisherman wanting a boy to work on his boat, or a girl to train in the weaving sheds, or he was buying slaves for his lord on another island. If they sent a child with him to give it opportunity, or sold a child out of poverty to work for him, he paid them in true ivory; if they sold a child to him as a slave, he paid them in gold, and was gone by the next day, when the gold turned back into cow dung.

He traveled far in the Archipelago, even out into the East Reach. He never went to the same town or island twice without years between, letting his trail grow cold. Even so he began to be spoken of. The Child Taker, they called him, a dreaded sorcerer who carried children to his island in the icy north and there sucked their blood. In villages on Way and Felkway they still tell children about the Child Taker, as an encouragement to distrust strangers.

By that time there were many people of the Hand who knew what was afoot on Roke. Young people came there sent by them. Men and women came to be taught and to teach. Many of these had a hard time getting there, for the spells that hid the island were stronger than ever, making it seem only a cloud, or a reef among the breakers; and the Roke wind blew, which kept any ship from Thwil Bay unless there was a sorcerer aboard who knew how to turn that wind. Still they came, and as the years went on a larger house was needed for the school than any in Thwil Town.

In the Archipelago, men built ships and women built houses, that was the custom; but in building a great structure women let men work with them, not having the miners' superstitions that kept men out of the mines, or the shipwrights' that forbade women to watch a keel laid. So both men and women of great power raised the Great House on Roke. Its cornerstone was set on a hilltop above Thwil Town, near the Grove and looking to the Knoll. Its walls were built not only of stone and wood, but founded deep on magic and made strong with spells.

Standing on that hill, Medra had said, "There is a vein of water, just under where I stand, that will not go dry." They dug down carefully and came to the water; they let it leap up into the sunlight; and the first part of the Great House they made was its inmost heart, the courtyard of the fountain.

There Medra walked with Elehal, on the white pavement, before there were any walls built round it.

She had planted a young rowan from the Grove beside the fountain. They came to be sure it was thriving. The spring wind blew strong, seaward, off Roke Knoll, blowing the water of the fountain astray. Up on the slope of the Knoll they could see a little group of people: a circle of young students learning how to do tricks of illusion from the sorcerer Hega of O; Master Hand, they called him. The sparkweed, past flowering, cast its ashes on the wind. There were streaks of grey in Ember's hair.

"Off you go, then," she said, "and leave us to settle this matter of the Rule." Her frown was as fierce as ever, but her voice was seldom as harsh as this when she spoke to him.

"I'll stay if you want, Elehal."

"I do want you to stay. But don't stay! You're a finder, you have to go find. It's only that agreeing on the Way—or the Rule, Waris wants us to call it—is twice the work of building the House. And causes ten times the quarrels. I wish I could get away from it! I wish I could just walk with you, like this . . . And I wish you wouldn't go north."

"Why do we quarrel?" he said rather despondently.

"Because there are more of us! Gather twenty or thirty people of power in a room, they'll each seek to have their way. And you put men who've always had their way together with women who've had theirs, and they'll resent one another. And then, too, there are some true and real divisions among us, Medra. They must be settled, and they can't be settled easily. Though a little goodwill would go a long way."

"Is it Waris?"

"Waris and several other men. And they *are* men, and they make that important beyond anything else. To them, the Old Powers are abominable. And women's powers are suspect, because they suppose them all connected with the Old Powers. As if those Powers were to be controlled or used by any mortal soul! But they put men where we put the world. And so they hold that a true wizard must be a man. And celibate."

"Ah, that," Medra said, rueful.

"That indeed. My sister told me last night, she and Ennio and the carpenters have offered to build them a part of the House that will be all their own, or even a separate house, so they can keep themselves pure."

"Pure?"

"It's not my word, it's Waris's. But they've refused. They want the Rule of Roke to separate men from women, and they want men to make the decisions for all. Now what compromise can we make with them? Why did they come here, if they won't work with us?"

"We should send away the men who won't."

"Away? In anger? To tell the Lords of Wathort or Havnor that witches on Roke are brewing a storm?"

"I forget—I always forget," he said, downcast again. "I forget the walls of the prison. I'm not such a fool when I'm outside them . . . When I'm here I can't believe it is a prison. But outside, without you, I remember . . . I don't want to go, but I have to go. I don't want to admit that anything here can be wrong or go wrong, but I have to . . . I'll go this time, and I will go north, Elehal. But when I come back I'll stay. What I need to find I'll find here. Haven't I found it already?"

"No," she said, "only me . . . But there's a great deal of seeking and finding to be done in the Grove. Enough to keep even you from being restless. Why north?"

"To reach out the Hand to Enlad and Éa. I've never gone there. We know nothing about their wizardries. *Enlad of the Kings, and bright Éa, eldest of isles!* Surely we'll find allies there."

"But Havnor lies between us," she said.

"I won't sail my boat across Havnor, dear love. I plan to go around it. By water." He could always make her laugh; he was the only one who could. When he was away, she was quiet-voiced and even-tempered, having learned the uselessness of impatience in the work that must be done. Sometimes she still scowled, sometimes she smiled, but she did not laugh. When she could, she went to the Grove alone, as she had always done. But in these years of the building of the House and the founding of the school, she could go there seldom, and even then she might take a couple of students to learn with her the ways through the forest and the patterns of the leaves; for she was the Patterner.

Tern left late that year on his journey. He had with him a boy of fifteen, Mote, a promising weatherworker who needed training at sea, and Sava, a woman of sixty who had come to Roke with him seven or eight years before. Sava had been one of the women of the Hand on the isle of Ark. Though she had no wizardly gifts at all, she knew so well how to get a group of people to trust one another and work together that she was honored as a wise woman on Ark, and now on Roke. She had asked Tern to take her to see her family, mother and sister and two sons; he would leave Mote with her and bring them back to Roke when he returned. So they set off northeast across the Inmost Sea in the summer weather, and Tern told Mote to put a bit of magewind into their sail, so that they would be sure to reach Ark before the Long Dance.

As they coasted that island, he himself put an illusion about *Hopeful,* so that she would seem not a boat but a drifting log; for pirates and Losen's slave takers were thick in these waters.

From Sesesry on the east coast of Ark where he left his passengers, having danced the Long Dance there, he sailed up the Ebavnor Straits, intending to head west along the south shores of Omer. He kept the illusion spell about his boat. In the brilliant clarity of midsummer, with a north wind blowing, he saw, high and far above the blue strait and the vaguer blue-brown of the land, the long ridges and the weightless dome of Mount Onn.

Look, Medra. Look!

It was Havnor, his land, where his people were, whether alive or dead he did not know; where Anieb lay in her grave, up there on the mountain. He had never been back, never come this close. It had been how long? Sixteen years, seventeen years. Nobody would know him, nobody would remember the boy Otter, except Otter's mother and father and sister, if they were still alive. And surely there were people of the Hand in the Great Port. Though he had not known of them as a boy, he should know them now.

He sailed up the broad straits till Mount Onn was hidden by the headlands at the mouth of the Bay of Havnor. He would not see it again unless he went through that narrow passage. Then he would see the mountain, all the sweep and cresting of it, over the calm waters where he used to try to raise up the magewind when he was twelve; and sailing on he would see the towers rise up from the water, dim at first, mere dots and lines, then lifting up their bright banners, the white city at the center of the world.

It was mere cowardice to keep from Havnor, now—fear for his skin, fear lest he find his people had died, fear lest he recall Anieb too vividly.

For there had been times when he felt that, as he had summoned her living, so dead she might summon him. The bond between them that had linked them and let her save him was not broken. Many times she had come into his dreams, standing silent as she stood when he first saw her in the reeking tower at Samory. And he had seen her, years ago, in the vision of the dying healer in Telio, in the twilight, beside the wall of stones.

He knew now, from Elehal and others on Roke, what that wall was. It lay between the living and the dead. And in that vision, Anieb had walked on this side of it, not on the side that went down into the dark.

Did he fear her, who had freed him?

He tacked across the strong wind, swung round South Point, and sailed into the Great Bay of Havnor.

Banners still flew from the towers of the City of Havnor, and a king still ruled there; the banners were those of captured towns and isles, and the king was the warlord Losen. Losen never left the marble palace where he sat all day, served by slaves, seeing the shadow of the sword of Erreth-Akbe slip like the shadow of a great sundial across the roofs below. He gave orders, and the slaves said, "It is done, your majesty." He held audiences, and old men came and said, "We obey, your majesty." He summoned his wizards, and the mage Early came, bowing low. "Make me walk!" Losen shouted, beating his paralysed legs with his weak hands.

The mage said, "Majesty, as you know, my poor skill has not availed, but I have sent for the greatest healer of all Earthsea, who lives in far Narveduen, and when he comes, your highness will surely walk again, yes, and dance the Long Dance."

Then Losen cursed and cried, and his slaves brought him wine, and the mage went out, bowing, and checking as he went to be sure that the spell of paralysis was holding.

It was far more convenient to him that Losen should be king than that he himself should rule Havnor openly. Men of arms didn't trust men of craft and didn't like to serve them. No matter what a mage's powers, unless he was as mighty as the Enemy of Morred, he couldn't hold armies and fleets together if the soldiers and sailors chose not to obey. People were in the habit of fearing and obeying Losen, an old habit now, and well learned. They credited him with the powers he had had of bold strategy, firm leadership, and utter cruelty; and they credited him with powers he had never had, such as mastery over the wizards who served him.

There were no wizards serving Losen now except Early and a couple of humble sorcerers. Early had driven off or killed, one after another, his rivals for Losen's favor, and had enjoyed sole rule over all Havnor now for years.

When he was Gelluk's prentice and assistant, he had encouraged his master in the study of the lore of Way, finding himself free while Gelluk was off doting on his quicksilver. But Gelluk's abrupt fate had shaken him. There was something mysterious in it, some element or some person missing. Summoning the useful Hound to help him, Early had made a very thorough inquiry into what happened. Where Gelluk was, of course, was no mystery. Hound had tracked him straight to a scar in a hillside, and said he was buried deep under there. Early had no wish to exhume him. But the boy who had been with him, Hound could not track: could not say whether he was under that hill with Gelluk, or had got clean away. He had left no spell traces as the mage did, said Hound, and it had rained very hard all the night after, and when Hound thought he had found the boy's tracks, they were a woman's; and she was dead.

Early did not punish Hound for his failure, but he remembered it. He was not used to failures and did not like them. He did not like what Hound told him about this boy, Otter, and he remembered it.

The desire for power feeds off itself, growing as it devours. Early suffered from hunger. He starved. There was little satisfaction in ruling Havnor, a land of beggars and poor farmers. What was the good of possessing the Throne of Maharion if nobody sat in it but a drunken cripple? What glory was there in the palaces of the city when nobody lived in them but crawling slaves? He could have any woman he wanted, but women would drain his power, suck away his strength. He wanted no woman near him. He craved an enemy: an opponent worth destroying.

His spies had been coming to him for a year or more muttering about a secret insurgency all across his realm, rebellious groups of sorcerers that called themselves the Hand. Eager to find his enemy, he had one such group investigated. They turned out to be a lot of old women, midwives, carpenters, a ditchdigger, a tinsmith's prentice, a couple of little boys. Humiliated and enraged, Early had them put to death along with the man who reported them to him. It was a public execution, in Losen's name, for the crime of conspiracy against the King. There had perhaps not been enough of that kind of intimidation lately. But it went against his grain. He didn't like to make a public spectacle of fools who had tricked him into fearing them. He would rather have dealt with them in his own way, in his own time. To be nourishing, fear must be immediate; he needed to see people afraid of him, hear their terror, smell it, taste it. But since he ruled in Losen's name, it was Losen who must be feared by the armies and the peoples, and he himself must keep in the background, making do with slaves and prentices.

Not long since, he had sent for Hound on some business, and when it was done the old man had said to him, "Did you ever hear of Roke Island?"

"South and west of Kamery. The Lord of Wathort's owned it for forty or fifty years."

Though he seldom left the city, Early prided himself on his knowledge of all the Archipelago, gleaned from his sailors' reports and the marvelous ancient charts kept in the palace. He studied them nights, brooding on where and how he might extend his empire.

Hound nodded, as if its location was all that had interested him in Roke.

"Well?"

"One of the old women you had tortured before they burned the lot, you know? Well, the fellow who did it told me. She talked about her son on Roke. Calling out to him to come, you know. But like as if he had the power to."

"Well?"

"Seemed odd. Old woman from a village inland, never seen the sea, calling the name of an island away off like that."

"The son was a fisherman who talked about his travels."

Early waved his hand. Hound sniffed, nodded, and left.

Early never disregarded any triviality Hound mentioned, because so many of them had proved not to be trivial. He disliked the old man for that, and because he was unshakable. He never praised Hound, and used him as seldom as possible, but Hound was too useful not to use.

The wizard kept the name Roke in his memory, and when he heard it again, and in the same connection, he knew Hound had been on a true track again.

Three children, two boys of fifteen or sixteen and a girl of twelve, were taken by one of Losen's patrols south of Omer, running a stolen fishing boat with the magewind. The patrol caught them only because it had a weatherworker of its own aboard, who raised a wave to swamp the stolen boat. Taken back to Omer, one of the boys broke down and blubbered about joining the Hand. Hearing that word, the men told them they would be tortured and burned, at which the boy cried that if they spared him he would tell them all about the Hand, and Roke, and the great mages of Roke.

"Bring them here," Early said to the messenger.

"The girl flew away, lord," the man said unwillingly.

"Flew away?"

"She took bird form. Osprey, they said. Didn't expect that from a girl so young. Gone before they knew it."

"Bring the boys, then," Early said with deadly patience.

They brought him one boy. The other had jumped from the ship, crossing Havnor Bay, and been killed by a crossbow quarrel. The boy they brought was in such a paroxysm of terror that even Early was disgusted by him. How could he frighten a creature already blind and beshatten with fear? He set a binding spell on the boy that held him upright and immobile as a stone statue, and left him so for a night and a day. Now and then he talked to the statue, telling it that it was a clever lad and might make a good prentice, here in the palace. Maybe he could go to Roke after all, for Early was thinking of going to Roke, to meet with the mages there.

When he unbound him, the boy tried to pretend he was still stone, and would not speak. Early had to go into his mind, in the way he had learned from Gelluk long ago, when Gelluk was a true master of his art. He found out what he could. Then the boy was no good for anything and had to be disposed of. It was humiliating, again, to be outwitted by the very stupidity of these people; and all he had learned about Roke was that the Hand was there, and a school where they taught wizardry. And he had learned a man's name.

The idea of a school for wizards made him laugh. A school for wild boars, he thought, a college for dragons! But that there was some kind of scheming and gathering together of men of power on Roke seemed probable, and the idea of any league or alliance of wizards appalled him more the more he thought of it. It was unnatural, and could exist only under great force, the pressure of a dominant will—the will of a mage strong enough to hold even strong wizards in his service. There was the enemy he wanted!

Hound was down at the door, they said. Early sent for him to come up. "Who's Tern?" he asked as soon as he saw the old man.

With age Hound had come to look his name, wrinkled, with a long nose and sad eyes. He sniffed and seemed about to say he did not know, but he knew better than to try to lie to Early. He sighed. "Otter," he said. "Him that killed old Whiteface."

"Where's he hiding?"

"Not hiding at all. Went about the city, talking to people. Went to see his mother in Endlane, round the mountain. He's there now."

"You should have told me at once," Early said.

"Didn't know you were after him. I've been after him a long time. He fooled me." Hound spoke without rancor.

"He tricked and killed a great mage, my master. He's dangerous. I want vengeance. Who did he talk to here? I want them. Then I'll see to him."

"Some old women down by the docks. An old sorcerer. His sister."

"Get them here. Take my men."

Hound sniffed, sighed, nodded.

There was not much to be got from the people his men brought to him. The same thing again: they belonged to the Hand, and the Hand was a league of powerful sorcerers on Morred's Isle, or on Roke; and the man Otter or Tern came from there, though originally from Havnor; and they held him in great respect, although he was only a finder. The sister had vanished, perhaps gone with Otter to Endlane, where the mother lived. Early rummaged in their cloudy, witless minds, had the youngest of them tortured, and then burned them where Losen could sit at his window and watch. The King needed some diversions.

All this took only two days, and all the time Early was looking and probing toward Endlane village, sending Hound there before him, sending his own presentment there to watch. When he knew where the man was he betook himself there very quickly, on eagle's wings; for

Early was a great shape-changer, so fearless that he would take even dragon form.

He knew it was well to use caution with this man. Otter had defeated Tinaral, and there was this matter of Roke. There was some strength in him or with him. Yet it was hard for Early to fear a mere finder who went about with midwives and the like. He could not bring himself to sneak and skulk. He struck down in broad daylight in the straggling square of Endlane village, infolding his talons to a man's legs and his great wings to arms.

A child ran bawling to its mammy. No one else was about. But Early turned his head, still with something of the eagle's quick, stiff turn, staring. Wizard knows wizard, and he knew which house his prey was in. He walked to it and flung the door open.

A slight, brown man sitting at the table looked up at him.

Early raised his hand to lay the binding spell on him. His hand was stayed, held immobile half lifted at his side.

This was a contest, then, a foe worth fighting! Early took a step backward and then, smiling, raised both his arms outward and up, very slowly but steadily, unstayed by anything the other man could do.

The house vanished. No walls, no roof, nobody. Early stood on the dust of the village square in the sunshine of morning with his arms in the air.

It was only illusion, of course, but it checked him a moment in his spell, and then he had to undo the illusion, bringing back the door frame around him, the walls and roof beams, the gleam of light on crockery, the hearth stones, the table. But nobody sat at the table. His enemy was gone.

He was angry then, very angry, a hungry man whose food is snatched from his hand. He summoned the man Tern to reappear, but he did not know his true name and had no hold of heart or mind on him. The summons went unanswered.

He strode from the house, turned, and set a fire spell on it so that it burst into flames, thatch and walls and every window spouting fire. Women ran out of it screaming. They had been hiding no doubt in the back room; he paid them no attention. "Hound," he thought. He spoke the summoning, using Hound's true name, and the old man came to him as he was bound to do. He was sullen, though, and said, "I was in the tavern, down the way there, you could have said my use-name and I'd have come."

Early looked at him once. Hound's mouth snapped shut and stayed shut.

"Speak when I let you," the wizard said. "Where is the man?"

Hound nodded northeastwards.

"What's there?"

Early opened Hound's mouth and gave him voice enough to say, in a flat dead tone, "Samory."

"What form is he in?"

"Otter," said the flat voice.

Early laughed. "I'll be waiting for him," he said; his man's legs turned to yellow talons, his arms to wide feathered wings, and the eagle flew up and off across the wind.

Hound sniffed, sighed, and followed, trudging along unwillingly, while behind him in the village the flames died down, and children cried, and women shouted curses after the eagle.

The danger in trying to do good is that the mind comes to confuse the intent of goodness with the act of doing things well.

That is not what the otter was thinking as it swam fast down the Yennava. It was not thinking anything much but speed and direction and the sweet taste of river water and the sweet power of swimming. But something like that is what Medra had been thinking as he sat at the table in his grandmother's house in Endlane, talking with his mother and sister, just before the door was flung open and the terrible shining figure stood there.

Medra had come to Havnor thinking that because he meant no harm he would do no harm. He had done irreparable harm. Men and women and children had died because he was there. They had died in torment, burned alive. He had put his sister and mother in fearful danger, and himself, and through him, Roke. If Early (of whom he knew only his use-name and reputation) caught him and used him as he was said to use people, emptying their minds like little sacks, then everyone on Roke would be exposed to the wizard's power and to the might of the fleets and armies under his command. Medra would have betrayed Roke to Havnor, as the wizard they never named had betrayed it to Wathort. Maybe that man, too, had thought he could do no harm.

Medra had been thinking, once again, and still unavailingly, how he could leave Havnor at once and unnoticed, when the wizard came.

Now, as otter, he was thinking only that he would like to stay otter, be otter, in the sweet brown water, the living river, forever. There is no death for an otter, only life to the end. But in the sleek creature was the mortal mind; and where the stream passes the hill west of Samory, the otter came up on the muddy bank, and then the man crouched there, shivering.

Where to now? Why had he come here?

He had not thought. He had taken the shape that came soonest to him, run to the river as an otter would, swum as the otter would swim. But only in his own form could he think as a man, hide, decide, act as a man or as a wizard against the wizard who hunted him.

He knew he was no match for Early. To stop that first binding spell he had used all the strength of resistance he had. The illusion and the shape-change were all the tricks he had to play. If he faced the wizard again he would be destroyed. And Roke with him. Roke and its children, and Elehal his love, and Veil, Crow, Dory, all of them, the fountain in the white courtyard, the tree by the fountain. Only the Grove would stand. Only the green hill, silent, immovable. He heard Elehal say to him, *Havnor lies between us.* He heard her say, *All the true powers, all the old powers, at root are one.*

He looked up. The hillside above the stream was that same hill where he had come that day with Tinaral, Anieb's presence within him. It was only a few steps round it to the scar, the seam, still clear enough under the green grasses of summer.

"Mother," he said, on his knees there, "Mother, open to me."

He laid his hands on the seam of earth, but there was no power in them.

"Let me in, mother," he whispered in the tongue that was as old as the hill. The ground shivered a little and opened.

He heard an eagle scream. He got to his feet. He leapt into the dark.

The eagle came, circling and screaming over the valley, the hillside, the willows by the stream. It circled, searching and searching, and flew back as it had come.

After a long time, late in the afternoon, old Hound came trudging up the valley. He stopped now and then and sniffed. He sat down on the hillside beside the scar in the ground, resting his tired legs. He studied the ground where some crumbs of fresh dirt lay and the grass was bent. He stroked the bent grass to straighten it. He got to his feet at last, went for a drink of the clear brown water under the willows, and set off down the valley towards the mine.

Medra woke in pain, in darkness. For a long time that was all there was. The pain came and went, the darkness remained. Once it lightened a little into a twilight in which he could dimly see. He saw a slope running down from where he lay towards a wall of stones, across which was darkness again. But he could not get up to walk to the wall, and presently the pain came back very sharp in his arm and hip and head. Then the darkness came around him, and then nothing.

Thirst: and with it pain. Thirst, and the sound of water running.

He tried to remember how to make light. Anieb said to him, plaintively, "Can't you make the light?" But he could not. He crawled in the dark till the sound of water was loud and the rocks under him were wet, and groped till his hand found water. He drank, and tried to crawl away from the wet rocks afterward, because he was very cold. One arm hurt and had no strength in it. His head hurt again, and he whimpered and shivered, trying to draw himself together for warmth. There was no warmth and no light.

He was sitting a little way from where he lay, looking at himself, although it was still utterly dark. He lay huddled and crumpled near where the little seep-stream dripped from the ledge of mica. Not far away lay another huddled heap, rotted red silk, long hair, bones. Beyond it the cavern stretched away. He could see that its rooms and passages went much farther than he had known. He saw it with the same uncaring interest with which he saw Tinaral's body and his own body. He felt a mild regret. It was only fair that he should die here with the man he had killed. It was right. Nothing was wrong. But something in him ached, not the sharp body pain, a long ache, lifelong.

"Anieb," he said.

Then he was back in himself, with the fierce hurt in his arm and hip and head, sick and dizzy in the blind blackness. When he moved, he whimpered; but he sat up. I have to live, he thought. I have to remember how to live. How to make light. I have to remember. I have to remember the shadows of the leaves.

How far does the forest go?

As far as the mind goes.

He looked up into the darkness. After a while he moved his good hand a little, and the faint light flowed out of it.

The roof of the cavern was far above him. The trickle of water dripping from the mica ledge glittered in short dashes in the werelight.

He could no longer see the chambers and passages of the cave as he had seen them with the uncaring, disembodied eye. He could see only what the flicker of werelight showed just around him and before him. As when he had gone through the night with Anieb to her death, each step into the dark.

He got to his knees, and thought then to whisper, "Thank you, mother." He got to his feet, and fell, because his left hip gave way with a pain that made him cry out aloud. After a while he tried again, and stood up. Then he started forward.

It took him a long time to cross the cavern. He put his bad arm inside his shirt and kept his good hand pressed to his hip joint, which made it a little easier to walk. The walls narrowed gradually to a passage. Here the roof was much lower, just above his head. Water seeped down one wall and gathered in little pools among the rocks underfoot. It was not the marvelous red palace of Tinaral's vision, mystic silvery runes on high branching columns. It was only the earth, only dirt, rock, water. The air was cool and still. Away from the dripping of the stream it was silent. Outside the gleam of werelight it was dark.

Medra bowed his head, standing there. "Anieb," he said, "can you come back this far? I don't know the way." He waited a while. He saw darkness, heard silence. Slow and halting, he entered the passage.

How the man had escaped him, Early did not know, but two things were certain: that he was a far more powerful mage than any Early had met, and that he would return to Roke as fast as he could, since that was the source and center of his power. There was no use trying to get there before him; he had the lead. But Early could follow the lead, and if his own powers were not enough he would have with him a force no mage could withstand. Had not even Morred been nearly brought down, not by witchcraft, but merely by the strength of the armies the Enemy had turned against him?

"Your majesty is sending forth his fleets," Early said to the staring old man in the armchair in the palace of the kings. "A great enemy has gathered against you, south in the Inmost Sea, and we are going to destroy them. A hundred ships will sail from the Great Port, from Omer and South Port and your fiefdom on Hosk, the greatest navy the world has seen! I shall lead them. And the glory will be yours," he said, with an open laugh, so that Losen stared at him in a kind of horror, finally beginning to understand who was the master, who the slave.

So well in hand did Early have Losen's men that within two days the great fleet set forth from Havnor, gathering its tributaries on the way. Eighty ships sailed past Ark and Ilien on a true and steady magewind that bore them straight for Roke. Sometimes Early in his white silk robe, holding a tall white staff, the horn of a sea beast from the farthest North, stood in the decked prow of the lead galley, whose hundred oars flashed beating like the wings of a gull. Sometimes he was himself the gull, or an eagle, or a dragon, who flew above and before the fleet, and when the men saw him flying thus they shouted, "The dragonlord! the dragonlord!"

They came ashore in Ilien for water and food. Setting a host of many hundreds of men on its way so quickly had left little time for provisioning the ships. They overran the towns along the west shore of Ilien, taking what they wanted, and did the same on Vissti and Kamery, looting what they could and burning what they left. Then the great fleet turned west, heading for the one harbor of Roke Island, the Bay of Thwil. Early knew of the harbor from the maps in Havnor, and knew there was a high hill above it. As they came nearer, he took dragon form and soared up high above his ships, leading them, gazing into the west for the sight of that hill.

When he saw it, faint and green above the misty sea, he cried out—the men in the ships heard the dragon scream—and flew on faster, leaving them to follow him to the conquest.

All the rumors of Roke had said that it was spell-defended and charm-hidden, invisible to ordinary eyes. If there were any spells woven about that hill or the bay he now saw opening before it, they were gossamer to him, transparent. Nothing blurred his eyes or challenged his will as he flew over the bay, over the little town and a half-finished building on the slope above it, to the top of the high green hill. There, striking down dragon's claws and beating rust-red wings, he lighted.

He stood in his own form. He had not made the change himself. He stood alert, uncertain.

The wind blew, the long grass nodded in the wind. Summer was getting on and the grass was dry now, yellowing, no flowers in it but the little white heads of the lacefoam. A woman came walking up the hill towards him through the long grass. She followed no path, and walked easily, without haste.

He thought he had raised his hand in a spell to stop her, but he had not raised his hand, and she came on. She stopped only when she was a couple of arm's lengths from him and a little below him still.

"Tell me your name," she said, and he said, "Teriel."

"Why did you come here, Teriel?"

"To destroy you."

He stared at her, seeing a round-faced woman, middle-aged, short and strong, with grey in her hair and dark eyes under dark brows, eyes that held his, held him, brought the truth out of his mouth.

"Destroy us? Destroy this hill? The trees there?" She looked down to a grove of trees not far from the hill. "Maybe Segoy who made them could unmake them. Maybe the earth will destroy herself. Maybe she'll destroy herself through our hands, in the end. But not through yours. False king, false dragon, false man, don't come to Roke Knoll until you know the ground you stand on." She made one gesture of her hand, downward to the earth. Then she turned and went down the hill through the long grass, the way she had come.

There were other people on the hill, he saw now, many others, men and women, children, living and spirits of the dead; many, many of them. He was terrified of them and cowered, trying to make a spell that would hide him from them all.

But he made no spell. He had no magic left in him. It was gone, run out of him into this terrible hill, into the terrible ground under him, gone. He was no wizard, only a man like the others, powerless.

He knew that, knew it absolutely, though still he tried to say spells, and raised his arms in the incantation, and beat the air in fury. Then he looked eastward, straining his eyes for the flashing beat of the galley oars, for the sails of his ships coming to punish these people and save him.

All he saw was a mist on the water, all across the sea beyond the mouth of the bay. As he watched it thickened and darkened, creeping out over the slow waves.

Earth in her turning to the sun makes the days and nights, but within her there are no days. Medra walked through the night. He was very lame, and could not always keep up the werelight. When it failed he had to stop and sit down and sleep. The sleep was never death, as he thought it was. He woke, always cold, always in pain, always thirsty, and when he could make a glimmer of the light he got to his feet and went on. He never saw Anieb but he knew she was there. He followed her. Sometimes there were great rooms. Sometimes there were pools of motionless water. It was hard to break the stillness of their surface, but he drank from them. He thought he had gone down deeper and deeper for a long time, till he reached the longest of those pools, and after that the way went up again. Sometimes now Anieb followed him. He could say her name, though she did not answer. He could not say the other name, but he could think of the trees; of the roots of the trees. This was the kingdom of the roots of the trees. How far does the forest go? As far as forests go. As long as the lives, as deep as the roots of the trees. As long as leaves cast shadows. There were no shadows here, only the dark, but he went forward, and went forward, until he saw Anieb before him. He saw the flash of her eyes, the cloud of her curling hair. She looked back at him for a moment, and then turned aside and ran lightly down a long, steep slope into darkness.

Where he stood it was not wholly dark. The air moved against his face. Far ahead, dim, small, there was a light that was not werelight. He went forward. He had been crawling for a long time now, dragging the right leg, which would not bear his weight. He went forward. He smelled the wind of evening and saw the sky of evening through the branches and leaves of trees. An arched oak root formed the mouth of the cave, no bigger than a man or a badger needed to crawl through. He crawled through. He lay there under the root of the tree, seeing the light fade and a star or two come out among the leaves.

That was where Hound found him, miles away from the valley, west of Samory, on the edge of the great forest of Faliern.

"Got you," the old man said, looking down at the muddy, lax body. He added, "Too late," regretfully. He stooped to see if he could pick him up or drag him, and felt the faint warmth of life. "You're tough," he said. "Here, wake up. Come on. Otter, wake up."

He recognised Hound, though he could not sit up and could barely speak. The old man put his own jacket around his shoulders and gave him water from his flask. Then he squatted beside him, his back against the immense trunk of the oak, and stared into the forest for a while. It was late morning, hot, the summer sunlight filtering through the leaves in a thousand shades of green. A squirrel scolded, far up in the oak, and a jay replied. Hound scratched his neck and sighed.

"The wizard's off on the wrong track, as usual," he said at last. "Said you'd gone to Roke Island and he'd catch you there. I said nothing."

He looked at the man he knew only as Otter.

"You went in there, that hole, with the old wizard, didn't you? Did you find him?"

Medra nodded.

"Hmn," Hound went, a short, grunting laugh. "You find what you look for, don't you? Like me." He saw that his companion was in distress, and said, "I'll get you out of here. Fetch a carter from the village down there, when I've got my breath. Listen. Don't fret. I haven't hunted you all these years to give you to Early. The way I gave you to Gelluk. I was sorry for that. I thought about it. What I said to you about men of a craft sticking together. And who we work for. Couldn't see that I had much choice about that. But having done you a disfavor, I thought if I came across you again I'd do you a favor, if I could. As one finder to the other, see?"

Otter's breath was coming hard. Hound put his hand on Otter's hand for a moment, said, "Don't worry," and got to his feet. "Rest easy," he said.

He found a carter who would carry them down to Endlane. Otter's mother and sister were living with cousins while they rebuilt their burned house as best they could. They welcomed him with disbelieving joy. Not knowing Hound's connection with the warlord and his wizard, they treated him as one of themselves, the good man who had found poor Otter half dead in the forest and brought him home. A wise man, said Otter's mother Rose, surely a wise man. Nothing was too good for such a man.

Otter was slow to recover, to heal. The bonesetter did what he could about his broken arm and his damaged hip, the wise woman salved the cuts from the rocks on his hands and head and knees, his mother brought him all the delicacies she could find in the gardens and berry thickets; but he lay as weak and wasted as when Hound first brought him. There was no heart in him, the wise woman of Endlane said. It was somewhere else, being eaten up with worry or fear or shame.

"So where is it?" Hound said.

Otter, after a long silence, said, "Roke Island."

"Where old Early went with the great fleet. I see. Friends there. Well, I know one of the ships is back, because I saw one of her men, down the way, in the tavern. I'll go ask about. Find out if they got to Roke and what happened there. What I can tell you is that it seems old Early is late coming home. Hmn, hmn," he went, pleased with his joke. "Late coming home," he repeated, and got up. He looked at Otter, who was not much to look at. "Rest easy," he said, and went off.

He was gone several days. When he returned, riding in a horse-drawn cart, he had such a look about him that Otter's sister hurried in to tell him, "Hound's won a battle or a fortune! He's riding behind a city horse, in a city cart, like a prince!"

Hound came in on her heels. "Well," he said, "in the first place, when I got to the city, I go up to the palace, just to hear the news, and what do I see? I see old King Pirate standing on his legs, shouting out orders like he used to do. Standing up! Hasn't stood for years. Shouting orders! And some of 'em did what he said, and some of 'em didn't. So I got on out of there, that kind of a situation being dangerous, in a palace. Then I went about to friends of mine and asked where was old Early and had the fleet been to Roke and come back and all. Early, they said, nobody knew about Early. Not a sign of him nor from him. Maybe I could find him, they said, joking me, hmn. They know I love him. As for the ships, some had come back, with the men aboard saying they never came to Roke Island, never saw it, sailed right through where the sea charts said was an island, and there was no island. Then there were some men from one of the great galleys. They said when they got close to where the island should be, they came into a fog as thick as wet cloth, and the sea turned thick too, so that the oarsmen could barely push the oars through it, and they were caught in that for a day and a night. When they got out, there wasn't another ship of all the fleet on the sea, and the slaves were near rebelling, so the master brought her home as quick as he could. Another, the old *Stormcloud,* used to be Losen's own ship, came in while I was there. I talked to some men off her. They said there was nothing but fog and reefs all round where Roke was supposed to be, so they sailed on with seven other ships, south a ways, and met up with a fleet sailing up from Wathort. Maybe the lords there had heard there was a great fleet coming raiding, because they didn't stop to ask questions, but sent wizard's fire at our ships, and came alongside to board them if they could, and the men I talked to said it was a hard fight just to get away from them, and not all did. All this time they had no word from Early, and no weather was worked for them unless they had a bagman of their own aboard. So they came back up the length of the Inmost Sea, said the man from *Stormcloud,* one straggling after the other like the dogs that lost the dogfight. Now, do you like the news I bring you?"

Otter had been struggling with tears; he hid his face. "Yes," he said, "thanks."

"Thought you might. As for King Losen," Hound said, "who knows." He sniffed and sighed. "If I was him I'd retire," he said. "I think I'll do that myself."

Otter had got control of his face and voice. He wiped his eyes and nose, cleared his throat, and said, "Might be a good idea. Come to Roke. Safer."

"Seems to be a hard place to find," Hound said.

"I can find it," said Otter.

IV. Medra

There was an old man by our door
Who opened it to rich or poor;
Many came there both small and great,
But few could pass through Medra's Gate.
So runs the water away, away,
So runs the water away.

Hound stayed in Endlane. He could make a living as a finder there, and he liked the tavern, and Otter's mother's hospitality.

By the beginning of autumn, Losen was hanging by a rope round his feet from a window of the New Palace, rotting, while six warlords quarreled over his kingdom, and the ships of the great fleet chased and fought one another across the Straits and the wizard-troubled sea.

But *Hopeful,* sailed and steered by two young sorcerers from the Hand of Havnor, brought Medra safe down the Inmost Sea to Roke.

Ember was on the dock to meet him. Lame and very thin, he came to her and took her hands, but he could not lift his face to hers. He said, "I have too many deaths on my heart, Elehal."

"Come with me to the Grove," she said.

They went there together and stayed till the winter came. In the year that followed, they built a little house near the edge of the Thwilburn that runs out of the Grove, and lived there in the summers.

They worked and taught in the Great House. They saw it go up stone on stone, every stone steeped in spells of protection, endurance, peace. They saw the Rule of Roke established, though never so firmly as they might wish, and always against opposition; for mages came from other islands and rose up from among the students of the school, women and men of power, knowledge, and pride, sworn by the Rule to work together and for the good of all, but each seeing a different way to do it.

Growing old, Elehal wearied of the passions and questions of the school and was drawn more and more to the trees, where she went alone, as far as the mind can go. Medra walked there too, but not so far as she, for he was lame.

After she died, he lived a while alone in the small house near the Grove.

One day in autumn he came back to the school. He went in by the garden door, which gives on the path through the fields to Roke Knoll. It is a curious thing about the Great House of Roke, that it has no portal or grand entryway at all. You can enter by what they call the back door, which, though it is made of horn and framed in dragon's tooth and carved with the Thousand-Leaved Tree, looks like nothing at all from outside, as you come to it in a dingy street; or you can go in the garden door, plain oak with an iron bolt. But there is no front door.

He came through the halls and stone corridors to the inmost place, the marble-paved courtyard of the fountain, where the tree Elehal had planted now stood tall, its berries reddening.

Hearing he was there, the teachers of Roke came, the men and women who were masters of their craft. Medra had been the Master Finder, until he went to the Grove. A young woman now taught that art, as he had taught it to her.

"I've been thinking," he said. "There are eight of you. Nine's a better number. Count me as a master again, if you will."

"What will you do, Master Tern?" asked the Summoner, a grey-haired mage from Ilien.

"I'll keep the door," Medra said. "Being lame, I won't go far from it. Being old, I'll know what to say to those who come. Being a finder, I'll find out if they belong here."

"That would spare us much trouble and some danger," said the young Finder.

"How will you do it?" the Summoner asked.

"I'll ask them their name," Medra said. He smiled. "If they'll tell me, they can come in. And when they think they've learned everything, they can go out again. If they can tell me my name."

So it was. For the rest of his life, Medra kept the doors of the Great House on Roke. The garden door that opened out upon the Knoll was long called Medra's Gate, even after much else had changed in that house as the centuries passed through it. And still the ninth Master of Roke is the Doorkeeper.

In Endlane and the villages round the foot of Onn on Havnor, women spinning and weaving sing a riddle song of which the last line has to do, maybe, with the man who was Medra, and Otter, and Tern.

Three things were that will not be:
Soléa's bright isle above the wave,
A dragon swimming in the sea,
A seabird flying in the grave.

Darkrose and Diamond

A Boat Song from West Havnor

Where my love is going
There will I go.
Where his boat is rowing
I will row.

We will laugh together,
Together we will cry.
If he lives I will live,
If he dies I die.

Where my love is going
There will I go.
Where his boat is rowing
I will row.

In the west of Havnor, among hills forested with oak and chestnut, is the town of Glade. A while ago, the rich man of that town was a merchant called Golden. Golden owned the mill that cut the oak boards for the ships they built in Havnor South Port and Havnor Great Port; he owned the biggest chestnut groves; he owned the carts and hired the carters that carried the timber and the chestnuts over the hills to be sold. He did very well from trees, and when his son was born, the mother said, "We could call him Chestnut, or Oak, maybe?" But the father said, "Diamond," diamond being in his estimation the one thing more precious than gold.

So little Diamond grew up in the finest house in Glade, a fat, bright-eyed baby, a ruddy, cheerful boy. He had a sweet singing voice, a true ear, and a love of music, so that his mother, Tuly, called him Songsparrow and Skylark, among other loving names, for she never really did like "Diamond." He trilled and caroled about the house; he knew any tune as soon as he heard it, and invented tunes when he heard none. His mother had the wise woman Tangle teach him *The Creation of Éa* and *The Deed of the Young King,* and at Sunreturn when he was eleven years old he sang *The Winter Carol* for the Lord of the Western Land, who was visiting his domain in the hills above Glade. The Lord and his Lady praised the boy's singing and gave him a tiny gold box with a diamond set in the lid, which seemed a kind and pretty gift to Diamond and his mother. But Golden was a bit impatient with the singing and the trinkets. "There are more important things for you to do, son," he said. "And greater prizes to be earned."

Diamond thought his father meant the business—the loggers, the sawyers, the sawmill, the chestnut groves, the pickers, the carters, the carts—all that work and talk and planning, those complicated, adult matters. He never felt that it had much to do with him, so how was he to have as much to do with it as his father expected? Maybe he'd find out when he grew up.

But in fact Golden wasn't thinking only about the business. He had observed something about his son that made him not exactly set his eyes higher than the business, but glance above it from time to time, and then shut his eyes.

At first he thought Diamond had a knack such as many children had and then lost, a stray spark of magery. When he was a little boy, Golden himself had been able to make his own shadow shine and sparkle. His family had praised him for the trick and made him show it off to visitors; and then when he was seven or eight he lost the hang of it and never could do it again.

When he saw Diamond come down the stairs without touching the stairs, he thought his eyes had deceived him; but a few days later, he saw the child float up the stairs, just a finger gliding along the oaken banister. "Can you do that coming down?" Golden asked, and Diamond said, "Oh, yes, like this," and sailed back down smooth as a cloud on the south wind.

"How did you learn to do that?"

"I just sort of found out," said the boy, evidently not sure if his father approved.

Golden did not praise the boy, not wanting to make him self-conscious or vain about what might be a passing, childish gift, like his sweet treble voice. There was too much fuss already made over that.

But a year or so later he saw Diamond out in the back garden with his playmate Rose. The children were squatting on their haunches, heads close together, laughing. Something intense or uncanny about them made him pause at the window on the stairs landing and watch them. A thing between them was leaping up and down, a frog? a toad? a big cricket? He went out into the garden and came up near them, moving so quietly, though he was a big man, that they in their absorption did not hear him. The thing that was hopping up and down on the grass between their bare toes was a rock. When Diamond raised his hand the rock jumped up in the air, and when he shook his hand a little the rock hovered in the air, and when he flipped his fingers downward it fell to earth.

"Now you," Diamond said to Rose, and she started to do what he had done, but the rock only twitched a little. "Oh," she whispered, "there's your dad."

"That's very clever," Golden said.

"Di thought it up," Rose said.

Golden did not like the child. She was both outspoken and defensive, both rash and timid. She was a girl, and a year younger than Diamond, and a witch's daughter. He wished his son would play with boys his own age, his own sort, from the respectable families of Glade. Tuly insisted on calling the witch "the wise woman," but a witch was a witch and her daughter was no fit companion for Diamond. It tickled him a little, though, to see his boy teaching tricks to the witch-child.

"What else can you do, Diamond?" he asked.

"Play the flute," Diamond said promptly, and took out of his pocket the little fife his mother had given him for his twelfth birthday. He put it to his lips, his fingers danced, and he played a sweet, familiar tune from the western coast, "Where My Love Is Going."

"Very nice," said the father. "But anybody can play the fife, you know."

Diamond glanced at Rose. The girl turned her head away, looking down.

"I learned it really quickly," Diamond said.

Golden grunted, unimpressed.

"It can do it by itself," Diamond said, and held out the fife away from his lips. His fingers danced on the stops, and the fife played a short jig. It hit several false notes and squealed on the last high note. "I haven't got it right yet," Diamond said, vexed and embarrassed.

"Pretty good, pretty good," his father said. "Keep practicing." And he went on. He was not sure what he ought to have said. He did not want to encourage the boy to spend any more time on music, or with this girl; he spent too much already, and neither of them would help him get anywhere in life. But this gift, this undeniable gift—the rock hovering, the unblown fife— Well, it would be wrong to make too much of it, but probably it should not be discouraged.

In Golden's understanding, money was power, but not the only power. There were two others, one equal, one greater. There was birth. When the Lord of the Western Land came to his domain near Glade, Golden was glad to show him fealty. The Lord was born to govern and to keep the peace, as Golden was born to deal with commerce and wealth, each in his place; and each, noble or common, if he served well and honestly, deserved honor and respect. But there were also lesser lords whom Golden could buy and sell, lend to or let beg, men born noble who deserved neither fealty nor honor. Power of birth and power of money were contingent, and must be earned lest they be lost.

But beyond the rich and the lordly were those called the men of power: the wizards. Their power, though little exercised, was absolute. In their hands lay the fate of the long-kingless kingdom of the Archipelago.

If Diamond had been born to that kind of power, if that was his gift, then all Golden's dreams and plans of training him in the business, and having him help in expanding the carting route to a regular trade with South Port, and buying up the chestnut forests above Reche—all such plans dwindled into trifles. Might Diamond go (as his mother's uncle had gone) to the School of Wizards on Roke Island? Might he (as that uncle had done) gain glory for his family and dominion over lord and commoner, becoming a mage in the Court of the Lords Regent in the Great Port of Havnor? Golden all but floated up the stairs himself, borne on such visions.

But he said nothing to the boy and nothing to the boy's mother. He was a consciously close-mouthed man, distrustful of visions until they could be made acts; and she, though a dutiful, loving wife and mother and housekeeper, already made too much of Diamond's talents and accomplishments. Also, like all women, she was inclined to babble and gossip, and indiscriminate in her friendships. The girl Rose hung about with Diamond because Tuly encouraged Rose's mother, the witch Tangle, to visit, consulting her every time Diamond had a hangnail, and telling her more than she or anyone ought to know about Golden's household. His business was none of the witch's business.

On the other hand, Tangle might be able to tell him if his son in fact showed promise, had a talent for magery . . . but he flinched away from the thought of asking her, asking a witch's opinion on anything, least of all a judgment on his son.

He resolved to wait and watch. Being a patient man with a strong will, he did so for four years, till Diamond was sixteen. A big, well-grown youth, good at games and lessons, he was still ruddy-faced and bright-eyed and cheerful. He had taken it hard when his voice changed, the sweet treble going all untuned and hoarse. Golden had hoped that that was the end of his singing, but the boy went on wandering about with itinerant musicians, ballad singers and such, learning all their trash. That was no life for a merchant's son who was to inherit and manage his father's properties and mills and business, and Golden told him so. "Singing time is over, son," he said. "You must think about being a man."

Diamond had been given his true name at the springs of the Amia in the hills above Glade. The wizard Hemlock, who had known his great-uncle the mage, came up from South Port to name him. And Hemlock was invited to his nameday party the year after, a big party, beer and food for all, and new clothes, a shirt or skirt or shift for every child, which was an old custom in the West of Havnor, and dancing on the village green in the warm autumn evening. Diamond had many friends, all the boys his age in town and all the girls too. The young people danced, and some of them had a bit too much beer, but nobody misbehaved very badly, and it was a merry and memorable night. The next morning Golden told his son again that he must think about being a man.

"I have thought some about it," said the boy, in his husky voice.

"And?"

"Well, I," said Diamond, and stuck.

"I'd always counted on your going into the family business," Golden said. His tone was neutral, and Diamond said nothing. "Have you had any ideas of what you want to do?"

"Sometimes."

"Did you talk at all to Master Hemlock?"

Diamond hesitated and said, "No." He looked a question at his father.

"I talked to him last night," Golden said. "He said to me that there are certain natural gifts which it's not only difficult but actually wrong, harmful, to suppress."

The light had come back into Diamond's dark eyes.

"The master said that such gifts or capacities, untrained, are not only wasted, but may be dangerous. The art must be learned, and practiced, he said."

Diamond's face shone.

"But, he said, it must be learned and practiced for its own sake."

Diamond nodded eagerly.

"If it's a real gift, an unusual capacity, that's even more true. A witch with her love potions can't do much harm, but even a village sorcerer, he said, must take care, for if the art is used for base ends, it becomes weak and noxious . . . Of course, even a sorcerer gets paid. And wizards, as you know, live with lords, and have what they wish."

Diamond was listening intently, frowning a little.

"So, to be blunt about it, if you have this gift, Diamond, it's of no use, directly, to our business. It has to be cultivated on its own terms, and kept under control—learned and mastered. Only then, he said, can your teachers begin to tell you what to do with it, what good it will do you. Or others," he added conscientiously.

There was a long pause.

"I told him," Golden said, "that I had seen you, with a turn of your hand and a single word, change a wooden carving of a bird into a bird that flew up and sang. I've seen you make a light glow in thin air. You didn't know I was watching. I've watched and said nothing for a long time. I didn't want to make too much of mere childish play. But I believe you have a gift, perhaps a great gift. When I told Master Hemlock what I'd seen you do, he agreed with me. He said that you may go study with him in South Port for a year, or perhaps longer."

"Study with Master Hemlock?" said Diamond, his voice up half an octave.

"If you wish."

"I, I, I never thought about it. Can I think about it? For a while—a day?"

"Of course," Golden said, pleased with his son's caution. He had thought Diamond might leap at the offer, which would have been natural, perhaps, but painful to the father, the owl who had—perhaps—hatched out an eagle.

For Golden looked on the art magic with genuine humility as something quite beyond him—not a mere toy, such as music or tale telling, but a practical business of immense potential, which his business could never quite equal. And he was also, though he wouldn't have put it that way, afraid of wizards. A bit contemptuous of sorcerers, with their sleights and illusions and gibble-gabble, but afraid of wizards.

"Does Mother know?" Diamond asked.

"She will when the time comes. She has no part to play in your decision, Diamond. Women know nothing of these matters and have nothing to do with them. You must make your choice alone, as a man. Do you understand that?" Golden was earnest, seeing his chance to begin to wean the lad from his mother. She as a woman would cling, but he as a man must learn to let go. And Diamond nodded sturdily enough to satisfy his father, though he had a thoughtful look.

"Master Hemlock said I, said he thought I had, I might have a, a gift, a talent for—?"

Golden reassured him that the wizard had actually said so, though of course what kind of gift remained to be seen. The boy's modesty was a great relief to him. He had half-consciously dreaded that Diamond would triumph over him, asserting his power right away—that mysterious, dangerous, incalculable power against which Golden's wealth and mastery and dignity shrank to impotence.

"Thank you, Father," the boy said. Golden embraced him and left, well pleased with him.

Their meeting place was in the sallows, the willow thickets down by the Amia as it ran below the smithy. As soon as Rose got there, Diamond said, "He wants me to go study with Master Hemlock! What am I going to do?"

"Study with the wizard?"

"He thinks I have this huge great talent. For magic."

"Who does?"

"Father does. He saw some of the stuff we were practicing. But he says Hemlock says I should come study with him because it might be dangerous not to. Oh," and Diamond beat his head with his hands.

"But you do have a talent."

He groaned and scoured his scalp with his knuckles. He was sitting on the dirt in their old play place, a kind of bower deep in the willows, where they could hear the stream running over the stones nearby and the clang-clang of the smithy further off. The girl sat down facing him.

"Look at all the stuff you can do," she said. "You couldn't do any of it if you didn't have a gift."

"A little gift," Diamond said indistinctly. "Enough for tricks."

"How do you know that?"

Rose was very dark-skinned, with a cloud of crinkled hair, a thin mouth, an intent, serious face. Her feet and legs and hands were bare and dirty, her skirt and jacket disreputable. Her dirty toes and fingers were delicate and elegant, and a necklace of amethysts gleamed under the torn, buttonless jacket. Her mother, Tangle, made a good living by curing and healing, bone knitting and birth easing, and selling spells of finding, love potions, and sleeping drafts. She could afford to dress herself and her daughter in new clothes, buy shoes, and keep clean, but it didn't occur to her to do so. Nor was housekeeping one of her interests. She and Rose lived mostly on boiled chicken and fried eggs, as she was often paid in poultry. The yard of their two-room house was a wilderness of cats and hens. She liked cats, toads, and jewels. The amethyst necklace had been payment for the safe delivery of a son to Golden's head forester. Tangle herself wore armfuls of bracelets and bangles that flashed and crashed when she flicked out an impatient spell. At times she wore a kitten on her shoulder. She was not an attentive mother. Rose had demanded, at seven years old, "Why did you have me if you didn't want me?"

"How can you deliver babies properly if you haven't had one?" said her mother.

"So I was practice," Rose snarled.

"Everything is practice," Tangle said. She was never ill-natured. She seldom thought to do anything much for her daughter, but never hurt her, never scolded her, and gave her whatever she asked for, dinner, a toad of her own, the amethyst necklace, lessons in witchcraft. She would have provided new clothes if Rose had asked for them, but she never did. Rose had looked after herself from an early age; and this was one of the reasons Diamond loved her. With her, he knew what freedom was. Without her, he could attain it only when he was hearing and singing and playing music.

"I do have a gift," he said now, rubbing his temples and pulling his hair.

"Stop destroying your head," Rose told him.

"I know Tarry thinks I do."

"Of course you do! What does it matter what Tarry thinks? You already play the harp about nine times better than he ever did."

This was another of the reasons Diamond loved her.

"Are there any wizard musicians?" he asked, looking up.

She pondered. "I don't know."

"I don't either. Morred and Elfarran sang to each other, and he was a mage. I think there's a Master Chanter on Roke, that teaches the lays and the histories. But I never heard of a wizard being a musician."

"I don't see why one couldn't be." She never saw why something could not be. Another reason he loved her.

"It always seemed to me they're sort of alike," he said, "magic and music. Spells and tunes. For one thing, you have to get them just exactly right."

"Practice," Rose said, rather sourly. "I know." She flicked a pebble at Diamond. It turned into a butterfly in midair. He flicked a butterfly back at her, and the two flitted and flickered a moment before they fell back to earth as pebbles. Diamond and Rose had worked out several such variations on the old stone-hopping trick.

"You ought to go, Di," she said. "Just to find out."

"I know."

"What if you got to be a wizard! Oh! Think of the stuff you could teach me! Shape-changing— We could be anything. Horses! Bears!"

"Moles," Diamond said. "Honestly, I feel like hiding underground. I always thought Father was going to make me learn his kind of stuff, after I got my name. But all this year he's kept sort of holding off. I guess he had this in mind all along. But what if I go down there and I'm not any better at being a wizard than I am at bookkeeping? Why can't I do what I know I *can* do?"

"Well, why can't you do it all? The magic and the music, anyhow? You can always hire a bookkeeper."

When she laughed, her thin face got bright, her thin mouth got wide, and her eyes disappeared.

"Oh, Darkrose," Diamond said, "I love you."

"Of course you do. You'd better. I'll witch you if you don't."

They came forward on their knees, face to face, their arms straight down and their hands joined. They kissed each other all over their faces. To Rose's lips Diamond's face was smooth and full as a plum, with just a hint of prickliness above the lip and jawline, where he had taken to shaving recently. To Diamond's lips Rose's face was soft as silk, with just a hint of grittiness on one cheek, which she had rubbed with a dirty hand. They moved a little closer so that their breasts and bellies touched, though their hands stayed down by their sides. They went on kissing.

"Darkrose," he breathed in her ear, his secret name for her.

She said nothing, but breathed very warm in his ear, and he moaned. His hands clenched hers. He drew back a little. She drew back.

They sat back on their ankles.

"Oh Di," she said, "it will be awful when you go."

"I won't go," he said. "Anywhere. Ever."

But of course he went down to Havnor South Port, in one of his father's carts driven by one of his father's carters, along with Master

Hemlock. As a rule, people do what wizards advise them to do. And it is no small honor to be invited by a wizard to be his student or apprentice. Hemlock, who had won his staff on Roke, was used to having boys come to him begging to be tested and, if they had the gift for it, taught. He was a little curious about this boy whose cheerful good manners hid some reluctance or self-doubt. It was the father's idea, not the boy's, that he was gifted. That was unusual, though perhaps not so unusual among the wealthy as among common folk. At any rate he came with a very good prenticing fee paid beforehand in gold and ivory. If he had the makings of a wizard Hemlock would train him, and if he had, as Hemlock suspected, a mere childish flair, then he'd be sent home with what remained of his fee. Hemlock was an honest, upright, humorless, scholarly wizard with little interest in feelings or ideas. His gift was for names. "The art begins and ends in naming," he said, which indeed is true, although there may be a good deal between the beginning and the end.

So Diamond, instead of learning spells and illusions and transformations and all such gaudy tricks, as Hemlock called them, sat in a narrow room at the back of the wizard's narrow house on a narrow back street of the old city, memorising long, long lists of words, words of power in the Language of the Making. Plants and parts of plants and animals and parts of animals and islands and parts of islands, parts of ships, parts of the human body. The words never made sense, never made sentences, only lists. Long, long lists.

His mind wandered. "Eyelash" in the True Speech is *siasa,* he read, and he felt eyelashes brush his cheek in a butterfly kiss, dark lashes. He looked up startled and did not know what had touched him. Later when he tried to repeat the word, he stood dumb.

"Memory, memory," Hemlock said. "Talent's no good without memory!" He was not harsh, but he was unyielding. Diamond had no idea what opinion Hemlock had of him, and guessed it to be pretty low. The wizard sometimes had him come with him to his work, mostly laying spells of safety on ships and houses, purifying wells, and sitting on the councils of the city, seldom speaking but always listening. Another wizard, not Roke-trained but with the healer's gift, looked after the sick and dying of South Port. Hemlock was glad to let him do so. His own pleasure was in studying and, as far as Diamond could see, doing no magic at all. "Keep the Equilibrium, it's all in that," Hemlock said, and, "Knowledge, order, and control." Those words he said so often that they made a tune in Diamond's head and sang themselves over and over: knowledge, or-der, and contro———l . . .

When Diamond put the lists of names to tunes he made up, he learned them much faster; but then the tune would come as part of the name, and he would sing out so clearly—for his voice had re-established itself as a strong, dark tenor—that Hemlock winced. Hemlock's was a very silent house.

Mostly the pupil was supposed to be with the master, or studying the lists of names in the room where the lore-books and word-books were, or asleep. Hemlock was a stickler for early abed and early afoot. But now and then Diamond had an hour or two free. He always went down to the docks and sat on a pier side or a water stair and thought about Darkrose. As soon as he was out of the house and away from Master Hemlock, he began to think about Darkrose, and went on thinking about her and very little else. It surprised him a little. He thought he ought to be homesick, to think about his mother. He did think about his mother quite often, and often was homesick, lying on his cot in his bare and narrow little room after a scanty supper of cold pea porridge—for this wizard, at least, did not live in such luxury as Golden had imagined. Diamond never thought about Darkrose, nights. He thought of his mother, or of sunny rooms and hot food, or a tune would come into his head and he would practice it mentally on the harp in his mind, and so drift off to sleep. Darkrose would come to his mind only when he was down at the docks, staring out at the water of the harbor, the piers, the fishing boats, only when he was outdoors and away from Hemlock and his house.

So he cherished his free hours as if they were actual meetings with her. He had always loved her, but had not understood that he loved her beyond anyone and anything. When he was with her, even when he was down on the docks thinking of her, he was alive. He never felt entirely alive in Master Hemlock's house and presence. He felt a little dead. Not dead, but a little dead.

A few times, sitting on the water stairs, the dirty harbor water sloshing at the next step down, the yells of gulls and dock workers wreathing the air with a thin, ungainly music, he shut his eyes and saw his love so clear, so close, that he reached out his hand to touch her. If he reached out his hand in his mind only, as when he played the mental harp, then indeed he touched her. He felt her hand in his, and her cheek, warm-cool, silken-gritty, lay against his mouth. In his mind he spoke to her, and in his mind she answered, her voice, her husky voice saying his name, "Diamond . . ."

But as he went back up the streets of South Port he lost her. He swore to keep her with him, to think of her, to think of her that night, but she faded away. By the time he opened the door of Master Hemlock's house he was reciting lists of names, or wondering what would be for dinner, for he was hungry most of the time. Not till he could take an hour and run back down to the docks could he think of her.

So he came to feel that those hours were true meetings with her, and he lived for them, without knowing what he lived for until his feet were on the cobbles, and his eyes on the harbor and the far line of the sea. Then he remembered what was worth remembering.

The winter passed by, and the cold early spring, and with the warm late spring came a letter from his mother, brought by a carter. Diamond read it and took it to Master Hemlock, saying, "My mother wonders if I might spend a month at home this summer."

"Probably not," the wizard said, and then, appearing to notice Diamond, put down his pen and said, "Young man, I must ask you if you wish to continue studying with me."

Diamond had no idea what to say. The idea of its being up to him had not occurred to him. "Do you think I ought to?" he asked at last.

"Probably not," the wizard said.

Diamond expected to feel relieved, released, but found he felt rejected, ashamed.

"I'm sorry," he said, with enough dignity that Hemlock glanced up at him.

"You could go to Roke," the wizard said.

"To Roke?"

The boy's drop-jawed stare irritated Hemlock, though he knew it shouldn't. Wizards are used to overweening confidence in the young of their kind. They expect modesty to come later, if at all. "I said Roke." Hemlock's tone said he was unused to having to repeat himself. And then, because this boy, this soft-headed, spoiled, moony boy had endeared himself to Hemlock by his uncomplaining patience, he took pity on him and said, "You should either go to Roke or find a wizard to teach you what you need. Of course you need what I can teach you. You need the names. The art begins and ends in naming. But that's not your gift. You have a poor memory for words. You must train it diligently. However, it's clear that you do have capacities, and that they need cultivation and discipline, which another man can give you better than I can." So does modesty breed modesty, sometimes, even in unlikely places. "If you were to go to Roke, I'd send a letter with you drawing you to the particular attention of the Master Summoner."

"Ah," said Diamond, floored. The Summoner's art is perhaps the most arcane and dangerous of all the arts of magic.

"Perhaps I am wrong," said Hemlock in his dry, flat voice. "Your gift may be for Pattern. Or perhaps it's an ordinary gift for shaping and transformation. I'm not certain."

"But you are—I do actually—"

"Oh yes. You are uncommonly slow, young man, to recognise your own capacities." It was spoken harshly, and Diamond stiffened up a bit.

"I thought my gift was for music," he said.

Hemlock dismissed that with a flick of his hand. "I am talking of the True Art," he said. "Now I will be frank with you. I advise you to write your parents—I shall write them too—informing them of your decision to go to the school on Roke, if that is what you decide; or to the Great Port, if the Mage Restive will take you on, as I think he will, with my recommendation. But I advise against visiting home. The entanglement of family, friends, and so on is precisely what you need to be free of. Now, and henceforth."

"Do wizards have no family?"

Hemlock was glad to see a bit of fire in the boy. "They are one another's family," he said.

"And no friends?"

"They may be friends. Did I say it was an easy life?" A pause. Hemlock looked directly at Diamond. "There was a girl," he said.

Diamond met his gaze for a moment, looked down, and said nothing.

"Your father told me. A witch's daughter, a childhood playmate. He believed that you had taught her spells."

"She taught me."

Hemlock nodded. "That is quite understandable, among children. And quite impossible now. Do you understand that?"

"No," Diamond said.

"Sit down," said Hemlock. After a moment Diamond took the stiff, high-backed chair facing him.

"I can protect you here, and have done so. On Roke, of course, you'll be perfectly safe. The very walls, there . . . But if you go home, you must be willing to protect yourself. It's a difficult thing for a young man, very difficult—a test of a will that has not yet been steeled, a mind that has not yet seen its true goal. I very strongly advise that you not take that risk. Write your parents, and go to the Great Port, or to Roke. Half your year's fee, which I'll return to you, will see to your first expenses."

Diamond sat upright and still. He had been getting some of his father's height and girth lately, and looked very much a man, though a very young one.

"What did you mean, Master Hemlock, in saying that you had protected me here?"

"Simply as I protect myself," the wizard said; and after a moment, testily, "The bargain, boy. The power we give for our power. The lesser state of being we forgo. Surely you know that every true man of power is celibate."

There was a pause, and Diamond said, "So you saw to it . . . that I . . ."

"Of course. It was my responsibility as your teacher."

Diamond nodded. He said, "Thank you." Presently he stood up. "Excuse me, Master," he said. "I have to think."

"Where are you going?"

"Down to the waterfront."

"Better stay here."

"I can't think, here."

Hemlock might have known then what he was up against; but having told the boy he would not be his master any longer, he could not in conscience command him. "You have a true gift, Essiri," he said, using the name he had given the boy in the springs of the Amia, a word that in the Old Speech means Willow. "I don't entirely understand it. I think you don't understand it at all. Take care! To misuse a gift, or to refuse to use it, may cause great loss, great harm."

Diamond nodded, suffering, contrite, unrebellious, unmovable.

"Go on," the wizard said, and Diamond went.

Later Hemlock knew he should never have let the boy leave the house. He had underestimated Diamond's willpower, or the strength of the spell the girl had laid on him. Their conversation was in the morning; Hemlock went back to the ancient cantrip he was annotating; it was not till supper time that he thought about his pupil, and not until he had eaten supper alone that he admitted that Diamond had run away.

Hemlock was loath to practice any of the lesser arts of magic. He did not put out a finding spell, as any sorcerer might have done. Nor did he call to Diamond in any way. He was angry; perhaps he was hurt. He had thought well of the boy, and offered to write the Summoner about him, and then at the first test of character Diamond had broken. "Glass," the wizard muttered. At least this weakness proved he was not dangerous. Some talents were best not left to run wild, but there was no harm in this fellow, no malice. No ambition. "No spine," said Hemlock to the silence of the house. "Let him crawl home to his mother."

Still it rankled him that Diamond had let him down flat, without a word of thanks or apology. So much for good manners, he thought.

As she blew out the lamp and got into bed, the witch's daughter heard an owl calling, the little, liquid hu-hu-hu-hu that made people call them laughing owls. She heard it with a mournful heart. That had been their signal, summer nights, when they sneaked out to meet in the willow grove down on the banks of the Amia, when everybody else was sleeping. She would not think of him at night. Back in the winter she had sent to him night after night. She had learned her mother's spell of sending, and knew that it was a true spell. She had sent him her touch, her voice saying his name, again and again. She had met a wall of air and silence. She touched nothing. He had walled her out. He would not hear.

Several times, all of a sudden, in the daytime, there had been a moment when she had known him close in mind and could touch him if she reached out. But at night she knew only his blank absence, his refusal of her. She had stopped trying to reach him months ago, but her heart was still very sore.

"Hu-hu-hu," said the owl, under her window, and then it said, "Darkrose!" Startled from her misery, she leapt out of bed and opened the shutters.

"Come on out," whispered Diamond, a shadow in the starlight.

"Mother's not home. Come in!" She met him at the door.

They held each other tight, hard, silent for a long time. To Diamond it was as if he held his future, his own life, his whole life, in his arms.

At last she moved, and kissed his cheek, and whispered, "I missed you, I missed you, I missed you. How long can you stay?"

"As long as I like."

She kept his hand and led him in. He was always a little reluctant to enter the witch's house, a pungent, disorderly place thick with the mysteries of women and witchcraft, very different from his own clean comfortable home, even more different from the cold austerity of the wizard's house. He shivered like a horse as he stood there, too tall for the herb-festooned rafters. He was very highly strung, and worn out, having walked forty miles in sixteen hours without food.

"Where's your mother?" he asked in a whisper.

"Sitting with old Ferny. She died this afternoon, Mother will be there all night. But how did you get here?"

"Walked."

"The wizard let you visit home?"

"I ran away."

"Ran away! Why?"

"To keep you."

He looked at her, that vivid, fierce, dark face in its rough cloud of hair. She wore only her shift, and he saw the infinitely delicate, tender rise of her breasts. He drew her to him again, but though she hugged him she drew away again, frowning.

"Keep me?" she repeated. "You didn't seem to worry about losing me all winter. What made you come back now?"

"He wanted me to go to Roke."

"To Roke?" She stared. "To Roke, Di? Then you really do have the gift—you could be a sorcerer?"

To find her on Hemlock's side was a blow.

"Sorcerers are nothing to him. He means I could be a wizard. Do magery. Not just witchcraft."

"Oh I see," Rose said after a moment. "But I don't see why you ran away."

They had let go of each other's hands.

"Don't you understand?" he said, exasperated with her for not understanding, because he had not understood. "A wizard can't have anything to do with women. With witches. With all that."

"Oh, I know. It's beneath them."

"It's not just beneath them—"

"Oh, but it is. I'll bet you had to unlearn every spell I taught you. Didn't you?"

"It isn't the same kind of thing."

"No. It isn't the High Art. It isn't the True Speech. A wizard mustn't soil his lips with common words. 'Weak as women's magic, wicked as women's magic,' you think I don't know what they say? So, why did you come back here?"

"To see you!"

"What for?"

"What do you think?"

"You never sent to me, you never let me send to you, all the time you were gone. I was just supposed to wait until you got tired of playing wizard. Well, I got tired of waiting." Her voice was nearly inaudible, a rough whisper.

"Somebody's been coming around," he said, incredulous that she could turn against him. "Who's been after you?"

"None of your business if there is! You go off, you turn your back on me. Wizards can't have anything to do with what I do, what my mother does. Well, I don't want anything to do with what you do, either, ever. So go!"

Starving, frustrated, misunderstood, Diamond reached out to hold her again, to make her body understand his body, repeating that first, deep embrace that had held all the years of their lives in it. He found himself standing two feet back, his hands stinging and his ears ringing and his eyes dazzled. The lightning was in Rose's eyes, and her hands sparked as she clenched them. "Never do that again," she whispered.

"Never fear," Diamond said, turned on his heel, and strode out. A string of dried sage caught on his head and trailed after him.

He spent the night in their old place in the sallows. Maybe he hoped she would come, but she did not come, and he soon slept in sheer weariness. He woke in the first, cold light. He sat up and thought. He looked at life in that cold light. It was a different matter from what he had believed it. He went down to the stream in which he had been named. He drank, washed his hands and face, made himself look as decent as he could, and went up through the town to the fine house at the high end, his father's house.

After the first outcries and embraces, the servants and his mother sat him right down to breakfast. So it was with warm food in his belly and a certain chill courage in his heart that he faced his father, who had been out before breakfast seeing off a string of timber carts to the Great Port.

"Well, son!" They touched cheeks. "So Master Hemlock gave you a vacation?"

"No, sir. I left."

Golden stared, then filled his plate and sat down. "Left," he said.

"Yes, sir. I decided that I don't want to be a wizard."

"Hmf," said Golden, chewing. "Left of your own accord? Entirely? With the Master's permission?"

"Of my own accord entirely, without his permission."

Golden chewed very slowly, his eyes on the table. Diamond had seen his father look like this when a forester reported an infestation in the chestnut groves, and when he found a mule dealer had cheated him.

"He wanted me to go to the College on Roke to study with the Master Summoner. He was going to send me there. I decided not to go."

After a while Golden asked, still looking at the table, "Why?"

"It isn't the life I want."

Another pause. Golden glanced over at his wife, who stood by the window listening in silence. Then he looked at his son. Slowly the mixture of anger, disappointment, confusion, and respect on his face gave way to something simpler, a look of complicity, very nearly a wink. "I see," he said. "And what did you decide you want?"

A pause. "This," Diamond said. His voice was level. He looked neither at his father nor his mother.

"Hah!" said Golden. "Well! I will say I'm glad of it, son." He ate a small pork pie in one mouthful. "Being a wizard, going to Roke, all that, it never seemed real, not exactly. And with you off there, I didn't know what all this was for, to tell you the truth. All my business. If you're here, it adds up, you see. It adds up. Well! But listen here, did you just run off from the wizard? Did he know you were going?"

"No. I'll write him," Diamond said, in his new, level voice.

"He won't be angry? They say wizards have short tempers. Full of pride."

"He's angry," Diamond said, "but he won't do anything."

So it proved. Indeed, to Golden's amazement, Master Hemlock sent back a scrupulous two-fifths of the prenticing fee. With the packet, which was delivered by one of Golden's carters who had taken a load of spars down to South Port, was a note for Diamond. It said, "True art requires a single heart." The direction on the outside was the Hardic rune for willow. The note was signed with Hemlock's rune, which had two meanings: the hemlock tree, and suffering.

Diamond sat in his own sunny room upstairs, on his comfortable bed, hearing his mother singing as she went about the house. He held the wizard's letter and reread the message and the two runes many times. The cold and sluggish mind that had been born in him that morning down in the sallows accepted the lesson. No magic. Never again. He had never given his heart to it. It had been a game to him, a game to play with Darkrose. Even the names of the True Speech that he had learned in the wizard's house, though he knew the beauty and the power that lay in them, he could let go, let slip, forget. That was not his language.

He could speak his language only with her. And he had lost her, let her go. The double heart has no true speech. From now on he could talk only the language of duty: getting and spending, outlay and income, the profit and the loss.

And beyond that, nothing. There had been illusions, little spells, pebbles that turned to butterflies, wooden birds that flew on living wings for a minute or two. There had never been a choice, really. There was only one way for him to go.

Golden was immensely happy and quite unconscious of it. "Old man's got his jewel back," said the carter to the forester. "Sweet as new butter, he is." Golden, unaware of being sweet, thought only how sweet life was. He had bought the Reche grove, at a very stiff price to be sure, but at least old Lowbough of Easthill hadn't got it, and now he and Diamond could dcvclop it as it ought to be developed. In among the chestnuts there were a lot of pines, which could be felled and sold for masts and spars and small lumber, and replanted with chestnut seedlings. It would in time be a pure stand like the Big Grove, the heart of his chestnut kingdom. In time, of course. Oak and chestnut don't shoot up overnight like alder and willow. But there was time. There was time, now. The boy was barely seventeen, and he himself just forty-five. In his prime. He had been feeling old, but that was nonsense. He was in his prime. The oldest trees, past bearing, ought to come out with the pines. Some good wood for furniture could be salvaged from them.

"Well, well, well," he said to his wife, frequently, "all rosy again, eh? Got the apple of your eye back home, eh? No more moping, eh?"

And Tuly smiled and stroked his hand.

Once instead of smiling and agreeing, she said, "It's lovely to have him back, but," and Golden stopped hearing. Mothers were born to worry about their children, and women were born never to be content. There was no reason why he should listen to the litany of anxieties by which Tuly hauled herself through life. Of course she thought a merchant's life wasn't good enough for the boy. She'd have thought being King in Havnor wasn't good enough for him.

"When he gets himself a girl," Golden said, in answer to whatever it was she had been saying, "he'll be all squared away. Living with the wizards, you know, the way they are, it set him back a bit. Don't worry about Diamond. He'll know what he wants when he sees it!"

"I hope so," said Tuly.

"At least he's not seeing the witch's girl," said Golden. "That's done with." Later on it occurred to him that neither was his wife seeing the witch any more. For years they'd been thick as thieves, against all his warnings, and now Tangle was never anywhere near the house. Women's friendships never lasted. He teased her about it. Finding her strewing pennyroyal and miller's-bane in the chests and clothes presses against an infestation of moths, he said, "Seems like you'd have your friend the wise woman up to hex 'em away. Or aren't you friends any more?"

"No," his wife said in her soft, level voice, "we aren't."

"And a good thing too!" Golden said roundly. "What's become of that daughter of hers, then? Went off with a juggler, I heard?"

"A musician," Tuly said. "Last summer."

"A nameday party," said Golden. "Time for a bit of play, a bit of music and dancing, boy. Nineteen years old. Celebrate it!"

"I'll be going to Easthill with Sul's mules."

"No, no, no. Sul can handle it. Stay home and have your party. You've been working hard. We'll hire a band. Who's the best in the country? Tarry and his lot?"

"Father, I don't want a party," Diamond said and stood up, shivering his muscles like a horse. He was bigger than Golden now, and when he moved abruptly it was startling. "I'll go to Easthill," he said, and left the room.

"What's that all about?" Golden said to his wife, a rhetorical question. She looked at him and said nothing, a non-rhetorical answer.

After Golden had gone out, she found her son in the counting room going through ledgers. She looked at the pages. Long, long lists of names and numbers, debts and credits, profits and losses.

"Di," she said, and he looked up. His face was still round and a bit peachy, though the bones were heavier and the eyes were melancholy.

"I didn't mean to hurt Father's feelings," he said.

"If he wants a party, he'll have it," she said. Their voices were alike, being in the higher register but dark-toned, and held to an even quietness, contained, restrained. She perched on a stool beside his at the high desk.

"I can't," he said, and stopped, and went on, "I really don't want to have any dancing."

"He's matchmaking," Tuly said, dry, fond.

"I don't care about that."

"I know you don't."

"The problem is . . ."

"The problem is the music," his mother said at last.

He nodded.

"My son, there is no reason," she said, suddenly passionate, "there is *no* reason why you should give up everything you love!"

He took her hand and kissed it as they sat side by side.

"Things don't mix," he said. "They ought to, but they don't. I found that out. When I left the wizard. I thought I could be everything. You know—do magic, play music, be Father's son, love Rose . . . It doesn't work that way. Things don't mix."

"They do, they do," Tuly said. "Everything is hooked together, tangled up!"

"Maybe things are, for women. But I . . . I can't be double-hearted."

"Double-hearted? You? You gave up wizardry because you knew that if you didn't, you'd betray it."

He took the word with a visible shock, but did not deny it.

"But why," she demanded, "why did you give up music?"

"I have to have a single heart. I can't play the harp while I'm bargaining with a mule breeder. I can't make ballads while I'm figuring what we have to pay the pickers to keep 'em from hiring out to Lowbough!" His voice shook a little now, a vibrato, and his eyes were not sad, but angry.

"So you put a spell on yourself," she said, "just as that wizard put one on you. A spell to keep you safe. To keep you with the mule breeders, and the nut pickers, and these." She struck the ledger full of lists of names and figures, a flicking, dismissive tap. "A spell of silence," she said.

After a long time the young man said, "What else can I do?"

"I don't know, my dear. I do want you to be safe. I do love to see your father happy and proud of you. But I can't bear to see you unhappy, without pride! I don't know. Maybe you're right. Maybe for a man it's only one thing ever. But I miss hearing you sing."

She was in tears. They hugged, and she stroked his thick, shining hair and apologised for being cruel, and he hugged her again and said she was the kindest mother in the world, and so she went off. But as she left she turned back a moment and said, "Let him have the party, Di. Let yourself have it."

"I will," he said, to comfort her.

Golden ordered the beer and food and fireworks, but Diamond saw to hiring the musicians.

"Of course I'll bring my band," Tarry said, "fat chance I'd miss it! You'll have every tootler in the west of the world here for one of your dad's parties."

"You can tell 'em you're the band that's getting paid."

"Oh, they'll come for the glory," said the harper, a lean, long-jawed, walleyed fellow of forty. "Maybe you'll have a go with us yourself, then? You had a hand for it, before you took to making money. And the voice not bad, if you'd worked on it."

"I doubt it," Diamond said.

"That girl you liked, witch's Rose, she's running about with Labby, I hear. No doubt they'll come by."

"I'll see you then," said Diamond, looking big and handsome and indifferent, and walked off.

"Too high and mighty these days to stop and talk," said Tarry, "though I taught him all he knows of harping. But what's that to a rich man?"

Tarry's malice had left Diamond's nerves raw, and the thought of the party weighed on him till he lost his appetite. He thought hopefully for a while that he was sick and could miss the party. But the day came, and he was there. Not so evidently, so eminently, so flamboyantly there as his father, but present, smiling, dancing. All his childhood friends were there too, half of them married by now to the other half, it seemed, but there was still plenty of flirting going on, and several pretty girls were always near him. He drank a good deal of Gadge Brewer's excellent beer, and found he could endure the music if he was dancing to it and talking and laughing while he danced. So he danced with all the pretty girls in turn, and then again with whichever one turned up again, which all of them did.

It was Golden's grandest party yet, with a dancing floor built on the town green down the way from Golden's house, and a tent for the old folks to eat and drink and gossip in, and new clothes for the children, and jugglers and puppeteers, some of them hired and some of them coming by to pick up whatever they could in the way of coppers and free beer. Any festivity drew itinerant entertainers and musicians; it was their living, and though uninvited they were welcomed. A tale singer with a droning voice and a droning bagpipe was singing *The Deed of the Dragonlord* to a group of people under the big oak on the hilltop. When Tarry's band of harp, fife, viol, and drum took time off for a breather and a swig, a new group hopped up onto the dance floor. "Hey, there's Labby's band!" cried the pretty girl nearest Diamond. "Come on, they're the best!"

Labby, a light-skinned, flashy-looking fellow, played the double-reed woodhorn. With him were a violist, a tabor player, and Rose, who played fife. Their first tune was a stampy, fast and brilliant, too fast for some of the dancers. Diamond and his partner stayed in, and people cheered and clapped them when they finished the dance, sweating and panting. "Beer!" Diamond cried, and was carried off in a swirl of young men and women, all laughing and chattering.

He heard behind him the next tune start up, the viol alone, strong and sad as a tenor voice: "Where My Love Is Going."

He drank a mug of beer down in one draft, and the girls with him watched the muscles in his strong throat as he swallowed, and they laughed and chattered, and he shivered all over like a cart horse stung by flies. He said, "Oh! I can't—!" He bolted off into the dusk beyond the lanterns hanging around the brewer's booth. "Where's he going?" said one, and another, "He'll be back," and they laughed and chattered.

The tune ended. "Darkrose," he said, behind her in the dark. She turned her head and looked at him. Their heads were on a level, she sitting cross-legged up on the dance platform, he kneeling on the grass.

"Come to the sallows," he said.

She said nothing. Labby, glancing at her, set his woodhorn to his lips. The drummer struck a triple beat on his tabor, and they were off into a sailor's jig.

When she looked around again Diamond was gone.

Tarry came back with his band in an hour or so, ungrateful for the respite and much the worse for beer. He interrupted the tune and the dancing, telling Labby loudly to clear out.

"Ah, pick your nose, harp picker," Labby said, and Tarry took offense, and people took sides, and while the dispute was at its brief height, Rose put her fife in her pocket and slipped away.

Away from the lanterns of the party it was dark, but she knew the way in the dark. He was there. The willows had grown, these two years. There was only a little space to sit among the green shoots and the long, falling leaves.

The music started up, distant, blurred by wind and the murmur of the river running.

"What did you want, Diamond?"

"To talk."

They were only voices and shadows to each other.

"So," she said.

"I wanted to ask you to go away with me," he said.

"When?"

"Then. When we quarreled. I said it all wrong. I thought . . ." A long pause. "I thought I could go on running away. With you. And play music. Make a living. Together. I meant to say that."

"You didn't say it."

"I know. I said everything wrong. I did everything wrong. I betrayed everything. The magic. And the music. And you."

"I'm all right," she said.

"Are you?"

"I'm not really good on the fife, but I'm good enough. What you didn't teach me, I can fill in with a spell, if I have to. And the band, they're all right. Labby isn't as bad as he looks. Nobody fools with me. We make a pretty good living. Winters, I go stay with Mother and help her out. So I'm all right. What about you, Di?"

"All wrong."

She started to say something, and did not say it.

"I guess we were children," he said. "Now . . ."

"What's changed?"

"I made the wrong choice."

"Once?" she said. "Or twice?"

"Twice."

"Third time's the charm."

Neither spoke for a while. She could just make out the bulk of him in the leafy shadows. "You're bigger than you were," she said. "Can you still make a light, Di? I want to see you."

He shook his head.

"That was the one thing you could do that I never could. And you never could teach me."

"I didn't know what I was doing," he said. "Sometimes it worked, sometimes it didn't."

"And the wizard in South Port didn't teach you how to make it work?"

"He only taught me names."

"Why can't you do it now?"

"I gave it up, Darkrose. I had to either do it and nothing else, or not do it. You have to have a single heart."

"I don't see why," she said. "My mother can cure a fever and ease a childbirth and find a lost ring, maybe that's nothing compared to what the wizards and the dragonlords can do, but it's not nothing, all the same. And she didn't give up anything for it. Having me didn't stop her. She had me so that she could *learn* how to do it! Just because I learned how to play music from you, did I have to give up saying spells? I can bring a fever down now too. Why should you have to stop doing one thing so you can do the other?"

"My father," he began, and stopped, and gave a kind of laugh. "They don't go together," he said. "The money and the music."

"The father and the witch-girl," said Darkrose.

Again there was silence between them. The leaves of the willows stirred.

"Would you come back to me?" he said. "Would you go with me, live with me, marry me, Darkrose?"

"Not in your father's house, Di."

"Anywhere. Run away."

"But you can't have me without the music."

"Or the music without you."

"I would," she said.

"Does Labby want a harper?"

She hesitated; she laughed. "If he wants a fife player," she said.

"I haven't practiced ever since I left, Darkrose," he said. "But the music was always in my head, and you . . ." She reached out her hands to him. They knelt facing, the willow leaves moving across their hair. They kissed each other, timidly at first.

In the years after Diamond left home, Golden made more money than he had ever done before. All his deals were profitable. It was as if good fortune stuck to him and he could not shake it off. He grew immensely wealthy.

He did not forgive his son. It would have made a happy ending, but he would not have it. To leave so, without a word, on his nameday night, to go off with the witch-girl, leaving all the honest work undone, to be a vagrant musician, a harper twanging and singing and grinning for pennies—there was nothing but shame and pain and anger in it for Golden. So he had his tragedy.

Tuly shared it with him for a long time, since she could see her son only by lying to her husband, which she found hard to do. She wept to think of Diamond hungry, sleeping hard. Cold nights of autumn were a misery to her. But as time went on and she heard him spoken of as Diamond the sweet singer of the West of Havnor, Diamond who had harped and sung to the great lords in the Tower of the Sword, her heart grew lighter. And once, when Golden was down at South Port, she and Tangle took a donkey cart and drove over to Easthill, where they heard Diamond sing the *Lay of the Lost Queen,* while Rose sat with them, and Little Tuly sat on Tuly's knee. And if not a happy ending, that was a true joy, which may be enough to ask for, after all.

The Bones of the Earth

IT WAS RAINING AGAIN, and the wizard of Re Albi was sorely tempted to make a weather spell, just a little, small spell, to send the rain on round the mountain. His bones ached. They ached for the sun to come out and shine through his flesh and dry them out. Of course he could say a pain spell, but all that would do was hide the ache for a while. There was no cure for what ailed him. Old bones need the sun. The wizard stood still in the doorway of his house, between the dark room and the rain-streaked open air, preventing himself from making a spell, and angry at himself for preventing himself and for having to be prevented.

He never swore—men of power do not swear, it is not safe—but he cleared his throat with a coughing growl, like a bear. A moment later a thunderclap rolled off the hidden upper slopes of Gont Mountain, echoing round from north to south, dying away in the cloud-filled forests.

A good sign, thunder, Dulse thought. It would stop raining soon. He pulled up his hood and went out into the rain to feed the chickens.

He checked the henhouse, finding three eggs. Red Bucca was setting. Her eggs were about due to hatch. The mites were bothering her, and she looked scruffy and jaded. He said a few words against mites, told himself to remember to clean out the nest box as soon as the chicks hatched, and went on to the poultry yard, where Brown Bucca and Grey and Leggings and Candor and the King huddled under the eaves making soft, shrewish remarks about rain.

"It'll stop by midday," the wizard told the chickens. He fed them and squelched back to the house with three warm eggs. When he was a child he had liked to walk in mud. He remembered enjoying the cool of it rising between his toes. He still liked to go barefoot, but no longer enjoyed mud; it was sticky stuff, and he disliked stooping to clean his feet before going into the house. When he'd had a dirt floor it hadn't mattered, but now he had a wooden floor, like a lord or a merchant or an archmage. To keep the cold and damp out of his bones. Not his own notion. Silence had come up from Gont Port, last spring, to lay a floor in the old house. They had had one of their arguments about it. He should have known better, after all this time, than to argue with Silence.

"I've walked on dirt for seventy-five years," Dulse had said. "A few more won't kill me!"

To which Silence of course made no reply, letting him hear what he had said and feel its foolishness thoroughly.

"Dirt's easier to keep clean," he said, knowing the struggle already lost. It was true that all you had to do with a good hard-packed clay floor was sweep it and now and then sprinkle it to keep the dust down. But it sounded silly all the same.

"Who's to lay this floor?" he said, now merely querulous.

Silence nodded, meaning himself.

The boy was in fact a workman of the first order, carpenter, cabinetmaker, stonelayer, roofer; he had proved that when he lived up here as Dulse's student, and his life with the rich folk of Gont Port had not softened his hands. He brought the boards from Sixth's mill in Re Albi, driving Gammer's ox team; he laid the floor and polished it the next day, while the old wizard was up at Bog Lake gathering simples. When Dulse came home there it was, shining like a dark lake itself. "Have to wash my feet every time I come in," he grumbled. He walked in gingerly. The wood was so smooth it seemed soft to the bare sole. "Satin," he said. "You didn't do all that in one day without a spell or two. A village hut with a palace floor. Well, it'll be a sight, come winter, to see the fire shine in that! Or do I have to get me a carpet now? A fleecefell, on a golden warp?"

Silence smiled. He was pleased with himself.

He had turned up on Dulse's doorstep a few years ago. Well, no, twenty years ago it must be, or twenty-five. A while ago now. He had been truly a boy then, long-legged, rough-haired, soft-faced. A set mouth, clear eyes. "What do you want?" the wizard had asked, knowing what he wanted, what they all wanted, and keeping his eyes from those clear eyes. He was a good teacher, the best on Gont, he knew that. But he was tired of teaching, didn't want another prentice underfoot. And he sensed danger.

"To learn," the boy whispered.

"Go to Roke," the wizard said. The boy wore shoes and a good leather vest. He could afford or earn ship's passage to the school.

"I've been there."

At that Dulse looked him over again. No cloak, no staff.

"Failed? Sent away? Ran away?"

The boy shook his head at each question. He shut his eyes; his mouth was already shut. He stood there, intensely gathered, suffering: drew breath: looked straight into the wizard's eyes.

"My mastery is here, on Gont," he said, still speaking hardly above a whisper. "My master is Heleth."

At that the wizard whose true name was Heleth stood as still as he did, looking back at him, till the boy's gaze dropped.

In silence Dulse sought the boy's name, and saw two things: a fir cone, and the rune of the Closed Mouth. Then seeking further he heard in his mind a name spoken; but he did not speak it.

"I'm tired of teaching and talking," he said. "I need silence. Is that enough for you?"

The boy nodded once.

"Then to me you are Silence," the wizard said. "You can sleep in the nook under the west window. There's an old pallet in the woodhouse. Air it. Don't bring mice in with it." And he stalked off towards the Overfell, angry with the boy for coming and with himself for giving in; but it was not anger that made his heart pound. Striding along—he could stride, then—with the sea wind pushing at him always from the left and the early sunlight on the sea out past the vast shadow of the mountain, he thought of the Mages of Roke, the masters of the art magic, the professors of mystery and power. "He was too much for 'em, was he? And he'll be too much for me," he thought, and smiled. He was a peaceful man, but he did not mind a bit of danger.

He stopped then and felt the dirt under his feet. He was barefoot, as usual. When he was a student on Roke, he had worn shoes. But he had come back home to Gont, to Re Albi, with his wizard's staff, and kicked his shoes off. He stood still and felt the dust and rock of the cliff-top path under his feet, and the cliffs under that, and the roots of the island in the dark under that. In the dark under the waters all islands touched and were one. So his teacher Ard had said, and so his teachers on Roke had said. But this was his island, his rock, his dirt. His wizardry grew out of it. "My mastery is here," the boy had said, but it went deeper than mastery. That, perhaps, was something Dulse could teach him: what went deeper than mastery. What he had learned here, on Gont, before he ever went to Roke.

And the boy must have a staff. Why had Nemmerle let him leave

Roke without one, empty-handed as a prentice or a witch? Power like that shouldn't go wandering about unchanneled and unsignaled.

My teacher had no staff, Dulse thought, and at the same moment thought, The boy wants his staff from me. Gontish oak, from the hands of a Gontish wizard. Well, if he earns it I'll make him one. If he can keep his mouth closed. And I'll leave him my lore-books. If he can clean out a henhouse, and understand the Glosses of Danemer, and keep his mouth closed.

The new student cleaned out the henhouse and hoed the bean patch, learned the meaning of the Glosses of Danemer and the Arcana of the Enlades, and kept his mouth closed. He listened. He heard what Dulse said; sometimes he heard what Dulse thought. He did what Dulse wanted and what Dulse did not know he wanted. His gift was far beyond Dulse's guidance, yet he had been right to come to Re Albi, and they both knew it.

Dulse thought sometimes in those years about sons and fathers. He had quarreled with his own father, a sorcerer-prospector, over his choice of Ard as his teacher. His father had shouted that a student of Ard's was no son of his, had nursed his rage, died unforgiving.

Dulse had seen young men weep for joy at the birth of a first son. He had seen poor men pay witches a year's earnings for the promise of a healthy boy, and a rich man touch his gold-bedizened baby's face and whisper, adoring, "My immortality!" He had seen men beat their sons, bully and humiliate them, spite and thwart them, hating the death they saw in them. He had seen the answering hatred in the sons' eyes, the threat, the pitiless contempt. And seeing it, Dulse knew why he had never sought reconciliation with his father.

He had seen a father and son work together from daybreak to sundown, the old man guiding a blind ox, the middle-aged man driving the iron-bladed plough, never a word spoken. As they started home the old man laid his hand a moment on the son's shoulder.

He had always remembered that. He remembered it now, when he looked across the hearth, winter evenings, at the dark face bent above a lore-book or a shirt that needed mending. The eyes cast down, the mouth closed, the spirit listening.

"Once in his lifetime, if he's lucky, a wizard finds somebody he can talk to." Nemmerle had said that to Dulse a night or two before Dulse left Roke, a year or two before Nemmerle was chosen Archmage. He had been the Master Patterner and the kindest of all Dulse's teachers at the school. "I think, if you stayed, Heleth, we could talk."

Dulse had been unable to answer at all for a while. Then, stammering, guilty at his ingratitude and incredulous at his obstinacy—

"Master, I would stay, but my work is on Gont. I wish it was here, with you—"

"It's a rare gift, to know where you need to be, before you've been to all the places you don't need to be. Well, send me a student now and then. Roke needs Gontish wizardry. I think we're leaving things out, here, things worth knowing . . ."

Dulse had sent students on to the school, three or four of them, nice lads with a gift for this or that; but the one Nemmerle waited for had come and gone of his own will, and what they had thought of him on Roke Dulse did not know. And Silence, of course, did not say. It was evident that he had learned there in two or three years what some boys learned in six or seven and many never learned at all. To him it had been mere groundwork.

"Why didn't you come to me first?" Dulse had demanded. "And then go to Roke, to put a polish on it?"

"I didn't want to waste your time."

"Did Nemmerle know you were coming to work with me?"

Silence shook his head.

"If you'd deigned to tell him your intentions, he might have sent a message to me."

Silence looked stricken. "Was he your friend?"

Dulse paused. "He was my master. Would have been my friend, perhaps, if I'd stayed on Roke. Have wizards friends? No more than they have wives, or sons, I suppose . . . Once he said to me that in our trade it's a lucky man who finds someone to talk to . . . Keep that in mind. If you're lucky, one day you'll have to open your mouth."

Silence bowed his rough, thoughtful head.

"If it hasn't rusted shut," Dulse added.

"If you ask me to, I'll talk," the young man said, so earnest, so willing to deny his whole nature at Dulse's request that the wizard had to laugh.

"I asked you not to," he said. "And it's not my need I spoke of. I talk enough for two. Never mind. You'll know what to say when the time comes. That's the art, eh? What to say, and when to say it. And the rest is silence."

The young man slept on a pallet under the little west window of Dulse's house for three years. He learned wizardry, fed the chickens, milked the cow. He suggested, once, that Dulse keep goats. He had not said anything for a week or so, a cold, wet week of autumn. He said, "You might keep some goats."

Dulse had the big lore-book open on the table. He had been trying to reweave one of the Acastan Spells, much broken and made powerless by the Emanations of Fundaur centuries ago. He had just begun to get a sense of the missing word that might fill one of the gaps, he almost had it, and— "You might keep some goats," Silence said.

Dulse considered himself a wordy, impatient man with a short temper. The necessity of not swearing had been a burden to him in his youth, and for thirty years the imbecility of prentices, clients, cows, and chickens had tried him sorely. Prentices and clients were afraid of his tongue, though cows and chickens paid no attention to his outbursts. He had never been angry at Silence before. There was a very long pause.

"What for?"

Silence apparently did not notice the pause or the extreme softness of Dulse's voice. "Milk, cheese, roast kid, company," he said.

"Have you ever kept goats?" Dulse asked, in the same soft, polite voice.

Silence shook his head.

He was in fact a town boy, born in Gont Port. He had said nothing about himself, but Dulse had asked around a bit. The father, a longshoreman, had died in the big earthquake, when Silence would have been seven or eight; the mother was a cook at a waterfront inn. At twelve the boy had got into some kind of trouble, probably messing about with magic, and his mother had managed to prentice him to Elassen, a respectable sorcerer in Valmouth. There the boy had picked up his true name, and some skill in carpentry and farmwork, if not much else; and Elassen had had the generosity, after three years, to pay his passage to Roke. That was all Dulse knew about him.

"I dislike goat cheese," Dulse said.

Silence nodded, acceptant as always.

From time to time in the years since then, Dulse remembered how he hadn't lost his temper when Silence asked about keeping goats; and each time the memory gave him a quiet satisfaction, like that of finishing the last bite of a perfectly ripe pear.

After spending the next several days trying to recapture the missing word, he had set Silence to studying the Acastan Spells. Together they finally worked it out, a long toil. "Like ploughing with a blind ox," Dulse said.

Not long after that he gave Silence the staff he had made for him of Gontish oak.

And the Lord of Gont Port had tried once again to get Dulse to come down to do what needed doing in Gont Port, and Dulse had sent Silence down instead, and there he had stayed.

And Dulse was standing on his own doorstep, three eggs in his hand and the rain running cold down his back.

How long had he been standing here? Why was he standing here? He had been thinking about mud, about the floor, about Silence. Had he been out walking on the path above the Overfell? No, that was years ago, years ago, in the sunlight. It was raining. He had fed the chickens, and come back to the house with three eggs, they were still warm in his hand, silky brown lukewarm eggs, and the sound of thunder was still in his mind, the vibration of thunder was in his bones, in his feet. Thunder?

No. There had been a thunderclap, a while ago. This was not thunder. He had had this queer feeling and had not recognised it, back—when? long ago, back before all the days and years he had been thinking of. When, when had it been?—before the earthquake. Just before the earthquake. Just before a half mile of the coast at Essary slumped into the sea, and people died crushed in the ruins of their villages, and a great wave swamped the wharfs at Gont Port.

He stepped down from the doorstep onto the dirt so that he could feel the ground with the nerves of his soles, but the mud slimed and fouled any messages the dirt had for him. He set the eggs down on the doorstep, sat down beside them, cleaned his feet with rainwater from the pot by the step, wiped them dry with the rag that hung on the handle of the pot, rinsed and wrung out the rag and hung it on the handle of the pot, picked up the eggs, stood up slowly, and went into his house.

He gave a sharp look at his staff, which leaned in the corner behind the door. He put the eggs in the larder, ate an apple quickly because he was hungry, and took up his staff. It was yew, bound at the foot with copper, worn to satin at the grip. Nemmerle had given it to him.

"Stand!" he said to it in its language, and let go of it. It stood as if he had driven it into a socket.

"To the root," he said impatiently, in the Language of the Making. "To the root!"

He watched the staff that stood on the shining floor. In a little while he saw it quiver very slightly, a shiver, a tremble.

"Ah, ah, ah," said the old wizard.

"What should I do?" he said aloud after a while.

The staff swayed, was still, shivered again.

"Enough of that, my dear," Dulse said, laying his hand on it. "Come now. No wonder I kept thinking about Silence. I should send for him . . . send to him . . . No. What did Ard say? Find the center, find the center. That's the question to ask. That's what to do . . ." As he muttered on to himself, routing out his heavy cloak, setting water to boil on the small fire he had lighted earlier, he wondered if he had always talked to himself, if he had talked all the time when Silence lived with him. No. It had become a habit after Silence left, he thought, with the bit of his mind that went on thinking the ordinary thoughts of life, while the rest of it made preparations for terror and destruction.

He hard-boiled the three new eggs and one already in the larder and put them into a pouch along with four apples and a bladder of resinated wine, in case he had to stay out all night. He shrugged arthritically into his heavy cloak, took up his staff, told the fire to go out, and left.

He no longer kept a cow. He stood looking into the poultry yard, considering. The fox had been visiting the orchard lately. But the chickens would have to forage if he stayed away. They must take their chances, like everyone else. He opened their gate a little. Though the rain was no more than a misty drizzle now, they stayed hunched up under the henhouse eaves, disconsolate. The King had not crowed once this morning.

"Have you anything to tell me?" Dulse asked them.

Brown Bucca, his favorite, shook herself and said her name a few times. The others said nothing.

"Well, take care. I saw the fox on the full-moon night," Dulse said, and went on his way.

As he walked he thought; he thought hard; he recalled. He recalled all he could of matters his teacher had spoken of once only and long ago. Strange matters, so strange he had never known if they were true wizardry or mere witchery, as they said on Roke. Matters he certainly had never heard about on Roke, nor had he ever spoken about them there, maybe fearing the Masters would despise him for taking such things seriously, maybe knowing they would not understand them, because they were Gontish matters, truths of Gont. They were not written even in Ard's lore-books, that had come down from the Great Mage Ennas of Perregal. They were all word of mouth. They were home truths.

"If you need to read the Mountain," his teacher had told him, "go to the Dark Pond at the top of Semere's cow pasture. You can see the ways from there. You need to find the center. See where to go in."

"Go in?" the boy Dulse had whispered.

"What could you do from outside?"

Dulse was silent for a long time, and then said, "How?"

"Thus." And Ard's long arms stretched out and upward in the invocation of what Dulse would know later was a great spell of Transforming. Ard spoke the words of the spell awry, as teachers of wizardry must do lest the spell operate. Dulse knew the trick of hearing them aright and remembering them. When Ard was done, Dulse had repeated the words in his mind in silence, half-sketching the strange, awkward gestures that were part of them. All at once his hand stopped.

"But you can't undo this!" he said aloud.

Ard nodded. "It is irrevocable."

Dulse knew no transformation that was irrevocable, no spell that could not be unsaid, except the Word of Unbinding, which is spoken only once.

"But why—?"

"At need," Ard said.

Dulse knew better than to ask for explanation. The need to speak such a spell could not come often; the chance of his ever having to use it was very slight. He let the terrible spell sink down in his mind and be hidden and layered over with a thousand useful or beautiful or enlightening mageries and charms, all the lore and rules of Roke, all the wisdom of the books Ard had bequeathed him. Crude, monstrous, useless, it lay in the dark of his mind for sixty years, like the cornerstone of an earlier, forgotten house down in the cellar of a mansion full of lights and treasures and children.

The rain had ceased, though mist still hid the peak and shreds of cloud drifted through the high forests. Though not a tireless walker like Silence, who would have spent his life wandering in the forests of Gont Mountain if he could, Dulse had been born in Re Albi and knew the roads and ways around it as part of himself. He took the shortcut at Rissi's well and came out before midday on Semere's high pasture, a level step on the mountainside. A mile below it, all in sunlight now, the farm buildings stood in the lee of a hill across which a flock of sheep moved like a cloud-shadow. Gont Port and its bay were hidden under the steep, knotted hills that stood inland above the city.

Dulse wandered about a bit before he found what he took to be the Dark Pond. It was small, half mud and reeds, with one vague, boggy path to the water, and no tracks on that but goat hoofs. The water was dark, though it lay out under the bright sky and far above the peat soils. Dulse followed the goat tracks, growling when his foot slipped in the mud and he wrenched his ankle to keep from falling. At the brink of the water he stood still. He stooped to rub his ankle. He listened.

It was absolutely silent.

No wind. No birdcall. No distant lowing or bleating or call of voice. As if all the island had gone still. Not a fly buzzed.

He looked at the dark water. It reflected nothing.

Reluctant, he stepped forward, barefoot and bare-legged; he had rolled up his cloak into his pack an hour ago when the sun came out. Reeds brushed his legs. The mud was soft and sucking under his feet, full of tangling reed-roots. He made no noise as he moved slowly out into the pool, and the circles of ripples from his movement were slight and small. It was shallow for a long way. Then his cautious foot felt no bottom, and he paused.

The water shivered. He felt it first on his thighs, a lapping like the tickling touch of fur; then he saw it, the trembling of the surface all over the pond. Not the round ripples he made, which had already died away, but a ruffling, a roughening, a shudder, again, and again.

"Where?" he whispered, and then said the word aloud in the language all things understand that have no other language.

There was the silence. Then a fish leapt from the black, shaking water, a white-grey fish the length of his hand, and as it leapt it cried out in a small, clear voice, in that same language, "Yaved!"

The old wizard stood there. He recollected all he knew of the names of Gont, brought all its slopes and cliffs and ravines into his mind, and in a minute he saw where Yaved was. It was the place where the ridges parted, just inland from Gont Port, deep in the knot of hills above the city. It was the place of the fault. An earthquake centered there could shake the city down, bring avalanche and tidal wave, close the cliffs of the bay together like hands clapping. Dulse shivered, shuddered all over like the water of the pool.

He turned and made for the shore, hasty, careless where he set his feet and not caring if he broke the silence by splashing and breathing hard. He slogged back up the path through the reeds till he reached dry ground and coarse grass, and heard the buzz of midges and crickets. He sat down then on the ground, hard, for his legs were shaking.

"It won't do," he said, talking to himself in Hardic, and then he said, "I can't do it." Then he said, "I can't do it by myself."

He was so distraught that when he made up his mind to call Silence he could not think of the opening of the spell, which he had known for sixty years; then when he thought he had it, he began to speak a Summoning instead, and the spell had begun to work before he realised what he was doing and stopped and undid it word by word.

He pulled up some grass and rubbed at the slimy mud on his feet and legs. It was not dry yet, and only smeared about on his skin. "I hate mud," he whispered. Then he snapped his jaws and stopped trying to clean his legs. "Dirt, dirt," he said, gently patting the ground he sat on. Then, very slow, very careful, he began to speak the spell of calling.

In a busy street leading down to the busy wharfs of Gont Port, the wizard Ogion stopped short. The ship's captain beside him walked on several steps and turned to see Ogion talking to the air.

"But I will come, master!" he said. And then after a pause, "How soon?" And after a longer pause, he told the air something in a language the ship's captain did not understand, and made a gesture that darkened the air about him for an instant.

"Captain," he said, "I'm sorry, I must wait to spell your sails. An earthquake is near. I must warn the city. Do you tell them down there, every ship that can sail make for the open sea. Clear out past the Armed Cliffs! Good luck to you." And he turned and ran back up the street, a tall, strong man with rough greying hair, running now like a stag.

Gont Port lies at the inner end of a long narrow bay between steep shores. Its entrance from the sea is between two great headlands, the Gates of the Port, the Armed Cliffs, not a hundred feet apart. The people of Gont Port are safe from sea-pirates. But their safety is their danger: the long bay follows a fault in the earth, and jaws that have opened may shut.

When he had done what he could to warn the city, and seen all the gate guards and port guards doing what they could to keep the few roads out from becoming choked and murderous with panicky people, Ogion shut himself into a room in the signal tower of the Port, locked the door, for everybody wanted him at once, and sent a sending to the Dark Pond in Semere's cow pasture up on the Mountain.

His old master was sitting in the grass near the pond, eating an apple. Bits of eggshell flecked the ground near his legs, which were caked with drying mud. When he looked up and saw Ogion's sending he smiled a wide, sweet smile. But he looked old. He had never looked so old. Ogion had not seen him for over a year, having been busy; he was always busy in Gont Port, doing the business of the lords and people, never a chance to walk in the forests on the mountainside or to come sit with Heleth in the little house at Re Albi and listen and be still. Heleth was an old man, near eighty now; and he was frightened. He smiled with joy to see Ogion, but he was frightened.

"I think what we have to do," he said without preamble, "is try to hold the fault from slipping much. You at the Gates and me at the inner end, in the Mountain. Working together, you know. We might be able to. I can feel it building up, can you?"

Ogion shook his head. He let his sending sit down in the grass near Heleth, though it did not bend the stems of the grass where it stepped or sat. "I've done nothing but set the city in a panic and send the ships out of the bay," he said. "What is it you feel? How do you feel it?"

They were technical questions, mage to mage. Heleth hesitated before answering.

"I learned about this from Ard," he said, and paused again.

He had never told Ogion anything about his first teacher, a sorcerer of no fame even in Gont, and perhaps of ill fame. Ogion knew only that Ard had never gone to Roke, had been trained on Perregal, and that some mystery or shame darkened the name. Though he was talkative, for a wizard, Heleth was silent as a stone about some things. And so Ogion, who respected silence, had never asked him about his teacher.

"It's not Roke magic," the old man said. His voice was dry, a little forced. "Nothing against the balance, though. Nothing sticky."

That had always been his word for evil doings, spells for gain, curses, black magic: "sticky stuff."

After a while, searching for words, he went on: "Dirt. Rocks. It's a dirty magic. Old. Very old. As old as Gont Island."

"The Old Powers?" Ogion murmured.

Heleth said, "I'm not sure."

"Will it control the earth itself?"

"More a matter of getting in with it, I think. Inside." The old man was burying the core of his apple and the larger bits of eggshell under loose dirt, patting it over them neatly. "Of course I know the words, but I'll have to learn what to do as I go. That's the trouble with the big spells, isn't it? You learn what you're doing while you do it. No chance to practice." He looked up. "Ah—there! You feel that?"

Ogion shook his head.

"Straining," Heleth said, his hand still absently, gently patting the dirt as one might pat a scared cow. "Quite soon now, I think. Can you hold the Gates open, my dear?"

"Tell me what you'll be doing—"

But Heleth was shaking his head: "No," he said. "No time. Not your kind of thing." He was more and more distracted by whatever it was he sensed in the earth or air, and through him Ogion too felt that gathering, intolerable tension.

They sat unspeaking. The crisis passed. Heleth relaxed a little and even smiled. "Very old stuff," he said, "what I'll be doing. I wish now I'd thought about it more. Passed it on to you. But it seemed a bit crude. Heavy-handed . . . She didn't say where she'd learned it. Here, of course . . . There are different kinds of knowledge, after all."

"She?"

"Ard. My teacher." Heleth looked up, his face unreadable, its expression possibly sly. "You didn't know that? No, I suppose I never mentioned it. I wonder what difference it made to her wizardry, her being a woman. Or to mine, my being a man . . . What matters, it seems to me, is whose house we live in. And who we let enter the house. This kind of thing— There! There again—"

His sudden tension and immobility, the strained face and inward look, were like those of a woman in labor when her womb contracts. That was Ogion's thought, even as he asked, "What did you mean, 'in the Mountain'?"

The spasm passed; Heleth answered, "Inside it. There at Yaved." He pointed to the knotted hills below them. "I'll go in, try to keep things from sliding around, eh? I'll find out how when I'm doing it, no doubt. I think you should be getting back to yourself. Things are tightening up." He stopped again, looking as if he were in intense pain, hunched and clenched. He struggled to stand up. Unthinking, Ogion held out his hand to help him.

"No use," said the old wizard, grinning, "you're only wind and sunlight. Now I'm going to be dirt and stone. You'd best go on. Farewell, Aihal. Keep the—keep the mouth open, for once, eh?"

Ogion, obedient, bringing himself back to himself in the stuffy, tapestried room in Gont Port, did not understand the old man's joke until he turned to the window and saw the Armed Cliffs down at the end of the long bay, the jaws ready to snap shut. "I will," he said, and set to it.

"What I have to do, you see," the old wizard said, still talking to Silence because it was a comfort to talk to him even if he was no longer there, "is get into the mountain, right inside. But not the way a sorcerer-prospector does, not just slipping about between things and looking and tasting. Deeper. All the way in. Not the veins, but the bones. So," and standing there alone in the high pasture, in the noon light, Heleth opened his arms wide in the gesture of invocation that opens all the greater spells; and he spoke.

Nothing happened as he said the words Ard had taught him, his old witch-teacher with her bitter mouth and her long, lean arms, the words spoken awry then, spoken truly now.

Nothing happened, and he had time to regret the sunlight and the sea wind, and to doubt the spell, and to doubt himself, before the earth rose up around him, dry, warm, and dark.

In there he knew he should hurry, that the bones of the earth ached to move, and that he must become them to guide them, but he could not hurry. There was on him the bewilderment of any transformation.

He had in his day been fox, and bull, and dragonfly, and knew what it was to change being. But this was different, this slow enlargement. I am vastening, he thought.

He reached out towards Yaved, towards the ache, the suffering. As he came closer to it he felt a great strength flow into him from the west, as if Silence had taken him by the hand after all. Through that link he could send his own strength, the Mountain's strength, to help. I didn't tell him I wasn't coming back, he thought, his last words in Hardic, his last grief, for he was in the bones of the mountain now. He knew the arteries of fire, and the beat of the great heart. He knew what to do. It was in no tongue of man that he said, "Be quiet, be easy. There now, there. Hold fast. So, there. We can be easy."

And he was easy, he was still, he held fast, rock in rock and earth in earth in the fiery dark of the mountain.

It was their mage Ogion whom the people saw stand alone on the roof of the signal tower on the wharf, when the streets ran up and down in waves, the cobbles bursting out of them, and walls of clay brick puffed into dust, and the Armed Cliffs leaned together, groaning. It was Ogion they saw, his hands held out before him, straining, parting: and the cliffs parted with them, and stood straight, unmoved. The city shuddered and stood still. It was Ogion who stopped the earthquake. They saw it, they said it.

"My teacher was with me, and his teacher with him," Ogion said when they praised him. "I could hold the Gate open because he held the Mountain still." They praised his modesty and did not listen to him. Listening is a rare gift, and men will have their heroes.

When the city was in order again, and the ships had all come back, and the walls were being rebuilt, Ogion escaped from praise and went up into the hills above Gont Port. He found the queer little valley called Trimmer's Dell, the true name of which in the Language of the Making was Yaved, as Ogion's true name was Aihal. He walked about there all one day, as if seeking something. In the evening he lay down on the ground and talked to it. "You should have told me. I could have said goodbye," he said. He wept then, and his tears fell on the dry dirt among the grass stems and made little spots of mud, little sticky spots.

He slept there on the ground, with no pallet or blanket between him and the dirt. At sunrise he got up and walked by the high road over to Re Albi. He did not go into the village, but past it to the house that stood alone north of the other houses at the beginning of the Overfell. The door stood open.

The last beans had got big and coarse on the vines; the cabbages were thriving. Three hens came clucking and pecking around the dusty dooryard, a red, a brown, a white; a grey hen was setting her clutch in the henhouse. There were no chicks, and no sign of the cock, the King, Heleth had called him. The king is dead, Ogion thought. Maybe a chick is hatching even now to take his place. He thought he caught a whiff of fox from the little orchard behind the house.

He swept out the dust and leaves that had blown in the open doorway across the floor of polished wood. He set Heleth's mattress and blanket in the sun to air. "I'll stay here a while," he thought. "It's a good house." After a while he thought, "I might keep some goats."

On the High Marsh

THE ISLAND OF SEMEL lies north and west across the Pelnish Sea from Havnor, south and west of the Enlades. Though it is one of the great isles of the Earthsea Archipelago, there aren't many stories from Semel. Enlad has its glorious history, and Havnor its wealth, and Paln its ill repute, but Semel has only cattle and sheep, forests and little towns, and the great silent volcano called Andanden standing over all.

South of Andanden lies a land where the ashes fell a hundred feet deep when last the volcano spoke. Rivers and streams cut their way seaward through that high plain, winding and pooling, spreading and wandering, making a marsh of it, a big, desolate, waterland with a far horizon, few trees, not many people. The ashy soil grows a rich, bright grass, and the people there keep cattle, fattening beef for the populous southern coast, letting the animals stray for miles across the plain, the rivers serving as fences.

As mountains will, Andanden makes the weather. It gathers clouds around it. The summer is short, the winter long, out on the high marsh.

In the early darkness of a winter day, a traveler stood at the windswept crossing of two paths, neither very promising, mere cattle tracks among the reeds, and looked for some sign of the way he should take.

As he came down the last slope of the mountain, he had seen houses here and there out in the marshlands, a village not far away. He had thought he was on the way to the village, but had taken a wrong turning somewhere. Tall reeds rose up close beside the paths, so that if a light shone anywhere he could not see it. Water chuckled softly somewhere near his feet. He had used up his shoes walking round

Andanden on the cruel roads of black lava. The soles were worn right through, and his feet ached with the icy damp of the marsh paths.

It grew darker quickly. A haze was coming up from the south, blotting out the sky. Only above the huge, dim bulk of the mountain did stars burn clearly. Wind whistled in the reeds, soft, dismal.

The traveler stood at the crossway and whistled back at the reeds.

Something moved on one of the tracks, something big, dark, in the darkness.

"Are you there, my dear?" said the traveler. He spoke in the Old Speech, the Language of the Making. "Come along, then, Ulla," he said, and the heifer came a step or two towards him, towards her name, while he walked to meet her. He made out the big head more by touch than sight, stroking the silken dip between her eyes, scratching her forehead at the roots of the nubbin horns. "Beautiful, you are beautiful," he told her, breathing her grassy breath, leaning against her large warmth. "Will you lead me, dear Ulla? Will you lead me where I need to go?"

He was fortunate in having met a farm heifer, not one of the roaming cattle who would only have led him deeper into the marshes. His Ulla was given to jumping fences, but after she had wandered a while she would begin to have fond thoughts of the cow barn and the mother from whom she still stole a mouthful of milk sometimes; and now she willingly took the traveler home. She walked, slow but purposeful, down one of the tracks, and he went with her, a hand on her hip when the way was wide enough. When she waded a knee-deep stream, he held on to her tail. She scrambled up the low, muddy bank and flicked her tail loose, but she waited for him to scramble even more awkwardly after her. Then she plodded gently on. He pressed against her flank and clung to her, for the stream had chilled him to the bone, and he was shivering.

"Moo," said his guide, softly, and he saw the dim, small square of yellow light just a little to his left.

"Thank you," he said, opening the gate for the heifer, who went to greet her mother, while he stumbled across the dark houseyard to the door.

It would be Berry at the door, though why he knocked she didn't know. "Come in, you fool!" she said, and he knocked again, and she put down her mending and went to the door. "Can you be drunk already?" she said, and then saw him.

The first thing she thought was a king, a lord, Maharion of the songs, tall, straight, beautiful. The next thing she thought was a beggar, a lost man, in dirty clothes, hugging himself with shivering arms.

He said, "I lost my way. Have I come to the village?" His voice was hoarse and harsh, a beggar's voice, but not a beggar's accent.

"It's a half mile on," said Gift.

"Is there an inn?"

"Not till you'd come to Oraby, a ten-twelve miles on south." She considered only briefly. "If you need a room for the night, I have one. Or San might, if you're going to the village."

"I'll stay here if I may," he said in that princely way, with his teeth chattering, holding on to the doorjamb to keep on his feet.

"Take your shoes off," she said, "they're soaking. Come in then." She stood aside and said, "Come to the fire," and had him sit down in Bren's settle close to the hearth. "Stir the fire up a bit," she said. "Will you have a bit of soup? It's still hot."

"Thank you, mistress," he muttered, crouching at the fire. She brought him a bowl of broth. He drank from it eagerly yet warily, as if long unaccustomed to hot soup.

"You came over the mountain?"

He nodded.

"Whatever for?"

"To come here," he said. He was beginning to tremble less. His bare feet were a sad sight, bruised, swollen, sodden. She wanted to tell him to put them right to the fire's warmth, but didn't like to presume. Whatever he was, he wasn't a beggar by choice.

"Not many come here to the High Marsh," she said. "Peddlers and such. But not in winter."

He finished his soup, and she took the bowl. She sat down in her place, the stool by the oil lamp to the right of the hearth, and took up her mending. "Get warm through, and then I'll show you your bed," she said. "There's no fire in that room. Did you meet weather, up on the mountain? They say there's been snow."

"Some flurries," he said. She got a good look at him now in the light of lamp and fire. He was not a young man, thin, not as tall as she had thought. It was a fine face, but there was something wrong, something amiss. He looks ruined, she thought, a ruined man.

"Why would you come to the Marsh?" she asked. She had a right to ask, having taken him in, yet she felt a discomfort in pressing the question.

"I was told there's a murrain among the cattle here." Now that he wasn't all locked up with cold his voice was beautiful. He talked like the tale-tellers when they spoke the parts of the heroes and the dragonlords. Maybe he was a teller or a singer? But no; the murrain, he had said.

"There is."

"I may be able to help the beasts."

"You're a curer?"

He nodded.

"Then you'll be more than welcome. The plague is terrible among the cattle. And getting worse."

He said nothing. She could see the warmth coming into him, untying him.

"Put your feet up to the fire," she said abruptly. "I have some old shoes of my husband's." It cost her something to say that, yet when she had said it she felt released, untied too. What was she keeping Bren's shoes for, anyhow? They were too small for Berry and too big for her. She'd given away his clothes, but kept the shoes, she didn't know what for. For this fellow, it would seem. Things came round if you could wait for them, she thought. "I'll set 'em out for you," she said. "Yours are perished."

He glanced at her. His dark eyes were large, deep, opaque like a horse's eyes, unreadable.

"He's dead," she said, "two years. The marsh fever. You have to watch out for that, here. The water. I live with my brother. He's in the village, at the tavern. We keep a dairy. I make cheese. Our herd's been all right," and she made the sign to avert evil. "I keep 'em close in. Out on the ranges, the murrain's very bad. Maybe the cold weather'll put an end to it."

"More likely to kill the beasts that sicken with it," the man said. He sounded a bit sleepy.

"I'm called Gift," she said. "My brother's Berry."

"Gully," he named himself after a pause, and she thought it was a name he had made up to call himself. It did not fit him. Nothing about him fit together, made a whole. Yet she felt no distrust of him. She was easy with him. He meant no harm to her. She thought there was kindness in him, the way he spoke of the animals. He would have a way with them, she thought. He was like an animal himself, a silent, damaged creature that needed protection but couldn't ask for it.

"Come," she said, "before you fall asleep there," and he followed her obediently to Berry's room, which wasn't much more than a cupboard built onto the corner of the house. Her room was behind the chimney. Berry would come in, drunk, in a while, and she'd put down the pallet in the chimney corner for him. Let the traveler have a good bed for a night. Maybe he'd leave a copper or two with her when he went on. There was a terrible shortage of coppers in her household these days.

He woke, as he always did, in his room in the Great House. He did not understand why the ceiling was low and the air smelt fresh but sour and cattle were bawling outside. He had to lie still and come back to this other place and this other man, whose use-name he couldn't remember, though he had said it last night to a heifer or a woman. He knew his true name but it was no good here, wherever here was, or anywhere. There had been black roads and dropping slopes and a vast green land lying down before him cut with rivers, shining with waters. A cold wind blowing. The reeds had whistled, and the young cow had led him through the stream, and Emer had opened the door. He had known her name as soon as he saw her. But he must use some other name. He must not call her by her name. He must remember what name he had told her to call him. He must not be Irioth, though he was Irioth. Maybe in time he would be another man. No; that was wrong; he must be this man. This man's legs ached and his feet hurt. But it was a good bed, a feather bed, warm, and he need not get out of it yet. He drowsed a while, drifting away from Irioth.

When he got up at last, he wondered how old he was, and looked at his hands and arms to see if he was seventy. He still looked forty, though he felt seventy and moved like it, wincing. He got his clothes on, foul as they were from days and days of travel. There was a pair of shoes under the chair, worn but good, strong shoes, and a pair of knit wool stockings to go with them. He put the stockings on his battered feet and limped into the kitchen. Emer stood at the big sink, straining something heavy in a cloth.

"Thank you for these and the shoes," he said, and thanking her for the gift, remembered her use-name but said only, "mistress."

"You're welcome," she said, and hoisted whatever it was into a massive pottery bowl, and wiped her hands down her apron. He knew nothing at all about women. He had not lived where women were since he was ten years old. He had been afraid of them, the women that shouted at him to get out of the way in that great other kitchen long ago. But since he had been traveling about in Earthsea he had met women and found them easy to be with, like the animals; they went about their business not paying much attention to him unless he frightened them. He tried not to do that. He had no wish or reason to frighten them. They were not men.

"Would you like some fresh curds? It makes a good breakfast."

She was eyeing him, but not for long, and not meeting his eyes. Like an animal, like a cat, she was, sizing him up but not challenging. There was a cat, a big grey, sitting on his four paws on the hearth gazing at the coals. Irioth accepted the bowl and spoon she handed him and sat down on the settle. The cat jumped up beside him and purred.

"Look at that," said the woman. "He's not friendly with most folk."

"It's the curds."

"He knows a curer, maybe."

It was peaceful here with the woman and the cat. He had come to a good house.

"It's cold out," she said. "Ice on the trough this morning. Will you be going on, this day?"

There was a pause. He forgot that he had to answer in words. "I'd stay if I might," he said. "I'd stay here."

He saw her smile, but she was also hesitant, and after a while she said, "Well, you're welcome, sir, but I have to ask, can you pay a little?"

"Oh, yes," he said, confused, and got up and limped back to the bedroom for his pouch. He brought her a piece of money, a little Enladian crownpiece of gold.

"Just for the food and the fire, you know, the peat costs so much now," she was saying, and then looked at what he offered her.

"Oh, sir," she said, and he knew he had done wrong.

"There's nobody in the village could change that," she said. She looked up into his face for a moment. "The whole village together couldn't change that!" she said, and laughed. It was all right, then, though the word "change" rang and rang in his head.

"It hasn't been changed," he said, but he knew that was not what she meant. "I'm sorry," he said. "If I stayed a month, if I stayed the winter, would that use it up? I should have a place to stay, while I work with the beasts."

"Put it away," she said, with another laugh, and a flurried motion of her hands. "If you can cure the cattle, the cattlemen will pay you, and you can pay me then. Call that surety, if you like. But put it away, sir! It makes me dizzy to look at it. —Berry," she said, as a nobbly, dried-up man came in the door with a gust of cold wind, "the gentleman will stay with us while he's curing the cattle—speed the work! He's given us surety of payment. So you'll sleep in the chimney corner, and him in the room. This is my brother Berry, sir."

Berry ducked his head and muttered. His eyes were dull. It seemed to Irioth that the man had been poisoned. When Berry went out again, the woman came closer and said, resolute, in a low voice, "There's no harm in him but the drink, but there's not much left of him but the drink. It's eaten up most of his mind, and most of what we have. So, do you see, put up your money where he won't see it, if you don't mind, sir. He won't come looking for it. But if he saw it, he'd take it. He often doesn't know what he's doing, do you see."

"Yes," Irioth said. "I understand. You are a kind woman." She was talking about him, about his not knowing what he was doing. She was forgiving him. "A kind sister," he said. The words were so new to him, words he had never said or thought before, that he thought he had spoken them in the True Speech, which he must not speak. But she only shrugged, with a frowning smile.

"Times I could shake his fool head off," she said, and went back to her work.

He had not known how tired he was until he came to haven. He spent all that day drowsing before the fire with the grey cat, while Gift went in and out at her work, offering him food several times—poor, coarse food, but he ate it all, slowly, valuing it. Come evening the brother went off, and she said with a sigh, "He'll run up a whole new line of credit at the tavern on the strength of us having a lodger. Not that it's your fault."

"Oh, yes," Irioth said. "It was my fault." But she forgave; and the grey cat was pressed up against his thigh, dreaming. The cat's dreams came into his mind, in the low fields where he spoke with the animals, the dusky places. The cat leapt there, and then there was milk, and the deep soft thrilling. There was no fault, only the great innocence. No need for words. They would not find him here. He was not here to find. There was no need to speak any name. There was nobody but her, and the cat dreaming, and the fire flickering. He had come over the dead mountain on black roads, but here the streams ran slow among the pastures.

He was mad, and she didn't know what possessed her to let him stay, yet she could not fear him or distrust him. What did it matter if he was mad? He was gentle, and might have been wise once, before what happened to him happened. And he wasn't so mad as all that. Mad in patches, mad at moments. Nothing in him was whole, not even his madness. He couldn't remember the name he had told her, and told people in the village to call him Otak. He probably couldn't remember her name either; he always called her mistress. But maybe that was his courtesy. She called him sir, in courtesy, and because neither Gully or

Otak seemed names well suited to him. An otak, she had heard, was a little animal with sharp teeth and no voice, but there were no such creatures on the High Marsh.

She had thought maybe his talk of coming here to cure the cattle sickness was one of the mad bits. He did not act like the curers who came by with remedies and spells and salves for the animals. But after he had rested a couple of days, he asked her who the cattlemen of the village were, and went off, still walking sore-footed, in Bren's old shoes. It made her heart turn in her, seeing that.

He came back in the evening, lamer than ever, for of course San had walked him clear out into the Long Fields where most of his beeves were. Nobody had horses but Alder, and they were for his cowboys. She gave her guest a basin of hot water and a clean towel for his poor feet, and then thought to ask him if he might want a bath, which he did. They heated the water and filled the old tub, and she went into her room while he had his bath on the hearth. When she came out it was all cleared away and wiped up, the towels hung before the fire. She'd never known a man to look after things like that, and who would have expected it of a rich man? Wouldn't he have servants, where he came from? But he was no more trouble than the cat. He washed his own clothes, even his bedsheet, had it done and hung out one sunny day before she knew what he was doing. "You needn't do that, sir, I'll do your things with mine," she said.

"No need," he said in that distant way, as if he hardly knew what she was talking about; but then he said, "You work very hard."

"Who doesn't? I like the cheese making. There's an interest to it. And I'm strong. All I fear is getting old, when I can't lift the buckets and the molds." She showed him her round, muscular arm, making a fist and smiling. "Pretty good for fifty years old!" she said. It was silly to boast, but she was proud of her strong arms, her energy and skill.

"Speed the work," he said gravely.

He had a way with her cows that was wonderful. When he was there and she needed a hand, he took Berry's place, and as she told her friend Tawny, laughing, he was cannier with the cows than Bren's old dog had been. "He talks to 'em, and I'll swear they consider what he says. And that heifer follows him about like a puppy." Whatever he was doing out on the ranges with the beeves, the cattlemen were coming to think well of him. Of course they would grab at any promise of help. Half San's herd was dead. Alder would not say how many head he had lost. The bodies of cattle were everywhere. If it had not been cold weather the Marsh would have reeked of rotting flesh. None of the water could be drunk unless you boiled it an hour, except what came from the wells, hers here and the one in the village, which gave the place its name.

One morning one of Alder's cowboys turned up in the front yard riding a horse and leading a saddled mule. "Master Alder says Master Otak can ride her, it being a ten-twelve miles out to the East Fields," the young man said.

Her guest came out of the house. It was a bright, misty morning, the marshes hidden by gleaming vapors. Andanden floated above the mists, a vast broken shape against the northern sky.

The curer said nothing to the cowboy but went straight to the mule, or hinny, rather, being out of San's big jenny by Alder's white horse. She was a whitey roan, young, with a pretty face. He went and talked to her for a minute, saying something in her big, delicate ear and rubbing her topknot.

"He does that," the cowboy said to Gift. "Talks at 'em." He was amused, disdainful. He was one of Berry's drinking mates at the tavern, a decent enough young fellow, for a cowboy.

"Is he curing the cattle?" she asked.

"Well, he can't lift the murrain all at once. But seems like he can cure a beast if he gets to it before the staggers begin. And those not struck yet, he says he can keep it off 'em. So the master's sending him all about the range to do what can be done. It's too late for many."

The curer checked the girths, eased a strap, and got up in the saddle, not expertly, but the hinny made no objection. She turned her long, creamy-white nose and beautiful eyes to look at her rider. He smiled. Gift had never seen him smile.

"Shall we go?" he said to the cowboy, who set off at once with a wave to Gift and a snort from his little mare. The curer followed. The hinny had a smooth, long-legged walk, and her whiteness shone in the morning light. Gift thought it was like seeing a prince ride off, like something out of a tale, the mounted figures that walked through bright mist across the vague dun of the winter fields, and faded into the light, and were gone.

It was hard work out in the pastures. "Who doesn't do hard work?" Emer had asked, showing her round, strong arms, her hard, red hands. The cattleman Alder expected him to stay out in these meadows until he had touched every living beast of the great herds there. Alder had sent two cowboys along. They made a camp of sorts, with a groundcloth and a half tent. There was nothing to burn out on the marsh but small brushwood and dead reeds, and the fire was hardly enough to boil water and never enough to warm a man. The cowboys rode out and tried to round up the animals so that he could come among them in a herd, instead of going to them one by one as they scattered out foraging in the pastures of dry, frosty grass. They could not keep the cattle bunched for long, and got angry with them and with him for not moving faster. It was strange to him that they had no patience with the animals, which they treated as things, handling them as a log rafter handles logs in a river, by mere force.

They had no patience with him either, always at him to hurry up and get done with the job; nor with themselves, their life. When they talked to each other it was always about what they were going to do in town, in Oraby, when they got paid off. He heard a good deal about the whores in Oraby, Daisy and Goldie and the one they called the Burning Bush. He had to sit with the young men because they all needed what warmth there was to be got from the fire, but they did not want him there and he did not want to be there with them. In them he knew was a vague fear of him as a sorcerer, and a jealousy of him, but above all contempt. He was old, other, not one of them. Fear and jealousy he knew and shrank from, and contempt he remembered. He was glad he was not one of them, that they did not want to talk to him. He was afraid of doing wrong to them.

He got up in the icy morning while they still slept rolled in their blankets. He knew where the cattle were nearby, and went to them. The sickness was very familiar to him now. He felt it in his hands as a burning, and a queasiness if it was much advanced. Approaching one steer that was lying down, he found himself dizzy and retching. He came no closer, but said words that might ease the dying, and went on.

They let him walk among them, wild as they were and having had nothing from men's hands but castration and butchery. He had a pleasure in their trust in him, a pride in it. He should not, but he did. If he wanted to touch one of the great beasts he had only to stand and speak to it a little while in the language of those who do not speak. "Ulla," he said, naming them. "Ellu. Ellua." They stood, big, indifferent; sometimes one looked at him for a long time. Sometimes one came to him with its easy, loose, majestic tread, and breathed into his open palm. All those that came to him he could cure. He laid his hands on them, on the stiff-haired, hot flanks and neck, and sent the healing into his hands with the words of power spoken over and over. After a while the beast would give a shake, or toss its head a bit, or step on. And he would drop his hands and stand there, drained and blank, for a while. Then there would be another one, big, curious, shyly bold, muddy-coated, with the sickness in it like a prickling, a tingling, a hotness in his hands, a dizziness. "Ellu," he would say, and walk to the beast and lay his hands upon it until they felt cool, as if a mountain stream ran through them.

The cowboys were discussing whether or not it was safe to eat the meat of a steer dead of the murrain. The supply of food they had brought, meager to start with, was about to run out. Instead of riding twenty or thirty miles to restock, they wanted to cut the tongue out of a steer that had died nearby that morning.

He had forced them to boil any water they used. Now he said, "If you eat that meat, in a year you'll begin to get dizzy. You'll end with the blind staggers and die as they do."

They cursed and sneered, but believed him. He had no idea if what he said was true. It had seemed true as he said it. Perhaps he wanted to spite them. Perhaps he wanted to get rid of them.

"Ride back," he said. "Leave me here. There's enough food for one man for three or four days more. The hinny will bring me back."

They needed no persuasion. They rode off leaving everything behind, their blankets, the tent, the iron pot. "How do we get all that back to the village?" he asked the hinny. She looked after the two ponies and said what hinnies say. "Aaawww!" she said. She would miss the ponies.

"We have to finish the work here," he told her, and she looked at him mildly. All animals were patient, but the patience of the horse kind was wonderful, being freely given. Dogs were loyal, but there was more of obedience in it. Dogs were hierarchs, dividing the world into lords and commoners. Horses were all lords. They agreed to collude. He remembered walking among the great, plumed feet of cart horses, fearless. The comfort of their breath on his head. A long time ago. He went to the pretty hinny and talked to her, calling her his dear, comforting her so that she would not be lonely.

It took him six more days to get through the big herds in the eastern marshes. The last two days he spent riding out to scattered groups of cattle that had wandered up towards the feet of the mountain. Many of them were not infected yet, and he could protect them. The hinny carried him bareback and made the going easy. But there was nothing left for him to eat. When he rode back to the village he was lightheaded and weak-kneed. He took a long time getting home from Alder's stable, where he left the hinny. Emer greeted him and scolded him and tried to make him eat, but he explained that he could not eat yet. "As I stayed there in the sickness, in the sick fields, I felt sick. After a while I'll be able to eat again," he explained.

"You're crazy," she said, very angry. It was a sweet anger. Why could not more anger be sweet?

"At least have a bath!" she said.

He knew what he smelled like, and thanked her.

"What's Alder paying you for all this?" she demanded while the water was heating. She was still indignant, speaking more bluntly even than usual.

"I don't know," he said.

She stopped and stared at him.

"You didn't set a price?"

"Set a price?" he flashed out. Then he remembered who he was not, and spoke humbly. "No. I didn't."

"Of all the innocence," Gift said, hissing the word. "He'll skin you." She dumped a kettleful of steaming water into the bath. "He has ivory," she said. "Tell him ivory it has to be. Out there ten days starving in the cold to cure his beasts! San's got nothing but copper, but Alder can pay you in ivory. I'm sorry if I'm meddling in your business. Sir." She flung out the door with two buckets, going to the pump. She would not use the stream water for anything at all, these days. She was wise, and kind. Why had he lived so long among those who were not kind?

"We'll have to see," said Alder, the next day, "if my beasts are cured. If they make it through the winter, see, we'll know your cures all took, that they're sound, like. Not that I doubt it, but fair's fair, right? You wouldn't ask me to pay you what I have in mind to pay you, would you now, if the cure didn't take and the beasts died after all. Avert the chance! But I wouldn't ask you to wait all that time unpaid, neither. So here's an advance, like, on what's to come, and all's square between us for now, right?"

The coppers weren't decently in a bag, even. Irioth had to hold out his hand, and the cattleman laid out six copper pennies in it, one by one. "Now then! That's fair and square!" he said, expansive. "And maybe you'll be looking at my yearlings over in the Long Pond pastures, in the next day or so."

"No," Irioth said. "San's herd was going down fast when I left. I'm needed there."

"Oh, no, you're not, Master Otak. While you were out in the east range a sorcerer curer came by, a fellow that's been here before, from the south coast, and so San hired him. You work for me and you'll be paid well. Better than copper, maybe, if the beasts fare well!"

Irioth did not say yes, or no, or thanks, but went off unspeaking. The cattleman looked after him and spat. "Avert," he said.

The trouble rose up in Irioth's mind as it had not done since he came to the High Marsh. He struggled against it. A man of power had come to heal the cattle, another man of power. But a sorcerer, Alder had said. Not a wizard, not a mage. Only a curer, a cattle healer. I do not need to fear him. I do not need to fear his power. I do not need his power. I must see him, to be sure, to be certain. If he does what I do here there is no harm. We can work together. If I do what he does here. If he uses only sorcery and means no harm. As I do.

He walked down the straggling street of Purewells to San's house, which was about midway, opposite the tavern. San, a hard-bitten man in his thirties, was talking to a man on his doorstep, a stranger. When they saw Irioth they looked uneasy. San went into his house and the stranger followed.

Irioth came up onto the doorstep. He did not go in, but spoke in the open door. "Master San, it's about the cattle you have there between the rivers. I can go to them today." He did not know why he said this. It was not what he had meant to say.

"Ah," San said, coming to the door, and hemmed a bit. "No need, Master Otak. This here is Master Sunbright, come up to deal with the murrain. He's cured beasts for me before, the hoof rot and all. Being as how you have all one man can do with Alder's beeves, you see . . ."

The sorcerer came out from behind San. His name was Ayeth. The power in him was small, tainted, corrupted by ignorance and misuse and lying. But the jealousy in him was like a stinging fire. "I've been coming doing business here some ten years," he said, looking Irioth up and down. "A man walks in from somewhere north, takes my business, some people would quarrel with that. A quarrel of sorcerers is a bad thing. If you're a sorcerer, a man of power, that is. I am. As the good people here well know."

Irioth tried to say he did not want a quarrel. He tried to say that there was work for two. He tried to say he would not take the man's work from him. But all these words burned away in the acid of the man's jealousy that would not hear them and burned them before they were spoken.

Ayeth's stare grew more insolent as he watched Irioth stammer. He began to say something to San, but Irioth spoke.

"You have—" he said—"you have to go. Back." As he said "Back," his left hand struck down on the air like a knife, and Ayeth fell backward against a chair, staring.

He was only a little sorcerer, a cheating healer with a few sorry spells. Or so he seemed. What if he was cheating, hiding his power, a rival hiding his power? A jealous rival. He must be stopped, he must be bound, named, called. Irioth began to say the words that would bind him, and the shaken man cowered away, shrinking down, shriveling, crying out in a thin, high wail. It is wrong, wrong, I am doing the wrong, I am the ill, Irioth thought. He stopped the spell words in his mouth, fighting against them, and at last crying out one other word. Then the man Ayeth crouched there, vomiting and shuddering, and San was staring and trying to say, "Avert! Avert!" And no harm was done. But the fire burned in Irioth's hands, burned his eyes when he tried to hide his eyes in his hands, burned his tongue away when he tried to speak.

For a long time nobody would touch him. He had fallen down in a fit in San's doorway. He lay there now like a dead man. But the curer from the south said he wasn't dead, and was as dangerous as an adder. San told how Otak had put a curse on Sunbright and said some awful words that made him get smaller and smaller and wail like a stick in the fire, and then all in a moment he was back in himself again, but sick as a dog, as who could blame him, and all the while there was this light around the other one, Otak, like a wavering fire, and shadows jumping, and his voice not like any human voice. A terrible thing.

Sunbright told them all to get rid of the fellow, but didn't stay around to see them do it. He went back down the south road as soon as he'd gulped a pint of beer at the tavern, telling them there was no room for two sorcerers in one village and he'd be back, maybe, when that man, or whatever he was, had gone.

Nobody would touch him. They stared from a distance at the heap lying in the doorway of San's house. San's wife wept aloud up and down the street. "Bad cess! Bad cess!" she cried. "Oh, my babe will be born dead, I know it!"

Berry went and fetched his sister, after he had heard Sunbright's tale at the tavern, and San's version of it, and several other versions already current. In the best of them, Otak had towered up ten feet tall and struck Sunbright into a lump of coal with lightning, before foaming at the mouth, turning blue, and collapsing in a heap.

Gift hurried to the village. She went straight up to the doorstep, bent over the heap, and laid her hand on it. Everybody gasped and muttered, "Avert! Avert!" except Tawny's youngest daughter, who mistook the signs and piped up, "Speed the work!"

The heap moved, and roused up slowly. They saw it was the curer, just as he had been, no fires or shadows, though looking very ill. "Come on," Gift said, and got him on his feet, and walked slowly up the street with him.

The villagers shook their heads. Gift was a brave woman, but there was such a thing as being too brave. Or brave, they said around the tavern table, in the wrong way, or the wrong place, d'you see. Nobody should ought to meddle with sorcery that ain't born to it. Nor with sorcerers. You forget that. They seem the same as other folk. But they ain't like other folk. Seems there's no harm in a curer. Heal the foot rot, clear a caked udder. That's all fine. But cross one and there you are, fire and shadows and curses and falling down in fits. Uncanny. Always was uncanny, that one. Where'd he come from, anyhow? Answer me that.

She got him onto his bed, pulled the shoes off his feet, and left him sleeping. Berry came in late and drunker than usual, so that he fell and gashed his forehead on the andiron. Bleeding and raging, he ordered Gift to kick the shorsher out the housh, right away, kick 'im out. Then he vomited into the ashes and fell asleep on the hearth. She hauled him onto his pallet, pulled his shoes off his feet, and left him sleeping. She went to look at the other one. He looked feverish, and she put her hand on his forehead. He opened his eyes, looking straight into hers without expression. "Emer," he said, and closed his eyes again.

She backed away from him, terrified.

In her bed, in the dark, she lay and thought: He knew the wizard who named me. Or I said my name. Maybe I said it out loud in my sleep. Or somebody told him. But nobody knows it. Nobody ever knew my name but the wizard, and my mother. And they're dead, they're dead . . . I said it in my sleep . . .

But she knew better.

She stood with the little oil lamp in her hand, and the light of it shone red between her fingers and golden on her face. He said her name. She gave him sleep.

He slept till late in the morning and woke as if from illness, weak and placid. She was unable to be afraid of him. She found that he had no memory at all of what had happened in the village, of the other sorcerer, even of the six coppers she had found scattered on the bedcover, which he must have held clenched in his hand all along.

"No doubt that's what Alder gave you," she said. "The flint!"

"I said I'd see to his beasts at . . . at the pasture between the rivers, was it?" he said, getting anxious, the hunted look coming back into him, and he got up from the settle.

"Sit down," she said. He sat down, but he sat fretting.

"How can you cure when you're sick?" she said.

"How else?" he said.

But he quieted down again presently, stroking the grey cat.

Her brother came in. "Come on out," he said to her as soon as he saw the curer dozing on the settle. She stepped outside with him.

"Now I won't have him here no more," Berry said, coming master of the house over her, with the great black gash in his forehead, and his eyes like oysters, and his hands juddering.

"Where'll you go?" she said.

"It's him has to go."

"It's my house. Bren's house. He stays. Go or stay, it's up to you."

"It's up to me too if he stays or goes, and he goes. You haven't got all the sayso. All the people say he ought to go. He's not canny."

"Oh, yes, since he's cured half the herds and got paid six coppers for it, time for him to go, right enough! I'll have him here as long as I choose, and that's the end of it."

"They won't buy our milk and cheese," Berry whined.

"Who says that?"

"San's wife. All the women."

"Then I'll carry the cheeses to Oraby," she said, "and sell 'em there. In the name of honor, brother, go wash out that cut, and change your shirt. You stink of the pothouse." And she went back into the house. "Oh, dear," she said, and burst into tears.

"What's the matter, Emer?" said the curer, turning his thin face and strange eyes to her.

"Oh, it's no good, I know it's no good. Nothing's any good with a drunkard," she said. She wiped her eyes with her apron. "Was that what broke you," she said, "the drink?"

"No," he said, taking no offense, perhaps not understanding.

"Of course it wasn't. I beg your pardon," she said.

"Maybe he drinks to try to be another man," he said. "To alter, to change . . ."

"He drinks because he drinks," she said. "With some, that's all it is. I'll be in the dairy, now. I'll lock the house door. There's . . . there's been strangers about. You rest yourself. It's bitter out." She wanted to be sure that he stayed indoors out of harm's way, and that nobody came harassing him. Later on she would go into the village, have a word with some of the sensible people, and put a stop to this rubbishy talk, if she could.

When she did so, Alder's wife Tawny and several other people agreed with her that a squabble between sorcerers over work was nothing new and nothing to take on about. But San and his wife and the tavern crew wouldn't let it rest, it being the only thing of interest to talk about for the rest of the winter, except the cattle dying. "Besides,"

Tawny said, "my man's never averse to paying copper where he thought he might have to pay ivory."

"Are the cattle he touched keeping afoot, then?"

"So far as we can see, they are. And no new sickenings."

"He's a true sorcerer, Tawny," Gift said, very earnest. "I know it."

"That's the trouble, love," said Tawny. "And you know it! This is no place for a man like that. Whoever he is is none of our business, but why did he come here, is what you have to ask."

"To cure the beasts," Gift said.

Sunbright had not been gone three days when a new stranger appeared in town: a man riding up the south road on a good horse and asking at the tavern for lodging. They sent him to San's house, but San's wife screeched when she heard there was a stranger at the door, crying that if San let another witch-man in the door her baby would be born dead twice over. Her screaming could be heard for several houses up and down the street, and a crowd, that is, ten or eleven people, gathered between San's house and the tavern.

"Well, that won't do," said the stranger pleasantly. "I can't be bringing on a birth untimely. Is there maybe a room above the tavern?"

"Send him on out to the dairy," said one of Alder's cowboys. "Gift's taking whatever comes." There was some sniggering and shushing.

"Back that way," said the taverner.

"Thanks," said the traveler, and led his horse along the way they pointed.

"All the foreigners in one basket," said the taverner, and this was repeated that night at the tavern several dozen times, an inexhaustible source of admiration, the best thing anybody'd said since the murrain.

Gift was in the dairy, having finished the evening milking. She was straining the milk and setting out the pans. "Mistress," said a voice at the door, and she thought it was the curer and said, "Just a minute while I finish this," and then turning saw a stranger and nearly dropped the pan. "Oh, you startled me!" she said. "What can I do for you, then?"

"I'm looking for a bed for the night."

"No, I'm sorry, there's my lodger, and my brother, and me. Maybe San, in the village—"

"They sent me here. They said, 'All the foreigners in one basket.'" The stranger was in his thirties, with a blunt face and a pleasant look, dressed plain, though the cob that stood behind him was a good horse.

"Put me up in the cow barn, mistress, it'll do fine. It's my horse needs a good bed; he's tired. I'll sleep in the barn and be off in the morning. Cows are a pleasure to sleep with on a cold night. I'll be glad to pay you, mistress, if two coppers would suit, and my name's Hawk."

"I'm Gift," she said, a bit flustered, but liking the fellow. "All right, then, Master Hawk. Put your horse up and see to him. There's the pump, there's plenty of hay. Come on in the house after. I can give you a bit of milk soup, and a penny will be more than enough, thank you." She didn't feel like calling him sir, as she always did the curer. This one had nothing of that lordly way about him. She hadn't seen a king when she first saw him, as with the other one.

When she finished in the dairy and went to the house, the new fellow, Hawk, was squatting on the hearth, skillfully making up the fire. The curer was in his room asleep. She looked in, and closed the door.

"He's not too well," she said, speaking low. "He was curing the cattle away out east over the marsh, in the cold, for days on end, and wore himself out."

As she went about her work in the kitchen, Hawk lent her a hand now and then in the most natural way, so that she began to wonder if men from foreign parts were all so much handier about the house than the men of the Marsh. He was easy to talk with, and she told him about the curer, since there was nothing much to say about herself.

"They'll use a sorcerer and then ill-mouth him for his usefulness," she said. "It's not just."

"But he scared 'em, somehow, did he?"

"I guess he did. Another curer came up this way, a fellow that's been by here before. Doesn't amount to much that I can see. He did no good to my cow with the caked bag, two years ago. And his balm's just pig fat, I'd swear. Well, so, he says to Otak, you're taking my business. And maybe Otak says the same back. And they lose their tempers, and they did some black spells, maybe. I guess Otak did. But he did no harm to the man at all, but fell down in a swoon himself. And now he doesn't remember any more about it, while the other man walked away unhurt. And they say every beast he touched is standing yet, and hale. Ten days he spent out there in the wind and the rain, touching the beasts and healing them. And you know what the cattleman gave him? Six pennies! Can you wonder he was a little rageous? But I don't say . . ." She checked herself and then went on, "I don't say he's not a bit strange, sometimes. The way witches and sorcerers are, I guess. Maybe they have to be, dealing with such powers and evils as they do. But he is a true man, and kind."

"Mistress," said Hawk, "may I tell you a story?"

"Oh, are you a teller? Oh, why didn't you say so to begin with! Is that what you are then? I wondered, it being winter and all, and you being on the roads. But with that horse, I thought you must be a merchant. Can you tell me a story? It would be the joy of my life, and the longer the better! But drink your soup first, and let me sit down to hear . . ."

"I'm not truly a teller, mistress," he said with his pleasant smile, "but I do have a story for you." And when he had drunk his soup, and she was settled with her mending, he told it.

"In the Inmost Sea, on the Isle of the Wise, on Roke Island, where all magery is taught, there are nine Masters," he began.

She closed her eyes in bliss and listened.

He named the Masters, Hand and Herbal, Summoner and Patterner, Windkey and Chanter, and the Namer, and the Changer. "The Changer's and the Summoner's are very perilous arts," he said. "Changing, or transformation, you maybe know of, mistress. Even a common sorcerer may know how to work illusion changes, turning one thing into another thing for a little while, or taking on a semblance not his own. Have you seen that?"

"Heard of it," she whispered.

"And sometimes witches and sorcerers will say that they've summoned the dead to speak through them. Maybe a child the parents are grieving for. In the witch's hut, in the darkness, they hear it cry, or laugh . . ."

She nodded.

"Those are spells of illusion only, of seeming. But there are true changes, and true summonings. And these may be true temptations to the wizard! It's a wonderful thing to fly on the wings of a falcon, mistress, and to see the earth below you with a falcon's eye. And summoning, which is naming truly, is a great power. To know the true name is to have power, as you know, mistress. And the summoner's art goes straight to that. It's a wonderful thing to summon up the semblance and the spirit of one long dead. To see the beauty of Elfarran in the orchards of Soléa, as Morred saw it when the world was young . . ."

His voice had become very soft, very dark.

"Well, to my story. Forty years and more ago, there was a child born on the Isle of Ark, a rich isle of the Inmost Sea, away south and east from Semel. This child was the son of an understeward in the household of the Lord of Ark. Not a poor man's son, but not a child of much account. And the parents died young. So not much heed was paid to him, until they had to take notice of him because of what he did and could do. He was an uncanny brat, as they say. He had powers. He could light a fire or douse it with a word. He could make pots and pans fly through the air. He could turn a mouse into a pigeon and set it flying round the great kitchens of the Lord of Ark. And if he was crossed, or frightened, then he did harm. He turned a kettle of boiling water over a cook who had mistreated him."

"Mercy," whispered Gift. She had not sewn a stitch since he began.

"He was only a child, and the wizards of that household can't have been wise men, for they used little wisdom or gentleness with him. Maybe they were afraid of him. They bound his hands and gagged his mouth to keep him from making spells. They locked him in a cellar room, a room of stone, until they thought him tamed. Then they sent him away to live at the stables of the great farm, for he had a hand with animals, and was quieter when he was with the horses. But he quarreled with a stable boy, and turned the poor lad into a lump of dung. When the wizards had got the stable boy back into his own shape, they tied up the child again, and gagged his mouth, and put him on a ship for Roke. They thought maybe the Masters there could tame him."

"Poor child," she murmured.

"Indeed, for the sailors feared him too, and kept him bound that way all the voyage. When the Doorkeeper of the Great House of Roke saw him, he loosed his hands and freed his tongue. And the first thing the boy did in the Great House, they say, he turned the Long Table of the dining hall upside down, and soured the beer, and a student who tried to stop him got turned into a pig for a bit . . . But the boy had met his match in the Masters.

"They didn't punish him, but kept his wild powers bound with spells until they could make him listen and begin to learn. It took them a long time. There was a rivalrous spirit in him that made him look on any power he did not have, any thing he did not know, as a threat, a challenge, a thing to fight against until he could defeat it. There are many boys like that. I was one. But I was lucky. I learned my lesson young.

"Well, this boy did learn at last to tame his anger and control his power. And a very great power it was. Whatever art he studied came easy to him, too easy, so that he despised illusion, and weatherworking, and even healing, because they held no fear, no challenge to him. He saw no virtue in himself for his mastery of them. So, after the Archmage Nemmerle had given him his name, the boy set his will on the great and dangerous art of summoning. And he studied with the Master of that art for a long time.

"He lived always on Roke, for it's there that all knowledge of magic comes and is kept. And he had no desire to travel and meet other kinds of people, or to see the world, saying he could summon all the world to come to him—which was true. Maybe that's where the danger of that art lies.

"Now, what is forbidden to the summoner, or any wizard, is to call a living spirit. We can call to them, yes. We can send to them a voice or a presentment, a seeming, of ourself. But we do not summon them, in spirit or in flesh, to come to us. Only the dead may we summon. Only the shadows. You can see why this must be. To summon a living man is to have entire power over him, body and mind. No one, no matter how strong or wise or great, can rightly own and use another.

"But the spirit of rivalry worked in the boy as he grew to be a man. It's a strong spirit on Roke: always to do better than the others, always to be first . . . The art becomes a contest, a game. The end becomes a means to an end less than itself . . . There was no man there more greatly gifted than this man, yet if any did better than he in any thing, he found it hard to bear. It frightened him, it galled him.

"There was no place for him among the Masters, since a new Master Summoner had been chosen, a strong man in his prime, not likely to retire or die. Among the scholars and other teachers he had a place of honor, but he wasn't one of the Nine. He'd been passed over. Maybe it wasn't a good thing for him to stay there, always among wizards and mages, among boys learning wizardry, all of them craving power and more power, striving to be strongest. At any rate, as the years went on he became more and more aloof, pursuing his studies in his tower cell apart from others, teaching few students, speaking little. The Summoner would send gifted students to him, but many of the boys there scarcely knew of him. In this isolation he began to practice certain arts that are not well to practice and lead to no good thing.

"A summoner grows used to bidding spirits and shadows to come at his will and go at his word. Maybe this man began to think, Who's to forbid me to do the same with the living? Why have I the power if I cannot use it? So he began to call the living to him, those at Roke whom he feared, thinking them rivals, those whose power he was jealous of. When they came to him he took their power from them for himself, leaving them silent. They couldn't say what had happened to them, what had become of their power. They didn't know.

"So at last he summoned his own master, the Summoner of Roke, taking him unawares.

"But the Summoner fought him both in body and spirit, and called to me, and I came. Together we fought against the will that would destroy us."

Night had come. Gift's lamp had flickered out. Only the red glow of the fire shone on Hawk's face. It was not the face she had thought it. It was worn, and hard, and scarred all down one side. The hawk's face, she thought. She held still, listening.

"This is not a teller's tale, mistress. This is not a story you will ever hear anyone else tell.

"I was new at the business of being Archmage then. And younger than the man we fought, and maybe not afraid enough of him. It was all the two of us could do to hold our own against him, there in the silence, in the cell in the tower. Nobody else knew what was going on. We fought. A long time we fought. And then it was over. He broke. Like a stick breaking. He was broken. But he fled away. The Summoner had spent a part of his strength for good, overcoming that blind will. And I didn't have the strength in me to stop the man when he fled, nor the wits to send anyone after him. And not a shred of power left in me to follow him with. So he got away from Roke. Clean gone.

"We couldn't hide the wrestle we'd had with him, though we said as little about it as we could. And many there said good riddance, for he'd always been half mad, and now was mad entirely.

"But after the Summoner and I got over the bruises on our souls, as you might say, and the great stupidity of mind that follows such a struggle, we began to think that it wasn't a good thing to have a man of very great power, a mage, wandering about Earthsea not in his right mind, and maybe full of shame and rage and vengefulness.

"We could find no trace of him. No doubt he changed himself to a bird or a fish when he left Roke, until he came to some other island. And a wizard can hide himself from all finding spells. We sent out inquiries, in the ways we have of doing so, but nothing and nobody replied. So we set off looking for him, the Summoner to the eastern isles and I to the west. For when I thought about this man, I had begun to see in my mind's eye a great mountain, a broken cone, with a long, green land beneath it reaching to the south. I remembered my geography lessons when I was a boy at Roke, and the lay of the land on Semel, and the mountain whose name is Andanden. So I came to the High Marsh. I think I came the right way."

There was a silence. The fire whispered.

"Should I speak to him?" Gift asked in a steady voice.

"No need," said the man like a falcon. "I will." And he said, "Irioth."

She looked at the door of the bedroom. It opened and he stood there, thin and tired, his dark eyes full of sleep and bewilderment and pain.

"Ged," he said. He bowed his head. After a while he looked up and asked, "Will you take my name from me?"

"Why should I do that?"

"It means only hurt. Hate, pride, greed."

"I'll take those names from you, Irioth, but not your own."

"I didn't understand," Irioth said, "about the others. That they are other. We are all other. We must be. I was wrong."

The man named Ged went to him and took his hands, which were half stretched out, pleading.

"You went wrong. You've come back. But you're tired, Irioth, and the way's hard when you go alone. Come home with me."

Irioth's head drooped as if in utter weariness. All tension and passion had gone out of his body. But he looked up, not at Ged but at Gift, silent in the hearth corner.

"I have work here," he said.

Ged too looked at her.

"He does," she said. "He heals the cattle."

"They show me what I should do," Irioth said, "and who I am. They know my name. But they never say it."

After a while Ged gently drew the older man to him and held him in his arms. He said something quietly to him and let him go. Irioth drew a deep breath.

"I'm no good there, you see, Ged," he said. "I am, here. If they'll let me do the work." He looked again at Gift, and Ged did also. She looked at them both.

"What say you, Emer?" asked the one like a falcon.

"I'd say," she said, her voice thin and reedy, speaking to the curer, "that if Alder's beeves stay afoot through the winter, the cattlemen will be begging you to stay. Though they may not love you."

"Nobody loves a sorcerer," said the Archmage. "Well, Irioth! Did I come all this way for you in the dead of winter, and must go back alone?"

"Tell them—tell them I was wrong," Irioth said. "Tell them I did wrong. Tell Thorion—" He halted, confused.

"I'll tell him that the changes in a man's life may be beyond all the arts we know, and all our wisdom," said the Archmage. He looked at Emer again. "May he stay here, mistress? Is that your wish as well as his?"

"He's ten times the use and company to me my brother is," she said. "And a kind true man, as I told you. Sir."

"Very well, then. Irioth, my dear companion, teacher, rival, friend, farewell. Emer, brave woman, my honor and thanks to you. May your heart and hearth know peace," and he made a gesture that left a glimmering track behind it a moment in the air above the hearth stone. "Now I'm off to the cow barn," he said, and he was.

The door closed. It was silent except for the whisper of the fire.

"Come to the fire," she said. Irioth came and sat down on the settle.

"Was that the Archmage? Truly?"

He nodded.

"The Archmage of the world," she said. "In my cow barn. He should have my bed—"

"He won't," said Irioth.

She knew he was right.

"Your name is beautiful, Irioth," she said after a while. "I never knew my husband's true name. Nor he mine. I won't speak yours again. But I like to know it, since you know mine."

"Your name is beautiful, Emer," he said. "I will speak it when you tell me to."

Dragonfly

I. Iria

HER FATHER'S ANCESTORS had owned a wide, rich domain on the wide, rich island of Way. Claiming no title or court privilege in the days of the kings, through all the dark years after Maharion fell they held their land and people with firm hands, putting their gains back into the land, upholding some sort of justice, and fighting off petty tyrants. As order and peace returned to the Archipelago under the sway of the wise men of Roke, for a while yet the family and their farms and villages prospered. That prosperity and the beauty of the meadows and upland pastures and oak-crowned hills made the domain a byword, so that people said "as fat as a cow of Iria," or "as lucky as an Irian." The masters and many tenants of the domain added its name to their own, calling themselves Irian. But though the farmers and shepherds went on from season to season and year to year and generation to generation as steady and regenerative as the oaks, the family that owned the land altered and declined with time and chance.

A quarrel between brothers over their inheritance divided them. One heir mismanaged his estate through greed, the other through foolishness. One had a daughter who married a merchant and tried to run her estate from the city, the other had a son whose sons quarreled again, redividing the divided land. By the time the girl called Dragonfly was born, the domain of Iria, though still one of the loveliest regions of hill and field and meadow in all Earthsea, was a battleground of feuds and litigations. Farmlands went to weeds, farmsteads went unroofed, milking sheds stood unused, and shepherds followed their flocks over the mountain to better pastures. The old house that had been the center of the domain was half in ruins on its hill among the oaks.

Its owner was one of four men who called themselves Master of Iria. The other three called him Master of Old Iria. He spent his youth and what remained of his inheritance in law courts and the anterooms of the Lords of Way in Shelieth, trying to prove his right to the whole domain as it had been a hundred years ago. He came back unsuccessful and embittered and spent his age drinking the hard red wine from his last vineyard and walking his boundaries with a troop of ill-treated, underfed dogs to keep interlopers off his land.

He had married while he was in Shelieth, a woman no one at Iria knew anything about, for she came from some other island, it was said, somewhere in the west; and she never came to Iria, for she died in childbirth there in the city.

When he came home he had a three-year-old daughter with him. He turned her over to the housekeeper and forgot about her. When he was drunk sometimes he remembered her. If he could find her, he made her stand by his chair or sit on his knees and listen to all the wrongs that had been done to him and to the house of Iria. He cursed and cried and drank and made her drink too, pledging to honor her inheritance and be true to Iria. She swallowed the mouthful of wine, but she hated the curses and pledges and tears, and the slobbered caresses that followed them. She would escape, as soon as she could, if she could, and go down to the dogs and horses and cattle. She swore to them that she would be loyal to her mother, whom nobody knew or honored or was true to, except herself.

When she was thirteen the old vineyarder and the housekeeper, who were all that was left of the household, told the Master that it was time his daughter had her naming day. They asked if they should send for the sorcerer over at Westpool, or would their own village witch do. The Master of Iria fell into a screaming rage. "A village witch? A hex-hag to give Irian's daughter her true name? Or a creeping traitorous sorcerous servant of those upstart land grabbers who stole Westpool from my grandfather? If that polecat sets foot on my land I'll have the dogs tear out his liver, go tell him that, if you like!" And so on. Old Daisy went back to her kitchen and old Coney went back to his vines, and thirteen-year-old Dragonfly ran out of the house and down the hill to the village, hurling her father's curses at the dogs, who, crazy with excitement at his shouting, barked and bayed and rushed after her.

"Get back, you black-hearted bitch!" she yelled. "Home, you

crawling traitor!" And the dogs fell silent and went sidling back to the house with their tails down.

Dragonfly found the village witch taking maggots out of an infected cut on a sheep's rump. The witch's use-name was Rose, like a great many women of Way and other islands of the Hardic Archipelago. People who have a secret name that holds their power the way a diamond holds light may well like their public name to be ordinary, common, like other people's names.

Rose was muttering a rote spell, but it was her hands and her little short sharp knife that did most of the work. The ewe bore the digging knife patiently, her opaque, amber, slotted eyes gazing into silence; only she stamped her small left front foot now and then, and sighed.

Dragonfly peered close at Rose's work. Rose brought out a maggot, dropped it, spat on it, and probed again. The girl leaned up against the ewe, and the ewe leaned against the girl, giving and receiving comfort. Rose extracted, dropped, and spat on the last maggot, and said, "Just hand me that bucket now." She bathed the sore with salt water. The ewe sighed deeply and suddenly walked out of the yard, heading for home. She had had enough of medicine. "Bucky!" Rose shouted. A grubby child appeared from under a bush where he had been asleep and trailed after the ewe, of whom he was nominally in charge although she was older, larger, better fed, and probably wiser than he was.

"They said you should give me my name," said Dragonfly. "Father fell to raging. So that's that."

The witch said nothing. She knew the girl was right. Once the Master of Iria said he would or would not allow a thing, he never changed his mind, priding himself on his intransigence, since in his view only weak men said a thing and then unsaid it.

"Why can't I give myself my own true name?" Dragonfly asked, while Rose washed the knife and her hands in the salt water.

"Can't be done."

"Why not? Why does it have to be a witch or a sorcerer? What do you *do*?"

"Well," Rose said, and dumped out the salt water on the bare dirt of the small front yard of her house, which, like most witches' houses, stood somewhat apart from the village. "Well," she said, straightening up and looking about vaguely as if for an answer, or a ewe, or a towel. "You have to know something about the power, see," she said at last, and looked at Dragonfly with one eye. Her other eye looked a little off to the side. Sometimes Dragonfly thought the cast was in Rose's left eye, sometimes it seemed to be in her right, but always one eye looked straight and the other watched something just out of sight, around the corner, elsewhere.

"Which power?"

"The one," Rose said. As suddenly as the ewe had walked off, she went into her house. Dragonfly followed her, but only to the door. Nobody entered a witch's house uninvited.

"You said I had it," the girl said into the reeking gloom of the one-roomed hut.

"I said you have a strength in you, a great one," the witch said from the darkness. "And you know it too. What you are to do I don't know, nor do you. That's to find. But there's no such power as to name yourself."

"Why not? What's more yourself than your own true name?"

A long silence.

The witch emerged with a soapstone drop spindle and a ball of greasy wool. She sat down on the bench beside her door and set the spindle turning. She had spun a yard of grey-brown yarn before she answered.

"My name's myself. True. But what's a name, then? It's what another calls me. If there was no other, only me, what would I want a name for?"

"But," said Dragonfly and stopped, caught by the argument. After a while she said, "So a name has to be a gift?"

Rose nodded.

"Give me my name, Rose," the girl said.

"Your dad says not."

"I say to."

"He's the master here."

"He can keep me poor and stupid and worthless, but he can't keep me nameless!"

The witch sighed, like the ewe, uneasy and constrained.

"Tonight," Dragonfly said. "At our spring, under Iria Hill. What he doesn't know won't hurt him." Her voice was half coaxing, half savage.

"You ought to have your proper nameday, your feast and dancing, like any young 'un," the witch said. "It's at daybreak a name should be given. And then there ought to be music and feasting and all. A party. Not sneaking about at night and no one knowing . . ."

"I'll know. How do you know what name to say, Rose? Does the water tell you?"

The witch shook her iron-grey head once. "I can't tell you." Her "can't" did not mean "won't." Dragonfly waited. "It's the power, like I said. It comes just so." Rose stopped her spinning and looked up with one eye at a cloud in the west; the other looked a little northward of the sky. "You're there in the water, together, you and the child. You take away the child-name. People may go on using that name for a use-name, but it's not her name, nor ever was. So now she's not a child, and she has no name. So then you wait. In the water there. You open your mind up, like. Like opening the doors of a house to the wind. So it comes. Your tongue speaks it, the name. Your breath makes it. You give it to that child, the breath, the name. You can't think of it. You let it come to you. It must come through you and the water to her it belongs to. That's the power, the way it works. It's all like that. It's not a thing you do. You have to know how to let it do. That's all the mastery."

"Mages can do more than that," the girl said after a while.

"Nobody can do more than that," said Rose.

Dragonfly rolled her head round on her neck, stretching till the vertebrae cracked, restlessly stretching out her long arms and legs. "Will you?" she said.

After some time, Rose nodded once.

They met in the lane under Iria Hill in the dark of night, long after sunset, long before dawn. Rose made a dim glow of werelight so that they could find their way through the marshy ground around the spring without falling in a sinkhole among the reeds. In the cold darkness under a few stars and the black curve of the hill, they stripped and waded into the shallow water, their feet sinking deep in velvet mud. The witch touched the girl's hand, saying, "I take your name, child. You are no child. You have no name."

It was utterly still.

In a whisper the witch said, "Woman, be named. You are Irian."

For a moment longer they held still; then the night wind blew across their naked shoulders, and shivering, they waded out, dried themselves as well as they could, struggled barefoot and wretched through the sharp-edged reeds and tangling roots, and found their way back to the lane. And there Dragonfly spoke in a ragged, raging whisper: "How could you name me that!"

The witch said nothing.

"It isn't right. It isn't my true name! I thought my name would make me be me. But this makes it worse. You got it wrong. You're only a witch. You did it wrong. It's *his* name. He can have it. He's so proud of it, his stupid domain, his stupid grandfather. I don't want it. I won't have it. It isn't me. I still don't know who I am. I'm not Irian!" She fell silent abruptly, having spoken the name.

The witch still said nothing. They walked along in the darkness side by side. At last, in a placating, frightened voice, Rose said, "It came so . . ."

"If you ever tell it to anyone I'll kill you," Dragonfly said.

At that, the witch stopped walking. She hissed in her throat like a cat. "*Tell* anyone?"

Dragonfly stopped too. She said after a moment, "I'm sorry. But I feel like—I feel like you betrayed me."

"I spoke your true name. It's not what I thought it would be. And I don't feel easy about it. As if I'd left something unfinished. But it is your name. If it betrays you, then that's the truth of it." Rose hesitated and then spoke less angrily, more coldly: "If you want the power to betray me, Irian, I'll give you that. My name is Etaudis."

The wind had come up again. They were both shivering, their teeth chattering. They stood face to face in the black lane, hardly able to see where the other was. Dragonfly put out her groping hand and met the witch's hand. They put their arms round each other in a fierce, long embrace. Then they hurried on, the witch to her hut near the village, the heiress of Iria up the hill to her ruinous house, where all the dogs, who had let her go without much fuss, received her back with a clamor and racket of barking that woke everybody for a half mile round except the master, sodden drunk by his cold hearth.

II. Ivory

The Master of Iria of Westpool, Birch, didn't own the old house, but he did own the central and richest lands of the old domain. His father, more interested in vines and orchards than in quarrels with his relatives, had left Birch a thriving property. Birch hired men to manage the farms and wineries and cooperage and cartage and all, while he enjoyed his wealth. He married the timid daughter of the younger brother of the Lord of Wayfirth, and took infinite pleasure in thinking that his daughters were of noble blood.

The fashion of the time among the nobility was to have a wizard in their service, a genuine wizard with a staff and a grey cloak, trained on the Isle of the Wise; and so the Master of Iria of Westpool got himself a wizard from Roke. He was surprised how easy it was to get one, if you paid the price.

The young man, called Ivory, did not actually have his staff and cloak yet; he explained that he was to be made wizard when he went back to Roke. The Masters had sent him out in the world to gain experience, for all the classes in the school cannot give a man the experience he needs to be a wizard. Birch looked a little dubious at this, and Ivory reassured him that his training on Roke had equipped him with every kind of magic that could be needed in Iria of Westpool on Way. To prove it, he made it seem that a herd of deer ran through the dining hall, followed by a flight of swans, who marvelously soared in through the south wall and out through the north wall; and lastly a fountain in a silver basin sprang up in the center of the table, and when the master and his family cautiously imitated their wizard and filled their cups from it and tasted it, it was a sweet golden wine. "Wine of the Andrades," said the young man with a modest, complacent smile. By then the wife and daughters were entirely won over. And Birch thought the young man was worth his fee, although his own silent preference was for the dry red Fanian of his own vineyards, which got you drunk if you drank enough, while this yellow stuff was just honeywater.

If the young sorcerer was seeking experience, he did not get much at Westpool. Whenever Birch had guests from Kembermouth or from neighboring domains, the herd of deer, the swans, and the fountain of golden wine made their appearance. He also worked up some very pretty fireworks for warm spring evenings. But if the managers of the orchards and vineyards came to the master to ask if his wizard might put a spell of increase on the pears this year or maybe charm the black rot off the Fanian vines on the south hill, Birch said, "A wizard of Roke doesn't lower himself to such stuff. Go tell the village sorcerer to earn his keep!" And when the youngest daughter came down with a wasting cough, Birch's wife dared not trouble the wise young man about it, but sent humbly to Rose of Old Iria, asking her to come in by the back door and maybe make a poultice or sing a chant to bring the girl back to health.

Ivory never noticed that the girl was ailing, nor the pear trees, nor the vines. He kept himself to himself, as a man of craft and learning should. He spent his days riding about the countryside on the pretty black mare that his employer had given him for his use when he made it clear that he had not come from Roke to trudge about on foot in the mud and dust of country byways.

On his rides he sometimes passed an old house on a hill among great oaks. Once he turned off the village lane up the hill, but a pack of scrawny, evil-mouthed dogs came pelting and bellowing down at him. The mare was afraid of dogs and liable to buck and bolt, so after that he kept his distance. But he had an eye for beauty, and liked to look at the old house dreaming away in the dappled light of the early summer afternoons.

He asked Birch about the place. "That's Iria," Birch said—"Old Iria, I mean to say. I own that house by rights. But after a century of feuds and fights over it, my granddad let the place go to settle the quarrel. Though the master there would still be quarreling with me if he didn't keep too drunk to talk. Haven't seen the old man for years. He had a daughter, I think."

"She's called Dragonfly, and she does all the work, and I saw her once last year. She's tall, and as beautiful as a flowering tree," said the youngest daughter, Rose, who was busy crowding a lifetime of keen observation into the fourteen years that were all she was going to have for it. She broke off, coughing. Her mother shot an anguished, yearning glance at the wizard. Surely he would hear that cough, this time? He smiled at young Rose, and the mother's heart lifted. Surely he wouldn't smile so if Rose's cough was anything serious?

"Nothing to do with us, that lot at the old place," Birch said, displeased. The tactful Ivory asked no more. But he wanted to see the girl as beautiful as a flowering tree. He rode past Old Iria regularly. He tried stopping in the village at the foot of the hill to ask questions, but there was nowhere to stop and nobody would answer questions. A walleyed witch took one look at him and scuttled into her hut. If he went up to the house he would have to face the pack of hellhounds and probably a drunk old man. But it was worth the chance, he thought; he was bored out of his wits with the dull life at Westpool, and was never slow to take a risk. He rode up the hill till the dogs were yelling around him in a frenzy snapping at the mare's legs. She plunged and lashed out her hoofs at them, and he kept her from bolting only by a staying spell and all the strength in his arms. The dogs were leaping and snapping at his own legs now, and he was about to let the mare have her head when somebody came among the dogs shouting curses and beating them back with a strap. When he got the lathered, gasping mare to stand still, he saw the girl as beautiful as a flowering tree. She was very tall, very sweaty, with big hands and feet and mouth and nose and eyes, and a head of wild dusty hair. She was yelling, "Down! Back to the house, you carrion, you vile sons of bitches!" to the whining, cowering dogs.

Ivory clapped his hand to his right leg. A dog's tooth had ripped his breeches at the calf, and a trickle of blood came through.

"Is she hurt?" the woman said. "Oh, the traitorous vermin!" She was stroking down the mare's right foreleg. Her hands came away covered with blood-streaked horse sweat. "There, there," she said. "The brave girl, the brave heart." The mare put her head down and shivered all over with relief. "What did you keep her standing there in the middle of the dogs for?" the woman demanded furiously. She was kneeling at the horse's leg, looking up at Ivory. He was looking down at her from horseback, yet he felt short; he felt small.

She did not wait for an answer. "I'll walk her up," she said, standing, and put out her hand for the reins. Ivory saw that he was supposed to dismount. He did so, asking, "Is it very bad?" and peering at the horse's leg, seeing only bright, bloody foam.

"Come on then, my love," the young woman said, not to him. The mare followed her trustfully. They set off up the rough path round the hillside to an old stone and brick stableyard, empty of horses, inhabited only by nesting swallows that swooped about over the roofs calling their quick gossip.

"Keep her quiet," said the young woman, and left him holding the mare's reins in this deserted place. She returned after some time lugging a heavy bucket, and set to sponging off the mare's leg. "Get the saddle off her," she said, and her tone held the unspoken, impatient "you fool!" Ivory obeyed, half annoyed by this crude giantess and half intrigued. She did not put him in mind of a flowering tree at all, but she was in fact beautiful, in a large, fierce way. The mare submitted to her absolutely. When she said, "Move your foot!" the mare moved her foot. The woman wiped her down all over, put the saddle blanket back on her, and made sure she was standing in the sun. "She'll be all right," she said. "There's a gash, but if you'll wash it with warm salt water four or five times a day, it'll heal clean. I'm sorry." She said the last honestly, though grudgingly, as if she still wondered how he could have let his mare stand there to be assaulted, and she looked straight at him for the first time. Her eyes were clear orange-brown, like dark topaz or amber. They were strange eyes, right on a level with his own.

"I'm sorry too," he said, trying to speak carelessly, lightly.

"She's Irian of Westpool's mare. You're the wizard, then?"

He bowed. "Ivory, of Havnor Great Port, at your service. May I—"

She interrupted. "I thought you were from Roke."

"I am," he said, his composure regained.

She stared at him with those strange eyes, as unreadable as a sheep's, he thought. Then she burst out: "You lived there? You studied there? Do you know the Archmage?"

"Yes," he said with a smile. Then he winced and stooped to press his hand against his shin for a moment.

"Are you hurt too?"

"It's nothing," he said. In fact, rather to his annoyance, the cut had stopped bleeding.

The woman's gaze returned to his face.

"What is it—what is it like—on Roke?"

Ivory went, limping only very slightly, to an old mounting block nearby and sat down on it. He stretched his leg, nursing the torn place, and looked up at the woman. "It would take a long time to tell you what Roke is like," he said. "But it would be my pleasure."

"The man's a wizard, or nearly," said Rose the witch, "a Roke wizard! You must not ask him questions!" She was more than scandalized, she was frightened.

"He doesn't mind," Dragonfly reassured her. "Only he hardly ever really answers."

"Of course not!"

"Why of course not?"

"Because he's a wizard! Because you're a woman, with no art, no knowledge, no learning!"

"You could have taught me! You never would!"

Rose dismissed all she had taught or could teach with a flick of the fingers.

"Well, so I have to learn from him," said Dragonfly.

"Wizards don't teach women. You're besotted."

"You and Broom trade spells."

"Broom's a village sorcerer. This man is a wise man. He learned the High Arts at the Great House on Roke!"

"He told me what it's like," Dragonfly said. "You walk up through the town, Thwil Town. There's a door opening on the street, but it's shut. It looks like an ordinary door."

The witch listened, unable to resist the lure of secrets revealed and the contagion of passionate desire.

"And a man comes when you knock, an ordinary looking man. And he gives you a test. You have to say a certain word, a password, before he'll let you in. If you don't know it, you can never go in. But if he lets you in, then from inside you see that the door is entirely different—it's made out of horn, with a tree carved on it, and the frame is made out of a tooth, one tooth of a dragon that lived long, long before Erreth-Akbe, before Morred, before there were people in Earthsea. There were only dragons, to begin with. They found the tooth on Mount Onn, in Havnor, at the center of the world. And the leaves of the tree are carved so thin that the light shines through them, but the door's so strong that if the Doorkeeper shuts it no spell could ever open it. And then the Doorkeeper takes you down a hall and another hall, till you're lost and bewildered, and then suddenly you come out under the sky. In the Court of the Fountain, in the very deepest inside of the Great House. And that's where the Archmage would be, if he was there . . ."

"Go on," the witch murmured.

"That's all he really told me, yet," said Dragonfly, coming back to the mild, overcast spring day and the infinite familiarity of the village lane, Rose's front yard, her own seven milch ewes grazing on Iria Hill, the bronze crowns of the oaks. "He's very careful how he talks about the Masters."

Rose nodded.

"But he told me about some of the students."

"No harm in that, I suppose."

"I don't know," Dragonfly said. "To hear about the Great House is wonderful, but I thought the people there would be—I don't know. Of course they're mostly just boys when they go there. But I thought they'd be . . ." She gazed off at the sheep on the hill, her face troubled. "Some of them are really bad and stupid," she said in a low voice. "They get into the school because they're rich. And they study there just to get richer. Or to get power."

"Well, of course they do," said Rose, "that's what they're there for!"

"But power—like you told me about—that isn't the same as making people do what you want, or pay you—"

"Isn't it?"

"No!"

"If a word can heal, a word can wound," the witch said. "If a hand can kill, a hand can cure. It's a poor cart that goes only one direction."

"But on Roke, they learn to use power well, not for harm, not for gain."

"Everything's for gain some way, I'd say. People have to live. But what do I know? I make my living doing what I know how to do. But I don't meddle with the great arts, the perilous crafts, like summoning the dead," and Rose made the hand sign to avert the danger spoken of.

"Everything's perilous," Dragonfly said, gazing now through the sheep, the hill, the trees, into still depths, a colorless, vast emptiness like the clear sky before sunrise.

Rose watched her. She knew she did not know who Irian was or what she might be. A big, strong, awkward, ignorant, innocent, angry woman, yes. But ever since Irian was a child Rose had seen something more in her, something beyond what she was. And when Irian looked away from the world like that, she seemed to enter that place or time or being beyond herself, utterly beyond Rose's knowledge. Then Rose feared her, and feared for her.

"You take care," the witch said, grim. "Everything's perilous, right enough, and meddling with wizards most of all."

Through love, respect, and trust, Dragonfly would never disregard a warning from Rose; but she was unable to see Ivory as perilous. She didn't understand him, but the idea of fearing him, him personally, was not one she could keep in mind. She tried to be respectful, but it was impossible. She thought he was clever and quite handsome, but she didn't think much about him, except for what he could tell her. He knew what she wanted to know and little by little he told it to her, and then it was not really what she had wanted to know, but she wanted to know more. He was patient with her, and she was grateful to him for his patience, knowing he was much quicker than she. Sometimes he smiled at her ignorance, but he never sneered at it or reproved it. Like the witch, he liked to answer a question with a question; but the answers to Rose's questions were always something she'd always known, while the answers to his questions were things she had never imagined and found startling, unwelcome, even painful, altering her beliefs.

Day by day, as they talked in the old stableyard of Iria, where they had fallen into the habit of meeting, she asked him and he told her more, though reluctantly, always partially; he shielded his Masters, she thought, trying to defend the bright image of Roke, until one day he gave in to her insistence and spoke freely at last.

"There are good men there," he said. "Great and wise the Archmage certainly was. But he's gone. And the Masters . . . Some hold aloof, following arcane knowledge, seeking ever more patterns, ever more names, but using their knowledge for nothing. Others hide their ambition under the grey cloak of wisdom. Roke is no longer where power is in Earthsea. That's the Court in Havnor, now. Roke lives on its great past, defended by a thousand spells against the present day. And inside those spell-walls, what is there? Quarreling ambitions, fear of anything new, fear of young men who challenge the power of the old. And at the center, nothing. An empty courtyard. The Archmage will never return."

"How do you know?" she whispered.

He looked stern. "The dragon bore him away."

"You saw it? You saw that?" She clenched her hands, imagining that flight, not even hearing his reply.

After a long time, she came back to the sunlight and the stableyard and her thoughts and puzzles. "But even if he's gone," she said, "surely some of the Masters are truly wise?"

When he looked up and spoke it was with reluctance, with a hint of a melancholy smile. "All the mystery and wisdom of the Masters, when it's out in the daylight, doesn't amount to so much, you know. Tricks of the trade—wonderful illusions. But people don't want to know that. They want the illusions, thc mysteries. Who can blame them? There's so little in life that's beautiful or worthy."

As if to illustrate what he was saying, he had picked up a bit of brick from the broken pavement, and tossed it up in the air, and as he spoke it fluttered about their heads on delicate blue wings, a butterfly. He put out his finger and the butterfly lighted on it. He shook his finger and the butterfly fell to the ground, a fragment of brick.

"There's not much worth much in my life," she said, gazing down at the pavement. "All I know how to do is run the farm, and try to stand up and speak truth. But if I thought it was all tricks and lies even on Roke, I'd hate those men for fooling me, fooling us all. It can't be lies. Not all of it. The Archmage did go into the labyrinth among the Hoary Men and come back with the Ring of Peace. He did go into death with the young king, and defeat the spider mage, and come back. We know that on the word of the King himself. Even here, the harpers came to sing that song, and a teller came to tell it."

Ivory nodded. "But the Archmage lost all his power in the land of death. Maybe all magery was weakened then."

"Rose's spells work as well as ever," she said stoutly.

Ivory smiled. He said nothing, but she saw how petty the doings of a village witch appeared to him, who had seen great deeds and powers. She sighed and spoke from her heart—"Oh, if only I wasn't a woman!"

He smiled again. "You're a beautiful woman," he said, but plainly, not in the flattering way he had used with her at first, before she showed him she hated it. "Why would you be a man?"

"So I could go to Roke! And see, and learn! Why, why is it only men can go there?"

"So it was ordained by the first Archmage, centuries ago," said Ivory. "But . . . I too have wondered."

"You have?"

"Often. Seeing only boys and men, day after day, in the Great House and all the precincts of the school. Knowing that the townswomen are spell-bound from so much as setting foot on the fields about Roke Knoll. Once in years, perhaps, some great lady is allowed to come briefly into the outer courts . . . Why is it so? Are all women incapable of understanding? Or is it that the Masters fear them, fear to be corrupted— No, but fear that to admit women might change the rule they cling to—the purity of that rule—"

"Women can live chaste as well as men can," Dragonfly said bluntly. She knew she was blunt and coarse where he was delicate and subtle, but she did not know any other way to be.

"Of course," he said, his smile growing brilliant. "But witches aren't always chaste, are they? . . . Maybe that's what the Masters are afraid of. Maybe celibacy isn't as necessary as the Rule of Roke teaches. Maybe it's not a way of keeping the power pure, but of keeping the power to themselves. Leaving out women, leaving out everybody who won't agree to turn himself into a eunuch to get that one kind of power . . . Who knows? A she-mage! Now that would change everything, all the rules!"

She could see his mind dance ahead of hers, taking up and playing with ideas, transforming them as he had transformed brick into butterfly. She could not dance with him, she could not play with him, but she watched him in wonder.

"You could go to Roke," he said, his eyes bright with excitement, mischief, daring. Meeting her almost pleading, incredulous silence, he insisted—"You could. A woman you are, but there are ways to change your seeming. You have the heart, the courage, the will of a man. You could enter the Great House. I know it."

"And what would I do there?"

"What all the students do. Live alone in a stone cell and learn to be wise! It might not be what you dream it to be, but that, too, you'd learn."

"I couldn't. They'd know. I couldn't even get in. There's the Doorkeeper, you said. I don't know the word to say to him."

"The password, yes. But I can teach it to you."

"You can? Is it allowed?"

"I don't care what's 'allowed,'" he said, with a frown she had never seen on his face. "The Archmage himself said, *Rules are made to be broken.* Injustice makes the rules, and courage breaks them. I have the courage, if you do!"

She looked at him. She could not speak. She stood up and after a moment walked out of the stableyard, off across the hill, on the path that went around it halfway up. One of the dogs, her favorite, a big, ugly, heavy-headed hound, followed her. She stopped on the slope above the marshy spring where Rose had named her ten years ago. She stood there. The dog sat down beside her and looked up at her face. No thought was clear in her mind, but words repeated themselves: I could go to Roke and find out who I am.

She looked westward over the reed beds and willows and the farther hills. The whole western sky was empty, clear. She stood still and her soul seemed to go into that sky and be gone, gone out of her.

There was a little noise, the soft clip-clop of the black mare's hoofs, coming along the lane. Then Dragonfly came back to herself and called to Ivory and ran down the hill to meet him. "I will go," she said.

He had not planned or intended any such adventure, but crazy as it was, it suited him better the more he thought about it. The prospect of spending the long grey winter at Westpool sank his spirits like a stone. There was nothing here for him except the girl Dragonfly, who had come to fill his thoughts. Her massive, innocent strength had defeated him absolutely so far, but he did what she pleased in order to have her do at last what he pleased, and the game, he thought, was worth playing. If she ran away with him, the game was as good as won. As for the joke of it, the notion of actually getting her into the school on Roke disguised as a man, there was little chance of pulling it off, but it pleased him as a gesture of disrespect to all the piety and pomposity of the Masters and their toadies. And if somehow it succeeded, if he could actually get a woman through that door, even for a moment, what a sweet revenge it would be!

Money was a problem. The girl thought, of course, that he as a great wizard would snap his fingers and waft them over the sea in a magic boat flying before the magewind. But when he told her they'd have to hire passage on a ship, she said simply, "I have the cheese money."

He treasured her rustic sayings of that kind. Sometimes she frightened him, and he resented it. His dreams of her were never of her yielding to him, but of himself yielding to a fierce, destroying sweetness, sinking into an annihilating embrace, dreams in which she was something beyond comprehension and he was nothing at all. He woke from those dreams shaken and shamed. In daylight, when he saw her big, dirty hands, when she talked like a yokel, a simpleton, he regained his superiority. He only wished there were someone to repeat her sayings to, one of his old friends in the Great Port who would find them amusing. "I have the cheese money," he repeated to himself, riding back to Westpool, and laughed. "I do indeed," he said aloud. The black mare flicked her ear.

He told Birch that he had received a sending from his teacher on Roke, the Master Hand, and must go at once, on what business he could not say, of course, but it should not take long once he was there;

a half month to go, another to return; he would be back well before the Fallows at the latest. He must ask Master Birch to provide him an advance on his salary to pay for ship passage and lodging, since a wizard of Roke should not take advantage of people's willingness to give him whatever he needed, but pay his way like an ordinary man. As Birch agreed with this, he had to give Ivory a purse for his journey, the first real money he had had in his pocket for years: ten ivory counters carved with the Otter of Shelieth on one side and the Rune of Peace on the other in honor of King Lebannen. "Hello, little namesakes," he told them when he was alone with them. "You and the cheese money will get along nicely."

He told Dragonfly very little of his plans, largely because he made few, trusting to chance and his own wits, which seldom let him down if he was given a fair chance to use them. The girl asked almost no questions. "Will I go as a man all the way?" was one.

"Yes," he said, "but only disguised. I won't put a semblance spell on you till we're on Roke Island."

"I thought it would be a spell of change," she said.

"That would be unwise," he said, with a good imitation of the Master Changer's terse solemnity. "If need be, I'll do it, of course. But you'll find wizards very sparing of the great spells. For good reason."

"The Equilibrium," she said, accepting all he said in its simplest sense, as always.

"And perhaps because such arts have not the power they once had," he said. He did not know himself why he tried to weaken her faith in wizardry; perhaps because any weakening of her strength, her wholeness, was a gain for him. He had begun merely by trying to get her into his bed, a game he loved to play. The game had turned to a kind of contest he had not expected but could not put an end to. He was determined now not to win her, but to defeat her. He could not let her defeat him. He must prove to her and himself that his dreams were meaningless.

Quite early on, impatient with wooing her massive physical indifference, he had worked up a charm, a sorcerer's seduction spell of which he was contemptuous even as he made it, though he knew it was effective. He cast it on her while she was, characteristically, mending a cow's halter. The result had not been the melting eagerness it had produced in girls he had used it on in Havnor and Thwil. Dragonfly had gradually become silent and sullen. She ceased asking her endless questions about Roke and did not answer when he spoke. When he very tentatively approached her, taking her hand, she struck him away with a blow to the head that left him dizzy. He saw her stand up and stride out of the stableyard without a word, the ugly hound she favored trotting after her. The hound looked back at him with a grin.

She took the path to the old house. When his ears stopped ringing he stole after her, hoping the charm was working and that this was only her particularly uncouth way of leading him at last to her bed. Nearing the house, he heard crockery breaking. The father, the drunkard, came wobbling out looking scared and confused, followed by Dragonfly's loud, harsh voice—"Out of the house, you drunken, crawling traitor! You foul, shameless lecher!"

"She took my cup away," the Master of Iria said to the stranger, whining like a puppy, while his dogs yammered around him. "She broke it."

Ivory departed. He did not return for two days. On the third day he rode experimentally past Old Iria, and she came striding down to meet him. "I'm sorry, Ivory," she said, looking up at him with her smoky orange eyes. "I don't know what came over me the other day. I was angry. But not at you. I beg your pardon."

He forgave her gracefully. He did not try a love charm on her again.

Soon, he thought now, he would not need one. He would have real power over her. He had finally seen how to get it. She had given it into his hands. Her strength and her willpower were tremendous, but fortunately she was stupid, and he was not.

Birch was sending a carter down to Kembermouth with six barrels of ten-year-old Fanian ordered by the wine merchant there. He was glad to send his wizard along as bodyguard, for the wine was valuable, and though the young king was putting things to rights as fast as he could, there were still gangs of robbers on the roads. So Ivory left Westpool on the big wagon pulled by four big cart horses, jolting slowly along, his legs dangling. Down by Jackass Hill an uncouth figure rose up from the wayside and asked the carter for a lift. "I don't know you," the carter said, lifting his whip to warn the stranger off, but Ivory came round the wagon and said, "Let the lad ride, my good man. He'll do no harm while I'm with you."

"Keep an eye on him then, master," said the carter.

"I will," said Ivory, with a wink at Dragonfly. She, well disguised in dirt and a farmhand's old smock and leggings and a loathsome felt hat, did not wink back. She played her part even while they sat side by side dangling their legs over the tailgate, with six great halftuns of wine jolting between them and the drowsy carter, and the drowsy summer hills and fields slipping slowly, slowly past. Ivory tried to tease her, but she only shook her head. Maybe she was scared by this wild scheme, now she was embarked on it. There was no telling. She was solemnly, heavily silent. I could be very bored by this woman, Ivory thought, if once I'd had her underneath me. That thought stirred him almost unbearably, but when he looked back at her, his desire died away before her massive, actual presence.

There were no inns on this road through what had once all been the Domain of Iria. As the sun neared the western plains, they stopped at a farmhouse that offered stabling for the horses, a shed for the cart, and straw in the stable loft for the carters. The loft was dark and stuffy and the straw musty. Ivory felt no lust at all, though Dragonfly lay not three feet from him. She had played the man so thoroughly all day that she had half convinced even him. Maybe she'll fool the old men after all! he thought. He grinned at the thought, and slept.

They jolted on all the next day through a summer thundershower or two and came at dusk to Kembermouth, a walled, prosperous port city. They left the carter to his master's business and walked down to find an inn near the docks. Dragonfly looked about at the sights of the city in a silence that might have been awe or disapproval or mere stolidity. "This is a nice little town," Ivory said, "but the only city in the world is Havnor."

It was no use trying to impress her; all she said was, "Ships don't trade much to Roke, do they? Will it take a long time to find one to take us, do you think?"

"Not if I carry a staff," he said.

She stopped looking about and strode along in thought for a while. She was beautiful in movement, bold and graceful, her head carried high.

"You mean they'll oblige a wizard? But you aren't a wizard."

"That's a formality. We senior sorcerers may carry a staff when we're on Roke's business. Which I am."

"Taking *me* there?"

"Bringing them a student—yes. A student of great gifts!"

She asked no more questions. She never argued; it was one of her virtues.

That night, over supper at the waterfront inn, she asked with unusual timidity in her voice, "Do I have great gifts?"

"In my judgment, you do," he said.

She pondered—conversation with her was often a slow business—and said, "Rose always said I had power, but she didn't know what kind. And I . . . I know I do, but I don't know what it is."

"You're going to Roke to find out," he said, raising his glass to her. After a moment she raised hers and smiled at him, a smile so tender and radiant that he said spontaneously, "And may what you find be all you seek!"

"If I do, it will be thanks to you," she said. In that moment he loved her for her true heart, and would have foresworn any thought of her but as his companion in a bold adventure, a gallant joke.

They had to share a room at the crowded inn with two other travelers, but Ivory's thoughts were perfectly chaste, though he laughed at himself a little for it.

Next morning he picked a sprig of an herb from the kitchen garden of the inn and spelled it into the semblance of a fine staff, copper-shod and his own height exactly. "What is the wood?" Dragonfly asked, fascinated, when she saw it, and when he answered with a laugh, "Rosemary," she laughed too.

They set off along the wharves, asking for a ship bound south that might take a wizard and his prentice to the Isle of the Wise, and soon enough they found a heavy trader bound for Wathort, whose master would carry the wizard for goodwill and the prentice for half price. Even half price was half the cheese money; but they would have the luxury of a cabin, for *Sea Otter* was a decked, two-masted ship.

As they were talking with her master a wagon drew up on the dock and began to unload six familiar halftun barrels. "That's ours," Ivory said, and the ship's master said, "Bound for Hort Town," and Dragonfly said softly, "From Iria."

She glanced back at the land then. It was the only time he ever saw her look back.

The ship's weatherworker came aboard just before they sailed, no Roke wizard but a weatherbeaten fellow in a worn sea cloak. Ivory flourished his staff a little in greeting him. The sorcerer looked him up and down and said, "One man works weather on this ship. If it's not me, I'm off."

"I'm a mere passenger, Master Bagman. I gladly leave the winds in your hands."

The sorcerer looked at Dragonfly, who stood straight as a tree and said nothing.

"Good," he said, and that was the last word he spoke to Ivory.

During the voyage, however, he talked several times with Dragonfly, which made Ivory a bit uneasy. Her ignorance and trustfulness could endanger her and therefore him. What did she and the bagman talk about? he asked, and she answered, "What is to become of us."

He stared.

"Of all of us. Of Way and Felkway, and Havnor, and Wathort, and Roke. All the people of the islands. He says that when King Lebannen was to be crowned, last autumn, he sent to Gont for the old Archmage to come crown him, and he wouldn't come. And there was no new Archmage. So the King put on his crown himself. And some say that's wrong, and he doesn't rightly hold the throne. But others say the King himself is the new Archmage. But he isn't a wizard, only a king. So others say the dark years will come again, when there was no rule of justice, and wizardry was used for evil ends."

After a pause Ivory said, "That old weatherworker says all this?"

"It's common talk, I think," said Dragonfly, with her grave simplicity.

The weatherworker knew his trade, at least. *Sea Otter* sped south; they met summer squalls and choppy seas, but never a storm or a troublesome wind. They put off and took on cargo at ports on the north shore of O, at Ilien, Leng, Kamery, and O Port, and then headed west to carry the passengers to Roke. And facing the west Ivory felt a little hollow at the pit of his stomach, for he knew all too well how Roke was guarded. He knew neither he nor the weatherworker could do anything at all to turn the Roke wind if it blew against them. And if it did, Dragonfly would ask why? why did it blow against them?

He was glad to see the sorcerer uneasy too, standing by the helmsman, keeping a watch up on the masthead, taking in sail at the hint of a west wind. But the wind held steady from the north. A thunder squall came pelting on that wind, and Ivory went down to the cabin, but Dragonfly stayed up on deck. She was afraid of the water, she had told him. She could not swim; she said, "Drowning must be a horrible thing— Not to breathe the air—" She had shuddered at the thought. It was the only fear she had ever shown of anything. But she disliked the low, cramped cabin, and had stayed on deck every day and slept there on the warm nights. Ivory had not tried to coax her into the cabin. He knew now that coaxing was no good. To have her he must master her; and that he would do, if only they could come to Roke.

He came up on deck again. It was clearing, and as the sun set, the clouds broke all across the west, showing a golden sky behind the high dark curve of a hill.

Ivory looked at that hill with a kind of longing hatred.

"That's Roke Knoll, lad," the weatherworker said to Dragonfly, who stood beside him at the rail. "We're coming into Thwil Bay now. Where there's no wind but the wind they want."

By the time they were well into the bay and had let down the anchor it was dark, and Ivory said to the ship's master, "I'll go ashore in the morning."

Down in their tiny cabin Dragonfly sat waiting for him, solemn as ever but her eyes blazing with excitement. "We'll go ashore in the morning," he repeated to her, and she nodded, acceptant.

She said, "Do I look all right?"

He sat down on his narrow bunk and looked at her sitting on her narrow bunk; they could not face each other directly, as there was no room for their knees. At O Port she had bought herself a decent shirt and breeches, at his suggestion, so as to look a more probable candidate for the school. Her face was windburnt and scrubbed clean. Her hair was braided and the braid clubbed, like Ivory's. She had got her hands clean too, and they lay flat on her thighs, long strong hands, like a man's.

"You don't look like a man," he said. Her face fell. "Not to me. You'll never look like a man to me. But don't worry. You will to them."

She nodded, with an anxious face.

"The first test is the great test, Dragonfly," he said. Every night as he lay alone in this cabin he had planned this conversation. "To enter the Great House. To go through that door."

"I've been thinking about it," she said, hurried and earnest. "Couldn't I just tell them who I am? With you there to vouch for me—to say even if I am a woman, I have some gift—and I'd promise to take the vow and make the spell of celibacy, and live apart if they wanted me to—"

He was shaking his head all through her speech. "No, no, no, no. Hopeless. Useless. Fatal!"

"Even if you—"

"Even if I argued for you. They won't listen. The Rule of Roke forbids women to be taught any high art, any word of the Language of the Making. It's always been so. They will not listen. So they must be shown! And we'll show them, you and I. We'll teach them. You must have courage, Dragonfly. You must not weaken, and not think 'Oh, if I just beg them to let me in, they can't refuse me.' They can, and will. And if you reveal yourself, they will punish you. And me." He put a ponderous emphasis on the last word, and inwardly murmured, "Avert."

She gazed at him from her unreadable eyes, and finally asked, "What must I do?"

"Do you trust me, Dragonfly?"

"Yes."

"Will you trust me entirely, wholly—knowing that the risk I take for you is greater even than your risk in this venture?"

"Yes."

"Then you must tell me the word you will speak to the Doorkeeper."

She stared. "But I thought you'd tell it to me—the password."

"The password he will ask you for is your true name."

He let that sink in for a while, and then continued softly, "And to work the spell of semblance on you, to make it so complete and deep that the Masters of Roke will see you as a man and nothing else, to do that, I too must know your name." He paused again. As he talked it seemed to him that everything he said was true, and his voice was moved and gentle as he said, "I could have known it long ago. But I chose not to use those arts. I wanted you to trust me enough to tell me your name yourself."

She was looking down at her hands, clasped now on her knees. In the faint reddish glow of the cabin lantern her lashes cast very delicate, long shadows on her cheeks. She looked up, straight at him. "My name is Irian," she said.

He smiled. She did not smile.

He said nothing. In fact he was at a loss. If he had known it would be this easy, he could have had her name and with it the power to make her do whatever he wanted, days ago, weeks ago, with a mere pretense at this crazy scheme—without giving up his salary and his precarious respectability, without this sea voyage, without having to go all the way to Roke for it! For he saw the whole plan now was folly. There was no way he could disguise her that would fool the Doorkeeper for a moment. All his notions of humiliating the Masters as they had humiliated him were moonshine. Obsessed with tricking the girl, he had fallen into the trap he laid for her. Bitterly he recognised that he was always believing his own lies, caught in nets he had elaborately woven. Having once made a fool of himself on Roke, he had come back to do it all over again. A great, desolate anger swelled up in him. There was no good, no good in anything.

"What's wrong?" she asked. The gentleness of her deep, husky voice unmanned him, and he hid his face in his hands, fighting against the shame of tears.

She put her hand on his knee. It was the first time she had ever touched him. He endured it, the warmth and weight of her touch that he had wasted so much time wanting.

He wanted to hurt her, to shock her out of her terrible, ignorant kindness, but what he said when he finally spoke was "I only wanted to make love to you."

"You did?"

"Did you think I was one of their eunuchs? That I'd castrate myself with spells so I could be holy? Why do you think I don't have a staff? Why do you think I'm not at the school? Did you believe everything I said?"

"Yes," she said. "I'm sorry." Her hand was still on his knee. She said, "We can make love if you want."

He sat up, sat still.

"What are you?" he said to her at last.

"I don't know. It's why I wanted to come to Roke. To find out."

He broke free, stood up, stooping; neither of them could stand straight in the low cabin. Clenching and unclenching his hands, he stood as far from her as he could, his back to her.

"You won't find out. It's all lies, shams. Old men playing games with words. I wouldn't play their games, so I left. Do you know what I did?" He turned, showing his teeth in a rictus of triumph. "I got a girl, a town girl, to come to my room. My cell. My little stone celibate cell. It had a window looking out on a back street. No spells—you can't make spells with all their magic going on. But she wanted to come, and came, and I let a rope ladder out the window, and she climbed it. And we were at it when the old men came in! I showed 'em! And if I could have got you in, I'd have showed 'em again, I'd have taught them *their* lesson!"

"Well, I'll try," she said.

He stared.

"Not for the same reasons as you," she said, "but I still want to. And we came all this way. And you know my name."

It was true. He knew her name: Irian. It was like a coal of fire, a burning ember in his mind. His thought could not hold it. His knowledge could not use it. His tongue could not say it.

She looked up at him, her sharp, strong face softened by the shadowy lantern light. "If it was only to make love you brought me here, Ivory," she said, "we can do that. If you still want to."

Wordless at first, he simply shook his head. After a while he was able to laugh. "I think we've gone on past . . . that possibility . . ."

She looked at him without regret, or reproach, or shame.

"Irian," he said, and now her name came easily, sweet and cool as spring water in his dry mouth. "Irian, here's what you must do to enter the Great House . . ."

III. Azver

He left her at the corner of the street, a narrow, dull, somehow sly-looking street that slanted up between featureless walls to a wooden door in a higher wall. He had put his spell on her, and she looked like a man, though she did not feel like one. She and Ivory took each other in their arms, because after all they had been friends, companions, and he had done all this for her. "Courage!" he said, and let her go. She walked up the street and stood before the door. She looked back then, but he was gone.

She knocked.

After a while she heard the latch rattle. The door opened. A middle-aged man stood there. "What can I do for you?" he said. He did not smile, but his voice was pleasant.

"You can let me into the Great House, sir."

"Do you know the way in?" His almond-shaped eyes were attentive, yet seemed to look at her from miles or years away.

"This is the way in, sir."

"Do you know whose name you must tell me before I let you in?"

"My own, sir. It is Irian."

"Is it?" he said.

That gave her pause. She stood silent. "It's the name the witch Rose of my village on Way gave me, in the spring under Iria Hill," she said at last, standing up and speaking truth.

The Doorkeeper looked at her for what seemed a long time. "Then it is your name," he said. "But maybe not all your name. I think you have another."

"I don't know it, sir."

After another long time she said, "Maybe I can learn it here, sir."

The Doorkeeper bowed his head a little. A very faint smile made crescent curves in his cheeks. He stood aside. "Come in, daughter," he said.

She stepped across the threshold of the Great House.

Ivory's spell of semblance dropped away like a cobweb. She was and looked herself.

She followed the Doorkeeper down a stone passageway. Only at the end of it did she think to turn back to see the light shine through the thousand leaves of the tree carved in the high door in its bone-white frame.

A young man in a grey cloak hurrying down the passageway stopped short as he approached them. He stared at Irian; then with a brief nod he went on. She looked back at him. He was looking back at her.

A globe of misty, greenish fire drifted swiftly down the corridor at eye level, apparently pursuing the young man. The Doorkeeper waved his hand at it, and it avoided him. Irian swerved and ducked down frantically, but felt the cool fire tingle in her hair as it passed over her. The Doorkeeper glanced round, and now his smile was wider. Though he said nothing, she felt he was aware of her, concerned for her. She stood up and followed him.

He stopped before an oak door. Instead of knocking he sketched a little sign or rune on it with the top of his staff, a light staff of some greyish wood. The door opened as a resonant voice behind it said, "Come in!"

"Wait here a little, if you please, Irian," the Doorkeeper said, and went into the room, leaving the door wide open behind him. She could see bookshelves and books, a table piled with more books and ink pots and writings, two or three boys seated at the table, and the grey-haired, stocky man the Doorkeeper spoke to. She saw the man's face change, saw his eyes shift to her in a brief, startled gaze, saw him question the Doorkeeper, low-voiced, intense.

They both came to her. "The Master Changer of Roke: Irian of Way," said the Doorkeeper.

The Changer stared openly at her. He was not as tall as she was. He stared at the Doorkeeper, and then at her again.

"Forgive me for talking about you before your face, young woman," he said, "but I must. Master Doorkeeper, you know I'd never question your judgment, but the Rule is clear. I have to ask what moved you to break it and let her come in."

"She asked to," said the Doorkeeper.

"But—" The Changer paused.

"When did a woman last ask to enter the school?"

"They know the Rule doesn't allow them."

"Did you know that, Irian?" the Doorkeeper asked her, and she said, "Yes, sir."

"So what brought you here?" the Changer asked, stern, but not hiding his curiosity.

"Master Ivory said I could pass for a man. Though I thought I should say who I was. I will be as celibate as anyone, sir."

Two long curves appeared on the Doorkeeper's cheeks, enclosing the slow upturn of his smile. The Changer's face remained stern, but he blinked, and after a little thought said, "I'm sure—yes— It was definitely the better plan to be honest. What Master did you speak of?"

"Ivory," said the Doorkeeper. "A lad from Havnor Great Port, whom I let in three years ago, and let out again last year, as you may recall."

"Ivory! That fellow that studied with the Hand?— Is he here?" the

Changer demanded of Irian, wrathily. She stood straight and said nothing.

"Not in the school," the Doorkeeper said, smiling.

"He fooled you, young woman. Made a fool of you by trying to make fools of us."

"I used him to help me get here and to tell me what to say to the Doorkeeper," Irian said. "I'm not here to fool anybody, but to learn what I need to know."

"I've often wondered why I let that boy in," said the Doorkeeper. "Now I begin to understand."

At that the Changer looked at him, and after pondering said soberly, "Doorkeeper, what have you in mind?"

"I think Irian of Way may have come to us seeking not only what she needs to know, but also what we need to know." The Doorkeeper's tone was equally sober, and his smile was gone. "I think this may be a matter for talk among the nine of us."

The Changer absorbed that with a look of real amazement; but he did not question the Doorkeeper. He said only, "But not among the students."

The Doorkeeper shook his head, agreeing.

"She can lodge in the town," the Changer said, with some relief.

"While we talk behind her back?"

"You won't bring her into the Council Room?" the Changer said in disbelief.

"The Archmage brought the boy Arren there."

"But— But Arren was King Lebannen—"

"And who is Irian?"

The Changer stood silent, and then he said quietly, with respect, "My friend, what is it you think to do, to learn? What is she, that you ask this for her?"

"Who are we," said the Doorkeeper, "that we refuse her without knowing what she is?"

"A woman," said the Master Summoner.

Irian had waited some hours in the Doorkeeper's chamber, a low, light, bare room with a window seat at a small-paned window looking out on the kitchen gardens of the Great House—handsome, well-kept gardens, long rows and beds of vegetables, greens, and herbs, with berry canes and fruit trees beyond. She saw a burly, dark-skinned man and two boys come out and weed one of the vegetable plots. It eased her mind to watch their careful work. She wished she could help them at it. The waiting and the strangeness were very difficult. Once the

Doorkeeper came in, bringing her a mug of water and a plate with cold meat and bread and scallions, and she ate because he told her to eat, but chewing and swallowing were hard work. The gardeners went away and there was nothing to watch out the window but the cabbages growing and the sparrows hopping, and now and then a hawk far up in the sky, and the wind moving softly in the tops of tall trees, on beyond the gardens.

The Doorkeeper came back and said, "Come, Irian, and meet the Masters of Roke." Her heart began to go at a cart-horse gallop. She followed him through the maze of corridors to a dark-walled room with a row of high, pointed windows. A group of men stood there. Every one of them turned to look at her as she came into the room.

"Irian of Way, my lords," said the Doorkeeper. They were all silent. He motioned her to come farther into the room. "The Master Changer you have met," he said to her. He named all the others, but she could not take in their names and masteries, except that the Master Herbal was the one she had supposed to be a gardener, and the youngest of them, a tall man with a stern, beautiful face that seemed carved out of dark stone, was the Master Summoner. It was he who spoke when the Doorkeeper was done. "A woman," he said.

The Doorkeeper nodded once, mild as ever.

"This is what you brought the Nine together for? This and no more?"

"This and no more," said the Doorkeeper.

"Dragons have been seen flying above the Inmost Sea. Roke has no archmage, and the islands no true-crowned king. There is real work to do," the Summoner said, and his voice too was like stone, cold and heavy. "When will we do it?"

There was an uncomfortable silence, as the Doorkeeper did not speak. At last a slight, bright-eyed man who wore a red tunic under his grey wizard's cloak said, "Do you bring this woman into the House as a student, Master Doorkeeper?"

"If I did, it would be up to you all to approve or disapprove," said he.

"Do you?" asked the man in the red tunic, smiling a little.

"Master Hand," said the Doorkeeper, "she asked to enter as a student, and I saw no reason to deny her."

"Every reason," said the Summoner.

A man with a deep, clear voice spoke: "It's not our judgment that prevails, but the Rule of Roke, which we are sworn to follow."

"I doubt the Doorkeeper would defy it lightly," said one whom Irian had not noticed till he spoke, though he was a big man, white-haired, rawboned, and crag-faced. Unlike the others, he looked at her as he spoke. "I am Kurremkarmerruk," he said to her. "As the Master Namer here, I make free with names, my own included. Who named you, Irian?"

"The witch Rose of our village, lord," she answered, standing straight, though her voice came out high-pitched and rough.

"Is she misnamed?" the Doorkeeper asked the Namer.

Kurremkarmerruk shook his head. "No. But . . ."

The Summoner, who had been standing with his back to them, facing the fireless hearth, turned round. "The names witches give each other are not our concern here," he said. "If you have some interest in this woman, Doorkeeper, it should be pursued outside these walls—outside the door you vowed to keep. She has no place here nor ever will. She can bring only confusion, dissension, and further weakness among us. I will speak no longer and say nothing else in her presence. The only answer to conscious error is silence."

"Silence is not enough, my lord," said one who had not spoken before. To Irian's eyes he was very strange-looking, having pale reddish skin, long pale hair, and narrow eyes the color of ice. His speech was also strange, stiff and somehow deformed. "Silence is the answer to everything, and to nothing," he said.

The Summoner lifted his noble, dark face and looked across the room at the pale man, but did not speak. Without a word or gesture he turned away again and left the room. As he walked slowly past Irian, she shrank back from him. It was as if a grave had opened, a winter grave, cold, wet, dark. Her breath stuck in her throat. She gasped a little for air. When she recovered herself, she saw the Changer and the pale man both watching her intently.

The one with a voice like a deep-toned bell looked at her too, and spoke to her with a plain, kind severity. "As I see it, the man who brought you here meant to do harm, but you do not. Yet being here, Irian, you do us and yourself harm. Everything not in its own place does harm. A note sung, however well sung, wrecks the tune it isn't part of. Women teach women. Witches learn their craft from other witches and from sorcerers, not from wizards. What we teach here is in a language not for women's tongues. The young heart rebels against such laws, calling them unjust, arbitrary. But they are true laws, founded not on what we want, but on what is. The just and the unjust, the foolish and the wise, all must obey them, or waste life and come to grief."

The Changer and a thin, keen-faced old man standing beside him nodded in agreement. The Master Hand said, "Irian, I am sorry. Ivory was my pupil. If I taught him badly, I did worse in sending him away. I thought him insignificant, and so harmless. But he lied to you and beguiled you. You must not feel shame. The fault was his and mine."

"I am not ashamed," Irian said. She looked at them all. She felt that she should thank them for their courtesy but the words would not come. She nodded stiffly to them, turned round, and strode out of the room.

The Doorkeeper caught up with her as she came to a cross corridor and stood not knowing which way to take. "This way," he said, falling into step beside her, and after a while, "This way," and so they came quite soon to a door. It was not made of horn and ivory. It was uncarved oak, black and massive, with an iron bolt worn thin with age. "This is the garden door," the mage said, unbolting it. "Medra's Gate, they used to call it. I keep both doors." He opened it. The brightness of the day dazzled Irian's eyes. When she could see clearly she saw a path leading from the door through the gardens and the fields beyond them; on past the fields were the high trees, and the swell of Roke Knoll was off to the right. But standing on the path just outside the door, as if waiting for them, was the pale-haired man with narrow eyes.

"Patterner," said the Doorkeeper, not at all surprised.

"Where do you send this lady?" said the Patterner in his strange speech.

"Nowhere," said the Doorkeeper. "I let her out as I let her in, at her desire."

"Will you come with me?" the Patterner said to Irian.

She looked at him and at the Doorkeeper and said nothing.

"I don't live in this House. In any house," the Patterner said. "I live there. The Grove. —Ah," he said, turning suddenly. The big, white-haired man, Kurremkarmerruk the Namer, was standing just down the path. He had not been standing there until the other mage said "Ah." Irian stared from one to the other in blank bewilderment.

"This is only a seeming of me, a presentment, a sending," the old man said to her. "I don't live here either. Miles off." He gestured northward. "You might come there when you're done with the Patterner here. I'd like to learn more about your name." He nodded to the other two mages and was not there. A bumblebee buzzed heavily through the air where he had been.

Irian looked down at the ground. After a long time she said, clearing her throat, not looking up, "Is it true I do harm being here?"

"I don't know," said the Doorkeeper.

"In the Grove is no harm," said the Patterner. "Come on. There is an old house, a hut. Old, dirty. You don't care, eh? Stay a while. You can see." And he set off down the path between the parsley and the bush beans. She looked at the Doorkeeper; he smiled a little. She followed the pale-haired man.

They walked a half mile or so. The round-topped knoll rose up full in the western sun on their right. Behind them the school sprawled grey and many-roofed on its lower hill. The grove of trees towered before them now. She saw oak and willow, chestnut and ash, and tall evergreens. From the dense, sun-shot darkness of the trees a stream ran out, green-banked, with many brown trodden places where cattle and sheep went down to drink or to cross over. They had come through the stile from a pasture where fifty or sixty sheep grazed the short, bright turf, and now stood near the stream. "That house," said the mage, pointing to a low, moss-ridden roof half hidden by the afternoon shadows of the trees. "Stay tonight. You will?"

He asked her to stay, he did not tell her to. All she could do was nod.

"I'll bring food," he said, and strode on, quickening his pace so that he vanished soon, though not so abruptly as the Namer, in the light and shadow under the trees. Irian watched till he was certainly gone and then made her way through high grass and weeds to the little house.

It looked very old. It had been rebuilt and rebuilt again, but not for a long time. Nor had anyone lived in it for a long time, from the still, lonesome air of it. Yet it had a pleasant air, as if those who had slept there slept peacefully. As for decrepit walls, mice, dust, cobwebs, and scant furniture, all that was quite homelike to Irian. She found a bald broom and swept out the mouse droppings. She unrolled her blanket on the plank bed. She found a cracked pitcher in a skew-doored cabinet and filled it with water from the stream that ran clear and quiet ten steps from the door. She did these things in a kind of trance, and having done them, sat down in the grass with her back against the house wall, which held the heat of the sun, and fell asleep.

When she woke, the Master Patterner was sitting nearby, and a basket was on the grass between them.

"Hungry? Eat," he said.

"I'll eat later, sir. Thank you," said Irian.

"I am hungry now," said the mage. He took a hard-boiled egg from the basket, cracked, shelled, and ate it.

"They call this the Otter's House," he said. "Very old. As old as the Great House. Everything is old, here. We are old—the Masters."

"You're not very," Irian said. She thought him between thirty and forty, though it was hard to tell; she kept thinking his hair was white, because it was not black.

"But I came far. Miles can be years. I am Kargish, from Karego. You know?"

"The Hoary Men!" said Irian, staring openly at him. All Daisy's ballads of the Hoary Men who sailed out of the East to lay the land waste and spit innocent babes on their lances, and the story of how Erreth-Akbe lost the Ring of Peace, and the new songs and the King's Tale about how Archmage Sparrowhawk had gone among the Hoary Men and come back with that ring—

"Hoary?" said the Patterner.

"Frosty. White," she said, looking away, embarrassed.

"Ah." Presently he said, "The Master Summoner is not old." And she got a sidelong look from those narrow, ice-colored eyes.

She said nothing.

"I think you feared him."

She nodded.

When she said nothing, and some time had passed, he said, "In the shadow of these trees is no harm. Only truth."

"When he passed me," she said in a low voice, "I saw a grave."

"Ah," said the Patterner.

He had made a little heap of bits of eggshell on the ground by his knee. He arranged the white fragments into a curve, then closed it into a circle. "Yes," he said, studying his eggshells; then, scratching up the earth a bit, he neatly and delicately buried them. He dusted off his hands. Again his glance flicked to Irian and away.

"You have been a witch, Irian?"

"No."

"But you have some knowledge."

"No. I don't. Rose wouldn't teach me. She said she didn't dare. Because I had power but she didn't know what it was."

"Your Rose is a wise flower," said the mage, unsmiling.

"But I know I have something to do. Something to be. That's why I wanted to come here. To find out. On the Isle of the Wise."

She was getting used to his strange face now and was able to read it. She thought that he looked sad. His way of speaking was harsh, quick, dry, peaceable. "The men of the Isle are not always wise, eh?" he said. "Maybe the Doorkeeper." He looked at her now, not glancing but squarely, his eyes catching and holding hers. "But there. In the wood. Under the trees. There is the old wisdom. Never old. I can't teach you. I can take you into the Grove." After a minute he stood up. "Yes?"

"Yes," she said uncertainly.

"The house is all right?"

"Yes—"

"Tomorrow," he said, and strode off.

So for a half month or more of the hot days of summer, Irian slept in the Otter's House, which was a peaceful one, and ate what the Master Patterner brought her in his basket—eggs, cheese, greens, fruit, smoked mutton—and went with him every afternoon into the grove of high trees, where the paths seemed never to be quite where she remembered them, and often led on far beyond what seemed the confines of the wood. They walked there in silence, and spoke seldom when they rested. The mage was a quiet man. Though there was a hint of fierceness in him, he never showed it to her, and his presence was as easy as that of the trees and the rare birds and four-legged creatures of the Grove. As he had said, he did not try to teach her. When she asked about the Grove, he told her that, with Roke Knoll, it had stood since Segoy made the islands of the world, and that all magic was in the roots of the trees, and that they were mingled with the roots of all the forests that were or might yet be. "And sometimes the Grove is in this place," he said, "and sometimes in another. But it is always."

She had never seen where he lived. He slept wherever he chose to, she imagined, in these warm summer nights. She asked him where the food they ate came from. What the school did not supply for itself, he said, the farmers round about provided, considering themselves well recompensed by the protections the Masters set on their flocks and fields and orchards. That made sense to her. On Way, the phrase "a wizard without his porridge" meant something unprecedented, unheard-of. But she was no wizard, and so, wanting to earn her porridge, she did her best to repair the Otter's House, borrowing tools from a farmer and buying nails and plaster in Thwil Town, for she still had half the cheese money.

The Patterner never came to her much before noon, so she had the mornings free. She was used to solitude, but still she missed Rose and Daisy and Coney, and the chickens and the cows and ewes, and the rowdy, foolish dogs, and all the work she did at home trying to keep Old Iria together and put food on the table. So she worked away unhurriedly every morning till she saw the mage come out from the trees with his sunlight-colored hair shining in the sunlight.

Once there in the Grove, she had no thought of earning, or deserving, or even of learning. To be there was enough, was all.

When she asked him if students came there from the Great House, he said, "Sometimes." Another time he said, "My words are nothing.

Hear the leaves." That was all he said that could be called teaching. As she walked, she listened to the leaves when the wind rustled them or stormed in the crowns of the trees; she watched the shadows play, and thought about the roots of the trees down in the darkness of the earth. She was utterly content to be there. Yet always, without discontent or urgency, she felt that she was waiting. And that silent expectancy was deepest and clearest when she came out of the shelter of the woods and saw the open sky.

Once, when they had gone a long way and the trees, dark evergreens she did not know, stood very high about them, she heard a call—a horn blowing, a cry?—remote, on the very edge of hearing. She stood still, listening towards the west. The mage walked on, turning only when he realised she had stopped.

"I heard—" she said, and could not say what she had heard.

He listened. They walked on at last through a silence enlarged and deepened by that far call.

She never went into the Grove without him, and it was many days before he left her alone within it. But one hot afternoon when they came to a glade among a stand of oaks, he said, "I will come back here, eh?" and walked off with his quick, silent step, lost almost at once in the dappled, shifting depths of the forest.

She had no wish to explore for herself. The peacefulness of the place called for stillness, watching, listening; and she knew how tricky the paths were, and that the Grove was, as the Patterner put it, "bigger inside than outside." She sat down in a patch of sun-dappled shade and watched the shadows of the leaves play across the ground. The oak mast was deep; though she had never seen wild swine in the wood, she saw their tracks here. For a moment she caught the scent of a fox. Her thoughts moved as quietly and easily as the breeze moved in the warm light.

Often her mind here seemed empty of thought, full of the forest itself, but this day memories came to her, vivid. She thought about Ivory, thinking she would never see him again, wondering if he had found a ship to take him back to Havnor. He had told her he'd never go back to Westpool; the only place for him was the Great Port, the King's City, and for all he cared the island of Way could sink in the sea as deep as Soléa. But she thought with love of the roads and fields of Way. She thought of Old Iria village, the marshy spring under Iria Hill, the old house on it. She thought about Daisy singing ballads in the kitchen, winter evenings, beating out the time with her wooden clogs; and old Coney in the vineyards with his razor-edge knife, showing her how to prune the vine "right down to the life in it"; and Rose, her

Etaudis, whispering charms to ease the pain in a child's broken arm. I have known wise people, she thought. Her mind flinched away from remembering her father, but the motion of the leaves and shadows drew it on. She saw him drunk, shouting. She felt his prying, tremulous hands on her. She saw him weeping, sick, shamed; and grief rose up through her body and dissolved, like an ache that melts away in a long stretch of the arms. He was less to her than the mother she had not known.

She stretched, feeling the ease of her body in the warmth, and her mind drifted back to Ivory. She had had no one in her life to desire. When the young wizard first came riding by so slim and arrogant, she wished she could want him; but she didn't and couldn't, and so she had thought him spell-protected. Rose had explained to her how wizards' spells worked "so that it never enters your head nor theirs, see, because it would take from their power, they say." But Ivory, poor Ivory, had been all too unprotected. If anybody was under a spell of chastity it must have been herself, for charming and handsome as he was she had never been able to feel a thing for him but liking, and her only lust had been to learn what he could teach her.

She considered herself, sitting in the deep silence of the Grove. No bird sang; the breeze was down; the leaves hung still. Am I ensorcelled? Am I a sterile thing, not whole, not a woman? she asked herself, looking at her strong bare arms, the soft swell of her breasts in the shadow under the throat of her shirt.

She looked up and saw the Hoary Man come out of a dark aisle of great oaks and come towards her across the glade.

He stopped in front of her. She felt herself blush, her face and throat burning, dizzy, her ears ringing. She sought words, anything to say, to turn his attention away from her, and could find nothing at all. He sat down near her. She looked down, as if studying the skeleton of a last-year's leaf by her hand.

What do I want? she asked herself, and the answer came not in words but throughout her whole body and soul: the fire, a greater fire than that, the flight, the flight burning—

She came back into herself, into the still air under the trees. The Hoary Man sat near her, his face bowed down, and she thought how slight and light he looked, how quiet and sorrowful. There was nothing to fear. There was no harm.

He looked over at her.

"Irian," he said, "do you hear the leaves?"

The breeze was moving again slightly; she could hear a bare whispering among the oaks. "A little," she said.

"Do you hear the words?"

"No."

She asked nothing and he said no more. Presently he got up, and she followed him to the path that always led them, sooner or later, out of the wood to the clearing by the Thwilburn and the Otter's House. When they came there, it was late afternoon. He went down to the stream and knelt to drink from it where it left the wood, above all the crossings. She did the same. Then sitting in the cool, long grass of the bank, he began to speak.

"My people, the Kargs, they worship gods. Twin gods, brothers. And the king there is also a god. But before the gods and after, always, are the streams. Caves, stones, hills. Trees. The earth. The darkness of the earth."

"The Old Powers," Irian said.

He nodded. "There, women know the Old Powers. Here too, witches. And the knowledge is bad—eh?"

When he added that little questioning "eh?" or "neh?" to the end of what had seemed a statement it always took her by surprise. She said nothing.

"Dark is bad," said the Patterner. "Eh?"

Irian drew a deep breath and looked at him eye to eye as they sat there. *"Only in dark the light,"* she said.

"Ah," he said. He looked away so that she could not see his expression.

"I should go," she said. "I can walk in the Grove, but not live there. It isn't my—my place. And the Master Chanter said I did harm by being here."

"We all do harm by being," said the Patterner.

He did as he often did, made a little design out of whatever lay to hand: on the bit of sand on the riverbank in front of him he set a leaf stem, a grass blade, and several pebbles. He studied them and re-arranged them. "Now I must speak of harm," he said.

After a long pause he went on. "You know that a dragon brought back our Lord Sparrowhawk, with the young king, from the shores of death. Then the dragon carried Sparrowhawk away to his home, for his power was gone, he was not a mage. So presently the Masters of Roke met to choose a new archmage, here, in the Grove, as always. But not as always.

"Before the dragon came, the Summoner too had returned from death, where he can go, where his art can take him. He had seen our lord and the young king there, in that country across the wall of stones. He said they would not come back. He said Lord Sparrowhawk had told him to come back to us, to life, to bear that word. So we grieved for our lord.

"But then came the dragon, Kalessin, bearing him living.

"The Summoner was among us when we stood on Roke Knoll and saw the Archmage kneel to King Lebannen. Then, as the dragon bore our friend away, the Summoner fell down.

"He lay as if dead, cold, his heart not beating, yet he breathed. The Herbal used all his art, but could not rouse him. 'He is dead,' he said. 'The breath will not leave him, but he is dead.' So we mourned him. Then, because there was dismay among us, and all my patterns spoke of change and danger, we met to choose a new warden of Roke, an archmage to guide us. And in our council we set the young king in the Summoner's place. To us it seemed right that he should sit among us. Only the Changer spoke against it at first, and then agreed.

"But we met, we sat, and we could not choose. We said this and said that, but no name was spoken. And then I . . ." He paused a while. "There came on me what my people call the *eduevanu,* the other breath. Words came to me and I spoke them. I said, *Hama Gondun!*— And Kurremkarmerruk told them this in Hardic: 'A woman on Gont.' But when I came back to my own wits, I could not tell them what that meant. And so we parted with no archmage chosen.

"The king left soon after, and the Master Windkey went with him. Before the king was to be crowned, they went to Gont and sought our lord Sparrowhawk, to find what that meant, 'a woman on Gont.' Eh? But they did not see him, only my countrywoman Tenar of the Ring. She said she was not the woman they sought. And they found no one, nothing. So Lebannen judged it to be a prophecy yet to be fulfilled. And in Havnor he set his crown on his own head.

"The Herbal, and I too, judged the Summoner dead. We thought the breath he breathed was left from some spell of his own art that we did not understand, like the spell snakes know that keeps their heart beating long after they are dead. Though it seemed terrible to bury a breathing body, yet he was cold, and his blood did not run, and no soul was in him. That was more terrible. So we made ready to bury him. And then, as he lay beside his grave, his eyes opened. He moved, and spoke. He said, 'I have summoned myself again into life, to do what must be done.' "

The Patterner's voice had grown rougher. He suddenly brushed the little design of pebbles apart with the palm of his hand.

"So when the Windkey returned from the king's crowning, we were nine again. But divided. For the Summoner said we must meet again and choose an archmage. The king had had no place among us, he said. And 'a woman on Gont,' whoever she may be, has no place among the men on Roke. Eh? The Windkey, the Chanter, the Changer, the Hand, say he is right. And as King Lebannen is a man returned from death, fulfilling that prophecy, they say so will the archmage be a man returned from death."

"But—" Irian said, and stopped.

After a while the Patterner said, "That art, summoning, you know, is terrible. It is always danger. Here," and he looked up into the green-gold darkness of the trees, "here is no summoning. No bringing back across the wall. No wall."

His face was a warrior's face, but when he looked into the trees it was softened, yearning.

"So," he said, "now he makes you his reason for our meeting. But I will not go to the Great House. I will not be summoned."

"He won't come here?"

"I think he will not walk in the Grove. Nor on Roke Knoll. On the Knoll, what is, is so."

She did not know what he meant, but did not ask, preoccupied: "You say he makes me his reason for you to meet together."

"Yes. To send away one woman, it takes nine mages." He very seldom smiled, and when he did it was quick and fierce. "We are to meet to uphold the Rule of Roke. And so to choose an archmage."

"If I went away—" She saw him shake his head. "I could go to the Namer—"

"You are safer here."

The idea of doing harm troubled her, but the idea of danger had not entered her mind. She found it inconceivable. "I'll be all right," she said. "So the Namer, and you—and the Doorkeeper?—"

"—do not wish Thorion to be archmage. Also the Master Herbal, though he digs and says little."

He saw Irian staring at him in amazement. "Thorion the Summoner speaks his true name," he said. "He died, eh?"

She knew that King Lebannen used his true name openly. He too had returned from death. Yet that the Summoner should do so continued to shock and disturb her as she thought about it.

"And the . . . the students?"

"Divided also."

She thought about the school, where she had been so briefly. From here, under the eaves of the Grove, she saw it as stone walls enclosing one kind of being and keeping out all others, like a pen, a cage. How could any of them keep their balance in a place like that?

The Patterner pushed four pebbles into a little curve on the sand

and said, "I wish the Sparrowhawk had not gone. I wish I could read what the shadows write. But all I can hear the leaves say is Change, change . . . Everything will change but them." He looked up into the trees again with that yearning look. The sun was setting. He stood up, bade her goodnight gently, and walked away, entering under the trees.

She sat on a while by the Thwilburn. She was troubled by what he had told her and by her thoughts and feelings in the Grove, and troubled that any thought or feeling could have troubled her there. She went to the house, set out her supper of smoked meat and bread and summer lettuce, and ate it without tasting it. She roamed restlessly back down the stream bank to the water. It was very still and warm in the late dusk, only the largest stars burning through a milky overcast. She slipped off her sandals and put her feet in the water. It was cool, but veins of sun warmth ran through it. She slid out of her clothes, the man's breeches and shirt that were all she had, and slipped naked into the water, feeling the push and stir of the current all along her body. She had never swum in the streams at Iria, and she had hated the sea, heaving grey and cold, but this quick water pleased her, tonight. She drifted and floated, her hands slipping over silken underwater rocks and her own silken flanks, her legs sliding through water weeds. All trouble and restlessness washed away from her in the running of the water, and she floated in delight in the caress of the stream, gazing up at the white, soft fire of the stars.

A chill ran through her. The water ran cold. Gathering herself together, her limbs still soft and loose, she looked up and saw on the bank above her the black figure of a man.

She stood straight up, naked, in the water.

"Get away!" she shouted. "Get away, you traitor, you foul lecher, or I'll cut the liver out of you!" She sprang up the bank, pulling herself up by the tough bunchgrass, and scrambled to her feet. No one was there. She stood afire, shaking with rage. She leapt back down the bank, found her clothes, and pulled them on, still swearing aloud—"You coward wizard! You traitorous son of a bitch!"

"Irian?"

"He was here!" she cried. "That foul heart, that Thorion!" She strode to meet the Patterner as he came into the starlight by the house. "I was bathing in the stream, and he stood there watching me!"

"A sending—only a seeming of him. It could not hurt you, Irian."

"A sending with eyes, a seeming with seeing! May he be—" She stopped, at a loss suddenly for the word. She felt sick. She shuddered, and swallowed the cold spittle that welled in her mouth.

The Patterner came forward and took her hands in his. His hands were warm, and she felt so mortally cold that she came close up against him for the warmth of his body. They stood so for a while, her face turned from him but their hands joined and their bodies pressed close. At last she broke free, straightening herself, pushing back her lank wet hair. "Thank you," she said. "I was cold."

"I know."

"I'm never cold," she said. "It was him."

"I tell you, Irian, he cannot come here, he cannot harm you here."

"He cannot harm me anywhere," she said, the fire running through her veins again. "If he tries to, I'll destroy him."

"Ah," said the Patterner.

She looked at him in the starlight, and said, "Tell me your name— Not your true name— Only a name I can call you. When I think of you."

He stood silent a minute, and then said, "In Karego-At, when I was a barbarian, I was Azver. In Hardic, that is a banner of war."

"Azver," she said. "Thank you."

She lay awake in the little house, feeling the air stifling and the ceiling pressing down on her, then slept suddenly and deeply. She woke as suddenly when the east was just getting light. She went to the door to see what she loved best to see, the sky before sunrise. Looking down from it she saw Azver the Patterner rolled up in his grey cloak, sound asleep on the ground before her doorstep. She withdrew noiselessly into the house. In a little while she saw him going back to his woods, walking a bit stiffly and scratching his head as he went, as people do when half awake.

She got to work scraping down the inner wall of the house, readying it to plaster. Just as the first sunlight struck in the window, there was a knock at her open door. Outside was the man she had thought was a gardener, the Master Herbal, looking solid and stolid, like a brown ox, beside the gaunt, grim-faced old Namer.

She came to the door and muttered some kind of greeting. They daunted her, these Masters of Roke; and also their presence meant that the peaceful time was over, the days of walking in the silent summer forest with the Patterner. That had come to an end last night. She knew it, but she did not want to know it.

"The Patterner sent for us," said the Master Herbal. He looked uncomfortable. Noticing a clump of weeds under the window, he said, "That's velver. Somebody from Havnor planted it here. Didn't know there was any on the island." He examined it attentively, and put some seed pods into his pouch.

Irian was studying the Namer covertly but equally attentively, trying to see if she could tell if he was what he had called a sending or was there in flesh and blood. Nothing about him appeared insubstantial, but she thought he was not there, and when he stepped into the slanting sunlight and cast no shadow, she knew it.

"Is it a long way from where you live, sir?" she asked.

He nodded. "Left myself halfway," he said. He looked up; the Patterner was coming towards them, wide awake now.

He greeted them and asked, "The Doorkeeper will come?"

"Said he thought he'd better keep the doors," said the Herbal. He closed his many-pocketed pouch carefully and looked around at the others. "But I don't know if he can keep a lid on the ant hill."

"What's up?" said Kurremkarmerruk. "I've been reading about dragons. Not paying attention to ants. But all the boys I had studying at the Tower left."

"Summoned," said the Herbal, drily.

"So?" said the Namer, more drily.

"I can tell you only how it seems to me," the Herbal said, reluctant, uncomfortable.

"Do that," the old mage said.

The Herbal still hesitated. "This lady is not of our council," he said at last.

"She is of mine," said Azver.

"She came to this place at this time," the Namer said. "And to this place, at this time, no one comes by chance. All any of us knows is how it seems to us. There are names behind names, my Lord Healer."

The dark-eyed mage bowed his head at that, and said, "Very well," evidently with relief at accepting their judgment over his own. "Thorion has been much with the other Masters, and with the young men. Secret meetings, inner circles. Rumors, whispers. The younger students are frightened, and several have asked me or the Doorkeeper if they may go—leave Roke. And we'd let them go. But there's no ship in port, and none has come into Thwil Bay since the one that brought you, lady, and sailed again next day for Wathort. The Windkey keeps the Roke wind against all. If the king himself should come, he could not land on Roke."

"Until the wind changes, eh?" said the Patterner.

"Thorion says Lebannen is not truly king, since no archmage crowned him."

"Nonsense! Not history!" said the old Namer. "The first archmage came centuries after the last king. Roke ruled in the kings' stead."

"Ah," said the Patterner. "Hard for the housekeeper to give up the keys when the owner comes home. Eh?"

"The Ring of Peace is healed," said the Herbal, in his patient, troubled voice, "the prophecy is fulfilled, the son of Morred is crowned, and yet we have no peace. Where have we gone wrong? Why can we not find the balance?"

"What does Thorion intend?" asked the Namer.

"To bring Lebannen here," said the Herbal. "The young men talk of 'the true crown.' A second coronation, here. By the Archmage Thorion."

"Avert!" Irian blurted out, making the sign to prevent word from becoming deed. None of the men smiled, and the Herbal belatedly made the same gesture.

"How does he hold them all?" the Namer said. "Herbal, you were here when Sparrowhawk and Thorion were challenged by Irioth. His gift was as great as Thorion's, I think. He used it to use men, to control them wholly. Is that what Thorion does?"

"I don't know," the Herbal said. "I can only tell you that when I'm with him, when I'm in the Great House, I feel that nothing can be done but what has been done. That nothing will change. Nothing will grow. That no matter what cures I use, the sickness will end in death." He looked around at them all like a hurt ox. "And I think it is true. There is no way to regain the Equilibrium but by holding still. We have gone too far. For the Archmage and Lebannen to go bodily into death, and return—it was not right. They broke a law that must not be broken. It was to restore the law that Thorion returned."

"What, to send them back into death?" the Namer said, and the Patterner, "Who is to say what is the law?"

"There is a wall," the Herbal said.

"That wall is not as deep-rooted as my trees," said the Patterner.

"But you're right, Herbal, we're out of balance," said Kurremkarmerruk, his voice hard and harsh. "When and where did we begin to go too far? What have we forgotten, turned our back on, overlooked?"

Irian looked from one to the other.

"When the balance is wrong, holding still is not good. It must get more wrong," said the Patterner. "Until—" He made a quick gesture of reversal with his open hands, down going up and up down.

"What's more wrong than to summon oneself back from death?" said the Namer.

"Thorion was the best of us all—a brave heart, a noble mind." The

Herbal spoke almost in anger. "Sparrowhawk loved him. So did we all."

"Conscience caught him," said the Namer. "Conscience told him he alone could set things right. To do it, he denied his death. So he denies life."

"And who shall stand against him?" said the Patterner. "I can only hide in my woods."

"And I in my tower," said the Namer. "And you, Herbal, and the Doorkeeper, are in the trap, in the Great House. The walls we built to keep all evil out. Or in, as the case may be."

"We are four against him," said the Patterner.

"They are five against us," said the Herbal.

"Has it come to this," the Namer said, "that we stand at the edge of the forest Segoy planted and talk of how to destroy one another?"

"Yes," said the Patterner. "What goes too long unchanged destroys itself. The forest is forever because it dies and dies and so lives. I will not let this dead hand touch me. Or touch the king who brought us hope. A promise was made, made through me. I spoke it—'A woman on Gont.' I will not see that word forgotten."

"Then should we go to Gont?" said the Herbal, caught in Azver's passion. "Sparrowhawk is there."

"Tenar of the Ring is there," said Azver.

"Maybe our hope is there," said the Namer.

They stood silent, uncertain, trying to cherish hope.

Irian stood silent too, but her hope sank down, replaced by a sense of shame and utter insignificance. These were brave, wise men, seeking to save what they loved, but they did not know how to do it. And she had no share in their wisdom, no part in their decisions. She drew away from them, and they did not notice. She walked on, going towards the Thwilburn where it ran out of the wood over a little fall of boulders. The water was bright in the morning sunlight and made a happy noise. She wanted to cry, but she had never been good at crying. She stood and watched the water, and her shame turned slowly into anger.

She came back towards the three men, and said, "Azver."

He turned to her, startled, and came forward a little.

"Why did you break your Rule for me? Was it fair to me, who can never be what you are?"

Azver frowned. "The Doorkeeper admitted you because you asked," he said. "I brought you to the Grove because the leaves of the trees spoke your name to me before you ever came here. *Irian,* they said, *Irian.* Why you came I don't know, but not by chance. The Summoner too knows that."

"Maybe I came to destroy him."

He looked at her and said nothing.

"Maybe I came to destroy Roke."

His pale eyes blazed then. "Try!"

A long shudder went through her as she stood facing him. She felt herself larger than he was, larger than she was, enormously larger. She could reach out one finger and destroy him. He stood there in his small, brave, brief humanity, his mortality, defenseless. She drew a long, long breath. She stepped back from him.

The sense of huge strength was draining out of her. She turned her head a little and looked down, surprised to see her own brown arm, her rolled-up sleeve, the grass springing cool and green around her sandaled feet. She looked back at the Patterner and he still seemed a fragile being. She pitied and honored him. She wanted to warn him of the peril he was in. But no words came to her at all. She turned round and went back to the stream bank by the little falls. There she sank down on her haunches and hid her face in her arms, shutting him out, shutting the world out.

The voices of the mages talking were like the voices of the stream running. The stream said its words and they said theirs, but none of them were the right words.

IV. Irian

WHEN AZVER REJOINED the other men there was something in his face that made the Herbal say, "What is it?"

"I don't know," he answered. "Maybe we should not leave Roke."

"Probably we can't," said the Herbal. "If the Windkey locks the winds against us . . ."

"I'm going back to where I am," Kurremkarmerruk said abruptly. "I don't like leaving myself about like an old shoe. I'll be here with you this evening." And he was gone.

"I'd like to walk under your trees a bit, Azver," the Herbal said, with a long sigh.

"Go on, Deyala. I'll stay here." The Herbal went off. Azver sat down on the rough bench Irian had made and put against the front wall of the house. He looked upstream at her, crouching motionless on the bank. Sheep in the field between them and the Great House blatted softly. The morning sun was getting hot.

His father had named him Banner of War. He had come west, leaving all he knew behind him. He had learned his true name from the trees of the Immanent Grove, and become the Patterner of Roke. All this year the patterns of the shadows and the branches and the roots, all the silent language of his forest, had spoken of destruction, of transgression, of all things changed. Now it was upon them, he knew. It had come with her.

She was in his charge, in his care, he had known that when he saw her. Though she came to destroy Roke, as she had said, he must serve her. He did so willingly. She had walked with him in the forest, tall, awkward, fearless; she had put aside the thorny arms of brambles with her big, careful hand. Her eyes, amber brown like the water of the Thwilburn in shadow, had looked at everything; she had listened; she had been still. He wanted to protect her and knew he could not. He had given her a little warmth when she was cold. He had nothing else to give her. Where she must go she would go. She did not understand danger. She had no wisdom but her innocence, no armor but her anger. Who are you, Irian? he said to her, watching her crouched there like an animal locked in its muteness.

The Herbal came back from the woods and sat with him a while, not speaking. In the middle of the day he went back to the Great House, agreeing to return with the Doorkeeper in the morning. They would ask all the other Masters to meet with them in the Grove. "But *he* won't come," Deyala said, and Azver nodded.

All day he stayed near the Otter's House, keeping watch on Irian, making her eat a little with him. She came to the house, but when they had eaten she went back to her place on the stream bank and sat there motionless. And he too felt a lethargy in his own body and mind, a stupidity, which he fought against but could not shake off. He thought of the Summoner's eyes, and then it was he that felt cold, cold through, though he was sitting in the full heat of the summer's day. We are ruled by the dead, he thought. The thought would not leave him.

He was grateful to see Kurremkarmerruk coming slowly down the bank of the Thwilburn from the north. The old man waded through the stream barefoot, holding his shoes in one hand and his tall staff in the other, snarling when he missed his footing on the rocks. He sat down on the near bank to dry his feet and put his shoes back on. "When I go back to the Tower," he said, "I'll ride. Hire a carter, buy a mule. I'm old, Azver."

"Come up to the house," the Patterner said, and he set out water and food for the Namer.

"Where's the girl?"

"Asleep." Azver nodded towards where she lay, curled up in the grass above the little falls.

The heat of the day was beginning to lessen and the shadows of the Grove lay across the grass, though the Otter's House was still in sunlight. Kurremkarmerruk sat on the bench with his back against the house wall, and Azver on the doorstep.

"We've come to the end of it," the old man said out of silence.

Azver nodded, in silence.

"What brought you here, Azver?" the Namer asked. "I've often thought of asking you. A long, long way to come. And you have no wizards in the Kargish lands."

"No. But we have the things wizardry is made of. Water, stones, trees, words . . ."

"But not the words of the Making."

"No. Nor dragons."

"Never?"

"Only in old tales from the farthest east, from the desert of Hur-at-Hur. Before the gods were. Before men were. Before men were men, they were dragons."

"Now that is interesting," said the old scholar, sitting up straighter. "I told you I've been reading about dragons. You know these rumors of them flying over the Inmost Sea as far east as Gont. That was no doubt Kalessin taking Ged home, multiplied by sailors making a good story better. But a boy here swore to me that his whole village had seen dragons flying, this spring, west of Mount Onn. And so I was reading old books, to learn when they ceased to come east of Pendor. And in an old Pelnish scroll, I came on your story, or something like it. That men and dragons were all one kind, but they quarreled. Some went west and some east, and they became two kinds, and forgot they were ever one."

"We went farthest east," Azver said. "But do you know what the leader of an army is, in my tongue?"

"*Edran,*" said the Namer promptly, and laughed. "Drake. Dragon . . ."

After a while he said, "I could chase an etymology on the brink of doom . . . But I think, Azver, that that's where we are. We won't defeat him."

"He has the advantage," Azver said, very dry.

"He does. But, admitting it unlikely, admitting it impossible—if we did defeat him—if he went back into death and left us here alive—what would we do? What comes next?"

After a long time, Azver said, "I have no idea."

"Your leaves and shadows tell you nothing?"

"Change, change," said the Patterner. "Transformation."

He looked up suddenly. The sheep, who had been grouped near the stile, were scurrying off, and someone was coming along the path from the Great House.

"A group of young men," said the Herbal, breathless, as he came to them. "Thorion's army. Coming here. To take the girl. To send her away." He stood and drew breath. "The Doorkeeper was speaking with them when I left. I think—"

"Here he is," said Azver, and the Doorkeeper was there, his smooth, yellow-brown face tranquil as ever.

"I told them," he said, "that if they went out Medra's Gate this day, they'd never go back through it into a house they knew. Some of them were for turning back, then. But the Windkey and the Chanter urged them on. They'll be along soon."

They could hear men's voices in the fields east of the Grove.

Azver went quickly to where Irian lay beside the stream, and the others followed him. She roused up and got to her feet, looking dull and dazed. They were standing around her, a kind of guard, when the group of thirty or more men came past the little house and approached them. They were mostly older students; there were five or six wizard's staffs among the crowd, and the Master Windkey led them. His thin, keen old face looked strained and weary, but he greeted the four mages courteously by their titles.

They greeted him, and Azver took the word— "Come into the Grove, Master Windkey," he said, "and we will wait there for the others of the Nine."

"First we must settle the matter that divides us," said the Windkey.

"That is a stony matter," said the Namer.

"The woman with you defies the Rule of Roke," the Windkey said. "She must leave. A boat is waiting at the dock to take her, and the wind, I can tell you, will stand fair for Way."

"I have no doubt of that, my lord," said Azver, "but I doubt she will go."

"My Lord Patterner, will you defy our Rule and our community, that has been one so long, upholding order against the forces of ruin? Will it be you, of all men, who break the pattern?"

"It is not glass, to break," Azver said. "It is breath, it is fire."

It cost him a great effort to speak.

"It does not know death," he said, but he spoke in his own language, and they did not understand him. He drew closer to Irian. He felt the warmth of her body. She stood staring, in that animal silence, as if she did not understand any of them.

"Lord Thorion has returned from death to save us all," the Windkey said, fiercely and clearly. "He will be Archmage. Under his rule Roke will be as it was. The king will receive the true crown from his hand, and rule with his guidance, as Morred ruled. No witches will defile sacred ground. No dragons will threaten the Inmost Sea. There will be order, safety, and peace."

None of the four mages with Irian answered him. In the silence, the men with him murmured, and a voice among them said, "Let us have the witch."

"No," Azver said, but could say nothing else. He held his staff of willow, but it was only wood in his hand.

Of the four of them, only the Doorkeeper moved and spoke. He took a step forward, looking from one young man to the next and the next. He said, "You trusted me, giving me your names. Will you trust me now?"

"My lord," said one of them with a fine, dark face and a wizard's oaken staff, "we do trust you, and therefore ask you to let the witch go, and peace return."

Irian stepped forward before the Doorkeeper could answer.

"I am not a witch," she said. Her voice sounded high, metallic, after the men's deep voices. "I have no art. No knowledge. I came to learn."

"We do not teach women here," said the Windkey. "You know that."

"I know nothing," Irian said. She took another step forward, facing the mage directly. "Tell me who I am."

"Learn your place, woman," the mage said with cold passion.

"My place," she said, slowly, the words dragging—"my place is on the hill. Where things are what they are. Tell the dead man I will meet him there."

The Windkey stood silent. The group of men muttered, angry, and some of them moved forward. Azver came between her and them, her words releasing him from the paralysis of mind and body that had held him. "Tell Thorion we will meet him on Roke Knoll," he said. "When he comes, we will be there. Now come with me," he said to Irian.

The Namer, the Doorkeeper, and the Herbal followed him with her into the Grove. There was a path for them. But when some of the young men started after them, there was no path.

"Come back," the Windkey said to the young men.

They turned back, uncertain. The low sun was still bright on the fields and the roofs of the Great House, but inside the wood it was all shadows.

"Witchery," they said, "sacrilege, defilement."

"Best come away," said the Master Windkey, his face set and somber, his keen eyes troubled. He set off back to the school, and they straggled after him, arguing and debating in frustration and anger.

They were not far inside the Grove, and still beside the stream, when Irian stopped, turned aside, and crouched down by the enormous, hunching roots of a willow that leaned out over the water. The four mages stood on the path.

"She spoke with the other breath," Azver said.

The Namer nodded.

"So we must follow her?" the Herbal asked.

This time the Doorkeeper nodded. He smiled faintly and said, "So it would seem."

"Very well," said the Herbal, with his patient, troubled look; and he went aside a little, and knelt to look at some small plant or fungus on the forest floor.

Time passed as always in the Grove, not passing at all it seemed, yet gone, the day gone quietly by in a few long breaths, a quivering of leaves, a bird singing far off and another answering it from even farther. Irian stood up slowly. She did not speak, but looked down the path, and then walked down it. The four men followed her.

They came out into the calm, open evening air. The west still held some brightness as they crossed the Thwilburn and walked across the fields to Roke Knoll, which stood up before them in a high dark curve against the sky.

"They're coming," the Doorkeeper said. Men were coming through the gardens and up the path from the Great House, the five mages, many students. Leading them was Thorion the Summoner, tall in his grey cloak, carrying his tall staff of bone-white wood, about which a faint gleam of werelight hovered.

Where the two paths met and joined to wind up to the heights of the Knoll, Thorion stopped and stood waiting for them. Irian strode forward to face him.

"Irian of Way," the Summoner said in his deep, clear voice, "that there may be peace and order, and for the sake of the balance of all things, I bid you now leave this island. We cannot give you what you ask, and for that we ask your forgiveness. But if you seek to stay here you forfeit forgiveness, and must learn what follows on transgression."

She stood up, almost as tall as he, and as straight. She said nothing for a minute and then spoke out in a high, harsh voice. "Come up onto the hill, Thorion," she said.

She left him standing at the waymeet, on level ground, and walked up the hill path for a little way, a few strides. She turned and looked back down at him. "What keeps you from the hill?" she said.

The air was darkening around them. The west was only a dull red line, the eastern sky was shadowy above the sea.

The Summoner looked up at Irian. Slowly he raised his arms and the white staff in the invocation of a spell, speaking in the tongue that all the wizards and mages of Roke had learned, the language of their art, the Language of the Making: "Irian, by your name I summon you and bind you to obey me!"

She hesitated, seeming for a moment to yield, to come to him, and then cried out, "I am not only Irian!"

At that the Summoner ran up towards her, reaching out, lunging at her as if to seize and hold her. They were both on the hill now. She towered above him impossibly, fire breaking forth between them, a flare of red flame in the dusk air, a gleam of red-gold scales, of vast wings—then that was gone, and there was nothing there but the woman standing on the hill path and the tall man bowing down before her, bowing slowly down to earth, and lying on it.

Of them all it was the Herbal, the healer, who was the first to move. He went up the path and knelt down by Thorion. "My lord," he said, "my friend."

Under the huddle of the grey cloak his hands found only a huddle of clothes and dry bones and a broken staff.

"This is better, Thorion," he said, but he was weeping.

The old Namer came forward and said to the woman on the hill, "Who are you?"

"I do not know my other name," she said. She spoke as he had spoken, as she had spoken to the Summoner, in the Language of the Making, the tongue the dragons speak.

She turned away and began to walk on up the hill.

"Irian," said Azver the Patterner, "will you come back to us?"

She halted and let him come up to her. "I will, if you call me," she said.

She reached out and touched his hand. He drew his breath sharply.

"Where will you go?" he said.

"To those who will give me my name. In fire, not water. My people."

"In the west," he said.

She said, "Beyond the west."

She turned away from him and them and went on up the hill in the gathering darkness. As she went farther from them they saw her, all of them, the great gold-mailed flanks, the spiked, coiling tail, the talons, the breath that was bright fire. On the crest of the knoll she paused a while, her long head turning to look slowly round the Isle of Roke, gazing longest at the Grove, only a blur of darkness in darkness now. Then with a rattle like the shaking of sheets of brass the wide, vaned wings opened and the dragon sprang up into the air, circled Roke Knoll once, and flew.

A curl of fire, a wisp of smoke drifted down through the dark air.

Azver the Patterner stood with his left hand holding his right hand, which her touch had burnt. He looked down at the men, who stood silent at the foot of the hill, staring after the dragon. "Well, my friends," he said, "what now?"

Only the Doorkeeper answered. He said, "I think we should go to our house, and open its doors."

A Description of Earthsea

Peoples and Languages

People

The Hardic Lands

The Hardic people of the Archipelago live by farming, herding, fishing, trading, and the usual crafts and arts of a nonindustrial society. Their population is stable and has never overcrowded the limited habitable land available to them. Famine is unknown and poverty seldom acute.

Small islands and villages are generally governed by a more or less democratic council or Parley, headed, or represented in dealings with other groups, by an elected Isleman or Islewoman. In the Reaches there is often no government other than the Isle Parley and the Town Parleys. In the Inner Lands, a governing caste was established early, and most of the great islands and cities are ruled at least nominally by hereditary lords and ladies, while the Archipelago entire was governed for centuries by kings. Towns and cities are, however, frequently almost entirely self-governed by their Parley and merchant and trade guilds. The great guilds, since their network covers all the Inner Lands, answer to no overlord or authority except the King in Havnor.

Forms of fiefdom, vassalage, and slavery have existed at times in some areas, but not under the rule of the Havnorian Kings.

The existence of magic as a recognised, effective power wielded by certain individuals, but not by all, shapes and influences all the institutions of the Hardic peoples, so that, much as ordinary life in the Archipelago seems to resemble that of nonindustrial peoples elsewhere, there are almost immeasurable differences. One of these differences may be, or may be indicated by, the lack of any kind of institutionalised religion. Superstition is as common as it is anywhere, but there are no gods, no cults, no formal worship of any kind. Ritual occurs only in traditional offerings at the sites of the Old Powers, in the great, universally celebrated annual festivals such as Sunreturn and the Long Dance, in the speaking and singing of the traditional songs and epics at these festivals, and, perhaps, in the performance of spells of magic.

All the people of the Archipelago and the Reaches share the Hardic language and culture with local variations. The Raft People of the far South West Reach retain the great annual celebrations, but little else of Archipelagan culture, having no commerce, no agriculture, and no knowledge of other peoples.

Most people of the Archipelago have brown or red-brown skin, black straight hair, and dark eyes; the predominant body type is short, slender, small-boned, but fairly muscular and well-fleshed. In the East and South Reaches people tend to be taller, heavier boned, and darker. Many Southerners have very dark brown skin. Most Archipelagan men have little or no facial hair.

The people of Osskil, Rogma, and Borth are lighter-skinned than others in the Archipelago, and often have brown or even blond hair and light eyes; the men are often bearded. Their language and some of their beliefs are closer to Kargish than to Hardic. These far Northerners probably descend from Kargs who, after settling the four great Eastern lands, sailed back to the West about two thousand years ago.

The Kargad Lands

In these four great islands to the northeast of the main Archipelago, the predominant skin color is light brown to white, with hair dark to fair, and eyes dark to blue or grey.

Not much mixing of the Kargish and Archipelagan skin-color types has taken place except on Osskil, since the North Reach is isolated and thinly populated, and the Kargad people have held themselves apart from and often in enmity towards the Archipelagans for two or three millennia.

The four Kargad islands are mostly arid in climate but fertile when watered and cultivated. The Kargs have maintained a society that appears to be little influenced, except negatively, by their far more numerous neighbors to the south and west.

Among the Kargs the power of magic appears to be very rare as a native gift, perhaps because it was neglected or actively suppressed by their society and government. Except as an evil to be dreaded and shunned, magic plays no recognised part in their society. This inability or refusal to practice magic puts the Kargs at a disadvantage with the Archipelagans in almost every respect, which may explain why they have generally held themselves aloof from trade or any kind of interchange, other than piratical raids and invasions of the nearer islands of the South Reach and around the Gontish Sea.

DRAGONS

Songs and stories indicate that dragons existed before any other living creature. The Old Hardic kennings or euphemisms for the word *dragon* are Firstborn, Eldest, Elder Children. (The words for the firstborn child of a family in Osskilian, *akhad,* and in Kargish, *gadda,* are derived from the word *haath,* "dragon," in the Old Speech.)

Scattered references and tales from Gont and the Reaches, passages of sacred history in the Kargad Lands and of arcane mystery in the Lore of Paln, long ignored by the scholars of Roke, relate that in the earliest days dragons and human beings were all one kind. Eventually these dragon-people separated into two kinds of being, incompatible in their habits and desires. Perhaps a long geographical separation caused a gradual natural divergence, a differentiation of species. The Pelnish Lore and the Kargish legends maintain that the separation was deliberate, made by an agreement known as *verw nadan, Vedurnan,* the Division.

These legends are best preserved in Hur-at-Hur, the easternmost of the Kargad Lands, where dragons have degenerated into animals without high intelligence. Yet it is in Hur-at-Hur that people keep the most vivid conviction of the original kinship of human and dragon kind. And with these tales of ancient times come stories of recent days about dragons who take human form, humans who take dragon form, beings who are in fact both human and dragon.

However the Division came about, from the beginning of historical time human beings have lived in the main Archipelago and the Kargad Lands east of it, while the dragons kept to the westernmost isles—and beyond. People have puzzled at their choosing the empty sea for their domain, since dragons are "creatures of wind and fire," who drown if plunged under the sea. But they have no need to touch down either on water or on earth; they live on the wing, aloft in air, sunlight, starlight. The only use a dragon has for the ground is some kind of rocky place where it can lay its eggs and rear the drakelets. The small, barren islets of the farthest West Reach suffice for this.

The Creation of Éa contains no clear references to an original unity and eventual separation of dragons and humans, but this may be because the poem in its presumed original form, in the Language of the Making, dated back to a time before the separation. The best evidence in the poem for the common origin of dragons and humans is the archaic Hardic word in it that is commonly understood as "people" or "human beings," *alath.* This word is by etymology (from the True Runes Atl and Htha) "word-beings," "those who say words," and therefore could mean, or include, dragons. Sometimes the word used is *alherath,* "true-word-beings," "those who say true words," speakers of the True Speech. This could mean human wizards, or dragons, or both. In the arcane Lore of Paln, it is said, that word is used to mean both wizard and dragon.

Dragons are born knowing the True Speech, or, as Ged put it, "the dragon and the speech of the dragon are one." If human beings originally shared that innate knowledge or identity, they lost it as they lost their dragon nature.

LANGUAGES

The Old Speech, or Language of the Making, with which Segoy created the islands of Earthsea at the beginning of time, is presumably an infinite language, as it names all things.

This language is innate to dragons, not to humans, as said above. There are exceptions. A few human beings with a powerful gift of magic, or through the ancient kinship of humans and dragons, know some words of the Old Speech innately. But the very great majority of people must learn the Old Speech. Hardic practitioners of the art magic learn it from their teachers. Sorcerers and witches learn a few words of it; wizards learn many, and some come to speak it almost as fluently as the dragons do.

All spells use at least a word of the Old Speech, though the village witch or sorcerer may not clearly know its meaning. Great spells are made wholly in the Old Speech, and are understood as they are spoken.

The Hardic language of the Archipelago, the Osskili tongue of Osskil, and the Kargish tongue, are all remote descendants of the Old

Speech. None of these languages serves for the making of spells of magic.

The people of the Archipelago speak Hardic. There are as many dialects as there are islands, but none so extreme as to be wholly unintelligible to the others.

Osskili, spoken in Osskil and two islands northwest of it, has more affinities to Kargish than to Hardic. Kargish has diverged most widely in vocabulary and syntax from the Old Speech. Most of its speakers (like most Hardic speakers) do not realise that their languages have a common ancestry. Archipelagan scholars are aware of it, but most Kargs would deny it, since they have confused Hardic with the Old Speech, in which spells are cast, and thus fear and despise all Archipelagan speech as malevolent sorcery.

WRITING

Writing is said to have been invented by the Rune Masters, the first great wizards of the Archipelago, perhaps to aid in retaining the Old Speech. The dragons have no writing.

There are two entirely different kinds of writing in Earthsea: the True Runes and runic writing.

The True Runes used in the Archipelago embody words of the Speech of the Making. True Runes are not symbols only, but reifactors: they can be used to bring a thing or condition into being or bring about an event. To write such a rune is to act. The power of the action varies with the circumstances. Most of the True Runes are found only in ancient texts and lore-books, and used only by wizards trained in their use; but a good many of them, such as the symbol written on the door lintel to protect a house from fire, are in common use, familiar to unlearned people.

Long after the invention of the True Runes, a related but nonmagical runic writing was developed for the Hardic language. This writing does not affect reality any more than any writing does; that is to say, indirectly, but considerably.

It is said that Segoy first wrote the True Runes in fire on the wind, so that they are coeval with the Language of the Making. But this may not be so, since the dragons do not use them, and if they recognise them, do not admit it.

Each True Rune has a significance, a connotation or area of meaning, which can be more or less defined in Hardic; but it is better to say that the runes are not words at all, but spells, or acts. Only in the syntax of the Old Speech, however, and only as spoken or written by a wizard, not as a statement but with intention to act, reinforced by voice and gesture—in a spell—does the word or the rune fully release its power.

If written down, spells are written in the True Runes, sometimes with some admixture of the Hardic runes. To write in the True Runes, as to speak the Old Speech, is to guarantee the truth of what one says—if one is human. Human beings cannot lie in that language. Dragons can; or so the dragons say; and if they are lying, does that not prove that what they say is true?

The spoken name of a True Rune may be the word it signifies in the Old Speech, or it may be one of the connotations of the rune translated into Hardic. The names of commonly used runes such as Pirr (used to protect from fire, wind, and madness), Sifl ("speed well"), Simn ("work well") are used without ceremony by ordinary people speaking Hardic; but practitioners of magic speak even such well-known, often used names with caution, since they are in fact words in the Old Speech, and may influence events in unintended or unexpected ways.

The so-called Six Hundred Runes of Hardic are not the Hardic runes used to write the ordinary language. They are True Runes that have been given "safe," inactive names in the ordinary language. Their true names in the Old Speech must be memorised in silence. The ambitious student of wizardry will go on to learn the "Further Runes," the "Runes of Éa," and many others. If the Old Speech is endless, so are the runes.

Ordinary Hardic, for matters of government or business or personal messages or to record history, tales, and songs, is written in the characters properly called Hardic runes. Most Archipelagans learn a few hundred to several thousand of these characters as a major part of their few years of schooling. Spoken or written, Hardic is useless for casting spells.

Literature and the Sources of History

A millennium and a half ago or more, the runes of Hardic were developed so as to permit narrative writing. From that time on, *The Creation of Éa, The Winter Carol,* the Deeds, the Lays, and the Songs, all of which began as sung or spoken texts, were written down and preserved as texts. They continue to exist in both forms. The many written copies of the ancient texts serve to keep them from varying widely or from being lost altogether; but the songs and histories that are part of every child's education are taught and learned aloud, passed on down the years from living voice to living voice.

Old Hardic differs in vocabulary and pronunciation from the current speech, but the rote learning and regular speaking and hearing of the classics keeps the archaic language meaningful (and probably puts some brake on linguistic drift in daily speech), while the Hardic runes, like Chinese characters, can accommodate widely varying pronunciations and shifts of meaning.

Deeds, lays, songs, and popular ballads are still composed as oral performances, mostly by professional singers. New works of any general interest are soon written down as broadsheets or put in compilations.

Whether performed or read silently, all such poems and songs are consciously valued for their content, not for their literary qualities, which range from high to nil. Loose regular meter, alliteration, stylised phrasing, and structuring by repetition are the principal poetic devices. Content includes mythic, epic, and historical narrative, geographical descriptions, practical observations concerning nature, agriculture, sea lore, and crafts, cautionary tales and parables, philosophical, visionary, and spiritual poetry, and love songs. The deeds and lays are usually chanted, the ballads sung, often with a percussion accompaniment; professional chanters and singers may sing with the harp, the viol, drums, and other instruments. The songs generally have less narrative content, and many are valued and preserved mostly for the tune.

Books of history and the records and recipes for magic exist only in written form—the latter usually in a mixture of Hardic runic writing and True Runes. Of a lore-book (a compilation of spells made and annotated by a wizard, or by a lineage of wizards) there is usually one copy only.

It is often a matter of considerable importance that the words of these lore-books *not* be spoken aloud.

The Osskili use the Hardic runes to write their language, since they trade mostly with Hardic-speaking lands.

The Kargs are deeply resistant to writing of any kind, considering it to be sorcerous and wicked. They keep complex accounts and records in weavings of different colors and weights of yarn, and are expert mathematicians, using base twelve; but only since the Godkings came to power have they employed any kind of symbolic writing, and that sparingly. Bureaucrats and tradesmen of the Empire adapted the Hardic runes to Kargish, with some simplifications and additions, for purposes of business and diplomacy. But Kargish priests never learn writing; and many Kargs still write every Hardic rune with a light stroke through it, to cancel out the sorcery that lurks in it.

History

Note on dates: Many islands have their own local count of years. The most widely used dating system in the Archipelago, which stems from the Havnorian Tale, *makes the year Morred took the throne the first year of history. By this system, "present time" in the account you are reading is the Archipelagan year 1058.*

The Beginnings

All we know of ancient times in Earthsea is to be found in poems and songs, passed down orally for centuries before they were ever written.

The Creation of Éa, the oldest and most sacred poem, is at least two thousand years old in the Hardic language; its original version may have existed millennia before that. Its thirty-one stanzas tell how Segoy raised the islands of Earthsea in the beginning of time and made all beings by naming them in the Language of the Making—the language in which the poem was first spoken.

The ocean, however, is older than the islands; so say the songs.

Before bright Éa was, before Segoy
bade the islands be,
the wind of dawn blew on the sea . . .

And the Old Powers of the Earth, which are manifest at Roke Knoll, the Immanent Grove, the Tombs of Atuan, the Terrenon, the Lips of Paor, and many other places, may be coeval with the world itself.

It may be that Segoy is or was one of the Old Powers of the Earth. It may be that Segoy is a name for the Earth itself. Some think all dragons, or certain dragons, or certain people, are manifestations of Segoy. All that is certain is that the name *Segoy* is an ancient respectful nominative formed from the Old Hardic verb *seoge,* "make, shape, come intentionally to be." From the same root comes the noun *esege,* "creative force, breath, poetry."

The Creation of Éa is the foundation of education in the Archipelago. By the age of six or seven, all children have heard the poem and most have begun to memorise it. An adult who doesn't know it by heart, so as to be able to speak or sing it with others and teach it to children, is considered grossly ignorant. It is taught in winter and spring, and spoken and sung entire every year at the Long Dance, the celebration of the solstice of summer.

A quotation from it stands at the head of *A Wizard of Earthsea*:

Only in silence the word,
only in dark the light,
only in dying life:
bright the hawk's flight
on the empty sky.

The beginning of the first stanza is quoted in *Tehanu*:

The making from the unmaking,
the ending from the beginning,
who shall know surely?
What we know is the doorway between them
that we enter departing.
Among all beings ever returning,
the eldest, the Doorkeeper, Segoy . . .

and the last line of the first stanza:

Then from the foam bright Éa broke.

History of the Archipelago

The Kings of Enlad

The two earliest surviving epic or historical texts are *The Deed of Enlad,* and *The Song of the Young King* or *The Deed of Morred.*

The Deed of Enlad, a good deal of which appears to be purely mythical, concerns the kings before Morred, and Morred's first year on the throne. The capital city of these rulers was Berila, on the island of Enlad.

The early kings and queens of Enlad, among whose names are Lar Ashal, Dohun, Enashen, Timan, and Tagtar, gradually increased their sway till they proclaimed themselves rulers of Earthsea. Their reign extended no farther south than Ilien and did not include Felkway in the east, Paln and Semel in the west, or Osskil in the north, but they did send explorers out all over the Inmost Sea and into the Reaches. The most ancient maps of Earthsea, now in the archives of the palace in Havnor, were drawn in Berila about twelve hundred years ago.

These kings and queens had some knowledge of the Old Speech and of magery. Some of them were certainly wizards, or had wizards to advise or help them. But magic in *The Deed of Enlad* is an erratic force, not to be relied on. Morred was the first man, and the first king, to be called Mage.

Morred

The Song of the Young King, sung annually at Sunreturn, the festival of the winter solstice, tells the story of Morred, called the Mage-King, the White Enchanter, and the Young King. Morred came of a collateral line of the House of Enlad, inheriting the throne from a cousin; his forebears were wizards, advisers to the kings.

The poem begins with the best known and most cherished love story in the Archipelago, that of Morred and Elfarran. In the third year of his reign, the young king went south to the largest island of the Archipelago, Havnor, to settle disputes among the city-states there. Returning in his "oarless longship," he came to the island Soléa and there saw Elfarran, the Islewoman or Lady of Soléa, "in the orchards in the spring." He did not continue on to Enlad, but stayed with Elfarran. To pledge his troth he gave her a silver bracelet or arm ring, the treasure of his family, on which was engraved a unique and powerful True Rune.

Morred and Elfarran married, and the poem describes their reign as a brief golden age, the foundation and touchstone of ethic and governance thereafter.

Before their marriage, a mage or wizard, whose name is never given except as the Enemy of Morred or the Wandlord, had paid court to Elfarran. Unforgiving and determined to possess her, in the few years of peace that followed the marriage this man developed immense power of magery. After five years he came forth and announced, in the words of the poem,

If Elfarran be not my own, I will unsay Segoy's word,
I will unmake the islands, the white waves will whelm all.

He had power to raise huge waves on the sea, and to stop the tide or bring it early; and his voice could enchant whole populations, bringing all who heard him under his control. So he turned Morred's people against him. Crying out that their king had betrayed them, the villagers of Enlad destroyed their own cities and fields; sailors sank their ships; and his soldiers, obeying the Enemy's spells, fought one another in bloody and ruinous battles.

While Morred sought to free his people from these spells and to confront his enemy, Elfarran returned with their year-old child to her native island, Soléa, where her own powers would be strongest. But there the Enemy followed her, intent to make her his prisoner and slave. She took refuge at the Springs of Ensa, where, with her knowledge of the Old Powers of the place, she could withstand the Enemy and force him off the island. "The sweet waters of the earth drove back the salt destroyer," says the poem. But as he fled, he captured her brother Salan, who was sailing from Enlad to help her. Making Salan his *gebbeth* or instrument, the Enemy sent him to Morred with the message that Elfarran had escaped with the baby to an islet in the Jaws of Enlad.

Trusting the messenger, Morred entered the trap. He barely escaped with his life. The Enemy pursued him from the east to the west of Enlad in a trail of ruin. On the Plains of Enlad, meeting the companions who had stayed loyal to him, most of them sailors who had brought their ships to Enlad to aid him, Morred turned and gave battle. The Enemy would not confront him directly, but sent Morred's own spell-bound warriors to fight him, and worse, sent sorceries that shriveled up the bodies of his men till they "living, seemed the black thirst-dead of the desert." To spare his people, Morred withdrew.

As he left the battlefield it began to rain, and he saw his enemy's true name written in raindrops in the dust.

Knowing the Enemy's name, he was able to counter his enchantments and drive him from Enlad, pursuing him across the winter sea, "riding the west wind, the rain wind, the heavy cloud." Each had met his match, and in their final confrontation, somewhere in the Sea of Éa, both perished.

In the rage of his agony the Enemy raised up a great wave and sent it speeding to overwhelm the island of Soléa. Elfarran knew this, as she knew the moment of Morred's death. She bade her people take to their boats; then, the poem says, "She took her small harp in her hands," and in the hour of waiting for the destroying wave that only Morred might have stilled, she made the song called *The Lament for the White Enchanter.* The island was drowned beneath the sea, and Elfarran with it. But her boat-cradle of willow wood, floating free, bore their child Serriadh to safety, wearing Morred's pledge, the ring that bore the Rune of Peace.

On maps of the Archipelago, the island Soléa is signified by a white space or a whirlpool.

After Morred, seven more kings and queens ruled from Enlad, and the realm increased steadily in size and prosperity.

The Kings of Havnor

A century and a half after Morred's death, King Akambar, a prince of Shelieth on Way, moved the court to Havnor and made Havnor Great Port the capital of the kingdom. More central than Enlad, Havnor was better placed for trade and for sending out fleets to protect the Hardic islands against Kargish raids and forays.

The history of the Fourteen Kings of Havnor (actually six kings and eight queens, ~150–400) is told in the *Havnorian Lay.* Tracing descent both through the male and the female lines, and intermarrying with various noble houses of the Archipelago, the royal house embraced five principalities: the House of Enlad, the oldest, tracing direct descent from Morred and Serriadh; the Houses of Shelieth, Éa, and Havnor; and lastly the House of Ilien. Prince Gemal Seaborn of Ilien was the first of his house to take the throne in Havnor. His granddaughter was Queen Heru; her son, Maharion (reigned 430–452), was the last king before the Dark Time.

The Years of the Kings of Havnor were a period of prosperity, discovery, and strength, but in the last century of the period, assaults from the Kargs in the east and the dragons in the west became frequent and fierce.

Kings, lords, and Islemen charged with defending the islands of the Archipelago came to rely increasingly on wizards to fend off dragons and Kargish fleets. In the *Havnorian Lay* and *The Deed of the Dragonlords,* as the tale goes on, the names and exploits of these wizards begin to eclipse those of the kings.

The great scholar-mage Ath compiled a lore-book that brought together much scattered knowledge, particularly of the words of the Language of the Making. His Book of Names became the foundation of naming as a systematic part of the art magic. Ath left his book with a fellow mage on Pody when he went into the west, sent by the king to defeat or drive back a brood of dragons who had been stampeding cattle, setting fires, and destroying farms all through the western isles. Somewhere west of Ensmer, Ath confronted the great dragon Orm. Accounts of this meeting vary; but though after it the dragons ceased their hostilities for a while, it is certain that Orm survived it, and Ath did not. His book, lost for centuries, is now in the Isolate Tower on Roke.

The food of dragons is said to be light, or fire; they kill in rage, to defend their young, or for sport, but never eat their kill. Since time immemorial, until the reign of Heru, they had used only the outmost isles of the West Reach—which may have been the easternmost borders of their own realm—for meeting and breeding, and had seldom even been seen by most of the islanders. Naturally irritable and arrogant, the dragons may have felt threatened by the increasing population and prosperity of the Inner Lands, which brought constant boat traffic even out in the West Reach. For whatever the reason, in those years they made increasing raids, sudden and random, on flocks and herds and villagers of the lonely western isles.

A tale of the *Vedurnan* or Division, known in Hur-at-Hur, says:

Men chose the yoke,
dragons the wing.
Men to own,
dragons no thing.

That is, human beings chose to have possessions and dragons chose not to. But, as there are ascetics among humans, some dragons are greedy for shining things, gold, jewels; one was Yevaud, who sometimes came among people in human form, and who made the rich Isle of Pendor into a dragon nursery, until driven back into the west by Ged. But the marauding dragons of the *Lay* and the songs seem to have been moved not so much by greed as by anger, a sense of having been cheated, betrayed.

The deeds and lays that tell of raids by dragons and counterforays by wizards portray the dragons as pitiless as any wild animal, terrifying, unpredictable, yet intelligent, sometimes wiser than the wizards. Though they speak the True Speech, they are endlessly devious. Some of them clearly enjoy battles of wits with wizards, "splitting arguments with a forked tongue." Like human beings, all but the greatest of them conceal their true names. In the lay *Hasa's Voyage,* the dragons appear as formidable but feeling beings, whose anger at the invading human fleet is justified by their love of their own desolate domain. They address the hero:

Sail home to the houses of the sunrise, Hasa.
Leave to our wings the long winds of the west,
leave us the air-sea, the unknown, the utmost . . .

Maharion and Erreth-Akbe

Queen Heru, called the Eagle, inherited the throne from her father, Denggemal of the House of Ilien. Her consort Aiman was of the House of Morred. When she had ruled thirty years she gave the crown to their son Maharion.

Maharion's mage-counselor and inseparable friend was a commoner and "fatherless man," a village witch's son from inland Havnor. The most beloved hero of the Archipelago, his story is told in *The Deed of Erreth-Akbe,* which bards sing at the Long Dance of midsummer.

Erreth-Akbe's gifts in magic became apparent when he was still a boy. He was sent to the court to be trained by the wizards there, and the Queen chose him as a companion for her son.

Maharion and Erreth-Akbe became "heart's brothers." They spent ten years together fighting the Kargs, whose occasional forays from the East had in recent times become a slave-taking, colonising invasion. Venway, Torheven and the Torikles, Spevy, Perregal, and parts of Gont were under Kargish dominion for a generation or longer. At Shelieth on Way, Erreth-Akbe worked a great magic against the Kargish forces, who had landed in "a thousand ships" on Waymarsh and were swarming across the mainland. Using an invocation of the Old Powers called the Waterlore (perhaps the same that Elfarran had used on Soléa against the Enemy), he turned the waters of the Fountains of Shelieth—sacred springs and pools in the gardens of the Lords of Way—into a flood that swept the invaders back to the seacoast, where Maharion's army awaited them. No ship of the fleet returned to Karego-At.

Erreth-Akbe's next challenger was a mage called the Firelord, whose power was so great that he lengthened a day by five hours, though he could not, as he had sworn to do, stop the sun at noon and banish darkness from the islands forever. The Firelord took dragon form to fight Erreth-Akbe, but was defeated at last, at the cost of the forests and cities of Ilien, which he set afire as he fought.

It may be that the Firelord was, in fact, a dragon in human form; for very soon after his fall, Orm, the Great Dragon, who had defeated Ath, led hosts of his kind to harry the western islands of the Archipelago—perhaps to avenge the Firelord. These fiery flights caused great terror, and hundreds of boats carried people fleeing from Paln and Semel to the Inner Islands; but the dragons were not doing as much damage as the Kargs, and Maharion judged the urgent danger lay in the east. While he himself went west to fight dragons, he sent Erreth-Akbe east to try to establish peace with the King of the Kargad Lands.

Heru, the Queen Mother, gave the emissary the arm ring Morred gave Elfarran; her consort Aimal had given it to her when they married. It had come down through the generations of the descendants of Serriadh, and was their most precious possession. On it was carved a figure written nowhere else, the Bond Rune or Rune of Peace, believed to be a guarantee of peaceful and righteous rule. "Let the Kargish king wear Morred's ring," the Queen Mother said. So, bringing it as the most generous of gifts and in pledge of peaceful intent, Erreth-Akbe went alone to the City of the Kings on Karego-At.

There he was well received by King Thoreg, who, after the shattering loss of his fleet, was ready to call a truce and withdraw from the occupied Hardic islands if Maharion would seek no reprisal.

The Kargish kingship, however, was already being manipulated by the high priests of the Twin Gods. Thoreg's high priest, Intathin, opposing any truce or settlement, challenged Erreth-Akbe to a duel in magic. Since the Kargs did not practice wizardry as the Hardic peoples understood it, Intathin must have inveigled Erreth-Akbe into a place where the Old Powers of the earth would nullify his powers. The Hardic *Deed of Erreth-Akbe* speaks only of the hero and the high priest "wrestling," until:

the weakness of the old darkness came into Erreth-Akbe's limbs,
the silence of the mother darkness into his mind.
Long he lay, forgetful of bright fame and brotherhood,
long, and on his breast lay the rune-ring broken.

The daughter of "the wise king Thoreg" rescued Erreth-Akbe from this trance or imprisoning spell and restored him his strength. He gave her the half of the Ring of Peace that remained to him. (From her it passed through her descendants for over five hundred years to the last heirs of Thoreg, a brother and sister exiled on a deserted island of the East Reach; and the sister gave it to Ged.) Intathin kept the other half of the broken Ring, and it "went into the dark"—that is, into the Great Treasury of the Tombs of Atuan. (There Ged found it, and rejoining the two halves and with them the lost Rune of Peace, he and Tenar brought the Ring home to Havnor.)

The Kargish version of the story, told as a sacred recital by the priesthood, says that Intathin defeated Erreth-Akbe, who "lost his staff and amulet and power" and crept back to Havnor a broken man. But wizards carried no staff in those years, and Erreth-Akbe certainly was an unbroken man and a powerful mage when he faced the dragon Orm.

King Maharion sought peace and never found it. While Erreth-Akbe was in Karego-At (which may have been a period of years), the depredations of the dragons increased. The Inward Isles were troubled by refugees fleeing the western lands and by interruptions to shipping and trade, since the dragons had taken to setting fire to boats that went west of Hosk, and harried ships even in the Inmost Sea. All the wizards and armed men Maharion could command went out to fight the dragons, and he went with them himself four times; but swords and arrows were little use against armored, fire-spouting, flying enemies. Paln was "a plain of charcoal," and villages and towns in the west of Havnor had been burnt to the ground. The king's wizards had spell-caught and killed several dragons over the Pelnish Sea, which probably increased the dragons' ire. Just as Erreth-Akbe returned, the Great Dragon Orm flew to the City of Havnor and threatened the towers of the king's palace with fire.

Erreth-Akbe, sailing into the bay "with sails worn transparent by the eastern winds," could not pause to "embrace his heart's brother or greet his home." Taking dragon form himself, he flew to battle with Orm over Mount Onn. "Flame and fire in the midnight air" could be seen from the palace in Havnor. They flew north, Erreth-Akbe in pursuit. Over the sea near Taon, Orm turned again and this time wounded the mage so that he had to come down to earth and take his own form. He came, with the dragon now following him, to the Old Island, Éa, the first land Segoy raised from the sea. On that sacred and powerful soil, he and Orm met. Ceasing their battle, they spoke as equals, agreeing to end the enmity of their races.

Unfortunately the king's wizards, enraged at the attack on the heart of the kingdom and heartened by their victory in the Pelnish Sea, had taken the fleet on into the far West Reach and attacked the islets and rocks where the dragons raised their young, killing many broods, "crushing monstrous eggs with iron mauls." Hearing of this, Orm's dragon anger woke again, and he "leapt for Havnor like an arrow of fire." (Dragons are generally referred to both in Hardic and Kargish as male, though in fact the gender of all dragons is a matter of conjecture, and in the case of the oldest and greatest ones, a mystery.)

Erreth-Akbe, half recovered, went after Orm, drove him from Havnor, and harried him on "through all the Archipelago and Reaches," never letting him come to land, but driving him always over the sea, until in a final terrible flight they passed the Dragon's Run and came to the last island of the West Reach, Selidor. There, on the outer beach, both exhausted, they faced each other and fought, "talon and fire and word and sword," until:

> *their blood ran mingled, making the sand red.*
> *Their breath ceased. Their bodies by the loud sea*
> *lay entangled. They entered death's land together.*

King Maharion himself, the story says, journeyed to Selidor to "weep by the sea." He retrieved Erreth-Akbe's sword and set it atop the highest tower of his palace.

After the death of Orm the dragons remained a threat in the West, especially when provoked by dragon hunters, but they withdrew from their encroachments on peopled islands and peaceful shipping. Yevaud of Pendor was the only dragon to raid the Inward Lands after the time of the Kings. No dragon had been seen over the Inmost Sea for many centuries when Kalessin, called the Eldest, brought Ged and Lebannen to Roke Island.

Maharion died a few years after Erreth-Akbe, having seen no peace established, and much unrest and dissent within his kingdom. It was widely said that since the Ring of Peace was lost there could be no true king of Earthsea. Mortally wounded in battle against the rebel lord Gehis of the Havens, Maharion spoke a prophecy: *"He shall inherit my throne who has crossed the dark land living and come to the far shores of the day."*

THE DARK TIME, THE HAND, AND ROKE SCHOOL

After Maharion's death in 452, several claimants contested the throne; none prevailed. Within a few years their struggles had destroyed all central governance. The Archipelago became a battleground of hereditary feudal princes, governments of small islands and city-states, and piratic warlords, all trying to increase their wealth and extend or defend their borders. Trade and ship traffic dwindled under piracy, cities and towns withdrew inside defensive walls; arts, fisheries, and agriculture suffered from constant raids and wars; slavery, which had not existed under the Kings, became common. Magic was the primary weapon in forays and battles. Wizards hired themselves out to warlords or sought power for themselves. Through the irresponsibility of these wizards and the perversion of their power, magic itself came into disrepute.

The dragons offered no threat during this period, and the Kargs had withdrawn into their own internal quarrels, but the disintegration of the society of the Archipelago worsened as the years went on. Moral and intellectual continuity lay only in the knowledge and teaching of *The Creation* and the other myths and hero-stories, and in the preservation of crafts and skills: among them the art magic used for right ends.

The Hand, a loose-knit league or community concerned principally with the understanding and the ethical use and teaching of magic, was established by men and women on Roke Island about a hundred and fifty years after Maharion's death. Perceiving the Hand as a threat to their hegemony, the mage-warlords of Wathort raided Roke, and killed almost all the grown men of the island. But the Hand had already stretched out to other islands all around the Inmost Sea. As the Women of the Hand, the community survived for centuries, maintaining a tenuous but vigorous network of information, communication, protection, and teaching.

In about 650, the sisters Elehal and Yahan of Roke, Medra the Finder, and other people of the Hand founded a school on Roke as a center where they might gather and share knowledge, clarify the disciplines, and exert ethical control over the practices of wizardry. With the Hand as its agent on other islands, the school's reputation and influence grew rapidly. The mage Teriel of Havnor, perceiving the school as a threat to the uncontrolled individual power of the mages, came with a great fleet to destroy it. He was destroyed, and his fleet scattered. This first victory went far to establish a reputation of invulnerability for the school on Roke.

Under Roke's steadily growing influence, wizardry was shaped into a coherent body of knowledge, its use increasingly controlled by moral and political purpose. Wizards trained at the school went to other islands of the Archipelago to work against warlords, pirates, and feuding nobles, preventing raids and forays, imposing penalties and settlements, enforcing boundaries, and protecting individuals, farms, towns, cities, and shipping, until social order was re-established. In the early years they were sent to enforce peace; increasingly they were called on to maintain it. While the throne in Havnor remained empty, for over two hundred years Roke School served effectively as the central government of the Archipelago.

The power of the Archmage of Roke was in many respects that of a king. Ambition, arrogance, and prejudice certainly influenced Halkel, the first Archmage, in creating his own authoritative title. Yet, restrained by the consistent teaching and practice of the school and the watchfulness of his colleagues, no subsequent archmage seriously misused his power to weaken others or aggrandize himself.

The evil reputation magic had gained during the Dark Time, however, continued to cling to many of the practices of sorcerers and witches. Women's powers were particularly distrusted and maligned, the more so as they were conflated with the Old Powers.

Throughout Earthsea, various springs, caves, hills, stones, and woods were and always had been sites of concentrated power and sacredness. All were locally feared or venerated; some were known far and wide.

Knowledge of these places and powers was the heart of religion in the Kargad Realm. In the Archipelago, the lore of the Old Powers was still part of the profound, common basis of thought and reverence. On all the islands, the arts mostly practiced by witches, such as midwifery, healing, animal husbandry, dousing, mining and metallurgy, planting and growing spells, love spells, and so on, often invoked or drew upon the Old Powers. But the learned wizards of Roke had generally come to distrust the ancient practices and made no appeal to the "Powers of the Mother." Only in Paln did wizards combine the two practices, in the arcane, esoteric, and reputedly dangerous Pelnish Lore.

Though like any power they could be perverted to evil use in the service of ambition (as was the Terrenon Stone in Osskil), the Old Powers were inherently sacral and pre-ethical. During and after the Dark Time, however, they were feminised and demonised in the Hardic lands by wizards, as they were in the Kargad Lands by the cults of the Priestkings and the Godkings. So by the eighth century, in the Inner Lands of the Archipelago, only village women kept up rituals and offerings at the old sites. They were despised or abused for doing so. Wizards kept clear of such places. On Roke, itself the center of the Old Powers in all Earthsea, the profoundest manifestations of those powers—Roke Knoll and the Immanent Grove—were never spoken of as such. Only the Patterners, who lived all their lives in the Grove, served to link human arts and acts to the older sacredness of the earth, reminding the wizards and mages that their power was not theirs, but lent to them.

History of the Kargad Lands

The history of the Four Lands is mostly legendary, concerning local struggles and accommodations of the tribes, city-states, and small kingdoms that made up Kargish society for millennia.

Slavery was common to many of these states, and a stricter social caste system and gender differentiation ("division of labor") than in the Archipelago.

Religion was a unifying element even among the most warlike tribes. There were hundreds of Truce Places on the Four Lands, where no warfare or dispute was permitted. Kargish religion was a domestic and community worship of the Old Powers, the chthonic or gaean forces manifest as spirits of place. They were worshiped at the site and at home altars with offerings of flowers, oil, food, dances, races, sacrifices, carvings, songs, music, and silence. Worship was both casual and ritual, private and communal. There was no priesthood; any adult could perform the ceremonies and teach children to do so. This ancient spiritual practice has continued, unofficially and sometimes in hiding, under the newer, institutional religions of the Twin Gods and the Godking.

Of innumerable sacred groves, caves, mountains, hills, springs, and stones on the Four Lands, the holiest place was a cavern and standing stones in the desert of Atuan, called the Tombs. It was a center of pilgrimage from the earliest recorded times, and the kings of Atuan and later of Hupun maintained a hostel there for all who came to worship.

Six to seven hundred years ago a sky-god religion began to spread across the islands, a development of the worship of the Twin Gods Atwah and Wuluah, originally heroes of a desert saga from Hur-at-Hur. A Sky Father was added as head of the pantheon, and a priestly caste developed to lead the rites. Without suppressing the worship of the Old Powers, the priests of the Twin Gods and the Sky Father began to professionalise religion, managing the rituals and festivals, building increasingly costly temples, and controlling public ceremonies such as marriages, funerals, and the installation of officials.

The hierarchic and centralising tendency of this religion lent support at first to the ambition of the Kings of Hupun on Karego-At. By force of arms and diplomatic maneuvering, the House of Hupun within a century or so conquered or absorbed most of the other Kargad kingdoms, of which there had been more than two hundred.

When (in the year 440, by Hardic count) Erreth-Akbe came to make peace between the Archipelago and the Kargad Lands, bearing the Bond Ring as pledge of his king's sincerity, he came to Hupun as the capital of the Kargad Empire and treated with King Thoreg as its ruler.

But for some decades the kings of Hupun had been in conflict with the high priest and his followers in Awabath, the Holy City, fifty miles from Hupun. The priests of the Twin Gods were in the process of wresting power from the kings and making Awabath not only the religious but the political center of the country. Erreth-Akbe's visit seems to have coincided with the final shift of power from the kings to the priests. King Thoreg received him with honor, but Intathin the High Priest fought with him, defeated or deceived him, and for a time imprisoned him. The Ring that was to bond the two kingdoms was broken.

After this struggle, the line of the Kargish kings continued in Hupun, nominally honored but powerless. The Four Lands were governed from Awabath. The high priests of the Twin Gods became Priestkings.

In the year 840 of the Archipelagan count, one of the two Priest-kings poisoned the other and declared himself to be the incarnation of the Sky Father, the Godking, to be worshiped in the flesh. Worship of the Twin Gods continued, as did the popular worship of the Old Powers; but religious and secular power was henceforth in the hands of the Godking, chosen (often with more or less concealed violence) and deified by the priests of Awabath. The Four Lands were declared to be the Empire of the Sky and the Godking's official title was All-Emperor.

The last heirs of the House of Hupun were a boy and girl, Ensar and Anthil. Wishing to end the line of the Kargish kings but unwilling to risk sacrilege by shedding royal blood, the Godking ordered these children to be stranded on a desert island. Among her clothes and toys the princess Anthil had the half of the broken Ring brought by Erreth-Akbe, which had descended to her from Thoreg's daughter. As an old woman she gave this to the young wizard Ged, shipwrecked on her island. Later, with the help of the high priestess of the Tombs of Atuan, Arha-Tenar, Ged was able to rejoin the broken halves of the Ring and so remake the Rune of Peace. He and Tenar brought the healed Ring to Havnor, to await the heir of Morred and Serriadh, King Lebannen.

Magic

Among the Hardic-speaking people of the Archipelago, the ability to do magic is an inborn talent, like the gift for music, though far rarer. Most people lack it entirely. In a few people, perhaps one in a hundred, it is a latent, cultivable talent. In a very few people it is manifest without training.

The gift for magic is empowered mainly by the use of the True Speech, the Language of the Making, in which the name of a thing is the thing.

This speech, innate to dragons, can be learned by human beings. Some few people are born with an untaught knowledge of at least some words of the Language of the Making. The teaching of it is the heart of the teaching of magic.

The true name of a person is a word in the True Speech. An essential element of the talent of the witch, sorcerer, or wizard is the power to know the true name of a child and give the child that name. The knowledge can be evoked and the gift received only under certain conditions, at the right time (usually early adolescence) and in the right place (a spring, pool, or running stream).

Since the name of the person is the person, in the most literal and absolute sense, anyone who knows it has real power, power of life and death, over the person. Often a true name is never known to anybody but the giver and to the owner, who both keep it secret all their life. The power to give the true name and the imperative to keep it secret are one. True names have been betrayed, but never by the name giver.

Some people of great innate and trained power are able to find out the true name of another, or even to have it come to them unsought. Since such knowledge can be betrayed or misused, it is immensely dangerous. Ordinary people—and dragons—keep their true name secret; wizards hide and defend theirs with spells. Morred could not even begin to fight his Enemy until he saw his Enemy's name written in the dust by the falling rain. Ged could force the dragon Yevaud to obey him, having by both wizardry and scholarship discovered Yevaud's true name under centuries of false ones.

Magic was a wild talent before the time of Morred, who as both king and mage established intellectual and moral discipline for the art magic, gathering wizards to work together at the court for the general good and to study the ethical bases and constraints of their practice. This harmony generally prevailed through the reign of Maharion. In the Dark Time, with no control over wizardly powers and widespread misuse of them, magic came into general disrepute.

THE SCHOOL ON ROKE

The school was founded in about 650, as described above. The Nine Masters or master-teachers of Roke were originally:

Windkey, master of the spells controlling weather
Hand, master of all illusions
Herbal, master of the arts of healing

Changer, master of the spells that transform matter and bodies
Summoner, master of the spells that call the spirits of the living and the dead
Namer, master of the knowledge of the True Speech
Patterner, dweller in the Immanent Grove, master of meaning and intent
Finder, master of the spells of finding, binding, and returning
Doorkeeper, master of the entering and leaving of the Great House

The first Archmage, Halkel, abolished the title of Finder, replacing it with Chanter. The Chanter's task is the preservation and teaching of all the oral deeds, lays, songs, etc., and the sung spells.

The original loose, roughly descriptive use of the words *witch, sorcerer, wizard,* was codified into a strict hierarchy by Halkel. Under his rules:

Witchery was restricted to women. All magic practiced by women was called "base craft," even when it included practices otherwise called "high arts," such as healing, chanting, changing, etc. Witches were to learn only from one another or from sorcerers. They were forbidden to enter Roke School, and Halkel discouraged wizards from teaching women anything at all. He specifically forbade the teaching of any word of the True Speech to women, and though this proscription was widely ignored, it led in the long run to a profound, long-lasting loss of knowledge and power among the women who practiced magic.

Sorcery was practiced by men—its only real distinction from witchery. Sorcerers trained one another, and had some knowledge of the True Speech. Sorcery included both base crafts as defined by Halkel (finding, mending, dowsing, animal healing, etc.) and some high arts (human healing, chanting, weatherworking). A student who showed a gift for sorcery and was sent to Roke for training would first study the high arts of sorcery, and if successful in them might pursue his training in the art magic, especially in naming, summoning, and patterning, and so become a wizard.

A *wizard,* as Halkel defined the term, was a man who received his staff from a teacher, himself a wizard, who had taken special responsibility for his training. It was usually the Archmage who gave a student his staff and made him wizard. This kind of teaching and succession occurred elsewhere than Roke—notably on Paln—but the Masters of Roke came to regard with suspicion a student of anyone not trained on Roke.

Mage remained an essentially undefined term: a wizard of great power.

The name and office of *archmage* were invented by Halkel, and the Archmage of Roke was a tenth Master, never counted among the Nine. A vital ethical and intellectual force, the archmage also exerted considerable political power. On the whole this power was used benevolently. Maintaining Roke as a strong centralising, normalising, pacific element in Archipelagan society, the archmages sent out sorcerers and wizards trained to understand the ethical practice of magic and to protect communities from drought, plague, invaders, dragons, and the unscrupulous use of their art.

Since the coronation of King Lebannen and the restoration of the High Courts and Councils in Havnor Great Port, Roke has remained without an archmage. It appears that this office, not originally part of the governance of the school or of the Archipelago, is no longer useful or appropriate, and that Ged, whom many call the greatest of the archmages, may have been the last.

Celibacy and Wizardry

Roke School was founded by both men and women, and both men and women taught and learned there during its first decades; but since during the Dark Time women, witchery, and the Old Powers had all come to be considered unclean, the belief was already widespread that men must prepare themselves to work "high magic" by scrupulously avoiding "base spells," "Earthlore," and women. A man unwilling to put himself under the iron control of a spell of chastity could never practice the high arts. He could be no more than a common sorcerer. Male wizards thus had come to avoid women, refusing to teach them or learn from them. Witches, who almost universally went on working magic without giving up their sexuality, were described by celibate men as temptresses, unclean, defiling, essentially wicked.

When in 730 the first Archmage of Roke, Halkel of Way, excluded women from the school, among his Nine Masters only the Patterner and the Doorkeeper protested; they were overruled. For more than three centuries, no woman taught or studied at the school on Roke. During those centuries, wizardry was an honored art, conferring status and power, while witchery was an unclean and ignorant superstition, practiced by women, paid for by peasants.

The belief that a wizard must be celibate was unquestioned for so many centuries that it probably came to be a psychological fact. Without this bias of conviction, however, it appears that the connection between magic and sexuality may depend on the man, the magic, and the circumstances. There is no doubt that so great a mage as Morred was a husband and father.

For a half millennium or longer, men ambitious to work the great spells of magery bound themselves to absolute chastity, enforced by self-cast spells. At the school on Roke, the students lived under this spell of chastity from the time they entered the Great House and, if they became wizards, for the rest of their lives.

Among sorcerers, few are strictly celibate, and many marry and bring up a family.

Women who work magic may practice periods of celibacy as well as fasting and other disciplines believed to purify and concentrate power; but most witches lead active sexual lives, having more freedom than most village women and less need to fear abuse. Many pledge "witch-troth" with another witch or an ordinary woman. They do not often marry men, and if they do, they are likely to choose a sorcerer.

The Other Wind

Farther west than west
beyond the land
my people are dancing
on the other wind.

—The Song of the Woman of Kemay

Contents

CHAPTER I

Mending the Green Pitcher

SAILS LONG AND WHITE as swan's wings carried the ship *Farflyer* through summer air down the bay from the Armed Cliffs toward Gont Port. She glided into the still water landward of the jetty, so sure and graceful a creature of the wind that a couple of townsmen fishing off the old quay cheered her in, waving to the crewmen and the one passenger standing in the prow.

He was a thin man with a thin pack and an old black cloak, probably a sorcerer or small tradesman, nobody important. The two fishermen watched the bustle on the dock and the ship's deck as she made ready to unload her cargo, and only glanced at the passenger with a bit of curiosity when as he left the ship one of the sailors made a gesture behind his back, thumb and first and last finger of the left hand all pointed at him: *May you never come back!*

He hesitated on the pier, shouldered his pack, and set off into the streets of Gont Port. They were busy streets, and he got at once into the Fish Market, abrawl with hawkers and hagglers, paving stones glittering with fish scales and brine. If he had a way, he soon lost it among the carts and stalls and crowds and the cold stares of dead fish.

A tall old woman turned from the stall where she had been insulting the freshness of the herring and the veracity of the fishwife. Seeing her glaring at him, the stranger said unwisely, "Would you have the kindness to tell me the way I should go for Re Albi?"

"Why, go drown yourself in pig slop for a start," said the tall woman and strode off, leaving the stranger wilted and dismayed. But the fishwife, seeing a chance to seize the high moral ground, blared out, "Re Albi is it? Re Albi you want, man? Speak up then! The Old

Mage's house, that would be what you'd want at Re Albi. Yes it would. So you go out by the corner there, and up Elvers Lane there, see, till you reach the tower . . ."

Once he was out of the market, broad streets led him uphill and past the massive watchtower to a town gate. Two stone dragons large as life guarded it, teeth the length of his forearm, stone eyes glaring blindly out over the town and the bay. A lounging guard told him just turn left at the top of the road and he'd be in Re Albi. "And keep on through the village for the Old Mage's house," the guard said.

So he went trudging up the road, which was pretty steep, looking up as he went to the steeper slopes and far peak of Gont Mountain that overhung its island like a cloud.

It was a long road and a hot day. He soon had his black cloak off and went on bareheaded in his shirtsleeves, but he had not thought to find water or buy food in the town, or had been too shy to, maybe, for he was not a man familiar with cities or at ease with strangers.

After several long miles he caught up to a cart which he had seen far up the dusty way for a long time as a dark blot in a white blot of dust. It creaked and screaked along at the pace of a pair of small oxen that looked as old, wrinkled, and unhopeful as tortoises. He greeted the carter, who resembled the oxen. The carter said nothing, but blinked.

"Might there be a spring of water up the road?" the stranger asked.

The carter slowly shook his head. After a long time he said, "No." A while later he said, "There ain't."

They all plodded along. Discouraged, the stranger found it hard to go any faster than the oxen, about a mile an hour, maybe.

He became aware that the carter was wordlessly reaching something out to him: a big clay jug wrapped round with wicker. He took it, and finding it very heavy, drank his fill of the water, leaving it scarcely lighter when he passed it back with his thanks.

"Climb on," said the carter after a while.

"Thanks. I'll walk. How far might it be to Re Albi?"

The wheels creaked. The oxen heaved deep sighs, first one, then the other. Their dusty hides smelled sweet in the hot sunlight.

"Ten mile," the carter said. He thought, and said, "Or twelve." After a while he said, "No less."

"I'd better walk on, then," said the stranger.

Refreshed by the water, he was able to get ahead of the oxen, and they and the cart and the carter were a good way behind him when he heard the carter speak again. "Going to the Old Mage's house," he said. If it was a question, it seemed to need no answer. The traveler walked on.

When he started up the road it had still lain in the vast shadow of the mountain, but when he turned left to the little village he took to be Re Albi, the sun was blazing in the western sky and under it the sea lay white as steel.

There were scattered small houses, a small dusty square, a fountain with one thin stream of water falling. He made for that, drank from his hands again and again, put his head under the stream, rubbed cool water through his hair and let it run down his arms, and sat for a while on the stone rim of the fountain, observed in attentive silence by two dirty little boys and a dirty little girl.

"He ain't the farrier," one of the boys said.

The traveler combed his wet hair back with his fingers.

"He'll be going to the Old Mage's house," said the girl, "stupid."

"Yerraghh!" said the boy, drawing his face into a horrible lopsided grimace by pulling at it with one hand while he clawed the air with the other.

"You watch it, Stony," said the other boy.

"Take you there," said the girl to the traveler.

"Thanks," he said, and stood up wearily.

"Got no staff, see," said one boy, and the other said, "Never said he did." Both watched with sullen eyes as the stranger followed the girl out of the village to a path that led north through rocky pastures that dropped down steep to the left.

The sun glared on the sea. His eyes dazzled, and the high horizon and the blowing wind made him dizzy. The child was a little hopping shadow ahead of him. He stopped.

"Come on," she said, but she too stopped. He came up to her on the path. "There," she said. He saw a wooden house near the cliff's edge, still some way ahead.

"I ain't afraid," the girl said. "I fetch their eggs lots of times for Stony's dad to carry to market. Once she gave me peaches. The old lady. Stony says I stole 'em but I never. Go on. She ain't there. Neither of 'em is."

She stood still, pointing to the house.

"Nobody's there?"

"The old man is. Old Hawk, he is."

The traveler went on. The child stood watching him till he went round the corner of the house.

Two goats stared down at the stranger from a steep fenced field. A scatter of hens and half-grown chicks pecked and conversed softly in long grass under peach and plum trees. A man was standing on a short ladder against the trunk of one of the trees; his head was in the leaves, and the traveler could see only his bare brown legs.

"Hello," the traveler said, and after a while said it again a bit louder.

The leaves shook and the man came briskly down the ladder. He carried a handful of plums, and when he got off the ladder he batted away a couple of bees drawn by the juice. He came forward, a short, straight-backed man, grey hair tied back from a handsome, timeworn face. He looked to be seventy or so. Old scars, four white seams, ran from his left cheekbone down to the jaw. His gaze was clear, direct, intense. "They're ripe," he said, "though they'll be even better tomorrow." He held out his handful of little yellow plums.

"Lord Sparrowhawk," the stranger said huskily. "Archmage."

The old man gave a curt nod of acknowledgment. "Come into the shade," he said.

The stranger followed him, and did what he was told: he sat down on a wooden bench in the shade of the gnarled tree nearest the house; he accepted the plums, now rinsed and served in a wicker basket; he ate one, then another, then a third. Questioned, he admitted that he had eaten nothing that day. He sat while the master of the house went into it, coming out presently with bread and cheese and half an onion. The guest ate the bread and cheese and onion and drank the cup of cold water his host brought him. The host ate plums to keep him company.

"You look tired. How far have you come?"

"From Roke."

The old man's expression was hard to read. He said only, "I wouldn't have guessed that."

"I'm from Taon, lord. I went from Taon to Roke. And there the Lord Patterner told me I should come here. To you."

"Why?"

It was a formidable gaze.

"Because you *walked across the dark land living* . . ." The stranger's husky voice died away.

The old man picked up the words: "*And came to the far shores of the day.* Yes. But that was spoken in prophecy of the coming of our King, Lebannen."

"You were with him, lord."

"I was. And he gained his kingdom there. But I left mine there. So don't call me by any title. Hawk, or Sparrowhawk, as you please. And how shall I call you?"

The man murmured his use-name: "Alder."

Food and drink and shade and sitting down had clearly eased him, but he still looked exhausted. He had a weary sadness in him; his face was full of it.

The old man had spoken to him with a hard edge in his voice, but that was gone when he said, "Let's put off talking for a bit. You've sailed near a thousand miles and walked fifteen uphill. And I've got to water the beans and the lettuce and all, since my wife and daughter left the garden in my charge. So rest a while. We can talk in the cool of the evening. Or the cool of the morning. There's seldom as much hurry as I used to think there was."

When he came back by half an hour later his guest was flat on his back asleep in the cool grass under the peach trees.

The man who had been Archmage of Earthsea stopped with a bucket in one hand and a hoe in the other and looked down at the sleeping stranger.

"Alder," he said under his breath. "What's the trouble you bring with you, Alder?"

It seemed to him that if he wanted to know the man's true name he would know it only by thinking, by putting his mind to it, as he might have done when he was a mage.

But he did not know it, and thinking would not give it to him, and he was not a mage.

He knew nothing about this Alder and must wait to be told. "Never trouble trouble," he told himself, and went on to water the beans.

As soon as the sun's light was cut off by a low rock wall that ran along the top of the cliff near the house, the cool of the shadow roused the sleeper. He sat up with a shiver, then stood up, a bit stiff and bewildered, with grass seed in his hair. Seeing his host filling buckets at the well and lugging them to the garden, he went to help him.

"Three or four more ought to do it," said the ex-Archmage, doling out water to the roots of a row of young cabbages. The smell of wet dirt was pleasant in the dry, warm air. The westering light came golden and broken over the ground.

They sat on a long bench beside the house door to see the sun go down. Sparrowhawk had brought out a bottle and two squat, thick cups of greenish glass. "My wife's son's wine," he said. "From Oak Farm, in Middle Valley. A good year, seven years back." It was a flinty red wine that warmed Alder right through. The sun set in calm clarity. The wind was down. Birds in the orchard trees made a few closing remarks.

Alder had been amazed when he learned from the Master Patterner of Roke that the Archmage Sparrowhawk, that man of legend, who had brought the king home from the realm of death and then flown off on a dragon's back, was still alive. Alive, said the Patterner, and living on his home island, Gont. "I tell you what not many know," the Patterner had said, "for I think you need to know it. And I think you will keep his secret."

"But then he is still Archmage!" Alder had said, with a kind of joy: for it had been a puzzle and concern to all men of the art that the wise men of Roke Island, the school and center of magery in the Archipelago, had not in all the years of King Lebannen's rule named an Archmage to replace Sparrowhawk.

"No," the Patterner had said. "He is not a mage at all."

The Patterner had told him a little of how Sparrowhawk had lost his power, and why; and Alder had had time to ponder it all. But still, here, in the presence of this man who had spoken with dragons, and brought back the Ring of Erreth-Akbe, and crossed the kingdom of the dead, and ruled the Archipelago before the king, all those stories and songs were in his mind. Even as he saw him old, content with his garden, with no power in him or about him but that of a soul made by a long life of thought and action, he still saw a great mage. And so it troubled him considerably that Sparrowhawk had a wife.

A wife, a daughter, a stepson . . . Mages had no family. A common sorcerer like Alder might marry or might not, but the men of true power were celibate. Alder could imagine this man riding a dragon, that was easy enough, but to think of him as a husband and father was another matter. He couldn't manage it. He tried. He asked, "Your— wife— She's with her son, then?"

Sparrowhawk came back from far away. His eyes had been on the western gulfs. "No," he said. "She's in Havnor. With the king."

After a while, coming all the way back, he added, "She went there with our daughter just after the Long Dance. Lebannen sent for them, to take counsel. Maybe on the same matter that brings you here to me. We'll see . . . But the truth is, I'm tired this evening, and not much disposed to weighing heavy matters. And you look tired too. So a bowl of soup, maybe, and another glass of wine, and sleep? And we'll talk in the morning."

"All with pleasure, lord," Alder said, "but for the sleep. That's what I fear."

It took the old man a while to register this, but then he said, "You fear to sleep?"

"Dreams."

"Ah." A keen glance from the dark eyes under eyebrows grown tangled and half grey. "You had a good nap there in the grass, I think."

"The sweetest sleep I've had since I left Roke Island. I'm grateful to you for that boon, lord. Maybe it will return tonight. But if not, I struggle with my dream, and cry out, and wake, and am a burden to anyone near me. I'll sleep outside, if you permit."

Sparrowhawk nodded. "It'll be a pleasant night," he said.

It was a pleasant night, cool, the sea wind mild from the south, the stars of summer whitening all the sky except where the broad, dark summit of the mountain loomed. Alder put down the pallet and sheepskin his host gave him, in the grass where he had slept before.

Sparrowhawk lay in the little western alcove of the house. He had slept there as a boy, when it was Ogion's house and he was Ogion's prentice in wizardry. Tehanu had slept there these last fifteen years, since she had been his daughter. With her and Tenar gone, when he lay in his and Tenar's bed in the dark back corner of the single room he felt his solitude, so he had taken to sleeping in the alcove. He liked the narrow cot built out from the thick house wall of timbers, right under the window. He slept well there. But this night he did not.

Before midnight, wakened by a cry, voices outside, he leapt up and went to the door. It was only Alder struggling with nightmare, amid sleepy protests from the henhouse. Alder shouted in the thick voice of dream and then woke, starting up in panic and distress. He begged his host's pardon and said he would sit up a while under the stars. Sparrowhawk went back to bed. He was not wakened again by Alder, but he had a bad dream of his own.

He was standing by a wall of stone near the top of a long hillside of dry grey grass that ran down from dimness into the dark. He knew he had been there before, had stood there before, but he did not know when, or what place it was. Someone was standing on the other side of the wall, the downhill side, not far away. He could not see the face, only that it was a tall man, cloaked. He knew that he knew him. The man spoke to him, using his true name. He said, "You will soon be here, Ged."

Cold to the bone, he sat up, staring to see the space of the house about him, to draw its reality around him like a blanket. He looked out the window at the stars. The cold came into his heart then. They were not the stars of summer, beloved, familiar, the Cart, the Falcon, the Dancers, the Heart of the Swan. They were other stars, the small, still stars of the dry land, that never rise or set. He had known their names, once, when he knew the names of things.

"Avert!" he said aloud and made the gesture to turn away misfortune that he had learned when he was ten years old. His gaze went to the open doorway of the house, the corner behind the door, where he thought to see darkness taking shape, clotting together and rising up.

But his gesture, though it had no power, woke him. The shadows behind the door were only shadows. The stars out the window were the stars of Earthsea, paling in the first reflection of the dawn.

He sat holding his sheepskin up round his shoulders, watching those stars fade as they dropped west, watching the growing brightness, the colors of light, the play and change of coming day. There was a grief in him, he did not know why, a pain and yearning as for something dear and lost, forever lost. He was used to that; he had held much dear, and lost much; but this sadness was so great it did not seem to be his own. He felt a sadness at the very heart of things, a grief even in the coming of the light. It clung to him from his dream, and stayed with him when he got up.

He lit a little fire in the big hearth and went to the peach trees and the henhouse to gather breakfast. Alder came in from the path that ran north along the cliff top; he had gone for a walk at first light, he said. He looked jaded, and Sparrowhawk was struck again by the sadness in his face, which echoed the deep aftermood of his own dream.

They had a cup of the warmed barley gruel the country people of Gont drink, a boiled egg, a peach; they ate by the hearth, for the morning air in the shadow of the mountain was too cold for sitting outdoors. Sparrowhawk looked after his livestock: fed the chickens, scattered grain for doves, let the goats into the pasture. When he came back they sat again on the bench in the dooryard. The sun was not over the mountain yet, but the air had grown dry and warm.

"Now tell me what brings you here, Alder. But since you came by Roke, tell me first if things are well in the Great House."

"I did not enter it, my lord."

"Ah." A neutral tone but a sharp glance.

"I was only in the Immanent Grove."

"Ah." A neutral tone, a neutral glance. "Is the Patterner well?"

"He told me, 'Carry my love and honor to my lord and say to him: I wish we walked in the Grove together as we used to do.' "

Sparrowhawk smiled a little sadly. After a while he said, "So. But he sent you to me with more to say than that, I think."

"I will try to be brief."

"Man, we have all day before us. And I like a story told from the beginning."

So Alder told him his story from the beginning.

He was a witch's son, born in the town of Elini on Taon, the Isle of the Harpers.

Taon is at the southern end of the Sea of Éa, not far from where Soléa lay before the sea whelmed it. That was the ancient heart of Earthsea. All those islands had states and cities, kings and wizards, when Havnor was a land of feuding tribesmen and Gont a wilderness ruled by bears. People born on Éa or Ebéa, Enlad or Taon, though they may be a ditchdigger's daughter or a witch's son, consider themselves to be descendants of the Elder Mages, sharing the lineage of the warriors who died in the dark years for Queen Elfarran. Therefore they often have a fine courtesy of manner, though sometimes an undue haughtiness, and a generous, uncalculating turn of mind and speech, a way of soaring above mere fact and prose, which those whose minds stay close to merchandise distrust. "Kites without strings," say the rich men of Havnor of such people. But they do not say it in the hearing of the king, Lebannen of the House of Enlad.

The best harps in Earthsea are made on Taon, and there are schools of music there, and many famous singers of the Lays and Deeds were born or learned their art there. Elini, however, is just a market town in the hills, with no music about it, Alder said; and his mother was a poor woman, though not, as he put it, hungry poor. She had a birthmark, a red stain from the right eyebrow and ear clear down over her shoulder. Many women and men with such a blemish or difference about them become witches or sorcerers perforce, "marked for it," people say. Blackberry learned spells and could do the most ordinary kind of witchery; she had no real gift for it, but she had a way about her that was almost as good as the gift itself. She made a living, and trained her son as well as she could, and saved enough to prentice him to the sorcerer who gave him his true name.

Of his father Alder said nothing. He knew nothing. Blackberry had never spoken of him. Though seldom celibate, witches seldom kept company more than a night or two with any man, and it was a rare thing for a witch to marry a man. Far more often two of them lived their lives together, and that was called witch marriage or she-troth. A witch's child, then, had a mother or two mothers, but no father. That went without saying, and Sparrowhawk asked nothing on that score; but he asked about Alder's training.

The sorcerer Gannet had taught Alder the few words he knew of the True Speech, and some spells of finding and illusion, at which Alder had shown, he said, no talent at all. But Gannet took enough interest in the boy to discover his true gift. Alder was a mender. He could rejoin. He could make whole. A broken tool, a knife blade or an axle snapped, a pottery bowl shattered: he could bring the fragments back together without joint or seam or weakness. So his master sent him about seeking various spells of mending, which he found mostly among witches of the island, and he worked with them and by himself to learn to mend.

"That is a kind of healing," Sparrowhawk said. "No small gift, nor easy craft."

"It was a joy to me," Alder said, with a shadow of a smile in his face. "Working out the spells, and finding sometimes how to use one of the True Words in the work . . . To put back together a barrel that's dried, the staves all fallen in from the hoops—that's a real pleasure, seeing it build up again, and swell out in the right curve, and stand there on its bottom ready for the wine . . . There was a harper from Meoni, a great harper, oh, he played like a storm on the high hills, like a tempest on the sea. He was hard on the harp strings, twanging and pulling them in the passion of his art, so they'd break at the very height and flight of the music. And so he hired me to be there near him when he played, and when he broke a string I'd mend it quick as the note itself, and he'd play on."

Sparrowhawk nodded with the warmth of a fellow professional talking shop. "Have you mended glass?" he asked.

"I have, but it's a long, nasty job," Alder said, "with all the tiny little bits and speckles glass goes to."

"But a big hole in the heel of a stocking can be worse," Sparrowhawk said, and they discussed mending for a while longer, before Alder returned to his story.

He had become a mender, then, a sorcerer with a modest practice and a local reputation for his gift. When he was about thirty, he went to the principal city of the island, Meoni, with the harper, who was playing for a wedding there. A woman sought him out in their lodging, a young woman, not trained as a witch; but she had a gift, she said, the same as his, and wanted him to teach her. And indeed she had a greater gift than his. Though she knew not a word of the Old Speech, she could put a smashed jug back together or mend a frayed-out rope just with the movements of her hands and a wordless song she sang under her breath, and she had healed broken limbs of animals and people, which Alder had never dared try to do.

So rather than his teaching her, they put their skills together and taught each other more than either had ever known. She came back to Elini and lived with Alder's mother Blackberry, who taught her various useful appearances and effects and ways of impressing customers, if not much actual witch knowledge. Lily was her name; and Lily and Alder worked together there and in all the hill towns nearby, as their reputation grew.

"And I came to love her," Alder said. His voice had changed when he began to speak of her, losing its hesitancy, growing urgent and musical.

"Her hair was dark, but with a shining of red gold in it," he said.

There was no way he could hide his love from her, and she knew it and returned it. Whether she was a witch now or not, she said she did not care; she said the two of them were born to be together, in their work and in their life; she loved him and would be married to him.

So they were married, and lived in very great happiness for a year, and half a second year.

"Nothing was wrong at all until the time came for the child to be born," Alder said. "But it was late, and then very late. The midwives tried to bring on the birth with herbs and spells, but it was as if the child would not let her bear it. It would not be separated from her. It would not be born. And it was not born. It took her with it."

After a while he said, "We had great joy."

"I see that."

"And my sorrow was in that degree."

The old man nodded.

"I could bear it," Alder said. "You know how it is. There was not much reason to be living that I could see, but I could bear it."

"Yes."

"But in the winter. Two months after her death. There was a dream came to me. She was in the dream."

"Tell it."

"I stood on a hillside. Along the top of the hill and running down the slope was a wall, low, like a boundary wall between sheep pastures. She was standing across the wall from me, below it. It was darker there."

Sparrowhawk nodded once. His face had gone rock hard.

"She was calling to me. I heard her voice saying my name, and I went to her. I knew she was dead, I knew it in the dream, but I was glad to go. I couldn't see her clear, and I went to her to see her, to be with her. And she reached out across the wall. It was no higher than my heart. I had thought she might have the child with her, but she did not. She was reaching her hands out to me, and so I reached out to her, and we took each other's hands."

"You touched?"

"I wanted to go to her, but I could not cross the wall. My legs would not move. I tried to draw her to me, and she wanted to come, it seemed as if she could, but the wall was there between us. We couldn't get over it. So she leaned across to me and kissed my mouth and said my name. And she said, 'Set me free!'

"I thought if I called her by her true name maybe I could free her, bring her across that wall, and I said, 'Come with me, Mevre!' But she said, 'That's not my name, Hara, that's not my name any more.' And she let go my hands, though I tried to hold her. She cried, 'Set me free, Hara!' But she was going down into the dark. It was all dark down that hillside below the wall. I called her name and her use-name and all the dear names I had had for her, but she went on away. So then I woke."

Sparrowhawk gazed long and keenly at his visitor. "You gave me your name, Hara," he said.

Alder looked a little stunned, and took a couple of long breaths, but he looked up with desolate courage. "Who could I better trust it with?" he said.

Sparrowhawk thanked him gravely. "I will try to deserve your trust," he said. "Tell me, do you know what that place is—that wall?"

"I did not know it then. Now I know you have crossed it."

"Yes. I've been on that hill. And crossed the wall, by the power and art I used to have. And I've gone down to the cities of the dead, and spoken to men I had known living, and sometimes they answered me. But Hara, you are the first man I ever knew or heard of, among all the great mages in the lore of Roke or Paln or the Enlades, who ever touched, who ever kissed his love across that wall."

Alder sat with his head bowed and his hands clenched.

"Will you tell me: what was her touch like? Were her hands warm? Was she cold air and shadow, or like a living woman? Forgive my questions."

"I wish I could answer them, my lord. On Roke the Summoner asked the same. But I can't answer truly. My longing for her was so great, I wished so much—it could be I wished her to be as she was in life. But I don't know. In dream not all things are clear."

"In dream, no. But I never heard of any man coming to the wall in dream. It is a place a wizard may seek to come to, if he must, if he's learned the way and has the power. But without the knowledge and the power, only the dying can—"

And then he broke off, remembering his dream of the night before.

"I took it for a dream," Alder said. "It troubled me, but I cherished it. It was like a harrow on my heart's ground to think of it, and yet I held to that pain, held it close to me. I wanted it. I hoped to dream again."

"Did you?"

"Yes. I dreamed again."

He looked unseeing into the blue gulf of air and ocean west of where they sat. Low and faint across the tranquil sea lay the sunlit hills of Kameber. Behind them the sun was breaking bright over the mountain's northern shoulder.

"It was nine days after the first dream. I was in that same place, but high up on the hill. I saw the wall below me across the slope. And I ran down the hill, calling out her name, sure of seeing her. There was someone there. But when I came close, I saw it wasn't Lily. It was a man, and he was stooping at the wall, as if he was repairing it. I said to him, 'Where is she, where is Lily?' He didn't answer or look up. I saw what he was doing. He wasn't working to mend the wall but to unbuild it, prying with his fingers at a great stone. The stone never moved, and he said, 'Help me, Hara!' Then I saw that it was my teacher, Gannet, who named me. He has been dead these five years. He kept prying and straining at the stone with his fingers, and said my name again—'Help me, set me free.' And he stood up and reached out to me across the wall, as she had done, and caught my hand. But his hand burned, with fire or with cold, I don't know, but the touch of it burned me so that I pulled away, and the pain and fear of it woke me from the dream."

He held his hand out as he spoke, showing a darkness on the back and palm like an old bruise.

"I've learned not to let them touch me," he said in a low voice.

Ged looked at Alder's mouth. There was a darkening across his lips too.

"Hara, you've been in mortal danger," he said, also softly.

"There is more."

Forcing his voice against silence, Alder went on with his story.

The next night when he slept again he found himself on that dim hill and saw the wall that dropped down from the hilltop across the slope. He went down towards it, hoping to find his wife there. "I didn't care if she couldn't cross it, if I couldn't, so long as I could see her and talk to her," he said. But if she was there he never saw her among all the others: for as he came closer to the wall he saw a crowd of shadowy people on the other side, some clear and some dim, some he seemed to know and others he did not know, and all of them reached out their hands to him as he approached and called him by his name: "Hara! let us come with you! Hara, set us free!"

"It's a terrible thing to hear one's true name called by strangers," Alder said, "and it's a terrible thing to be called by the dead."

He tried to turn and climb back up the hill, away from the wall; but his legs had the awful weakness of dream and would not carry him. He fell to his knees to keep himself from being drawn down to the wall, and called out for help, though there was no one to help him; and so he woke in terror.

Since then, every night that he slept deeply, he found himself standing on the hill in the dry grey grass above the wall, and the dead would crowd thick and shadowy below it, pleading and crying to him, calling his name.

"I wake," he said, "and I'm in my own room. I'm not there, on that hillside. But I know they are. And I have to sleep. I try to wake often, and to sleep in daylight when I can, but I have to sleep at last. And then I am there, and they are there. And I can't go up the hill. If I move it's always downhill, towards the wall. Sometimes I can turn my back to them, but then I think I hear Lily among them, crying to me. And I turn to look for her. And they reach out to me."

He looked down at his hands gripping each other.

"What am I to do?" he said.

Sparrowhawk said nothing.

After a long time Alder said, "The harper I told you of was a good friend to me. After a while he saw there was something amiss, and when I told him that I couldn't sleep for fear of my dreams of the dead, he urged me and helped me to take ship's passage to Éa, to speak to a grey wizard there." He meant a man trained in the School on Roke. "As soon as that wizard heard what my dreams were he said I must go to Roke."

"What is his name?"

"Beryl. He serves the Prince of Éa, who is Lord of the Isle of Taon."

The old man nodded.

"He had no help to give me, he said, but his word was as good as gold to the ship's master. So I went on the water again. That was a long journey, coasting clear round Havnor and down the Inmost Sea. I thought maybe being on the water, far from Taon, always farther, I might leave the dream behind me. The wizard on Éa called that place in my dream *the dry land,* and I thought maybe I'd be going away from it, going on the sea. But every night I was there on the hillside. And more than once in the night, as time went on. Twice, or three times, or every time my eyes close, I'm on the hill, and the wall below me, and the voices calling me. So I'm like a man crazy with the pain of a wound who can find peace only in sleep, but the sleep is my torment, with the pain and anguish of the wretched dead all crowding at the wall, and my fear of them."

The sailors soon began to shun him, he said, at night because he cried out and woke them with his miserable wakenings, and in daylight because they thought there was a curse on him or a gebbeth in him.

"And no relief for you on Roke?"

"In the Grove," Alder said, and his face changed entirely when he said the word.

Sparrowhawk's face had the same look for a moment.

"The Master Patterner took me there, under those trees, and I could sleep. Even at night I could sleep. In daylight, if the sun's on me—it was like that in the afternoon, yesterday, here—if the warmth of the sun's on me and the red of the sun shines through my eyelids, I don't fear to dream. But in the Grove there was no fear at all, and I could love the night again."

"Tell me how it was when you came to Roke."

Though hampered by weariness, anguish, and awe, Alder had the silver tongue of his island; and what he left out for fear of going on too long or telling the Archmage what he already knew, his listener could well imagine, remembering when he himself first came to the Isle of the Wise as a boy of fifteen.

When Alder left the ship at the docks at Thwil Town, one of the sailors had drawn the rune of the Closed Door on the top of the gangplank to prevent his ever coming back aboard. Alder noticed it, but he thought the sailor had good cause. He felt himself ill-omened; he felt he bore darkness in him. That made him shyer than he would have been in any case in a strange town. And Thwil was a very strange town.

"The streets lead you awry," Sparrowhawk said.

"They do that, my lord!—I'm sorry, my tongue will obey my heart, and not you—"

"Never mind. I was used to it once. I can be Lord Goatherd again, if it eases your speech. Go on."

Misdirected by those he asked, or misunderstanding the directions, Alder wandered about the hilly little labyrinth of Thwil Town with the School always in sight and never able to get to it, until, having reached despair, he came to a plain door in a bare wall on a dull square. After staring at it a while he recognised the wall was the one he had been trying to get to. He knocked, and a man with a quiet face and quiet eyes opened the door.

Alder was ready to say that he had been sent by the wizard Beryl of Éa with a message for the Master Summoner, but he didn't have a chance to speak. The Doorkeeper gazed at him a moment and said mildly, "You cannot bring them into this house, friend."

Alder did not ask who it was he could not bring with him. He knew. He had slept scarcely at all the past nights, snatching fragments of sleep and waking in terror, dozing off in the daylight, seeing the dry grass sloping down through the sunlit deck of the ship, the wall of stones across the waves of the sea. And waking, the dream was in him, with him, around him, veiled, and he could hear, always, faintly, through all the noises of wind and sea, the voices that cried his name. He did not know if he was awake now or asleep. He was crazy with pain and fear and weariness.

"Keep them out," he said, "and let me in, for pity's sake let me in!"

"Wait here," the man said, as gently as before. "There's a bench," pointing. And he closed the door.

Alder went and sat down on the stone bench. He remembered that, and he remembered some boys of fifteen or so looking curiously at him as they went by and entered that door, but what happened for some while after he could recall only in fragments.

The Doorkeeper came back with a young man with the staff and cloak of a Roke wizard. Then Alder was in a room, which he understood was in a lodging house. There the Master Summoner came and tried to talk with him. But Alder by then was not able to talk. Between sleep and waking, between the sunlit room and the dim grey hill, between the Summoner's voice speaking to him and the voices calling him across the wall, he could not think and he could not move, in the living world. But in the dim world where the voices called, he thought it would be easy to walk on down those few steps to the wall and let the reaching hands take him and hold him. If he was one of them they would let him be, he thought.

Then, as he remembered, the sunlit room was altogether gone, and he was on the grey hill. But with him stood the Summoner of Roke: a big, broad, dark-skinned man, with a great staff of yew wood that shimmered in the dim place.

The voices had ceased calling. The people, the crowding figures at the wall, were gone. He could hear a distant rustle and a kind of sobbing as they went down into the darkness, went away.

The Summoner stepped to the wall and put his hands on it.

The stones had been loosened here and there. A few had fallen and lay on the dry grass. Alder felt that he should pick them up and replace them, mend the wall, but he did not.

The Summoner turned to him and asked, "Who brought you here?"

"My wife, Mevre."

"Summon her here."

Alder stood dumb. At last he opened his mouth, but it was not his wife's true name that he spoke but her use-name, the name he had called her in life. He said it aloud, "Lily . . ." The sound of it was not like a white flower, but like a pebble dropping on dust.

No sound. Stars shone small and steady in the black sky. Alder had never looked up at the sky in this place before. He did not recognise the stars.

"Mevre!" said the Summoner, and in his deep voice spoke some words in the Old Speech.

Alder felt the breath go out of him and could barely stand. But nothing stirred on the long slope that led down to formless dark.

Then there was some movement, something lighter, coming up the hill, coming slowly nearer. Alder shook with fear and yearning, and whispered, "Oh my dear love."

But the figure as it came closer was too small to be Lily. He saw it was a child of twelve or so, girl or boy he could not tell. It paid no heed to him or the Summoner and never looked across the wall, but settled down just under it. When Alder came closer and looked down he saw the child was prying and pulling at the stones, trying to loosen one, then another.

The Summoner was whispering in the Old Speech. The child glanced up once indifferently and went on tugging at the stones with its thin fingers that seemed to have no strength in them.

This was so horrible to Alder that his head spun; he tried to turn away, and beyond that he could remember nothing till he woke in the sunny room, lying in bed, weak and sick and cold.

People looked after him: the aloof, smiling woman who kept the lodging house, and a brown-skinned, stocky old man who came with the Doorkeeper. Alder took him for a physician-sorcerer. Only after he had seen him with his staff of olive wood did he understand that he was the Herbal, the master of healing of the School on Roke.

His presence brought solace, and he was able to give Alder sleep. He brewed up a tea and had Alder drink it, and lighted some herb that burned slowly with a smell like the dark earth under pine woods, and sitting nearby began a long, soft chant. "But I must not sleep," Alder protested, feeling sleep coming into him like a great dark tide. The healer laid his warm hand on Alder's hand. Then peace came into Alder, and he slipped into sleep without fear. So long as the healer's hand was on his, or on his shoulder, it kept him from the dark hillside and the wall of stones.

He woke to eat a little, and soon the Master Herbal was there again with the tepid, insipid tea and the earth-smelling smoke and the dull untuneful chant and the touch of his hand; and Alder could have rest.

The healer had all his duties at the School, so could be there only some hours of the night. Alder got enough rest in three nights that he could eat and walk about the town a little in the day and think and talk coherently. On the fourth morning the three masters, the Herbal, the Doorkeeper, and the Summoner, came to his room.

Alder bowed to the Summoner with dread, almost distrust, in his heart. The Herbal was also a great mage, but his art was not altogether different from Alder's own craft, so they had a kind of understanding; and there was the great kindness of his hand. The Summoner, though, dealt not with bodily things but with the spirit, with the minds and wills of men, with ghosts, with meanings. His art was arcane, dangerous, full of risk and threat. And he had stood beside Alder there, not in the body, on the boundary, at the wall. With him the darkness and the fear returned.

None of the three mages said anything at first. If they had one thing in common, it was a great capacity for silence.

So Alder spoke, trying to say what was in his heart, for nothing less would do.

"If I did some wrong that brought me to that place, or brought my wife to me there, or the other souls, if I can mend or undo what I did, I will. But I don't know what it is I did."

"Or what you are," the Summoner said.

Alder was mute.

"Not many of us know who or what we are," said the Doorkeeper. "A glimpse is all we get."

"Tell us how you first went to the wall of stones," the Summoner said.

And Alder told them.

The mages listened in silence and said nothing for a while after he was done. Then the Summoner asked, "Have you thought what it means to cross that wall?"

"I know I could not come back."

"Only mages can cross the wall living, and only at utmost need. The Herbal may go with a sufferer all the way to that wall, but if the sick man crosses it, he does not follow."

The Summoner was so tall and broad-bodied and dark that, looking at him, Alder thought of a bear.

"My art of Summoning empowers us to call the dead back across the wall for a brief time, a moment, if there is need to do so. I myself question if any need could justify so great a breach in the law and balance of the world. I have never made that spell. Nor have I crossed the wall. The Archmage did, and the King with him, to heal the wound in the world the wizard called Cob made."

"And when the Archmage did not return, Thorion, who was our Summoner then, went down into the dry land to seek him," the Herbal said. "He came back, but changed."

"There is no need to speak of that," the big man said.

"Maybe there is," said the Herbal. "Maybe Alder needs to know it. Thorion trusted his strength too far, I think. He stayed there too long. He thought he could summon himself back into life, but what came back was only his skill, his power, his ambition—the will to live that gives no life. Yet we trusted him, because we had loved him. So he devoured us. Until Irian destroyed him."

Far from Roke, on the Isle of Gont, Alder's listener interrupted him— "What name was that?" Sparrowhawk asked.

"Irian, he said."

"Do you know that name?"

"No, my lord."

"Nor I." After a pause Sparrowhawk went on softly, as if unwillingly. "But I saw Thorion, there. In the dry land, where he had risked going to seek me. It grieved me to see him there. I said to him he might go back across the wall." His face went dark and grim. "That was ill spoken. All is spoken ill between the living and the dead. But I had loved him too."

They sat in silence. Sparrowhawk got up abruptly to stretch his arms and rub his thighs. They both moved about a bit. Alder got a drink of water from the well. Sparrowhawk fetched out a garden spade and the new handle to fit to it, and set to work smoothing the oaken shaft and tapering the end that would go in the socket.

He said, "Go on, Alder," and Alder went on with his story.

The two masters had been silent for a while after the Herbal spoke about Thorion. Alder got up the courage to ask them about a matter that had been much on his mind: how those who died came to the wall, and how the mages came there.

The Summoner answered promptly: "It is a spirit journey."

The old healer was more hesitant. "It's not in the body that we cross the wall, since the body of one who dies stays here. And if a mage goes there in vision, his sleeping body is still here, alive. And so we call that voyager . . . we call what makes that journey from the body, the soul, the spirit."

"But my wife took my hand," Alder said. He could not say again to them that she had kissed his mouth. "I felt her touch."

"So it seemed to you," the Summoner said.

"If they touched bodily, if a link was made," the Herbal said to the Summoner, "might that not be why the other dead can come to him, call to him, even touch him?"

"That is why he must resist them," said the Summoner, with a glance at Alder. His eyes were small, fiery.

Alder felt it as an accusation, and not a fair one. He said, "I try to resist them, my lord. I have tried. But there are so many of them—and she's with them—and they're suffering, crying out to me."

"They cannot suffer," the Summoner said. "Death ends all suffering."

"Maybe the shadow of pain is pain," said the Herbal. "There are mountains in that land, and they are called Pain."

The Doorkeeper had scarcely spoken until now. He said in his quiet, easy voice, "Alder is a mender, not a breaker. I don't think he can break that link."

"If he made it he can break it," the Summoner said.

"Did he make it?"

"I have no such art, my lord," Alder said, so frightened by what they were saying that he spoke angrily.

"Then I must go down among them," said the Summoner.

"No, my friend," said the Doorkeeper, and the old Herbal said, "You last of us all."

"But this is my art."

"And ours."

"Who then?"

The Doorkeeper said, "It seems Alder is our guide. Having come to us for help, maybe he can help us. Let us all go with him in his vision—to the wall, though not across it."

So that night, when late and fearfully Alder let sleep overcome him, and found himself on the grey hill, the others were with him: the Herbal, a warm presence in the chill; the Doorkeeper, elusive and silvery as starlight; and the massive Summoner, the bear, a dark strength.

This time they were standing not where the hill ran down into the dark, but on the near slope, looking up to the top. The wall in this place ran along the crest of the hill and was low, little more than knee height. Above it the sky with its few small stars was perfectly black.

Nothing moved.

It would be hard to walk uphill to the wall, Alder thought. Always before it had been below him.

But if he could go to it maybe Lily would be there, as she had been the first time. Maybe he could take her hand, and the mages would bring her back with him. Or he could step over the wall where it was so low and come to her.

He began to walk up the hill. It was easy, it was no trouble, he was almost there.

"Hara!"

The Summoner's deep voice called him back like a noose round his neck, a jerked leash. He stumbled, staggered forward one step more, almost at the wall, dropped to his knees and reached out to the stones. He was crying, "Save me!" but to whom? To the mages, or to the shadows beyond the wall?

Then hands were on his shoulders, living hands, strong and warm, and he was in his room, with the healer's hands indeed on his shoulders, and the werelight burning white around them. And there were four men in the room with him, not three.

The old Herbal sat down on the bed with him and soothed him a while, for he was shaking, shuddering, sobbing. "I can't do it," he kept saying, but still he did not know if he was talking to the mages or to the dead.

When the fear and pain began to lessen, he felt tired beyond bearing, and looked almost without interest at the man who had come into the room. His eyes were the color of ice, his hair and skin were white. A far Northerner, from Enwas or Bereswek, Alder thought him.

This man said to the mages, "What are you doing, my friends?"

"Taking risks, Azver," said the old Herbal.

"Trouble at the border, Patterner," said the Summoner.

Alder could feel the respect they had for this man, their relief that he was there, as they told him briefly what the trouble was.

"If he'll come with me, will you let him go?" the Patterner asked when they were done, and turning to Alder, "You need not fear your dreams in the Immanent Grove. And so we need not fear your dreams."

They all assented. The Patterner nodded and vanished. He was not there.

He had not been there; he had been a sending, a presentment. It was the first time Alder had seen the great powers of these masters made manifest, and it would have unnerved him if he had not been past amazement and fear.

He followed the Doorkeeper out into the night, through the streets, past the walls of the School, across fields under a high round hill, and along a stream singing its water music softly in the darkness of its banks. Ahead of them was a high wood, the trees crowned with grey starlight.

The Master Patterner came along the path to meet them, looking just as he had in the room. He and the Doorkeeper spoke for a minute, and then Alder followed the Patterner into the Grove.

"The trees are dark," Alder said to Sparrowhawk, "but it isn't dark under them. There is a light—a lightness there."

His listener nodded, smiling a little.

"As soon as I came there, I knew I could sleep. I felt as if I'd been asleep all along, in an evil dream, and now, here, I was truly awake: so I could truly sleep. There was a place he took me to, in among the roots of a huge tree, all soft with the fallen leaves of the tree, and he told me I could lie there. And I did, and I slept. I cannot tell you the sweetness of it."

The midday sun had grown strong; they went indoors, and the host set out bread and cheese and a bit of dried meat. Alder looked round him as they ate. The house had only the one long room with its little western alcove, but it was large and darkly airy, strongly built, with wide boards and beams, a gleaming floor, a deep stone fireplace. "This is a noble house," Alder said.

"An old one. They call it the Old Mage's house. Not for me, nor for my master Aihal who lived here, but for his master Heleth, who with him stilled the great earthquake. It's a good house."

Alder slept a while again under the trees with the sun shining on him through the moving leaves. His host rested too, but not long; when Alder woke, there was a good-sized basket of the small golden plums under the tree, and Sparrowhawk was up in the goat pasture mending a fence. Alder went to help him, but the job was done. The goats, however, were long gone.

"Neither of 'em's in milk," Sparrowhawk grumbled as they returned to the house. "They've got nothing to do but find new ways through the fence. I keep them for exasperation . . . The first spell I ever learned was to call goats from wandering. My aunt taught me. It's no more use to me now than if I sang them a love song. I'd better go see if they've got into the widower's vegetables. You don't have the kind of sorcery to charm a goat to come, do you?"

The two brown nannies were indeed invading a cabbage patch on the outskirts of the village. Alder repeated the spell Sparrowhawk told him:

Noth hierth malk man,
hiolk han merth han!

The goats gazed at him with alert disdain and moved away a little. Shouting and a stick got them out of the cabbages onto the path, and there Sparrowhawk produced some plums from his pocket. Promising, offering, and cajoling, he slowly led the truants back into their pasture.

"They're odd creatures," he said, latching the gate. "You never know where you are with a goat."

Alder thought that he never knew where he was with his host, but did not say it.

When they were sitting in the shade again, Sparrowhawk said, "The Patterner isn't a Northerner, he's a Karg. Like my wife. He was a warrior of Karego-At. The only man I know of who ever came from those lands to Roke. The Kargs have no wizards. They distrust all sorcery. But they've kept more knowledge of the Old Powers of the Earth than we have. This man, Azver, when he was young, he heard some tale of the Immanent Grove, and it came to him that the center of all the earth's powers must be there. So he left his gods and his native tongue behind him and made his way to Roke. He stood on our doorstep and said, 'Teach me to live in that forest!' And we taught him, till he began to teach us . . . So he became our Master Patterner. He's not a gentle man, but he is to be trusted."

"I never could fear him," Alder said. "It was easy to be with him. He'd take me far into the wood with him."

They were both silent, both thinking of the glades and aisles of that wood, the sunlight and starlight in its leaves.

"It is the heart of the world," Alder said.

Sparrowhawk looked up eastward at the slopes of Gont Mountain, dark with trees. "I'll go walking there," he said, "in the forest, come autumn."

After a while he said, "Tell me what counsel the Patterner had for you, and why he sent you here to me."

"He said, my lord, that you knew more of the . . . the dry land than any living man, and so maybe you would understand what it means that the souls there come to me as they do, begging me for freedom."

"Did he say how he thinks it came about?"

"Yes. He said that maybe my wife and I didn't know how to be parted, only how to be joined. That it was not my doing, but was maybe ours together, because we drew each to the other, like drops of quicksilver. But the Master Summoner didn't agree. He said that only a great power of magery could so transgress the order of the world. Because my old master Gannet also touched me across the wall, the Summoner said maybe it was a mage power in him which had been hidden or disguised in life, but now was revealed."

Sparrowhawk brooded a while. "When I lived on Roke," he said, "I might have seen it as the Summoner does. There I knew no power stronger than what we call magery. Not even the Old Powers of the Earth, I thought . . . If the Summoner you met is the man I think, he came as a boy to Roke. My old friend Vetch of Iffish sent him to study with us. And he never left. That's a difference between him and Azver the Patterner. Azver lived till he was grown as a warrior's son, a warrior himself, among men and women, in the thick of life. Matters that the walls of the School keep out, he knows in his flesh and blood. He knows that men and women love, make love, marry . . . Having lived these fifteen years outside the walls, I incline to think Azver might be on the better track. The bond between you and your wife is stronger than the division between life and death."

Alder hesitated. "I've thought it might be so. But it seems . . . shameless to think it. We loved each other, more than I can say we loved each other, but was our love greater than any other before us? Was it greater than Morred's and Elfarran's?"

"Maybe not less."

"How can that be?"

Sparrowhawk looked at him as if saluting something, and answered him with a care that made Alder feel honored. "Well," he said slowly, "sometimes there's a passion that comes in its springtime to ill fate or death. And because it ends in its beauty, it's what the harpers sing of and the poets make stories of: the love that escapes the years. That was the love of the Young King and Elfarran. That was your love, Hara. It wasn't greater than Morred's, but was his greater than yours?"

Alder said nothing, pondering.

"There's no less or greater in an absolute thing," Sparrowhawk said. "All or nothing at all, the true lover says, and that's the truth of it. My love will never die, he says. He claims eternity. And rightly. How can it die when it's life itself? What do we know of eternity but the glimpse we get of it when we enter in that bond?"

He spoke softly but with fire and energy; then he leaned back, and after a minute said, with a half smile, "Every oaf of a farm boy sings that, every young girl that dreams of love knows it. But it's not a thing the Masters of Roke are familiar with. The Patterner maybe knew it early. I learned it late. Very late. Not quite too late." He looked at Alder, the fire still in his eyes, challenging. "You had that," he said.

"I did." Alder drew a deep breath. Presently he said, "Maybe they're there together, in the dark land. Morred and Elfarran."

"No," Sparrowhawk said with bleak certainty.

"But if the bond is true, what can break it?"

"There are no lovers there."

"Then what are they, what do they do, there in that land? You've been there, you crossed the wall. You walked and spoke with them. Tell me!"

"I will." But Sparrowhawk said nothing for a while. "I don't like to think about it," he said. He rubbed his head and scowled. "You saw . . . You've seen those stars. Little, mean stars, that never move. No moon. No sunrise . . . There are roads, if you go down the hill. Roads and cities. On the hill there's grass, dead grass, but farther down there's only dust and rocks. Nothing grows. Dark cities. The multitudes of the dead stand in the streets, or walk on the roads to no end. They don't speak. They don't touch. They never touch." His voice was low and dry. "There Morred would pass Elfarran and never turn his head, and she wouldn't look at him . . . There's no rejoining there, Hara. No bond. The mother doesn't hold her child, there."

"But my wife came to me," Alder said, "she called my name, she kissed my mouth!"

"Yes. And since your love wasn't greater than any other mortal love, and since you and she aren't mighty wizards whose power might change the laws of life and death, therefore, therefore something else is in this. Something is happening, is changing. Though it happens through you and to you, you are its instrument and not its cause."

Sparrowhawk stood up and strode to the beginning of the path along the cliff and back to Alder; he was charged, almost quivering with tense energy, like a hawk about to stoop down on its prey.

"Did your wife not say to you, when you called her by her true name, *That is not my name any more—?*"

"Yes," Alder whispered.

"But how is that? We who have true names keep them when we die, it's our use-name that is forgotten . . . This is a mystery to the learned, I can tell you, but as well as we understand it, a true name is a word in the True Speech. That's why only one with the gift can know a child's name and give it. And the name binds the being—alive or dead. All the art of the Summoner lies in that . . . Yet when the master summoned your wife to come by her true name, she didn't come to him.

You called by her use-name, Lily, and she came to you. Did she come to you as to the one who knew her truly?"

He gazed at Alder keenly and yet as if he saw more than the man who sat with him. After a while he went on, "When my master Aihal died, my wife was here with him; and as he was dying he said to her, *It is changed, all changed.* He was looking across that wall. From which side I do not know.

"And since that time, indeed there have been changes—a king on Morred's throne, and no Archmage of Roke. But more than that, much more. I saw a child summon the dragon Kalessin, the Eldest: and Kalessin came to her, calling her daughter, as I do. What does that mean? What does it mean that dragons have been seen above the islands of the west? The king sent to us, sent a ship to Gont Port, asking my daughter Tehanu to come and take counsel with him concerning dragons. People fear that the old covenant is broken, that the dragons will come to burn fields and cities as they did before Erreth-Akbe fought with Orm Embar. And now, at the boundary of life and death, a soul refuses the bond of her name . . . I do not understand it. All I know is that it is changing. It is all changing."

There was no fear in his voice, only fierce exultation.

Alder could not share that. He had lost too much and was too worn out by his struggle against forces he could not control or comprehend. But his heart rose to that gallantry.

"May it change for the good, my lord," he said.

"Be it so," the old man said. "But change it must."

As the heat went out of the day, Sparrowhawk said he had to walk to the village. He carried the basket of plums with a basket of eggs nested in it.

Alder walked with him and they talked. When Alder understood that Sparrowhawk bartered fruit and eggs and the other produce of the little farm for barley and wheat flour, that the wood he burned was gathered patiently up in the forest, that his goats' not giving milk meant he must eke out last year's cheese, Alder was amazed: how could it be that the Archmage of Earthsea lived from hand to mouth? Did his own people not honor him?

When he went with him to the village, he saw women shut their doors when they saw the old man coming. The marketer who took his eggs and fruit tallied the count on his wooden tablet without a word, his face sullen and his eyes lowered. Sparrowhawk spoke to him pleasantly, "A good day to you then, Iddi," but got no answer.

"My lord," Alder asked as they walked home, "do they know who you are?"

"No," said the ex-Archmage, with a dry sidelong look. "And yes."

"But—" Alder did not know how to speak his indignation.

"They know I have no power of sorcery, but there's something uncanny about me. They know I live with a foreigner, a Kargish woman. They know the girl we call our daughter is something like a witch, but worse, because her face and hand were burnt away by fire, and because she herself burnt up the Lord of Re Albi, or pushed him off the cliff, or killed him with the evil eye—their stories vary. They honor the house we live in, though, because it was Aihal's and Heleth's house, and dead wizards are good wizards . . . You're a townsman, Alder, of an isle of Morred's kingdom. A village on Gont is another matter."

"But why do you stay here, lord? Surely the king would do you proper honor—"

"I want no honor," the old man said, with a violence that silenced Alder entirely.

They walked on. As they came to the house built at the cliff's edge he spoke again. "This is my eyrie," he said.

They had a glass of the red wine with supper, and another sitting out to watch the sun set. They did not talk much. Fear of the night, of the dream, was coming into Alder.

"I'm no healer," his host said, "but perhaps I can do what the Master Herbal did to let you sleep."

Alder looked his question.

"I've been thinking about it, and it seems to me maybe it was no spell at all that kept you away from that hillside, but just the touch of a living hand. If you like, we can try it."

Alder protested, but Sparrowhawk said, "I'm awake half most nights anyway." So the guest lay that night in the low bed in the back corner of the big room, and the host sat up beside him, watching the fire and dozing.

He watched Alder, too, and saw him fall asleep at last; and not long after that saw him start and shudder in his sleep. He put out his hand and laid it on Alder's shoulder as he lay half turned away. The sleeping man stirred a little, sighed, relaxed, and slept on.

It pleased Sparrowhawk that he could do this much. As good as a wizard, he told himself with mild sarcasm.

He was not sleepy; the tension was still in him. He thought about all Alder had told him, and what they had talked about in the afternoon. He saw Alder stand in the path by the cabbage patch saying the spell to call the goats, and the goats' haughty indifference to the powerless words. He remembered how he had used to speak the name of the sparrowhawk, the marsh hawk, the grey eagle, calling them down from the sky to him in a rush of wings to grasp his arm with iron talons and glare at him, eye to wrathful, golden eye . . . None of that any more. He could boast, calling this house his eyrie, but he had no wings.

But Tehanu did. The dragon's wings were hers to fly on.

The fire had burned out. He pulled his sheepskin over him more closely, leaning his head back against the wall, still keeping his hand on Alder's inert, warm shoulder. He liked the man and was sorry for him.

He must remember to ask him to mend the green pitcher, tomorrow.

The grass next to the wall was short, dry, dead. No wind blew to make it move or rustle.

He roused up with a start, half rising from the chair, and after a moment of bewilderment put his hand back on Alder's shoulder, grasping it a little, and whispered, "Hara! Come away, Hara." Alder shuddered, then relaxed. He sighed again, turned more onto his face and lay still.

Sparrowhawk sat with his hand on the sleeper's arm. How had he himself come there, to the wall of stones? He no longer had the power to go there. He had no way to find the way. As in the night before, Alder's dream or vision, Alder's voyaging soul had drawn him with it to the edge of the dark land.

He was wide awake now. He sat gazing at the greyish square of the west window, full of stars.

The grass under the wall . . . It did not grow farther down where the hill leveled out into the dim, dry land. He had said to Alder that down there was only dust, only rock. He saw that black dust, black rock. Dead stream beds where no water ever ran. No living thing. No bird, no field mouse cowering, no glitter and buzz of little insects, the creatures of the sun. Only the dead, with their empty eyes and silent faces.

But did birds not die?

A mouse, a gnat, a goat—a white-and-brown, clever-hoofed, yellow-eyed, shameless goat, Sippy who had been Tehanu's pet, and who had died last winter at a great age—where was Sippy?

Not in the dry land, the dark land. She was dead, but she was not there. She was where she belonged, in the dirt. In the dirt, in the light, in the wind, the leap of water from the rock, the yellow eye of the sun.

Then why, then why . . .

He watched Alder mend the pitcher. Fat-bellied and jade green, it had been a favorite of Tenar's; she had carried it all the way from Oak Farm, years ago. It had slipped from his hands the other day as he took it from the shelf. He had picked up the two big pieces of it and the little fragments with some notion of gluing them back together so it could sit out for looks, if never for use again. Every time he saw the pieces, which he had put into a basket, his clumsiness had outraged him.

Now, fascinated, he watched Alder's hands. Slender, strong, deft, unhurried, they cradled the shape of the pitcher, stroking and fitting and settling the pieces of pottery, urging and caressing, the thumbs coaxing and guiding the smaller fragments into place, reuniting them, reassuring them. While he worked he murmured a two-word, tuneless chant. They were words of the Old Speech. Ged knew and did not know their meaning. Alder's face was serene, all stress and sorrow gone: a face so wholly absorbed in time and task that timeless calm shone through it.

His hands separated from the pitcher, opening out from it like the sheath of a flower opening. It stood on the oak table, whole.

He looked at it with quiet pleasure.

When Ged thanked him, he said, "It was no trouble at all. The breaks were very clean. It's a well-made piece, and good clay. It's the shoddy work that costs to mend."

"I had a thought how you might find sleep," Ged said.

Alder had waked at first light and had got up, so that his host could go to his bed and sleep sound till broad day; but clearly the arrangement would not do for long.

"Come along with me," the old man said, and they set off inland on a path that skirted the goats' pasture and wound between knolls, little, half-tended fields, and inlets of the forest. Gont was a wild-looking place to Alder, ragged and random, the shaggy mountain always frowning and looming above.

"It seemed to me," Sparrowhawk said as they walked, "if I could do as well as the Master Herbal did, keeping you from the hill of the wall only by putting my hand on you, that there might be others who could help you. If you have no objection to animals."

"Animals?"

"You see," Sparrowhawk began, but got no further, interrupted by a strange creature bounding down the path towards them. It was bundled in skirts and shawls, feathers stuck out in all directions from its head, and it wore high leather boots. "O Mastawk, O Mastawk!" it shouted.

"Hello, then, Heather. Gently now," said Sparrowhawk. The woman stopped, rocking her body, her head-feathers waving, a large grin on her face. "She knowed you was a-coming!" she bawled. "She made that hawk's beak with her fingers like this, see, she did, and she told me go, go, with her hand! She knowed you was a-coming!"

"And so I am."

"To see us?"

"To see you. Heather, this is Master Alder."

"Mastalder," she whispered, quieting suddenly as she included Alder in her consciousness. She shrank, drew into herself, looked down at her feet.

She had no leather boots on. Her bare legs were coated from the knee down with smooth, brown, drying mud. Her skirts were bunched, caught up into the waistband.

"You've been frogging, have you, Heather?"

She nodded vacantly.

"I'll go tell Aunty," she said, beginning in a whisper and ending with a bellow, and bolted back the way she had come.

"She's a good soul," Sparrowhawk said. "She used to help my wife. She lives with our witch now and helps her. I don't think you'll object to entering a witch's house?"

"Never in the world, my lord."

"Many do. Nobles and common folk, wizards and sorcerers."

"Lily my wife was a witch."

Sparrowhawk bowed his head and walked in silence for a while. "How did she learn of her gift, Alder?"

"It was born in her. As a child she'd make a torn branch grow on the tree again, and other children brought her their broken toys to mend. But when her father saw her do that he would strike her hands. Her family were considerable persons in their town. Respectable persons," Alder said in his even, gentle voice. "They didn't want her consorting with witches. Since it would keep her from marriage with a respectable man. So she kept all her study to herself. And the witches of her town would have nothing to do with her, even when she sought to learn from them, for they were afraid of her father, you see. Then a rich man came to court her, for she was beautiful, as I told you, my lord. More beautiful than I could say. And her father told her she was to be married. She ran away that night. She lived by herself, wandering, for some years. A witch here and there took her in, but she kept herself by her skill."

"It's not a big island, Taon."

"Her father wouldn't seek her. He said no tinker witch was his daughter."

Again Sparrowhawk bowed his head. "So she heard of you, and came to you."

"But she taught me more than I could teach her," Alder said earnestly. "It was a great gift she had."

"I believe it."

They had come to a little house or big hut, set down in a dell, with witch hazel and broom in tangles about it, and a goat on the roof, and a flock of white-speckled black hens squawking away, and a lazy little sheepdog bitch standing up and thinking about barking and thinking better of it and waving her tail.

Sparrowhawk went to the low doorway, stooping to look in. "There you are, Aunty!" he said. "I've brought you a visitor. Alder, a man of sorcery from the Isle of Taon. His craft is mending, and he's a master, I can tell you, for I just watched him put back together Tenar's green pitcher, you know the one, that I like a clumsy old fool dropped and broke to pieces the other day."

He entered the hut, and Alder followed him. An old woman sat in a cushioned chair near the doorway where she could look out into the sunlight. Feathers stuck out of her wispy white hair. A speckled hen was settled in her lap. She smiled at Sparrowhawk with enchanting sweetness and nodded politely to the visitor. The hen woke, cackled, and departed.

"This is Moss," said Sparrowhawk, "a witch of many skills, the greatest of which is kindness."

So, Alder imagined, might the Archmage of Roke have introduced a great wizard to a great lady. He bowed. The old woman ducked her head and laughed a little.

She made a circling motion with her left hand, looking a query at Sparrowhawk.

"Tenar? Tehanu?" he said. "Still in Havnor with the king, so far as I know. They'll be having a fine time there, seeing all the sights of the great city and the palaces."

"I made us crowns," Heather shouted, bouncing out of the odorous, dark jumble farther inside the house. "Like kings and queens. See?" She preened the chicken feathers that stuck out of her thick hair at all angles. Aunty Moss, becoming aware of her own peculiar headdress, batted ineffectively at the feathers with her left hand and grimaced.

"Crowns are heavy," Sparrowhawk said. He gently plucked the feathers from the thin hair.

"Who's the queen, Mastawk?" Heather cried. "Who's the queen? Bannen's the king, who's the queen?"

"King Lebannen has no queen, Heather."

"Why not? He ought to. Why not?"

"Maybe he's looking for her."

"He'll marry Tehanu!" the woman shrieked, joyful. "He will!"

Alder saw Sparrowhawk's face change, close, become rock.

He said only, "I doubt it." He held the feathers he had taken from Moss's hair and stroked them softly. "I've come to you for a favor, as always, Aunty Moss," he said.

She reached her good hand out and took his hand with such tenderness that Alder was moved to the heart.

"I want to borrow one of your puppies."

Moss began to look sad. Heather, gawking beside her, puzzled it over for a minute and then shouted, "The puppies! Aunty Moss, the puppies! But they're all gone!"

The old woman nodded, looking forlorn, caressing Sparrowhawk's brown hand.

"Somebody wanted them?"

"The biggest one got out and maybe it ran up in the forest and some creature killed it for it never came back and then old Ramballs, he came and said he needs sheepdogs and he'd take both and train them and Aunty gave them to him because they chased the new chicks Snowflakes hatched and ate out house and home, they did, besides."

"Well, Rambles may have a bit of a job training them," Sparrowhawk said with a half smile. "I'm glad he's got them but sorry they're gone, since I wanted to borrow one for a night or two. They slept on your bed, didn't they, Moss?"

She nodded, still sad. Then, brightening a little, she looked up with her head to one side and mewed.

Sparrowhawk blinked, but Heather understood. "Oh! The kittens!" she shouted. "Little Grey had four, and Old Black he killed one before we could stop him, but there's still two or three somewhere round here, they sleep with Aunty and Biddy most every night now the little dogs are gone. Kitty! kitty! kitty! where are you, kitty, kitty?" And after a good deal of commotion and scrambling and piercing mews in the dark interior, she reappeared with a grey kitten clutched squirming and squealing in her hand. "Here's one!" she shouted, and threw it at Sparrowhawk. He caught it awkwardly. It instantly bit him.

"There, there now," he told it. "Calm down." A tiny, rumbling growl emerged from it, and it tried to bite him again. Moss gestured, and he set the little creature down in her lap. She stroked it with her slow heavy hand. It flattened out at once, stretched, looked up at her, and purred.

"May I borrow it for a while?"

The old witch raised her hand from the kitten in a royal gesture that said clearly: It is yours and welcome.

"Master Alder here is having troublesome dreams, you see, and I thought maybe having an animal with him nights might help to ease the trouble."

Moss nodded gravely and, looking up at Alder, slipped her hand under the kitten and lifted it towards him. Alder took it rather gingerly into his hands. It did not growl or bite. It scrambled up his arm and clung to his neck under his hair, which he wore loosely gathered at the nape.

As they walked back to the Old Mage's house, the kitten tucked inside Alder's shirt, Sparrowhawk explained. "Once, when I was new to the art, I was asked to heal a child with the redfever. I knew the boy was dying, but I couldn't bring myself to let him go. I tried to follow him. To bring him back. Across the wall of stones . . . And so, here in the body, I fell down by the bedside and lay like the dead myself. There was a witch there who guessed what the matter was, and she had me taken to my house and laid abed there. And in my house was an animal that had befriended me when I was a boy on Roke, a wild creature that came to me of its own will and stayed with me. An otak. Do you know them? I think there are none in the North."

Alder hesitated. He said, "I know of them only from the Deed that tells of how . . . how the mage came to the Court of the Terrenon in Osskil. And the otak tried to warn him of a gebbeth that walked with him. And he won free of the gebbeth, but the little animal was caught and slain."

Sparrowhawk walked on without speaking for twenty paces or so. "Yes," he said. "So. Well, my otak also saved my life when I was caught by my own folly on the wrong side of the wall, my body lying here and my soul astray there. The otak came to me and washed me, the way they wash themselves and their young, the way cats do, with a dry tongue, patiently, touching me and bringing me back with its touch, bringing me back into my body. And the gift the animal gave me was not only life but a knowledge as great as I ever learned on Roke . . . But you see, I forget all my learning.

"A knowledge, I say, but it's rather a mystery. What's the difference between us and the animals? Speech? All the animals have some way of speaking, saying *come* and *beware* and much else; but they can't tell stories, and they can't tell lies. While we can . . .

"But the dragons speak: they speak the True Speech, the language of the Making, in which there are no lies, in which to tell the story is to make it be! Yet we call the dragons animals . . .

"So maybe the difference isn't language. Maybe it's this: animals do neither good nor evil. They do as they must do. We may call what they do harmful or useful, but good and evil belong to us, who chose to choose what we do. The dragons are dangerous, yes. They can do harm, yes. But they're not evil. They're beneath our morality, if you will, like any animal. Or beyond it. They have nothing to do with it.

"We must choose and choose again. The animals need only be and do. We're yoked, and they're free. So to be with an animal is to know a little freedom . . .

"Last night, I was thinking of how witches often have a companion, a familiar. My aunt had an old dog that never barked. She called him Gobefore. And the Archmage Nemmerle, when I first came to Roke Island, had a raven that went with him everywhere. And I thought of a young woman I knew once who wore a little dragon-lizard, a harekki, for her bracelet. And so at last I thought of my otak. Then I thought, if what Alder needs to keep him on this side of the wall is the warmth of a touch, why not an animal? Since they see life, not death. Maybe a dog or cat is as good as a Master of Roke . . ."

So it proved. The kitten, evidently happy to be away from the household of dogs and tomcats and roosters and the unpredictable Heather, tried hard to show that it was a reliable and diligent cat, patrolling the house for mice, riding on Alder's shoulder under his hair when permitted, and settling right down to sleep purring under his chin as soon as he lay down. Alder slept all night without any dream he remembered, and woke to find the kitten sitting on his chest, washing its ears with an air of quiet virtue.

When Sparrowhawk tried to determine its sex, however, it growled and struggled. "All right," he said, getting his hand out of danger quickly. "Have it your way. It's either a male or a female, Alder, I'm certain of that."

"I won't name it, in any case," Alder said. "They go out like candle flames, little cats. If you've named one you grieve more for it."

That day at Alder's suggestion they went fence mending, walking the goat-pasture fence, Sparrowhawk on the inside and Alder on the outside. Whenever one of them found a place where the palings showed the beginning of rot or the tie laths had been weakened, Alder would run his hands along the wood, thumbing and tugging and smoothing and strengthening, a half-articulate chant almost inaudible in his throat and chest, his face relaxed and intent.

Once Sparrowhawk, watching him, murmured, "And I used to take it all for granted!"

Alder, lost in his work, did not ask him what he meant.

"There," he said, "that'll hold." And they moved on, followed closely by the two inquisitive goats, who butted and pushed at the repaired sections of fence as if to test them.

"I've been thinking," Sparrowhawk said, "that you might do well to go to Havnor."

Alder looked at him in alarm. "Ah," he said. "I thought maybe, if I have a way now to keep away from . . . that place . . . I could go home to Taon." He was losing faith in what he said as he said it.

"You might, but I don't think it would be wise."

Alder said reluctantly, "It is a great deal to ask of a kitten, to defend a man against the armies of the dead."

"It is."

"But I—what should I do in Havnor?" And, with sudden hope, "Would you go with me?"

Sparrowhawk shook his head once. "I stay here."

"The Lord Patterner . . ."

"Sent you to me. And I send you to those who should hear your tale and find out what it means . . . I tell you, Alder, I think in his heart the Patterner believes I am what I was. He believes I'm merely hiding here in the forests of Gont and will come forth when the need is greatest." The old man looked down at his sweaty, patched clothes and dusty shoes, and laughed. "In all my glory," he said.

"Beh," said the brown goat behind him.

"But all the same, Alder, he was right to send you here, since she'd have been here, if she hadn't gone to Havnor."

"The Lady Tenar?"

"*Hama Gondun.* So the Patterner himself called her," Sparrowhawk said, looking across the fence at Alder, his eyes unfathomable. "A woman on Gont. The Woman of Gont. Tehanu."

Chapter II

Palaces

When Alder came down to the docks, *Farflyer* was still there, taking on a cargo of timbers; but he knew he had worn out his welcome on that ship. He went to a small shabby coaster tied up next to her, the *Pretty Rose.*

Sparrowhawk had given him a letter of passage signed by the king and sealed with the Rune of Peace. "He sent it for me to use if I changed my mind," the old man had said with a snort. "It'll serve you." The ship's master, after getting his purser to read it for him, became quite deferential and apologised for the cramped quarters and the length of the voyage. *Pretty Rose* was going to Havnor, sure enough, but she was a coaster, trading small goods from port to port, and it might take her a month to work clear round the southeast coast of the Great Island to the King's City.

That was all right with him, Alder said. For if he dreaded the voyage, he feared its ending more.

New moon to half moon, the sea voyage was a time of peace for him. The grey kitten was a hardy traveler, busy mousing the ship all day but faithfully curling up under his chin or within hand's reach at night; and to his unceasing wonder, that little scrap of warm life kept him from the wall of stones and the voices calling him across it. Not wholly. Not so that he ever entirely forgot them. They were there, just through the veil of sleep in darkness, just through the brightness of the day. Sleeping out on deck those warm nights, he opened his eyes often to see that the stars moved, swinging to the rocking of the moored ship, following their courses through heaven to the west. He was still a haunted man. But for a half month of summer along the coasts of

Kameber and Barnisk and the Great Island he could turn his back on his ghosts.

For days the kitten hunted a young rat nearly as big as it was. Seeing it proudly and laboriously hauling the carcass across the deck, one of the sailors called it Tug. Alder accepted the name for it.

They sailed down the Ebavnor Straits and in through the portals of Havnor Bay. Across the sunlit water little by little the white towers of the city at the center of the world resolved out of the haze of distance. Alder stood at the prow as they came in and looking up saw on the pinnacle of the highest tower a flash of silver light, the Sword of Erreth-Akbe.

Now he wished he could stay aboard and sail on and not go ashore into the great city among great people with a letter for the king. He knew he was no fit messenger. Why had such a burden been laid on him? How could it be that a village sorcerer who knew nothing of high matters and deep arts was called on to make these journeys from land to land, from mage to monarch, from the living to the dead?

He had said something like that to Sparrowhawk. "It's all beyond me," he had said. The old man looked at him a while and then, calling him by his true name, said, "The world's vast and strange, Hara, but no vaster and no stranger than our minds are. Think of that sometimes."

Behind the city the sky darkened with a thunderstorm inland. The towers burned white against purple-black, and gulls soared like drifting sparks of fire above them.

Pretty Rose was moored, the gangplank run out. This time the sailors wished him well as he shouldered his pack. He picked up the covered poultry basket in which Tug crouched patiently, and went ashore.

The streets were many and crowded, but the way to the palace was plain, and he had no idea what to do except go there and say that he carried a letter for the king from the Archmage Sparrowhawk.

And that he did, many times.

From guard to guard, from official to official, from the broad outer steps of the palace to high anterooms, staircases with gilded banisters, inner offices with tapestried walls, across floors of tile and marble and oak, under ceilings coffered, beamed, vaulted, painted, he went repeating his talisman: "I come from Sparrowhawk who was the Archmage with a letter for the king." He would not give his letter up. A retinue, a crowd of suspicious, semi-civil, patronising, temporising, obstructive guards and ushers and officials kept gathering and thickening around him and followed and impeded his slow way into the palace.

Suddenly they were all gone. A door had opened. It closed behind him.

He stood alone in a quiet room. A wide window looked out over the roofs northwestward. The thundercloud had cleared and the broad grey summit of Mount Onn hovered above far hills.

Another door opened. A man came in, dressed in black, about Alder's age, quick moving, with a fine, strong face as smooth as bronze. He came straight to Alder: "Master Alder, I am Lebannen."

He put out his right hand to touch Alder's hand, palm against palm, as the custom was in Éa and the Enlades. Alder responded automatically to the familiar gesture. Then he thought he ought to kneel, or bow at least, but the moment to do so seemed to have passed. He stood dumb.

"You came from my Lord Sparrowhawk? How is he? Is he well?"

"Yes, lord. He sends you—" Alder hurriedly groped inside his jacket for the letter, which he had intended to offer to the king kneeling, when they finally showed him to the throne room where the king would be sitting on his throne—"this letter, my lord."

The eyes watching him were alert, urbane, as implacably keen as Sparrowhawk's, but withholding even more of the mind within. As the king took the letter Alder offered him, his courtesy was perfect. "The bearer of any word from him has my heart's thanks and welcome. Will you forgive me?"

Alder finally managed a bow. The king walked over to the window to read the letter.

He read it twice at least, then refolded it. His face was as impassive as before. He went to the door and spoke to someone outside it, then turned back to Alder. "Please," he said, "sit down with me. They'll bring us something to eat. You've been all afternoon in the palace, I know. If the gate captain had had the wits to send me word, I could have spared you hours of climbing the walls and swimming the moats they set around me . . . Did you stay with my Lord Sparrowhawk? In his house on the cliff's edge?"

"Yes."

"I envy you. I've never been there. I haven't seen him since we parted on Roke, half my lifetime ago. He wouldn't let me come to him on Gont. He wouldn't come to my crowning." Lebannen smiled as if nothing he said was of any moment. "He gave me my kingdom," he said.

Sitting down, he nodded to Alder to take the chair facing him across a little table. Alder looked at the tabletop, inlaid with curling patterns of ivory and silver, leaves and blossoms of the rowan tree twined about slender swords.

"Did you have a good voyage?" the king asked, and made other small talk while they were served plates of cold meat and smoked trout and lettuces and cheese. He set Alder a welcome example by eating with a good appetite; and he poured them wine, the palest topaz, in goblets of crystal. He raised his glass. "To my lord and dear friend," he said.

Alder murmured, "To him," and drank.

The king spoke about Taon, which he had visited a few years before—Alder remembered the excitement of the island when the king was in Meoni. And he spoke of some musicians from Taon who were in the city now, harpers and singers come to make music for the court; it might be Alder knew some of them; and indeed the names he said were familiar. He was very skilled at putting his guest at ease, and food and wine were a considerable help too.

When they were done eating, the king poured them another half glass of wine and said, "The letter concerns you, mostly. Did you know that?" His tone had not changed much from the small talk, and Alder was fuddled for a moment.

"No," he said.

"Do you have an idea what it deals with?"

"What I dream, maybe," Alder said, speaking low, looking down.

The king studied him for a moment. There was nothing offensive in his gaze, but he was more open in that scrutiny than most men would have been. Then he took up the letter and held it out to Alder.

"My lord, I read very little."

Lebannen was not surprised—some sorcerers could read, some could not—but he clearly and sharply regretted putting his guest at a disadvantage. The gold-bronze skin of his face went dusky red. He said, "I'm sorry, Alder. May I read you what he says?"

"Please, my lord," Alder said. The king's embarrassment made him, for a moment, feel the king's equal, and he spoke for the first time naturally and with warmth.

Lebannen scanned the salutation and some lines of the letter and then read aloud:

"'Alder of Taon who bears this to you is one called in dream and not by his own will to that land you and I crossed once together. He will tell you of suffering where suffering is past and change where no thing changes. We closed the door Cob opened. Now the wall itself maybe is to fall. He has been to Roke. Only Azver heard him. My Lord the King will hear and will act as wisdom instructs and need requires. Alder bears my lifelong honor and obedience to my Lord the King. Also my lifelong honor and regard to my lady Tenar. Also to my beloved daughter Tehanu a spoken message from me.' And he signs it with the rune of the Talon." Lebannen looked up from the letter into Alder's eyes and held his gaze. "Tell me what it is you dream," he said.

So once more Alder told his story.

He told it briefly and not very well. Though he had been in awe of Sparrowhawk, the ex-Archmage looked and dressed and lived like an old villager or farmer, a man of Alder's own kind and standing, and that simplicity had defeated all superficial timidity. But however kind and courteous the king might be, he looked like the king, he behaved like the king, he was the king, and to Alder the distance was insuperable. He hurried through as best he could and stopped with relief.

Lebannen asked a few questions. Lily and then Gannet had each touched Alder once: never since? And Gannet's touch had burned?

Alder held out his hand. The marks were almost invisible under a month's tan.

"I think the people at the wall would touch me if I came close to them," he said.

"But you keep away from them?"

"I have done so."

"And they are not people you knew in life?"

"Sometimes I think I know one or another."

"But never your wife?"

"There are so many of them, my lord. Sometimes I think she's there. But I can't see her."

To talk about it brought it near, too near. He felt the fear welling up in him again. He thought the walls of the room might melt away and the evening sky and the floating mountain-crown vanish like a curtain brushed aside, to leave him standing where he was always standing, on a dark hill by a wall of stones.

"Alder."

He looked up, shaken, his head swimming. The room seemed bright, the king's face hard and vivid.

"You'll stay here in the palace?"

It was an invitation, but Alder could only nod, accepting it as an order.

"Good. I'll arrange for you to give the message you bear to Mistress Tehanu tomorrow. And I know the White Lady will wish to talk with you."

He bowed. Lebannen turned away.

"My lord—"

Lebannen turned.

"May I have my cat with me?"

Not a flicker of a smile, no mockery. "Of course."

"My lord, I am sorry to my heart to bring news that troubles you!"

"Any word from the man who sent you is a grace to me and to its bearer. And I'd rather get bad news from an honest man than lies from a flatterer," Lebannen said, and Alder, hearing the true accent of his home islands in the words, was a little cheered.

The king went out, and at once a man looked in the door Alder had entered by. "I will take you to your chamber, if you will follow me, sir," he said. He was dignified, elderly, and well dressed, and Alder followed him without any idea whether he was a nobleman or a servant, and therefore not daring to ask him about Tug. In the room before the room where he had met the king, the officials and guards and ushers had absolutely insisted that he leave his poultry basket with them. It had been eyed with suspicion and inspected with disapproval by ten or fifteen officials already. He had explained ten or fifteen times that he had the cat with him because he had nowhere in the city to leave it. The anteroom where he had been compelled to set it down was far behind him, he had not seen it there as they went through, he would never find it now, it was half a palace away, corridors, hallways, passages, doors . . .

His guide bowed and left him in a small, beautiful room, tapestried, carpeted, a chair with an embroidered seat, a window that looked out to the harbor, a table on which stood a bowl of summer fruit and a pitcher of water. And the poultry basket.

He opened it. Tug emerged in a leisurely manner indicating his familiarity with palaces. He stretched, sniffed Alder's fingers in greeting, and went about the room examining things. He discovered a curtained alcove with a bed in it and jumped up on the bed. A discreet knock at the door. A young man entered carrying a large, flat, heavy wooden box with no lid. He bowed to Alder, murmuring, "Sand, sir." He placed the box in the far corner of the alcove. He bowed again and left.

"Well," Alder said, sitting down on the bed. He was not in the habit of talking to the kitten. Their relationship was one of silent, trustful touch. But he had to talk to somebody. "I met the king today," he said.

The king had all too many people to talk to before he could sit down on his bed. Chief among them were the emissaries of the High King of the

Kargs. They were about to take their leave, having accomplished their mission to Havnor, to their own satisfaction if not at all to Lebannen's.

He had looked forward to the visit of these ambassadors as the culmination of years of patient overture, invitation, and negotiation. For the first ten years of his reign he had been able to accomplish nothing at all with the Kargs. The God-King in Awabath rejected his offers of treaties and trade and sent his envoys back unheard, declaring that gods do not parley with vile mortals, least of all with accursed sorcerers. But the God-King's proclamations of universal divine empire were not followed by the threatened fleets of a myriad ships bearing plumed warriors to overrun the godless West. Even the pirate raids that had plagued the eastern isles of the Archipelago for so long gradually ceased. The pirates had become contrabanders, seeking to trade whatever unlicensed goods they could smuggle out of Karego-At for Archipelagan iron and steel and bronze, for the Kargad Lands were poor in mines and metal.

It was from these illicit traders that news first came of the rise of the High King.

On Hur-at-Hur, the big, poor, easternmost island of the Kargad Lands, a warlord, Thol, claiming descent from Thoreg of Hupun and from the God Wuluah, had made himself High King of that land. Next he had conquered Atnini, and then, with a fleet and an invading army drawn from both Hur-at-Hur and Atnini, he had claimed dominion over the rich central island, Karego-At. While his warriors were fighting their way towards Awabath, the capital city, the people of the city rose up against the tyranny of the God-King. They slaughtered the high priests, drove the bureaucrats out of the temples, threw the gates wide, and welcomed King Thol to the throne of Thoreg with banners and dancing in the streets.

The God-King fled with a remnant of his guards and hierophants to the Place of the Tombs on Atuan. There in the desert, in his temple by the earthquake-shattered ruins of the shrine of the Nameless Ones, one of his priest-eunuchs cut the God-King's throat.

Thol proclaimed himself High King of the Four Kargad Lands. As soon as he got word of that, Lebannen sent ambassadors to greet his brother king and assure him of the friendly disposition of the Archipelago.

Five years of difficult and tiresome diplomacy had ensued. Thol was a violent man on a threatened throne. In the wreckage of the theocracy, all control in his realm was chancy, all authority questionable. Lesser kings constantly declared themselves and had to be bought or beaten into obedience to the High King. Sectarians issued from shrines and caverns crying "Woe to the mighty!" and foretelling earthquake, tidal wave, plague upon the deicides. Ruling a troubled, divided empire, Thol could scarcely place any trust in the powerful and wealthy Archipelagans.

It meant nothing to him that their king talked about friendship, flourishing the Ring of Peace. Did not the Kargs have a claim to that ring? It had been made in ancient days in the West, but long ago, King Thoreg of Hupun had accepted it as a gift from the hero Erreth-Akbe, a sign of amity between the Kargad and Hardic lands. It had disappeared, and there had been war, not amity. But then the Hawk-Mage had found the ring and stolen it back, along with the Priestess of the Tombs of Atuan, and carried both off to Havnor. So much for the trustworthiness of the Archipelagans.

Through his envoys, Lebannen patiently and politely pointed out that the Ring of Peace had, to begin with, been Morred's gift to Elfarran, a cherished token of the Archipelago's most beloved king and queen. And a very sacred thing as well, for on it was the Bond rune, a mighty enchantment of blessing. Nearly four centuries ago, Erreth-Akbe had taken it to the Kargad Lands as a pledge of unbreakable peace. But the priests of Awabath had broken the pledge, and broken the Ring. Some forty years ago now, Sparrowhawk of Roke and Tenar of Atuan had healed the Ring. What, then, of the peace?

That had been the gist of his messages to King Thol.

And a month ago, just after the Long Dance of summer, a fleet of ships had come sailing straight down the Passage of Felkway, up the Ebavnor Straits, and in between the portals of Havnor Bay: long red ships with red sails, carrying plumed warriors, gorgeous-robed emissaries, and a few veiled women.

"Let the daughter of Thol the High King, who sits upon the Throne of Thoreg and whose ancestor was Wuluah, wear the Ring of Peace upon her arm, as Queen Elfarran of Soléa wore it, and this will be the sign of everlasting peace between the Western and the Eastern Isles."

That was the High King's message to Lebannen. It was written out in big Hardic runes on a scroll, but before handing it to King Lebannen, Thol's ambassador read it out loud, in public, at the reception of the emissaries at the court in Havnor, with the whole court there to do the Kargish envoys honor. Perhaps it was because the ambassador did not actually read Hardic, but spoke the words loudly and slowly from memory, that they had the tone of an ultimatum.

The princess said nothing. She stood among the ten handmaidens or slave girls who had accompanied her to Havnor and the flock of court ladies who had been hastily assigned to look after her and do her honor. She was veiled, entirely veiled, as was, it appeared, the custom of well-born women in Hur-at-Hur. The veils, red with lines of gold embroidery, fell straight down from a flat-brimmed hat or headdress, so that the princess appeared to be a red column or pillar, cylindrical, featureless, motionless, silent.

"The High King Thol does us great honor," Lebannen said in his clear, quiet voice; and then he paused. The court and the emissaries waited. "You are welcome here, princess," he said to the veiled figure. It did not stir.

"Let the princess be lodged in the River House, and let all be as she desires," Lebannen said.

The River House was a beautiful small palace at the northern edge of the city, fitted into the old city wall, with terraces built out over the little River Serrenen. Queen Heru had built it, and it was often called the Queen's House. When Lebannen came to the throne he had had it repaired and refurnished, along with the Palace of Maharion, called the New Palace, in which he held court. He used the River House only for summer festivities and sometimes as a retreat for himself for a few days.

A little rustle now went through his courtiers. The Queen's House?

After urbanities among the Kargish emissaries, Lebannen left the audience room. He went to his dressing room, where he could be as alone as a king can be, with his old servant, Oak, whom he had known all his life.

He slapped the gilded scroll down on a table. "Cheese in a rat trap," he said. He was shaking. He whipped the dagger he always wore out of its sheath and stabbed it straight down through the High King's message. "A pig in a poke," he said. "A piece of goods. The Ring on her arm and the collar round my neck."

Oak stared at him in blank dismay. Prince Arren of Enlad had never lost his temper. When he was a child he might have wept for a moment, one bitter sob, but that was all. He was too well trained, too well disciplined to give way to anger. And as king, a king who had earned his realm by crossing the land of the dead, he could be stern, but always, Oak thought, too proud, too strong for anger.

"They will not use me!" Lebannen said, stabbing the dagger down again, his face so black and blind with fury that the old man drew back from him in real fear.

Lebannen saw him. He always saw the people around him.

He sheathed his dagger. He said in a steadier voice, "Oak, by my name, I will destroy Thol and his kingdom before I let him use me as a footstool to his throne." Then he drew a long breath and sat down to let Oak lift the heavy, gold-weighted state robe from his shoulders.

Oak never breathed a word of this scene to anyone, but there was, of course, immediate and continuous speculation about the princess of the Kargs and what the king was going to do about her—or what, in fact, he had already done.

He had not said that he accepted the offer of the princess as his bride. For all agreed she had been offered to him as his bride; the language about Elfarran's Ring barely veiled the offer, or the bargain, or the threat. But he had not refused it, either. His response (endlessly analyzed) had been to say she was welcome, that all should be as she desired, and that she should live in the River House: the Queen's House. Surely that was significant? But on the other hand, why not in the New Palace? Why send her across the city?

Ever since Lebannen's coronation, ladies of noble houses and princesses of the old royal lineages of Enlad, Éa, and Shelieth had come to visit or to stay at the court. They had all been entertained most royally, and the king had danced at their weddings as, one by one, they settled for noblemen or wealthy commoners. It was well known that he liked the company of women and their counsel as well, that he would willingly flirt with a pretty girl and invite an intelligent woman to advise him, tease him, or console him. But no girl or woman had ever come near the rumor of a shadow of a chance of marrying him. And none had ever been lodged in the River House.

The king must have a queen, his advisors told him at regular intervals.

You really must marry, Arren, his mother had told him the last time he saw her alive.

The heir of Morred, will he have no heir? asked the common people.

To all of them he had said, in various words and ways: Give me time. I have the ruins of a kingdom to rebuild. Let me make a house worthy of a queen, a realm my child can rule. And because he was well loved and trusted, and still a young man, and for all his gravity a charming and persuasive one, he had escaped all the hopeful maidens. Until now.

What was under the stiff red veils? Who lived inside that unrevealing tent? The ladies assigned to the princess's entourage were besieged by questions. Was she pretty? Ugly? Was it true she was tall and thin, short and muscular, white as milk, pockmarked, one-eyed, yellow-haired, black-haired, forty-five years old, ten years old, a drooling cretin, a brilliant beauty?

Gradually the rumors began to run one way. She was young, though not a child; hair neither yellow nor black; pretty enough, said some of the ladies; coarse, said others. Spoke not a word of Hardic, they all said, and would not learn. Hid among her women, and when forced to leave her room, hid in her red tent-veils. The king had paid her a visit of courtesy. She had not bowed to him, or spoken, or made any sign, but stood there, said old Lady Iyesa in exasperation, "like a brick chimney."

He spoke to her through men who had served as his envoys in the Kargad Lands and through the Karg ambassador, who spoke fairly good Hardic. Laboriously he transmitted his compliments and queries as to her wishes and desires. The translators spoke to her women, whose veils were shorter and somewhat less impenetrable. Her women gathered round the motionless red pillar and mumbled and buzzed and returned to the translators, and the translators informed the king that the princess was content and required nothing.

She had been there a half month when Tenar and Tehanu arrived from Gont. Lebannen had sent a ship and a message begging them to come, shortly before the Kargad fleet brought the princess, and for reasons that had nothing to do with her or King Thol. But the first time he was alone with Tenar, he burst out, "What am I going to do with her? What can I do?"

"Tell me about it," Tenar said, looking somewhat amazed.

Lebannen had spent only a brief time with Tenar, though they had written a few letters over the years; he was not yet used to her hair being grey, and she seemed smaller than he remembered her; but with her he felt immediately, as he had fifteen years earlier, that he could say anything and she would understand.

"For five years I've built up trade and tried to keep on good terms with Thol, because he's a warlord and I don't want my kingdom pinched, as it was in Maharion's reign, between dragons in the west and warlords in the east. And because I rule in the Sign of Peace. And it went well enough, till this. Till he sends this girl out of the blue, saying if you want peace, give her Elfarran's Ring. Your Ring, Tenar! Yours and Ged's!"

Tenar hesitated a while. "She is his daughter, after all."

"What's a daughter to a barbarian king? Goods. A bargaining piece to buy advantage with. You know that! You were born there!"

It was unlike him to speak so, and he heard it himself. He knelt down suddenly, catching her hand and putting it over his eyes in sign of contrition. "Tenar, I'm sorry. This disturbs me beyond all reason. I can't see what to do."

"Well, so long as you do nothing, you have some leeway . . . Maybe the princess has some opinion of her own?"

"How can she? Hidden in that red sack? She won't talk, she won't look out, she might as well be a tent pole." He tried to laugh. His own uncontrollable resentment alarmed him and he tried to excuse it. "This came on just as I had troubling news from the west. It was for that that I asked you and Tehanu to come. Not to bother you with this foolishness."

"It isn't foolishness," Tenar said, but he brushed the topic away, dismissed it, and began to talk about dragons.

Since the news from the west had been troubling indeed, he had succeeded in not thinking about the princess at all, most of the time. He was aware that it was not his habit to handle matters of state by ignoring them. Manipulated, one manipulates others. Several days after their conversation, he asked Tenar to visit the princess, to try to get her to talk. After all, he said, they spoke the same language.

"Probably," Tenar said. "I never knew anybody from Hur-at-Hur. On Atuan, we called them barbarians."

He was chastised. But of course she did what he asked. Presently she reported that she and the princess spoke the same language, or nearly the same, and that the princess had not known that there were any other languages. She had thought all the people here, the courtiers and ladies, were malicious lunatics, mocking her by chattering and yapping like animals without human speech. As well as Tenar could tell, she had grown up in the desert, in King Thol's original domain on Hur-at-Hur, and had only been very briefly at the imperial court in Awabath before she was sent on to Havnor.

"She's frightened," Tenar said.

"So she hides in her tent. What does she think I am?"

"How could she know what you are?"

He scowled. "How old is she?"

"Young. But a woman."

"I can't marry her," he said, with sudden resolution. "I'll send her back."

"A returned bride is a dishonored woman. If you send her back, Thol might kill her to keep the dishonor from his house. He'll certainly consider that you intend to dishonor him."

The look of fury came into his face again.

Tenar forestalled him. "Barbarian customs," she said stiffly.

He strode up and down the room. "Very well. But I will not consider this girl as queen of the Kingdom of Morred. Can she be taught to speak Hardic? A few words, at least? Is she unteachable? I'll tell Thol that a Hardic king can't marry a woman who doesn't speak the language of the realm. I don't care if he doesn't like it, he needs the slap. And it buys me time."

"And you'll ask her to learn Hardic?"

"How can I ask her anything if she takes it all for gibberish? What possible use is there in my going to her? I thought perhaps you'd speak to her, Tenar . . . You must see what an imposition this is, using this girl to make Thol appear my equal, using the Ring—the Ring you brought us—as a trap! I cannot even seem to condone it. I'm willing to temporise, to delay, in order to keep the peace. Nothing more. Even that much deceit is vile. Tell the girl what you think best. I will have nothing to do with her."

And he went out in a righteous wrath, which cooled slowly into an uneasy feeling much resembling shame.

When the Kargish emissaries announced they would be leaving soon, Lebannen prepared a carefully worded message for King Thol. He expressed his appreciation of the honor of the princess's presence in Havnor and the pleasure he and his court would have in introducing her to the manners, customs, and language of his kingdom. He said nothing at all about the Ring, about marrying her, or about not marrying her.

It was in the evening after his conversation with the dream-troubled sorcerer from Taon that he met for the last time with the Kargs and gave them his letter to the High King. He read it aloud first, as the ambassador had read aloud Thol's letter to him.

The ambassador listened complacently. "The High King will be pleased," he said.

All the time he was talking amenities to the emissaries and displaying the gifts he was sending to Thol, Lebannen puzzled over this easy acceptance of his evasiveness. His thoughts all came to one conclusion: He knows I'm stuck with her. To which his mind made a passionate silent answer: Never.

He inquired whether the ambassador would be going by the River House to bid his princess farewell. The ambassador looked at him blankly, as if he had been asked if he was going to say goodbye to a package he had delivered. Lebannen felt the anger rising in his heart again. He saw the ambassador's face change a little, taking on a wary, placating look. He smiled and wished the emissaries a fair wind to the Kargad Lands. He went out of the audience chamber and to his own room.

Rites and ceremony hedged most of his acts, and as king he must be in public most of his life; but because he had come to a throne empty for centuries, a palace where there were no protocols, he had been able to have some things as he liked them. He had kept ceremony out of his bedroom. His nights were his own. He said good night to Oak, who would sleep in the anteroom, and shut the door. He sat down on his bed. He felt tired and angry and strangely desolate.

Around his neck he always wore a slight gold chain with a little pouch of cloth-of-gold on it. In the pouch was a pebble: a dull, black bit of rock, rough edged. He took it out and held it in his hand as he sat and thought.

He tried to turn his mind away from all this stupidity about the Kargish girl by thinking about the sorcerer Alder and his dreams. But all that came into his mind was a painful envy of Alder for having gone ashore on Gont, having talked with Ged, having stayed with him.

That was why he felt desolate. The man he called his lord, the man he had loved above all others, wouldn't let him come near, wouldn't come to him.

Did Ged believe that because he had lost his wizardly power, Lebannen must think less of him? must despise him?

Given the power that power had over the minds and hearts of men, it was not an implausible thought. But surely Ged knew him better, or at least thought better of him.

Was it that, having been truly Lebannen's lord and guide, Ged could not bear to be his subject? That might indeed be hard for the old man to bear: the blunt, irrevocable reversal of their status.

But Lebannen remembered very clearly how Ged had knelt to him, down on both knees, on Roke Knoll, in the shadow of the dragon and in the sight of the masters whose master Ged had been. He had stood up and kissed Lebannen, telling him to rule well, calling him *my lord and dear companion.*

"He gave me my kingdom," Lebannen had said to Alder. That had been the moment he gave it. Wholly, freely.

And that was why Ged wouldn't come to Havnor, wouldn't let Lebannen come to take counsel with him. He had handed over the power—wholly, freely. He would not even seem to meddle, to cast his shadow across Lebannen's light.

"He has done with doing," the Doorkeeper had said.

But Alder's story had moved Ged to send the man here, to Lebannen, asking him to act as need required.

It was indeed strange, Alder's story; and Ged's saying that maybe the wall itself was going to fall was stranger yet. What could it mean? And why should one man's dreams bear so much weight?

He himself had dreamed of the outskirts of the dry land, long ago, when he and Ged the Archmage were traveling together, before they ever came to Selidor.

And on that westernmost of all the islands he had followed Ged into the dry land. Across the wall of stones. Down to dim cities where the shadows of the dead stood in doorways or walked without aim or purpose in streets lit only by the moveless stars. With Ged he had walked across all that country, a weary way to a dark valley of dust and stones at the foot of the mountains whose only name was Pain.

He opened his palm, looked down at the little black stone he held, closed his hand on it again.

From the valley of the dry river, having done what they came to do, they had climbed up into the mountains, because there was no turning back. They had gone up the road forbidden to the dead, climbing, clambering over rocks that scored and burned their hands, till Ged could go no farther. Lebannen had carried him as far as he could, then crawled on with him to the end of darkness, the hopeless cliff of night. And so had come back, with him, into the sunlight and the sound of the sea breaking on the shores of life.

It was a long time since he had thought so vividly of that terrible journey. But the bit of black stone from those mountains was always over his heart.

And it seemed to him now that the memory of that land, the darkness of it, the dust, was always in his mind just under the bright various play and movement of the days, although he always looked away from it. He looked away because he could not bear the knowledge that in the end that was where he would come again: come alone, uncompanioned, and forever. To stand empty-eyed, unspeaking, in the shadows of a shadow city. Never to see sunlight, or drink water, or touch a living hand.

He got up abruptly, shaking off these morbid thoughts. He closed the stone in its pouch, made ready for bed, put out the lamp, and lay down. At once he saw it again: the dim grey land of dust and rock. It rose up far ahead into black, sharp peaks, but here it sloped away, always downward, to the right, into utter darkness. "What lies that way?" he had asked Ged as they walked on and on. His companion had said he did not know, that maybe that way there was no end.

Lebannen sat up, angered and alarmed by the relentless drift of his thought. His eyes sought the window. It looked north. He liked the view from Havnor across the hills to the tall, grey-headed mountain Onn. Farther north, unseen, across all the width of the Great Island and the Sea of Éa, was Enlad, his home.

Lying in bed he could see only the sky, a clear summer night sky, the Heart of the Swan riding high among lesser stars. His kingdom. The kingdom of light, of life, where the stars blossomed like white flowers in the east and drooped in their brightness to the west. He would not think of that other realm where the stars stayed still, where there was no power in a man's hand, and no right way to go because no way led anywhere.

Lying gazing at the stars, he turned his mind deliberately from those memories and from the thought of Ged. He thought of Tenar: the sound of her voice, the touch of her hand. Courtiers were ceremonious, cautious about how and when they touched the king. She was not. She laid her hand on his, laughing. She was bolder with him than his mother had been.

Rose, princess of the House of Enlad, had died of a fever two years ago, while he was on shipboard coming to make a royal visit to Berila on Enlad and the isles south of it. He had not known of her death till he came home to a city and a house in mourning.

His mother was there now in the dark country, the dry country. If he came there and passed her in the street she would not look at him. She would not speak to him.

He clenched his hands. He rearranged the cushions of his bed, tried to make himself easy, tried to set his mind away from there, to think of things that would keep him from going back there. To think of his mother living, her voice, her dark eyes under dark arched brows, her delicate hands.

Or to think of Tenar. He knew he had asked Tenar to come to Havnor not only to take counsel from her but because she was the mother that remained to him. He wanted that love, to give it and be given it. The ruthless love that makes no allowances, no conditions. Tenar's eyes were grey, not dark, but she looked right through him with a piercing tenderness undeceived by anything he said or did.

He knew he did well what he had been called to do. He knew he was good at playing king. But only with his mother and with Tenar had he ever known beyond any self-doubt what it was to be king.

Tenar had known him since he was a very young man, not yet crowned. She had loved him then and ever since, for his sake, for Ged's sake, and for her own. He was to her the son who never breaks your heart.

But she thought he might yet manage to, if he kept on being so rageful and dishonest about this poor girl from Hur-at-Hur.

She attended the final audience of the emissaries from Awabath. Lebannen had asked her to be there, and she was glad to come. Finding Kargs at the court when she came there at the beginning of summer, she had expected them to shun her or at least to eye her askance: the renegade priestess who with the thieving Hawk Mage had stolen the Ring of Erreth-Akbe from the treasury of the Tombs of Atuan and traitorously fled with it to Havnor. It was her doing that the Archipelago had a king again. The Kargs might well hold it against her.

And Thol of Hur-at-Hur had restored the worship of the Twin Gods and the Nameless Ones, whose greatest temple Tenar had despoiled. Her treason had been not only political but religious.

Yet that was long ago, forty years and more, almost the stuff of legend; and statesmen remember things selectively. Thol's ambassador had begged the honor of an audience with her and had greeted her with elaborately pious respect, some of which she thought was real. He called her Lady Arha, the Eaten One, the One Ever Reborn. She had not been called by those names for years, and they sounded very strange to her. But it gave her a keen, rueful pleasure to hear her native tongue and to find she could still speak it.

So she came to bid the ambassador and his company goodbye. She asked him to assure the High King of the Kargs that his daughter was well, and she looked admiringly a last time at the tall, rawboned men with their pale, braided hair, their plumed headdresses, their court armor of silver mesh interwoven with feathers. When she lived in the Kargad Lands she had seen few men of her own race. Only women and eunuchs had lived at the Place of the Tombs.

After the ceremony she escaped into the gardens of the palace. The summer night was warm and restless, flowering shrubs of the gardens stirring in the night wind. The sounds of the city outside the palace walls were like the murmur of a quiet sea. A couple of young courtiers were walking entwined under the arbors; not to disturb them, Tenar walked among the fountains and the roses at the other end of the garden.

Lebannen had left the audience scowling again. What was wrong with him? So far as she knew, he had never before rebelled against the obligations of his position. Certainly he knew that a king must marry and has little real choice as to whom he marries. He knew that a king who does not obey his people is a tyrant. He knew his people wanted a queen, wanted heirs to the throne. But he had done nothing about it.

Women of the court had been happy to gossip to Tenar about his several mistresses, none of whom had lost anything by being known as the king's lover. He had certainly managed all that quite well, but he couldn't expect to do so forever. Why was he so enraged by King Thol's offering him a perfectly appropriate solution?

Imperfectly appropriate, perhaps. The princess was something of a problem.

Tenar was going to have to try to teach the girl Hardic. And to find ladies willing to instruct her in the manners of the Archipelago and the etiquette of the court—something she certainly wasn't capable of herself. She had more sympathy with the princess's ignorance than with the courtiers' sophistication.

She resented Lebannen's failure or inability to take the girl's point of view. Couldn't he imagine what it was like for her? Brought up in the women's quarters of a warlord's fortress in a remote desert land, where she probably had never seen any man but her father and uncles and some priests; suddenly carried off from that changeless poverty and rigidity of life, by strangers, on a long and frightening sea voyage; abandoned among people whom she knew of only as irreligious and bloodthirsty monsters who dwelt on the far edge of the world, not truly human at all because they were wizards who could turn into animals and birds— And she was to marry one of them!

Tenar had been able to leave her own people and come to live among the monsters and wizards of the West because she had been with Ged, whom she loved and trusted. Even so it had not been easy; often her courage had failed. For all the welcome the people of Havnor had given her, the crowds and cheering and flowers and praise, the sweet names they called her, the White Lady, the Peace Bringer, Tenar of the Ring—for all that, she had cowered in her room in the palace those nights long ago, in misery because she was so lonely, and nobody spoke her language, and she didn't know any of the things they all knew. As soon as the rejoicings were over and the Ring was in its place she had begged Ged to take her away, and he had kept his promise, slipping away with her to Gont. There she had lived in the Old Mage's house as Ogion's ward and pupil, learning how to be an Archipelagan, till she saw the way she wanted to follow for herself as a woman grown.

She had been younger than this girl when she came to Havnor with the Ring. But she had not grown up powerless, as the princess had. Though her power as the One Priestess had been mostly ceremonial, nominal, she had taken real control of her fate when she broke with the grim ways of her upbringing and won freedom for her prisoner and herself. But the daughter of a warlord would have control over only trivial things. When her father made himself king she would be called princess, she would be given richer clothing, more slaves, more eunuchs, more jewelry, until she herself was given in marriage; but she would have no say in any of it. All she ever saw of the world outside the women's quarters would be through window slits in thick walls, through layers of red veiling.

Tenar counted herself lucky not to have been born on so backward and barbaric an island as Hur-at-Hur, never to have worn the *feyag*. But she knew what it was to grow up in the grip of an iron tradition. It behooved her to do what she could to help the princess, so long as she was in Havnor. But she didn't intend to stay here long.

Strolling in the garden, watching the fountains glimmer in starlight, she thought about how and when she could go home.

She did not mind the formalities of court life or the knowledge that under the civility simmered a stew of ambitions, rivalries, passions, complicities, collusions. She had grown up with rituals and hypocrisy and hidden politics, and none of it frightened or worried her. She was simply homesick. She wanted to be back on Gont, with Ged, in their house.

She had come to Havnor because Lebannen sent for her and Tehanu, and Ged if he would come; but Ged wouldn't come, and Tehanu wouldn't come without her. That did frighten and worry her. Could her daughter not break free from her? It was Tehanu's counsel Lebannen needed, not hers. But her daughter clung to her, as ill at ease, as out of place in the court of Havnor as the girl from Hur-at-Hur was, and like her, silent, in hiding.

So Tenar must play nursemaid, tutor, and companion now to both of them, two scared girls who didn't know how to take hold of their power, while she wanted no power on earth except the freedom to go home where she belonged and help Ged with the garden.

She wished they could grow white roses like these, at home. Their scent was so sweet in the night air. But it was too windy on the Overfell, and the sun was too strong in summer. And probably the goats would eat the roses.

She went back indoors at last and made her way through the eastern wing to the suite of rooms she shared with Tehanu. Her daughter was asleep, for it was late. A flame no bigger than a pearl burned on the wick of a tiny alabaster lamp. The high rooms were soft, shadowy. She blew out the lamp, got into bed, and soon sank towards sleep.

She was walking along a narrow, high-vaulted corridor of stone. She carried the alabaster lamp. Its faint oval of light died away into darkness in front of her and behind her. She came to the door of a room that opened off the corridor. Inside the room were people with the wings of birds. Some had the heads of birds, hawks and vultures. They stood or squatted motionless, not looking at her or at anything, with eyes encircled with white and red. Their wings were like huge black cloaks hanging down behind them. She knew they could not fly. They were so mournful, so hopeless, and the air in the room was so foul that she struggled to turn, to run away, but she could not move; and fighting that paralysis, she woke.

There were the warm shadows, the stars in the window, the scent of roses, the soft stir of the city, Tehanu's breathing as she slept.

Tenar sat up to shake off the remnants of the dream. It had been of the Painted Room in the Labyrinth of the Tombs, where she had first met Ged face to face, forty years ago. In the dream the paintings on the walls had come to life. Only it was not life. It was the endless, timeless unlife of those who died without rebirth: those accursed by the Nameless Ones: infidels, westerners, sorcerers.

After you died you were reborn. That was the sure knowledge in which she had been brought up. When as a child she was taken to the Tombs to be Arha, the Eaten One, they told her that she alone of all people had been and would be reborn as herself, life after life. Sometimes she had believed that, but not always, even when she was the priestess of the Tombs, and never since. But she knew what all the people of the Kargad Lands knew, that when they died they would return in a new body, the lamp that guttered out flickering up again that same instant elsewhere, in a woman's womb or the tiny egg of a minnow or a windborne seed of grass, coming back to be, forgetful of the old life, fresh for the new, life after life eternally.

Only those outcast by the earth itself, by the Old Powers, the dark sorcerers of the Hardic Lands, were not reborn. When they died—so said the Kargs—they did not rejoin the living world, but went to a dreary place of half being where, winged but flightless, neither bird nor human, they must endure without hope. How the priestess Kossil had relished telling her about the terrible fate of those boastful enemies of the God-King, their souls doomed to be cast out of the world of light forever!

But the afterlife Ged had told her of, where he said his people went, that changeless land of cold dust and shadow—was that any less dreary, any less terrible?

Unanswerable questions clamored in her mind: because she was no longer a Karg, because she had betrayed the sacred place, must she go to that dry land when she died? Must Ged go there? Would they pass each other there, uncaring? That was not possible. But what if he must go there, and she be reborn, so that their parting must be eternal?

She would not think about all that. It was clear enough why she had dreamed of the Painted Room, all these years after she had left all that behind her. It had to do with seeing the ambassadors, speaking Kargish again, of course. But still she lay upset, unnerved by the dream. She did not want to go back to the nightmares of her youth. She wanted to be back in the house on the Overfell, lying by Ged, hearing Tehanu's breath while she slept. When he slept Ged lay still as a stone; but the fire had left some damage in Tehanu's throat so there was a little harshness always in her breathing, and Tenar had listened to that, listened for it, night after night, year after year. That was life, that was life returning, that dear sound, that slight harsh breath.

Listening to it, she slept again at last. If she dreamed it was only of gulfs of air and the colors of morning moving in the sky.

Alder woke very early. His little companion had been restless all night, and so had he. He was glad to get up and go to the window and sit sleepily watching light come into the sky over the harbor, fishing boats set out and the sails of ships loom from a low mist in the great bay, and listening to the hum and bustle of the city making ready for the day. About the time he began to wonder if he should venture into the bewilderment of the palace to find what he was supposed to do, there was a knock on his door. A man brought in a tray of fresh fruit and bread, a jug of milk, and a small bowl of meat for the kitten. "I will come to conduct you to the king's presence when the fifth hour is told," he informed Alder solemnly, and then rather less formally told him how to get down into the palace gardens if he wanted a walk.

Alder knew of course that there were six hours from midnight to noon and six hours from noon to midnight, but had never heard the hours told, and wondered what the man meant.

He learned, presently, that here in Havnor four trumpeters went out on the high balcony from which rose the highest tower of the palace, the one that was topped with the slender steel blade of the hero's sword, and at the fourth and fifth hours before noon, and at noon, and at the first, second, and third hours after noon they blew their trumpets one to the west, one to the north, one to the east, one to the south. So the courtiers of the palace and the merchants and shippers of the city could arrange their doings and meet their appointments at the hour agreed. A boy he met walking in the gardens explained all this, a small, thin boy in a tunic that was too long for him. He explained that the trumpeters knew when to blow their trumpets because there were great sand clocks in the tower, as well as the Pendulum of Ath which hung down from high up in the tower and if set swinging just at the hour would cease to swing just as the next hour began. And he told Alder that the tunes the trumpeters played were all parts of the Lament for Erreth-Akbe that King Maharion wrote when he came back from Selidor, a different part for each hour, but only at noon did they play the whole tune through. And if you wanted to be somewhere at a certain hour, you should keep an eye on the balconies, because the trumpeters always came out a few minutes early, and if the sun was shining they held up their silver trumpets to flash and shine. The boy was called Rody and he had come with his father, the Lord of Metama on Ark, to stay a year in Havnor, and he went to school in the palace, and he was nine, and he missed his mother and his sister.

Alder was back in his room in time to meet his guide, less nervous than he might have been. The conversation with the child had reminded him that the sons of lords were children, that lords were men, and that it was not men he need fear.

His guide brought him through the palace corridors to a long, light room with windows all along one wall, looking out over Havnor's towers and fantastic bridges that arched over the canals and leapt from roof to roof and balcony to balcony across the streets. He half saw that panorama as he stood near the door, hesitant, not knowing if he should go forward to the group of people at the far end of the room.

The king saw him and came to him, greeted him kindly, led him to the others, and introduced them one by one.

There was a woman of fifty or so, small and very light-skinned, with greying hair and large grey eyes: Tenar, the king said smiling: Tenar of the Ring. She looked Alder in the eye and greeted him quietly.

There was a man of about the king's age, dressed in velvet and airy linens, with jewels on his belt and at his throat and a great ruby stud in his earlobe: Shipmaster Tosla, said the king. Tosla's face, dark as old oak wood, was keen and hard.

There was a middle-aged man, simply dressed, with a steady look that made Alder feel he could trust him: Prince Sege of the House of Havnor, said the king.

There was a man of forty or so who carried a wooden staff of his own height, by which Alder knew him as a wizard of the School on Roke. He had a rather worn face, fine hands, an aloof but courteous manner. Master Onyx, said the king.

There was a woman whom Alder took for a servant because she was very plainly dressed and stayed outside the group, turned half away as if looking out the windows. He saw the beautiful fall of her black hair, heavy and glossy as falling water, as Lebannen led her forward. "Tehanu of Gont," the king said, and his voice rang out like a challenge.

The woman looked straight at Alder for a moment. She was young; the left side of her face was smooth copper-rose, a dark bright eye under an arched eyebrow. The right side had been destroyed and was ridged, slabby scar, eyeless. Her right hand was like a raven's curled claw.

She put out her hand to Alder, in the manner of the people of Éa and the Enlades, as the others had done, but it was her left hand she held out. He touched his hand to hers, palm to palm. Hers was hot, fever hot. She looked at him again, an amazing glance from that one eye, bright, frowning, fierce. Then she looked down again and stood back as if she wished not to be one of them, wished not to be there.

"Master Alder bears a message for you from your father the Hawk of Gont," the king said, seeing the messenger stand wordless.

Tehanu did not lift her head. The glossy black hair almost hid the ruin of her face.

"My lady," Alder said, dry-mouthed and husky-voiced, "he bade me ask you two questions." He paused, only because he had to wet his lips and get his breath in a moment of panic that he had forgotten what he was to say; but the pause became a waiting silence.

Tehanu said, in a voice hoarser than his, "Ask them."

"He said to ask first: *Who are those who go to the dry land?* And as I took my leave of him, he said, 'Ask my daughter also: *Will a dragon cross the wall of stones?*'"

Tehanu nodded her head in acknowledgment and stepped back a little more, as if to carry her riddles away with her, away from them.

"The dry land," the king said, "and the dragons . . ."

His alert gaze went from face to face.

"Come," he said, "let's sit and talk."

"Perhaps we could talk down in the gardens?" said the little grey-eyed woman, Tenar. The king agreed at once. Alder heard Tenar say to him as they went, "She finds it hard to be indoors all day. She wants the sky."

Gardeners brought chairs for them in the shade of a huge old willow beside one of the pools. Tehanu went to stand by the pool, gazing down into the green water where a few big silver carp swam lazily.

Clearly she wanted to think over her father's message, not to talk, though she could hear what they said.

When the others were all settled, the king had Alder tell his story yet again. Their silence as they listened was compassionate, and he was able to speak without constraint or hurry. When he was done, they remained silent a while, and then the wizard Onyx asked him one question: "Did you dream last night?"

Alder said he had had no dream he could recall.

"I did," Onyx said. "I dreamed of the Summoner who was my teacher in the School on Roke. They say of him that he died twice: because he came back from that country across the wall."

"I dreamed of the spirits that are not reborn," Tenar said, very low.

Prince Sege said, "All night I thought I heard voices down in the city streets, voices I knew from my childhood, calling as they used to do. But when I listened, it was only watchmen or drunken sailors shouting."

"I never dream," said Tosla.

"I didn't dream of that country," the king said. "I remembered it. And couldn't cease remembering it."

He looked at the silent woman, Tehanu, but she only looked down into the pond and did not speak.

No one else spoke; and Alder could not stand it. "If I am a plague bringer, you must send me away!" he said.

The wizard Onyx spoke, not imperiously but with finality. "If Roke sent you to Gont, and Gont sent you to Havnor, Havnor is where you should be."

"Many heads make light thinking," said Tosla, sardonic.

Lebannen said, "Let's put dreams aside for a while. Our guest needs to know what we were concerned about before he came—why I begged Tenar and Tehanu to come, earlier this summer, and summoned Tosla from his voyaging to take counsel with us. Will you tell Alder of this matter, Tosla?"

The dark-faced man nodded. The ruby in his ear gleamed like a drop of blood.

"The matter is dragons," he said. "In the West Reach for some years now they've come to farms and villages on Ully and Usidero, flying low, seizing the roofs of houses with their talons, shaking them, terrifying the people. In the Toringates they've come twice now at harvest time and set the fields burning with their breath, and burnt haystacks and set the thatch of houses afire. They haven't struck at people, but people have died in the fires. They haven't attacked the houses of the lords of those islands, seeking after treasure, the way they did in the Dark Years, but only the villages and the fields. The same word came from a merchantman who'd been southwest as far as Simly trading for grain: dragons had come and burnt the crop just as they were harvesting.

"Then, last winter in Semel, two dragons settled on the summit of the volcano, Mount Andanden."

"Ah," said Onyx, and at the king's inquiring glance: "The wizard Seppel of Paln tells me that mountain was a most sacred place to the dragons, where they came to drink fire from the earth in ancient days."

"Well, they're back," said Tosla. "And they come down harrying the herds and flocks that are the wealth of the people there, not hurting the beasts but frightening them so they break loose and run wild. The people say they're young dragons, black and thin, without much fire yet.

"And in Paln, there are dragons living now in the mountains of the north part of the island, wild country without farms. Hunters used to go there to hunt mountain sheep and catch falcons to tame, but they've been driven out by the dragons, and no one goes near the mountains now. Maybe your Pelnish wizard knows about them?"

Onyx nodded. "He says flights of them have been seen above the mountains like the flights of wild geese."

"Between Paln and Semel, and the Island of Havnor, is only the width of the Pelnish Sea," said Prince Sege.

Alder was thinking that it was less than a hundred miles from Semel to his own island, Taon.

"Tosla set out to the Dragons' Run in his ship the *Tern,*" the king said.

"But got barely in sight of the easternmost of those isles before a swarm of the beasts came at me," Tosla said, with a hard grin. "They harried me as they do the cattle and sheep, swooping down to singe my sails, till I ran back where I came from. But that's nothing new."

Onyx nodded again. "Nobody but a dragonlord has ever sailed the Dragons' Run."

"I have," the king said, and suddenly smiled a broad, boyish smile. "But I was with a dragonlord . . . Now that's a time I've been thinking about. When I was in the West Reach with the Archmage, seeking Cob the necromancer, we passed Jessage, which lies even farther out than Simly, and we saw burned fields there. And in the Dragons' Run, we saw that they fought and killed one another like animals gone rabid."

After a time Prince Sege asked, "Could it be that some of those dragons did not recover from their madness in that evil time?"

"It's been fifteen years and more," Onyx said. "But dragons live very long. Maybe time passes differently for them."

Alder noticed that as the wizard spoke he glanced at Tehanu, standing apart from them by the pool.

"Yet only within the last year or two have they attacked people," said the prince.

"That they have not," Tosla said. "If a dragon wanted to destroy the people of a farm or village, who'd stop it? They've been after people's livelihood. Harvests, hayricks, farms, cattle. They're saying, *Begone—get out of the West!*"

"But why are they saying it with fire, with havoc?" the wizard demanded. "They can speak! They speak the Language of the Making. Morred and Erreth-Akbe talked with dragons. Our Archmage talked with them."

"Those we saw in the Dragons' Run," the king said, "had lost the power of speech. The breach Cob had made in the world was drawing their power from them, as it did from us. Only the great dragon Orm Embar came to us and spoke to the Archmage, telling him to go to Selidor . . ." He paused, his eyes far away. "And even from Orm Embar speech was taken, before he died." Again he looked away from them, a strange light in his face. "It was for us Orm Embar died. He opened the way for us into the dark land."

They were all silent for a while. Tenar's quiet voice broke the silence. "Once Sparrowhawk said to me—let me see if I can remember how he said it: that the dragon and the dragon's speech are one thing, one being. That a dragon does not learn the Old Speech, but *is* it."

"As a tern is flight. As a fish is swimming," Onyx said slowly. "Yes."

Tehanu was listening, standing motionless by the pool. They all looked at her now. The look on her mother's face was eager, urgent. Tehanu turned her head away.

"How do you make a dragon talk to you?" the king said. He said it lightly, as if it were a pleasantry, but it was followed by another silence. "Well," he said, "that's something I hope we can learn. Now, Master Onyx, while we're speaking of dragons, will you tell us your story of the girl who came to the School on Roke, for none but me has heard it yet."

"A girl in the School!" said Tosla, with a scoffing grin. "Things have changed on Roke!"

"Indeed they have," the wizard said, with a long cool look at the sailor. "This was some eight years ago. She came from Way, disguised as a young man, wanting to study the art magic. Of course her poor disguise didn't fool the Doorkeeper. Yet he let her in, and he took her part. At that time, the School was headed by the Master Summoner—the man," and he hesitated a moment, "the man of whom I told you I dreamed last night."

"Tell us something of that man, if you will, Master Onyx," the king said. "That was Thorion, who returned from death?"

"Yes. When the Archmage had been long gone and no word came, we feared he was dead. So the Summoner used his arts to go see if indeed he had crossed the wall. He stayed long there, so the masters feared for him too. But at last he woke, and said that the Archmage was there among the dead, and would not return himself but had bade Thorion return to govern Roke. Yet before long the dragon bore the Archmage Sparrowhawk living to us, with my lord Lebannen . . . Then when the Archmage had departed again, the Summoner fell down and lay as if life had gone out of him. The Master Herbal, with all his art, believed him dead. Yet as we made ready to bury him, he moved, and spoke, saying he had come back to life to do what must be done. So, since we were not able to choose a new Archmage, Thorion the Summoner governed the School." He paused. "When the girl came, though the Doorkeeper had admitted her, Thorion would not have her within the walls. He would have nothing to do with her. But the Master Patterner took her to the Grove, and she lived there some while at the edge of the trees, and walked with him among them. He and the Doorkeeper, and the Herbal, and Kurremkarmerruk the Namer, believed that there was a reason she had come to Roke, that she was a messenger or an agent of some great event, even if she herself didn't know it; and so they protected her. The other masters followed Thorion, who said she brought only dissension and ruin and should be driven out. I was a student then. It was a sore trouble to us to know that our masters, masterless, were quarreling."

"And over a girl," said Tosla.

Onyx's look at him this time was extremely cold. "Quite," he said. After a minute he took up his story. "To be brief, then, when Thorion sent a group of us to compel her to leave the island, she challenged him to meet her that evening on Roke Knoll. He came, and summoned her by her name to obey him: 'Irian,' he called her. But she said, 'I am not only Irian,' and speaking, she changed. She became—she took the form of a dragon. She touched Thorion and his body fell to dust. Then she climbed the hill, and watching her, we didn't know whether we saw a woman that burned like a fire, or a winged beast. But at the summit we saw her clearly, a dragon like a flame of red and gold. And she lifted up her wings and flew into the west."

His voice had grown soft and his face was full of the remembered awe. Nobody spoke.

The wizard cleared his throat. "Before she went up the hill the Namer asked her, 'Who are you?' She said she did not know her other name. The Patterner spoke to her, asking where she would go and whether she would come back. She said she was going beyond the west, to learn her name from her own people, but if he called her she would come."

In the silence, a hoarse, weak voice, like metal brushing on metal, spoke. Alder did not understand the words and yet they seemed familiar, as if he could almost remember what they meant.

Tehanu had come close to the wizard and was standing by him, bending to him, tense as a drawn bow. It was she who had spoken.

Startled and taken aback, the wizard stared up at her, got to his feet, backed off a step, and then controlling himself said, "Yes, those were her words: *My people, beyond the west.*"

"Call her. Oh, call her," Tehanu whispered, reaching out both her hands to him. Again he drew back involuntarily.

Tenar stood up and murmured to her daughter, "What is it, what is it, Tehanu?"

Tehanu stared round at them all. Alder felt as if he were a wraith she saw through. "Call her here," she said. She looked at the king. "Can you call her?"

"I have no such power. Perhaps the Patterner of Roke—perhaps you yourself—"

Tehanu shook her head violently. "No, no, no, no," she whispered. "I am not like her. I have no wings."

Lebannen looked at Tenar as if for guidance. Tenar looked miserably at her daughter.

Tehanu turned round and faced the king. "I'm sorry," she said, stiffly, in her weak, harsh voice. "I have to be alone, sir. I will think about what my father said. I will try to answer what he asked. But I have to be alone, please."

Lebannen bowed to her and glanced at Tenar, who went at once to her daughter and put an arm about her; and they went away on the sunny path by the pools and fountains.

The four men sat down again and said nothing for a few minutes.

Lebannen said, "You were right, Onyx," and to the others, "Master Onyx told me this tale of the woman-dragon Irian after I told him something about Tehanu. How as a child Tehanu summoned the dragon Kalessin to Gont, and spoke with the dragon in the Old Speech, and Kalessin called her daughter."

"Sire, this is very strange, this is a strange time, when a dragon is a woman, and when an untaught girl speaks in the Language of the Making!" Onyx was deeply and obviously shaken, frightened. Alder saw that, and wondered why he himself felt no such fear. Probably, he thought, because he did not know enough to be afraid, or what to be afraid of.

"But there are old stories," Tosla said. "Haven't you heard them on Roke? Maybe your walls keep them out. They're only tales simple people tell. Songs, even. There's a sailors' song, 'The Lass of Belilo,' that tells how a sailor left a pretty girl weeping in every port, until one of the pretty girls flew after his boat on wings of brass and snatched him out of it and ate him."

Onyx looked at Tosla with disgust. But Lebannen smiled and said, "The Woman of Kemay . . . The Archmage's old master, Aihal, called Ogion, told Tenar about her. She was an old village woman, and lived as such. She invited Ogion into her cottage and served him fish soup. But she said mankind and dragonkind had once been one. She herself was a dragon as well as a woman. And being a mage, Ogion saw her as a dragon."

"As you saw Irian, Onyx," said Lebannen.

Speaking stiffly and addressing himself to the king only, Onyx said, "After Irian left Roke, the Master Namer showed us passages in the most ancient lore-books which had always been obscure, but which could be understood to speak of beings both human and dragon. And of a quarrel or great division among them. But none of this is clear to our understanding."

"I hoped that Tehanu might make it clear," Lebannen said. His voice was even, so that Alder did not know whether he had given up or still held that hope.

A man was hurrying down the path to them, a grey-headed soldier of the king's guards. Lebannen looked round, stood up, went to him. They conferred for a minute, low-voiced. The soldier strode off again; the king turned back to his companions. "Here is news," he said, the ring of challenge in his voice again. "Over the west of Havnor there have been great flights of dragons. They have set forests afire, and a coaster's crew say people fleeing down to South Port told them the town of Resbel is burning."

That night the king's swiftest ship carried him and his party across the Bay of Havnor, running fast before the magewind Onyx raised. They came into the mouth of the Onneva River, under the shoulder of Mount Onn, at daybreak. With them eleven horses were disembarked, fine, strong, slender-legged creatures from the royal stables. Horses were rare on all the islands but Havnor and Semel. Tehanu knew donkeys well enough but had never seen a horse before. She had spent much of the night with them and their handlers, helping control and calm them. They were well-bred, mannerly horses but not used to sea voyages.

When it came time to mount them, there on the sands of the Onneva, Onyx was fairly daunted, and had to be coached and encouraged by the handlers, but Tehanu was up in the saddle as soon as the king. She put the reins in her crippled hand and did not use them, seeming to communicate with her mare by other means.

So the little caravan set off due west into the foothills of the Falierns, keeping up a good pace. It was the swiftest way to travel that Lebannen had at his disposal; to coast clear round South Havnor would take too long. They had the wizard Onyx with them to keep the weather favorable, clear the path of any obstacles, and defend them from any harm short of dragon fire. Against the dragons, if they encountered them, they had no defense at all, except perhaps Tehanu.

Taking counsel the evening before with his advisors and the officers of his guard, Lebannen had quickly concluded that there was no way to fight the dragons or protect the towns and fields from them: arrows were useless, shields were useless. Only the greatest mages had ever been able to defeat a dragon. He had no such mage in his service and knew of none now living, but he must defend his people as best he could, and he knew no way to do it but to try to parley with the dragons.

His majordomo had been shocked when he set off for the apartment where Tenar and Tehanu were: the king should send for those he wished to see, command them to come to him. "Not if he's going to beg from them," Lebannen said.

He told the startled maid who answered their door to ask if he might speak with the White Lady and the Woman of Gont. So they were known to the people of the palace and the city. That each bore her true name openly, as the king did, was so rare a matter, so defiant of rule and custom, of safety and propriety, that though people might know the name they were reluctant to say it and preferred to speak around it.

He was admitted, and having told them briefly the news he had received, said, "Tehanu, it may be that you alone in my kingdom can help me. If you can call to these dragons as you called to Kalessin, if you have any power over them, if you can speak to them and ask why they war on my people, will you do so?"

The young woman shrank from his words, turning towards her mother.

But Tenar did not offer her any shelter. She stood unmoving. After a while she said, "Tehanu, long ago I told you: when a king speaks to you, you answer. You were a child then, and didn't answer. You're not a child now."

Tehanu took a step back from them both. Like a child, she hung her head. "I can't call to them," she said in her faint, harsh voice. "I don't know them."

"Can you call Kalessin?" Lebannen asked.

She shook her head. "Too far away," she whispered. "I don't know where."

"But you are Kalessin's daughter," Tenar said. "Can you not speak to these dragons?"

She said wretchedly, "I don't know."

Lebannen said, "If there is any chance, Tehanu, that they'll talk to you, that you can talk to them, I beg you to take that chance. For I can't fight them, and don't know their language, and how can I find what they want of us from creatures who can destroy me with a breath, with a look? Will you speak for me, for us?"

She was silent. Then, so faintly he could barely hear it, she said, "Yes."

"Then make ready to travel with me. We leave by the fourth hour of the evening. My people will bring you to the ship. I thank you. And I thank you, Tenar!" he said, taking her hand a moment, but no longer, for he had much to see to before he went.

When he came down to the wharf, late and hurrying, there was the slender hooded figure. The last horse to be led aboard was snorting and bracing its feet, refusing to go up the gangplank. Tehanu seemed to be conferring with the handler. Presently she took the horse's bridle and talked to it a little, and they went up the gangplank quietly together.

Ships are small, crowded houses; Lebannen heard two of the hostlers talking softly on the afterdeck towards midnight. "She has the true hand," one said, and the other, a younger voice, "Aye, she does, but she's horrible to look at, ain't she?" The first one said, "If a horse don't mind it, why should you?" and the other, "I don't know, but I do."

Now, as they rode from the Onneva sands into the foothills, where the way widened, Tosla brought his horse up beside Lebannen's. "She's to be our interpreter, is she?" he asked.

"If she can."

"Well, she's braver than I'd have thought. If that happened to her the first time she talked with a dragon, it's likely to happen again."

"What do you mean?"

"She was half burnt to death."

"Not by a dragon."

"Who then?"

"The people she was born to."

"How was that?" Tosla asked with a grimace.

"Tramps, thieves. She was five or six years old. Whatever she did or they did, it ended in her being beaten unconscious and shoved into their campfire. Thinking, I suppose, she was dead or would die and it would be taken for an accident. They made off. Villagers found her, and Tenar took her in."

Tosla scratched his ear. "There's a pretty tale of human kindness. So she's no daughter of the old Archmage either? But then what do they mean saying she's a dragon's get?"

Lebannen had sailed with Tosla, had fought beside him years ago in the siege of Sorra, and knew him a brave, keen, coolheaded man. When Tosla's coarseness chafed him he blamed his own thin skin. "I don't know what they mean," he answered mildly. "All I know is, the dragon called her daughter."

"That Roke wizard of yours, that Onyx, is quick to say he's no use in this matter. But he can speak the Old Tongue, can't he?"

"Yes. He could wither you into ash with a few words of it. If he hasn't it's out of respect for me, not you, I think."

Tosla nodded. "I know that," he said.

They rode all that day at as quick a pace as the horses could keep, coming at nightfall to a little hill town where the horses could be fed and rested and the riders could sleep in variously uncomfortable beds. Those of them unused to riding now discovered they could barely walk. The people there had heard nothing about dragons, and were overwhelmed only by the terror and glory of a whole party of rich strangers riding in and wanting oats and beds and paying for them with silver and gold.

The riders set off again long before dawn. It was nearly a hundred miles from the sands of Onneva to Resbel. This second day would take them over the low pass of the Faliern Mountains and down the western side. Yenay, one of Lebannen's most trusted officers, rode well ahead of the others; Tosla was rear guard; Lebannen led the main group. He was jogging along half asleep in the dull quiet before dawn when hoofbeats coming towards him woke him. Yenay had come riding back. Lebannen looked up where the man was pointing.

They had just emerged from woods on the crest of an open hillside and could see through the clear half light all the way to the pass. The mountains to either side of it massed black against the dull reddish glow of a cloudy dawn.

But they were looking west.

"That's nearer than Resbel," Yenay said. "Fifteen miles, maybe."

Tehanu's mare, though small, was the finest of the lot, and had a strong conviction that she should lead the others. If Tehanu didn't hold her back she would keep sidling and overtaking till she was ahead of the line. The mare came up at once when Lebannen reined in his big horse, and so Tehanu was beside him now, looking where he looked.

"The forest is burning," he said to her.

He could see only the scarred side of her face, so she seemed to gaze blindly; but she saw, and her claw hand that held the reins was trembling. The burned child fears the fire, he thought.

What cruel, cowardly folly had possessed him to tell this girl, "Come talk to the dragons, save my skin!" and bring her straight into the fire?

"We will turn back," he said.

Tehanu raised her good hand, pointing. "Look," she said. "Look!"

A spark from a bonfire, a burning cinder rising over the black line of the pass, an eagle of flame soaring, a dragon flying straight at them.

Tehanu stood up in her stirrups and let out a piercing, scraping cry, like a sea bird's or a hawk's scream, but it was a word, one word: *"Medeu!"*

The great creature drew nearer with terrible speed, its long, thin wings beating almost lazily; it had lost the reflection of fire and looked black or bronze-colored in the growing light.

"Mind your horses," Tehanu said in her cracked voice, and just then Lebannen's grey gelding saw the dragon and started violently, tossing its head and backing. He could control it, but behind him one of the other horses let out a neigh of terror, and he heard them trampling and the handlers' voices. The wizard Onyx came running up and stood beside Lebannen's horse. Mounted or afoot, they stood and watched the dragon come.

Again Tehanu cried out that word. The dragon veered in its flight, slowed, came on, stopped and hovered in the air about fifty feet from them.

"Medeu!" Tehanu called, and the answer came like an echo prolonged: *"Me-de-uuu!"*

"What does it mean?" Lebannen asked, bending to Onyx.

"Sister, brother," the wizard whispered.

Tehanu was off her horse, had tossed the reins to Yenay, was walking forward down the slight slope to where the dragon hovered, its long wings beating quick and short like a hovering hawk's. But these wings were fifty feet from tip to tip, and as they beat they made a sound like kettledrums or rattles of brass. As she came closer to it, a little curl of fire escaped from the dragon's long, long-toothed, open mouth.

She held up her hand. Not the slender brown hand but the burned one, the claw. The scarring of her arm and shoulder kept her from raising it fully. She could reach barely as high as her head.

The dragon sank a little in the air, lowered its head, and touched her hand with its lean, flared, scaled snout. Like a dog, an animal greeting and sniffing, Lebannen thought; like a falcon stooping to the wrist; like a king bowing to a queen.

Tehanu spoke, the dragon spoke, both briefly, in their cymbal-shiver voices. Another exchange, a pause; the dragon spoke at length. Onyx listened intently. One more exchange of words. A wisp of smoke from the dragon's nostrils; a stiff, imperious gesture of the woman's crippled, withered hand. She spoke clearly two words.

"Bring her," the wizard translated in a whisper.

The dragon beat its wings hard, lowered its long head, and hissed, spoke again, then sprang up into the air, high over Tehanu, turned, wheeled once, and set off like an arrow to the west.

"It called her Daughter of the Eldest," the wizard whispered, as Tehanu stood motionless, watching the dragon go.

She turned around, looking small and fragile in that great sweep of hill and forest in the grey dawn light. Lebannen swung off his horse and hurried forward to her. He thought to find her drained and terrified, he put out his hand to help her walk, but she smiled at him. Her face, half terrible half beautiful, shone with the red light of the unrisen sun.

"They won't strike again. They will wait in the mountains," she said.

Then indeed she looked around as if she did not know where she was, and when Lebannen took her arm she let him do so; but the fire and the smile lingered in her face, and she walked lightly.

While the hostlers held the horses, already grazing on the dew-wet grass, Onyx, Tosla, and Yenay came round her, though they kept a respectful distance. Onyx said, "My Lady Tehanu, I have never seen so brave an act."

"Nor I," Tosla said.

"I was afraid," Tehanu said, in her voice that carried no emotion. "But I called him brother, and he called me sister."

"I could not understand all you said," the wizard said. "I have no such knowledge of the Old Speech as you. Will you tell us what passed between you?"

She spoke slowly, her eyes on the west where the dragon had flown. The dull red of the distant fire was paling as the east grew bright. "I said, 'Why are you burning the king's island?' And he said, 'It is time we have our own lands again.' And I said, 'Did the Eldest bid you take them with fire?' Then he said that the Eldest, Kalessin, had gone with Orm Irian beyond the west to fly on the other wind. And he said the young dragons who remained here on the winds of the world say men are oath breakers who stole the dragons' lands. They tell one another that Kalessin will never return, and they will wait no longer, but will drive men out of all the western lands. But lately Orm Irian has returned, and is on Paln, he said. And I told him to ask her to come. And he said she would come to Kalessin's daughter."

CHAPTER III

The Dragon Council

FROM THE WINDOW OF her room in the palace Tenar had watched the ship sail, carrying Lebannen and her daughter away into the night. She had not gone down to the wharf with Tehanu. It had been hard, very hard to refuse to come with her on this journey. Tehanu had begged, she who never asked for anything. She never cried, could not cry, but her breath had caught sobbing: "But I can't go, I *can't* go alone! Come with me, mother!"

"My love, my heart, if I could spare you this fear I would, don't you see I can't? I've done what I could do for you, my flame of fire, my star. The king is right—only you, you alone, can do this."

"But if you were just there, so I knew you were there—"

"I'm here, I'm always here. What could I do there but be a burden? You must travel fast, it will be a hard journey. I'd hold you back. And you might fear for me. You don't need me. I'm no use to you. You must learn that. You must go, Tehanu."

And she had turned away from her child and begun sorting out the clothing Tehanu should take, home clothes, not the fancy things they wore here in the palace: her stout shoes, her good cloak. If she wept while she did it, she did not let her daughter see it.

Tehanu stood as if bewildered, paralysed with fear. When Tenar gave her clothes to change into, she obeyed. When the king's lieutenant, Yenay, knocked and asked if he might conduct Mistress Tehanu down to the wharf, she stared at him like a dumb animal.

"Go now," Tenar said. She embraced her and laid her hand on the great scar that was half her face. "You are Kalessin's daughter as well as mine."

The girl held her very tightly for a long moment, let go, turned away without a word, and followed Yenay out the door.

Tenar stood feeling the chill of the night air where the heat of Tehanu's body and arms had been.

She went over to the window. Lights down on the dock, the coming and going of men, the hoof clatter of horses being led down the steep streets above the water. A tall ship was at the pier, a ship she knew, the *Dolphin.* She watched from the window and saw Tehanu on the dock. She saw her go aboard at last, leading a horse that had been balking, and saw Lebannen follow her. She saw the mooring lines cast off, the docile movement of the ship following the oared tug that towed her clear, the sudden fall and flowering of the white sails in the darkness. The light of the stern lantern trembled on the dark water, shrank slowly to a tiny drop of brightness, and was gone.

Tenar went about the room folding up the clothes Tehanu had worn, the silken shift and overskirt; she picked up the light sandals and held them to her cheek a while before she put them away.

She lay awake in the wide bed and saw before her mind's eye over and over again the same scene: a road, and Tehanu walking on it alone. And a knot, a net, a black writhing coiling mass descending from the sky, dragons swarming, fire licking and streaming from them at her, her hair burning, her clothes burning— No, Tenar said, no! it will not happen! She would force her mind away from that scene, until she saw it again, the road, and Tehanu walking on it alone, and the black, burning knot in the sky, coming closer.

When the first light began to turn the room grey she slept at last, exhausted. She dreamed that she was in the Old Mage's house on the Overfell, her house, and she was glad beyond all words to be there. She took the broom from behind the door to sweep the shining oaken floor, for Ged had let it get dusty. But there was a door at the back of the house that had not been there before. When she opened it she found a small, low room with stone walls painted white. Ged was crouching in the room, squatting with his arms on his knees and his hands hanging limp. His head was not a man's head but small, black, and beaked, a vulture's head. He said in a faint, hoarse voice, "Tenar, I have no wings." And when he said that, such anger and terror rose up in her that she woke, gasping, to see sunlight on the high wall of her palace room and hear the sweet clear trumpets telling the fourth hour of morning.

Breakfast was brought. She ate a little and talked with Berry, the elderly servant whom she had chosen from all the retinue of maids and ladies of honor Lebannen had offered her. Berry was an intelligent, competent woman, born in a village in inland Havnor, with whom Tenar got on better than with most of the ladies of the court. They were civil and respectful, but they didn't know what to do with her, how to talk to a woman who was half Kargish priestess, half farmwife from Gont. She saw that it was easier for them to be kind to Tehanu in her fierce timidity. They could be sorry for her. They could not be sorry for Tenar.

Berry, however, could be and was, and she gave Tenar considerable comfort that morning. "The king will bring her back safe and sound," she said. "Why, do you think he'd take the girl into a danger he couldn't get her out of? Never! Not him!" It was false comfort, but Berry so passionately believed it to be true that Tenar had to agree with her, which was a little solace in itself.

She needed something to do, for Tehanu's absence was everywhere. She resolved to go talk to the Kargish princess, to see if the girl was willing to learn a word of Hardic, or at least to tell Tenar her name.

In the Kargad Lands people did not have a true name that they kept secret, as the speakers of Hardic did. Like use-names here, Kargish names often had some meaning—Rose, Alder, Honor, Hope; or they were traditional, often the name of an ancestor. People spoke them openly and were proud of the antiquity of a name passed down from generation to generation. She had been taken too young from her parents to know why they had called her Tenar, but thought it might be for a grandmother or great-grandmother. That name had been taken from her when she was recognised as Arha, the Nameless One reborn, and she had forgotten it till Ged gave it back to her. To her, as to him, it was her true name; but it was not a word of the Old Speech; it gave no one any power over her, and she had never concealed it.

She was puzzled now why the princess did so. Her bondwomen called her only Princess, or Lady, or Mistress; the ambassadors had talked about her as the High Princess, Daughter of Thol, Lady of Hur-at-Hur, and so on. If all the poor girl had was titles, it was time she had a name.

Tenar knew it was not fitting for a guest of the king to go alone through the streets of Havnor, and she knew Berry had duties in the palace, so she asked for a servant to accompany her. She was provided with a charming footman, or footboy, for he was only about fifteen, who looked after her at the street crossings as if she were a doddering crone. She liked walking in the city. She had already found and admitted to herself, going to the River House, that it was easier without Tehanu beside her. People would look at Tehanu and look away, and Tehanu walked in stiff, suffering pride, hating their looks and their looking away, and Tenar suffered with her, maybe more than she herself did.

Now she was able to loiter and watch the street shows, the market booths, the various faces and clothing from all over the Archipelago, to go out of the direct way to let her footboy show her a street where the painted bridges from rooftop to rooftop made a kind of airy vaulted ceiling high above them, from which red-flowering vines looped down in festoons, and people put birdcages out the windows on gilt poles among the flowers, so that it all seemed a garden in the middle of the air. "Oh, I wish Tehanu could see this," she thought. But she could not think of Tehanu, of where she might be.

The River House, like the New Palace, dated from the reign of Queen Heru, five centuries ago. It had been in ruins when Lebannen came to the throne; he had rebuilt it with much care, and it was a lovely, peaceful place, sparsely furnished, with dark, polished, uncarpeted floors. Ranks of narrow door-windows slid aside to open up the whole side of a room to a view of the willows and the river, and one could walk out onto deep wooden balconies built over the water. Court ladies had told Tenar that it had been the place the king liked best to slip away to for a night of solitude or a night with a lover, which lent even more significance, they hinted, to his housing the princess there. Her own suspicion was that he had not wanted the princess under the same roof with him and had simply named the only other possible place for her, but maybe the court ladies were right.

Guards in their fine harness recognised and let her pass, footmen announced her and went off with her footboy to crack nuts and gossip, which seemed to be the principal occupation of footmen, and ladies-in-waiting came to greet her, grateful for any new face and gasping for more news of the king's expedition against the dragons. Having run the whole gamut she was admitted at last to the apartments of the princess.

On her two previous visits she had been kept waiting some while in an anteroom, and then the veiled bondwomen had brought her into an inner room, the only dim room in the whole airy house, where the princess had stood in her round-brimmed hat with the red veil hanging down all round it to the floor, looking permanently fixed there, built in, exactly as if she were a brick chimney, as Lady Iyesa had said.

This time it was different. As soon as she came into the anteroom there was shrieking within and the sound of people running in various directions. The princess burst through the door and with a wild cry flung her arms around Tenar. Tenar was small, and the princess, a tall, vigorous young woman full of emotion, knocked her right off her feet, but held her up in strong arms. "Oh Lady Arha, Lady Arha, save me, save me!" she was crying.

"Princess! What's wrong?"

The princess was in tears of terror or relief or both at once, and all Tenar could understand of her laments and pleas was a babble of dragons and sacrifice.

"There are no dragons near Havnor," she said sternly, disengaging herself from the girl, "and nobody is being sacrificed. What is all this about? What have you been told?"

"The women said the dragons were coming and they'd sacrifice a king's daughter and not a goat because they're sorcerers and I was afraid." The princess wiped her face, clenched her hands, and began trying to master the panic she had been in. It had been real, ungovernable terror, and Tenar was sorry for her. She did not let her pity show. The girl needed to learn to hold on to her dignity.

"Your women are ignorant and don't know enough Hardic to understand what people tell them. And you don't know any Hardic at all. If you did you'd know there's nothing to be afraid of. Do you see the people of the house here rushing about weeping and screaming?"

The princess stared at her. She wore no hat, no veils, and only a light shift-dress, for it was a hot day. It was the first time Tenar had seen her except as a dim form through the red veiling. Though the princess's eyes were swollen with tears and her face blotched, she was magnificent: tawny-haired, tawny-eyed, with round arms and full breasts and slender waist, a woman in her first full beauty and strength.

"But none of those people is going to be sacrificed," she said finally.

"Nobody is going to be sacrificed."

"Then why are the dragons coming?"

Tenar drew a deep breath. "Princess," she said, "there are a great many things we need to talk about. If you'll look at me as your friend—"

"I do," the princess said. She stepped forward and took Tenar's right arm in a very strong grasp. "You are my friend, I have no other friend, I will shed my blood for you."

Ridiculous as it was, Tenar knew it was true.

She returned the girl's grip as well as she could and said, "You are my friend. Tell me your name."

The princess's eyes got big. There was a little snot and blubber still on her upper lip. Her lower lip trembled. She said, with a deep breath, "Seserakh."

"Seserakh: my name is not Arha, but Tenar."

"Tenar," the girl said, and grasped her arm tighter.

"Now," Tenar said, trying to regain control of the situation, "I have walked a long way and I'm thirsty. Please let's sit down, and may I have some water to drink? And then we can talk."

"Yes," said the princess, and leapt out of the room like a hunting lioness. There were shouts and cries from the inner rooms, and more sounds of running. A bondwoman appeared, adjusting her veil shakily and gibbering something in such thick dialect Tenar could not understand her. "Speak in the accursed tongue!" shouted the princess from within, and the woman pitifully squeaked out in Hardic, "To sit? to drink? lady?"

Two chairs had been set in the middle of the dark, stuffy room, facing each other. Seserakh stood beside one of them.

"I should like to sit outside, in the shade, over the water," Tenar said. "If it please you, princess."

The princess shouted, the women scuttled, the chairs were carried out onto the deep balcony. They sat down side by side.

"That's better," Tenar said. It was still strange to her to be speaking Kargish. She had no difficulty with it at all, but she felt as if she were not herself, were somebody else speaking, an actor enjoying her role.

"You *like* the water?" the princess asked. Her face had returned to its normal color, that of heavy cream, and her eyes, no longer swollen, were bluish gold, or blue with gold flecks.

"Yes. You don't?"

"I hate it. There was no water where I lived."

"A desert? I lived in a desert too. Until I was sixteen. Then I crossed the sea and came west. I love the water, the sea, the rivers."

"Oh, the sea," Seserakh said, shrinking and putting her head in her hands. "Oh I hate it, I hate it. I vomited my soul out. Over and over and over. Days and days and days. I never want to see the sea again." She shot a quick glance through the willow boughs at the quiet, shallow stream below them. "This river is all right," she said distrustfully.

A woman brought a tray with a pitcher and cups, and Tenar had a long drink of cool water.

"Princess," she said, "we have a great deal to talk about. First: the dragons are still a long way away, in the west. The king and my daughter have gone to talk with them."

"To *talk* with them?"

"Yes." She had been going to say more, but she said, "Now please tell me about the dragons in Hur-at-Hur."

Tenar had been told as a child in Atuan that there were dragons in Hur-at-Hur. Dragons in the mountains, brigands in the deserts. Hur-at-

Hur was poor and far away and nothing good came from it but opals and turquoises and cedar logs.

Seserakh heaved a deep sigh. Tears came into her eyes. "It makes me cry to think about home," she said, with such pure simplicity of feeling that tears came into Tenar's eyes too. "Well, the dragons live up in the mountains. Two days, three days journey from Mesreth. It's all rocks up there and nobody bothers the dragons and they don't bother anybody. But once a year they come down, crawling down a certain way. It's a path, all smooth dust, made by their bellies crawling along it every year since time began. It's called the Dragons' Way." She saw that Tenar was listening with deep attention, and went on. "It's taboo to cross the Dragons' Way. You mustn't set foot on it at all. You have to go clear round it, south of the Place of the Sacrifice. They start crawling down it late in spring. On the fourth day of the fifth month they've all arrived at the Place of the Sacrifice. None of them is ever late. And everybody from Mesreth and the villages is there waiting for them. And then, when they've all come down the Dragons' Way, the priests begin the sacrifice. And that's . . . Don't you have the spring sacrifice, in Atuan?"

Tenar shook her head.

"Well, that's why I got scared, you see, because it can be a human sacrifice. If things weren't going well, they'd sacrifice a king's daughter. Otherwise it would just be some ordinary girl. But they haven't done even that for a long time. Not since I was little. Since my father defeated all the other kings. Since then, they've only sacrificed a she-goat and a ewe. And they catch the blood in bowls, and throw the fat into the sacred fire, and call to the dragons. And the dragons all come crawling up. They drink the blood and eat the fire." She shut her eyes for a moment; so did Tenar. "Then they go back up into the mountains, and we go back to Mesreth."

"How big are the dragons?"

Seserakh put her hands about a yard apart. "Sometimes bigger," she said.

"And they can't fly? Or speak?"

"Oh, no. Their wings are just little stubs. They make a kind of hissing. Animals can't talk. But they're sacred animals. They're the sign of life, because fire is life, and they eat fire and spit out fire. And they're sacred because they come to the spring sacrifice. Even if no people came, the dragons would come and gather at that place. We come there because the dragons do. The priests always tell all about that before the sacrifice."

Tenar absorbed this for a while. "The dragons here in the west," she said, "are large. Huge. And they can fly. They're animals, but they can speak. And they are sacred. And dangerous."

"Well," the princess said, "dragons may be animals, but they're more like us than the accursed-sorcerers are."

She said "accursed-sorcerers" all as one word and without any particular emphasis. Tenar remembered that phrase from her childhood. It meant the Dark Folk, the Hardic people of the Archipelago.

"Why is that?"

"Because the dragons are reborn! Like all the animals. Like us." Seserakh looked at Tenar with frank curiosity. "I thought since you were a priestess at the Most Sacred Place of the Tombs you'd know a lot more about all that than I do."

"But we had no dragons there," Tenar said. "I didn't learn anything about them at all. Please, my friend, tell me."

"Well, let me see if I can tell the story about it. It's a winter story. I guess it's all right to tell it in summer here. Everything here is all wrong anyway." She sighed. "Well, in the beginning, you know, in the first time, we were all the same, all the people and the animals, we did the same things. And then we learned how to die. And so we learned how to be reborn. Maybe as one kind of being, maybe another. But it doesn't matter so much because anyhow you'll die again and get reborn again and get to be everything sooner or later."

Tenar nodded. So far, the story was familiar to her.

"But the best things to get reborn as are people and dragons, because those are the sacred beings. So you try not to break the taboos, and you try to observe the Precepts, so you have a better chance to be a person again, or anyhow a dragon . . . If dragons here can talk and are so big, I can see why that would be a reward. Being one of ours never seemed like much to look forward to.

"But the story is about the accursed-sorcerers discovering the Vedurnan. That was a thing, I don't know what it was, that told some people that if they'd agree never to die and never be reborn, they could learn how to do sorcery. So they chose that, they chose the Vedurnan. And they went off into the west with it. And it turned them dark. And they live here. All these people here—they're the ones who chose the Vedurnan. They live, and they can do their accursed sorceries, but they can't die. Only their bodies die. The rest of them stays in a dark place and never gets reborn. And they look like birds. But they can't fly."

"Yes," Tenar whispered.

"You didn't learn about that on Atuan?"

"No," Tenar said.

Her mind was recalling the story the Woman of Kemay told

Ogion: in the beginning of time, mankind and the dragons had been one, but the dragons chose wildness and freedom, and mankind chose wealth and power. A choice, a separation. Was it the same story?

But the image in Tenar's heart was of Ged squatting in a stone room, his head small, black, beaked . . .

"The Vedurnan isn't that ring, is it, that they kept talking about, that I'm going to have to wear?"

Tenar tried to force her mind away from the Painted Room and from last night's dream to Seserakh's question.

"Ring?"

"Urthakby's ring."

"Erreth-Akbe. No. That ring is the Ring of Peace. And you'll wear it only if and when you're King Lebannen's queen. And you'll be a lucky woman to be that."

Seserakh's expression was curious. It was not sullen or cynical. It was hopeless, half humorous, patient, the expression of a woman decades older. "There is no luck about it, dear friend Tenar," she said. "I have to marry him. And so I will be lost."

"Why are you lost if you marry him?"

"If I marry him I have to give him my name. If he speaks my name, he steals my soul. That's what the accursed-sorcerers do. So they always hide their names. But if he steals my soul, I won't be able to die. I'll have to live forever without my body, a bird that can't fly, and never be reborn."

"That's why you hid your name?"

"I gave it to you, my friend."

"I honor the gift, my friend," Tenar said energetically. "But you can say your name to anybody you want, here. They can't steal your soul with it. Believe me, Seserakh. And you can trust him. He doesn't—he won't do you any harm."

The girl had caught her hesitation. "But he wishes he could," she said. "Tenar my friend, I know what I am, here. In that big city Awabath where my father is, I was a stupid ignorant desert woman. A *feyagat.* The city women sniggered and poked each other whenever they saw me, the barefaced whores. And here it's worse. I can't understand anybody and they can't understand me, and everything, everything is different! I don't even know what the food is, it's sorcerer food, it makes me dizzy. I don't know what the taboos are, there aren't any priests to ask, only sorcerer women, all black and barefaced. And I saw the way he looked at me. You can see out of the *feyag,* you know! I saw his face. He's very handsome, he looks like a warrior, but he's a black sorcerer and he hates me. Don't say he doesn't, because I know he does. And I think when he learns my name he'll send my soul to that place forever."

After a while, gazing into the moving branches of the willows over the softly moving water, feeling sad and weary, Tenar said, "What you need to do, then, princess, is learn how to make him like you. What else can you do?"

Seserakh shrugged mournfully.

"It would help if you understood what he said."

"Bagabba-bagabba. They all sound like that."

"And we sound like that to them. Come on, princess, how can he like you if all *you* can say to *him* is bagabba-bagabba? Look," and she held up her hand, pointed to it with the other, and said the word first in Kargish, then in Hardic.

Seserakh repeated both words in a dutiful tone. After a few more body parts she suddenly grasped the potentialities of translation. She sat up straighter. "How do sorcerers say 'king'?"

"Agni. It's a word of the Old Speech. My husband told me that."

She realised as she spoke that it was foolish to bring up the existence of yet a third language at this point; but that was not what caught the princess's attention.

"You have a husband?" Seserakh stared at her with luminous, leonine eyes, and laughed aloud. "Oh, how wonderful! I thought you were a priestess! Oh please, my friend, tell me about him! Is he a warrior? Is he handsome? Do you love him?"

After the king went dragon hunting, Alder had no idea what to do; he felt utterly useless, unjustified in staying in the palace eating the king's food, guilty for the trouble he had brought with him. He could not sit all day in his room, so he went out into the streets, but the splendor and activity of the city were daunting to him, and having no money or purpose all he could do was walk till he was tired. He would come back to the Palace of Maharion wondering if the stern-faced guards would readmit him. The nearest he came to peace was in the palace gardens. He hoped to meet Rody there again, but the child did not appear, and perhaps that was as well. Alder thought that he should not talk with people. The hands that reached to him from death would reach out to them.

On the third day after the king's departure he went down to walk among the garden pools. The day had been very hot; the evening was still and sultry. He brought Tug with him and let the little cat loose to stalk insects under the bushes, while he sat on a bench near the big willow and watched the silver-green glimmer of fat carp in the water. He felt lonely and discouraged; he felt his defense against the voices and the reaching hands was breaking down. What was the good of being here, after all? Why not go into the dream once and for all, go down that hill, be done with it? Nobody in the world would grieve for him, and his death would spare them this sickness he had brought with him. Surely they had enough to do fighting dragons. Maybe if he went there he would see Lily.

If he was dead they could not touch each other. The wizards said they would not even want to. They said the dead forgot what it was to be alive. But Lily had reached to him. At first, for a little while, maybe they would remember life long enough to look at each other, to see each other, even if they did not touch.

"Alder."

He looked up slowly at the woman who stood near him. The small grey woman, Tenar. He saw the concern in her face, but did not know why she was troubled. Then he remembered that her daughter, the burned girl, had gone with the king. Maybe there had been bad news. Maybe they were all dead.

"Are you ill, Alder?" she asked.

He shook his head. It was hard to talk. He understood now how easy it would be, in that other land, not to speak. Not to meet people's eyes. Not to be troubled.

She sat down on the bench beside him. "You look troubled," she said.

He made a vague gesture—it's all right, it's no matter.

"You were on Gont. With my husband Sparrowhawk. How was he? Was he looking after himself?"

"Yes," Alder said. He tried to answer more adequately. "He was the kindest of hosts."

"I'm glad to hear that," she said. "I worry about him. He keeps house as well as I do, but still, I didn't like leaving him alone . . . Please, would you tell me what he was doing while you were there?"

He told her that Sparrowhawk had picked the plums and taken them to sell, that the two of them had mended the fence, that Sparrowhawk had helped him sleep.

She listened intently, seriously, as if these small matters were as weighty as the strange events they had talked about here three days ago—the dead calling to a living man, a girl becoming a dragon, dragons setting fire to the islands of the west.

Indeed he did not know what weighed more heavily after all, the great strange things or the small common ones.

"I wish I could go home," the woman said.

"I could wish the same thing, but it would be in vain. I think I'll never go home again." He did not know why he said it, but heard himself say it and thought it was true.

She looked at him a minute with her quiet grey eyes and asked no question.

"I could wish my daughter would go home with me," she said, "but it would be in vain, too. I know she must go on. I don't know where."

"Will you tell me what gift it is that she has, what woman she is, that the king sent for her, and took her with him to meet the dragons?"

"Oh, if I knew what she is, I'd tell you," Tenar said, her voice full of grief and love and bitterness. "She's not my daughter born, as you may have guessed or known. She came to me a little child, saved from the fire, but only barely and not wholly saved . . . When Sparrowhawk came back to me she became his daughter too. And she kept both him and me from a cruel death, by summoning a dragon, Kalessin, called Eldest. And that dragon called her daughter. So she's the child of many and none, spared no pain yet spared from the fire. Who she is in truth I may never know. But I wish she were here now, safe with me!"

He wanted to reassure her, but his own heart was too low.

"Tell me a little more about your wife, Alder," she said.

"I cannot," he said at last into the silence that lay easily between them. "I would if I could, Lady Tenar. There's such a heaviness in me, and a dread and fear, tonight. I try to think of Lily, but there's only that dark desert going down and down, and I can't see her in it. All the memories I had of her, that were like water and breath to me, have gone into that dry place. I have nothing left."

"I am sorry," she whispered, and they sat again in silence. The dusk was deepening. It was windless, very warm. Lights in the palace shone through the carved window screens and the still, hanging foliage of the willows.

"Something is happening," Tenar said. "A great change in the world. Maybe nothing we knew will be left to us."

Alder looked up into the darkening sky. The towers of the palace stood clear against it, their pale marble and alabaster catching all the light left in the west. His eyes sought the sword blade mounted at the point of the highest tower and he saw it, faint silver. "Look," he said. At the sword's point, like a diamond or a drop of water, shone a star. As they watched the star moved free of the sword, rising straight above it.

There was a commotion, in the palace or outside the walls; voices; a horn sounded, a sharp imperative call.

"They've come back," Tenar said, and stood up. Excitement had come into the air, and Alder too stood up. Tenar hurried into the palace, from which the harbor could be seen. But before he took Tug back inside, Alder looked up again at the sword, now only a faint glimmer, and the star riding bright above it.

Dolphin came sailing up the harbor in that windless summer night, leaning forward, urgent, the magewind bellying out her sails. Nobody in the palace had looked for the king to return so soon, but nothing was out of order or unready when he came. The quay was instantly crowded with courtiers, off-duty soldiers, and townspeople ready to greet him, and song makers and harpers were waiting to hear how he had fought and defeated dragons so they could make ballads about it.

They were disappointed: the king and his party made straight for the palace, and the guards and sailors from the ship said only, "They went up into the country above Onneva Sands, and in two days they came back. The wizard sent out a message bird to us, for we were down at the Gates of the Bay by then, since we were going to meet them in South Port. We came back and there they were awaiting us at the river mouth, all unharmed. But we saw the smoke of forests afire over the South Falierns."

Tenar was in the crowd on the quay, and Tehanu went straight to her. They embraced fiercely. But as they walked up the street among the lights and the rejoicing voices, Tenar was still thinking, "It has changed. She has changed. She'll never come home."

Lebannen walked among his guards. Charged with tension and energy, he was regal, warlike, radiant. "Erreth-Akbe," people called out, seeing him, and "Son of Morred!" On the steps of the palace he turned and faced them all. He had a strong voice to use when he wanted it, and it rang out now silencing the tumult. "Listen, people of Havnor! The Woman of Gont has spoken for us with a chief among the dragons. They have pledged a truce. One of them will come to us. A dragon will come here, to the City of Havnor, to the Palace of Maharion. Not to destroy, but to parley. The time has come when men and dragons must meet and talk. So I tell you: when the dragon comes, do not fear it, do not fight it, do not flee it, but welcome it in the Sign of Peace. Greet it as you would greet a great lord come in peace from afar. And have no fear. For we are well protected by the Sword of Erreth-Akbe, by the Ring of Elfarran, and by the Name of Morred. And by my own name I promise you, so long as I live I will defend this city and this realm!"

They listened in a breathless hush. A burst of cheers and shouts followed on his words as he turned and strode into the palace. "I thought it best to give them some warning," he said in his usual quiet voice to Tehanu, and she nodded. He spoke to her as to a comrade, and she behaved as such. Tenar and the courtiers nearby saw this.

He ordered that his full Council meet in the morning at the fourth hour, and then they all dispersed, but he kept Tenar with him a minute while Tehanu went on. "It's she who protects us," he said.

"Alone?"

"Don't fear for her. She is the dragon's daughter, the dragon's sister. She goes where we can't go. Don't fear for her, Tenar."

She bowed her head in acceptance. "I thank you for bringing her safe back to me," she said. "For a while."

They were apart from other people, in the corridor that led to the western apartments of the palace. Tenar looked up at the king and said, "I've been talking about dragons with the princess."

"The princess," he said blankly.

"She has a name. I can't tell it to you, since she believes you might use it to destroy her soul."

He scowled.

"In Hur-at-Hur there are dragons. Small, she says, and wingless, and they don't speak. But they're sacred. The sacred sign and pledge of death and rebirth. She reminded me that my people don't go where your people do when they die. That dry land Alder tells of, it's not where we go. The princess, and I, and the dragons."

Lebannen's face changed from wary reserve to intense attention. "Ged's questions to Tehanu," he said in a low voice. "Are these the answers?"

"I know only what the princess told me, or reminded me. I'll speak with Tehanu about these things tonight."

He frowned, pondering; then his face cleared. He stooped and kissed Tenar's cheek, bidding her good night. He strode off and she watched him go. He melted her heart, he dazzled her, but she was not blinded. "He's still afraid of the princess," she thought.

The throne room was the oldest room in the Palace of Maharion. It had been the hall of Gemal Sea-Born, Prince of Ilien, who became king in Havnor and of whose lineage came Queen Heru and her son Maharion. The Havnorian Lay says:

A hundred warriors, a hundred women
sat in the great hall of Gemal Sea-Born
at the king's table, courtly in talk,

handsome and generous gentry of Havnor,
no warriors braver, no women more beautiful.

Around this hall for over a century Gemal's heirs had built an ever larger palace, and lastly Heru and Maharion had raised above it the Tower of Alabaster, the Tower of the Queen, the Tower of the Sword.

These still stood; but though the people of Havnor had stoutly called it the New Palace all through the long centuries since Maharion's death, it was old and half in ruins when Lebannen came to the throne. He had rebuilt it almost entirely, and richly. The merchants of the Inner Isles, in their first joy at having a king and laws again to protect their trading, had set his revenue high and offered him yet more money for all such undertakings; for the first few years of his reign they had not even complained that taxation was destroying their business and would leave their children destitute. So he had been able to make the New Palace new again, and splendid. But the throne room, once the beamed ceiling was rebuilt, the stone walls replastered, the narrow, high-set windows reglazed, he left in its old starkness.

Through the brief false dynasties and the Dark Years of tyrants and usurpers and pirate lords, through all the insults of time and ambition, the throne of the kingdom had stood at the end of the long room: a wooden chair, high-backed, on a plain dais. It had once been sheathed in gold. That was long gone; the small golden nails had left rents in the wood where they had been torn out. Its silken cushions and hangings had been stolen or destroyed by moth and mouse and mold. Nothing showed it to be what it was but the place where it stood and a shallow carving on the back, a heron flying with a twig of rowan in its beak. That was the crest of the House of Enlad.

The kings of that house had come from Enlad to Havnor eight hundred years ago. Where Morred's High Seat is, they said, the kingdom is.

Lebannen had it cleaned, the decayed wood repaired and replaced, oiled and burnished back to dark satin, but left it unpainted, ungilt, bare. Some of the rich people who came to admire their expensive palace complained about the throne room and the throne. "It looks like a barn," they said, and, "Is it Morred's High Seat or an old farmer's chair?"

To which some said the king had replied, "What is a kingdom without the barns that feed it and the farmers to grow the grain?" Others said he had replied, "Is my kingdom gauds of gilt and velvet or does it stand by the strength of wood and stone?" Still others said he had said nothing except that he liked it the way it was. And it being his royal buttocks that sat on the uncushioned throne, his critics did not get the last word on the matter.

Into that stern and high-beamed hall, on a cool morning of late summer sea fog, filed the King's Council: ninety-one men and women, a hundred if all had been there. All had been chosen by the king, some to represent the great noble and princely houses of the Inner Isles, pledged vassals of the Crown; some to speak for the interests of other islands and parts of the Archipelago; some because the king had found them or hoped to find them useful and trustworthy counselors of state. There were merchants, shippers, and factors of Havnor and the other great port cities of the Sea of Éa and the Inmost Sea, splendid in their conscious gravity and their dark robes of heavy silk. There were masters from the workers' guilds, flexible and canny bargainers, notable among them a pale-eyed, hard-handed woman, the chief of the miners of Osskil. There were Roke wizards like Onyx, with grey cloaks and wooden staffs. There was also a Pelnish wizard, called Master Seppel, who carried no staff and of whom people mostly steered clear, though he seemed mild enough. There were noblewomen, young and old, from the kingdom's fiefs and principalities, some in silks of Lorbanery and pearls from the Isles of Sand, and two Islandwomen, stout, plain, and dignified, one from Iffish and one from Korp, to speak for the people of the East Reach. There were some poets, some learned people from the old colleges of Éa and the Enlades, and several captains of soldiery or of the king's ships.

All these councillors the king had chosen. At the end of two or three years he would ask them to serve again or send them home with thanks and in honor, and replace them. All laws and taxations, all judgments brought before the throne, he discussed with them, taking their counsel. They would then vote on his proposal, and only with the consent of the majority was it enacted. There were those who said the council was nothing but the king's pets and puppets, and so indeed it might have been. He mostly got his way if he argued for it. Often he expressed no opinion and let the council make the decision. Many councillors had found that if they had enough facts to support their opposition and made a good argument, they might sway the others and even persuade the king. So debates within the various divisions and special bodies of the council were often hotly contested, and even in full session the king had several times been opposed, argued with, and voted down. He was a good diplomat, but an indifferent politician.

He found his council served him well, and people of power had come to respect it. Common folk did not pay much attention to it. They centered their hopes and attention on the king's person. There were a thousand lays and ballads about the son of Morred, the prince who rode the dragon back from death to the shores of day, the hero of Sorra, wielder of the Sword of Serriadh, the Rowan Tree, the Tall Ash of Enlad, the well-loved king who ruled in the Sign of Peace. But it was hard going to make songs about councillors debating shipping taxes.

Unsung, then, they filed in and took their seats on the cushioned benches facing the uncushioned throne. They stood again as the king came in. With him came the Woman of Gont, whom most of them had seen before so that her appearance caused no stir, and a slight man in rusty black. "Looks like a village sorcerer," a merchant from Kamery said to a shipwright from Way, who answered, "No doubt," in a resigned, forgiving tone. The king was loved also by many of the councillors, or at least liked; he had after all put power in their hands, and even if they felt no obligation to be grateful to him, they respected his judgment.

The elderly Lady of Ebéa hurried in late, and Prince Sege, who presided over protocol, told the council to be seated. They all sat down. "Hear the king," Sege said, and they listened.

He told them, and for many it was the first real news of these matters, about the dragons' attacks on West Havnor, and how he had set out with the Woman of Gont, Tehanu, to parley with them.

He kept them in suspense while he spoke of the earlier attacks by dragons on the islands of the west, and told them briefly Onyx's tale of the girl who turned into a dragon on Roke Knoll, and reminded them that Tehanu was claimed as daughter by Tenar of the Ring, by the one-time Archmage of Roke, and by the dragon Kalessin, on whose back the king himself had been borne from Selidor.

Then finally he told them what had happened at the pass in the Faliern Mountains at dawn three days ago.

He ended by saying, "That dragon carried Tehanu's message to Orm Irian in Paln, who then must make the long flight here, three hundred miles or more. But dragons are swifter than any ship even with the magewind. We may look for Orm Irian at any time."

Prince Sege asked the first question, knowing the king would welcome it: "What do you hope to gain, my lord, by parley with a dragon?"

The answer was prompt: "More than we can ever gain by trying to fight it. It is a hard thing to say, but it is the truth: against the anger of these great creatures, if indeed they were to come against us in any number, we have no true defense. Our wise men tell us there is maybe one place that could stand against them, Roke Island. And on Roke there is maybe one man who could face the wrath of even a single dragon and not be destroyed. Therefore we must try to find out the cause of their anger and, by removing it, make peace with them."

"They are animals," said the old Lord of Felkway. "Men cannot reason with animals, make peace with them."

"Have we not the Sword of Erreth-Akbe, who slew the Great Dragon?" cried a young councillor.

He was answered at once by another: "And who slew Erreth-Akbe?"

Debate in the council tended to be tumultuous, though Prince Sege kept strict rule, not letting anyone interrupt another or speak for more than one turn of the two-minute sandglass. Babblers and droners were cut off by a crash of the prince's silver-tipped staff and his call to the next speaker. So they talked and shouted back and forth at a fast pace, and all the things that had to be said and many things that did not need to be said were said, and refuted, and said again. Mostly they argued that they should go to war, fight the dragons, defeat them.

"A band of archers on one of the king's warships could bring them down like ducks," cried a hot-blooded merchant from Wathort.

"Are we to grovel before mindless beasts? Are there no heroes left among us?" demanded the imperious Lady of O-tokne.

To that, Onyx made a sharp reply: "Mindless? They speak the Language of the Making, in the knowledge of which our art and power lies. They are beasts as we are beasts. Men are animals that speak."

A ship's captain, an old, far-traveled man, said, "Then isn't it you wizards who should be talking with them? Since you know their speech, and maybe share their powers? The king spoke of a young untaught girl who turned into a dragon. But mages can take that form at will. Couldn't the Masters of Roke speak with the dragons or fight with them, if need be, evenly matched?"

The wizard from Paln stood up. He was a short man with a soft voice. "To take the form is to be the being, captain," he said politely. "A mage can look like a dragon. But true Change is a risky art. Especially now. A small change in the midst of great changes is like a breath against the wind . . . But we have here among us one who need use no art, and yet can speak for us to dragons better than any man could do. If she will speak for us."

At that, Tehanu stood up from her bench at the foot of the dais. "I will," she said. And sat down again.

That brought a pause to the discussion for a minute, but soon they were all at it again.

The king listened and did not speak. He wanted to know the temper of his people.

The sweet silver trumpets high on the Tower of the Sword played all their tune four times, telling the sixth hour, noon. The king stood, and Prince Sege declared a recess until the first hour of the afternoon.

A lunch of fresh cheese and summer fruits and greens was set out in a room in Queen Heru's Tower. There Lebannen invited Tehanu and Tenar, Alder, Sege, and Onyx; and Onyx, with the king's permission, brought with him the Pelnish wizard Seppel. They sat and ate together, talking little and quietly. The windows looked over all the harbor and the north shoreline of the bay fading off into a bluish haze that might be either the remnants of the morning fog or smoke from the forest fires in the west of the island.

Alder remained bewildered at being included among the king's intimates and brought into his councils. What had he to do with dragons? He could neither fight with them nor talk with them. The idea of such mighty beings was great and strange to him. At moments the boasts and challenges of the councillors seemed to him like a yapping of dogs. He had seen a young dog once on a beach barking and barking at the ocean, rushing and snapping at the ebb wave, running back from the breaker with its wet tail between its legs.

But he was glad to be with Tenar, who put him at ease, and whom he liked for her kindness and courage, and he found now that he was also at ease with Tehanu.

Her disfigurement made it seem that she had two faces. He could not see them both at one time, only the one or the other. But he had got used to that and it did not disquiet him. His mother's face had been half masked by its wine-red birthmark. Tehanu's face reminded him of that.

She seemed less restless and troubled than she had been. She sat quietly, and a couple of times she spoke to Alder, sitting next to her, with a shy comradeliness. He felt that, like him, she was there not by choice but because she had forgone choice, driven to follow a way she did not understand. Maybe her way and his went together, for a while at least. The idea gave him courage. Knowing only that there was something he had to do, something begun that must be finished, he felt that whatever it might be, it would be better done with her than without her. Perhaps she was drawn to him out of the same loneliness.

But her conversation was not of such deep matters. "My father gave you a kitten," she said to him as they left the table. "Was it one of Aunty Moss's?"

He nodded, and she asked, "The grey one?"

"Yes."

"That was the best cat of the litter."

"She's getting fat, here."

Tehanu hesitated and then said timidly, "I think it's a he."

Alder found himself smiling. "He's a good companion. A sailor named him Tug."

"Tug," she said, and looked satisfied.

"Tehanu," the king said. He had sat down beside Tenar in the deep window seat. "I didn't call on you in council today to speak of the questions Lord Sparrowhawk asked you. It was not the time. Is it the place?"

Alder watched her. She considered before answering. She glanced once at her mother, who made no answering sign.

"I'd rather speak to you here," she said in her hoarse voice. "And maybe to the Princess of Hur-at-Hur."

After a brief pause the king said pleasantly, "Shall I send for her?"

"No, I can go see her. Afterward. I haven't much to say, really. My father asked, *Who goes to the dry land when they die?* And my mother and I talked about it. And we thought, people go there, but do the beasts? Do birds fly there? Are there trees, does the grass grow? Alder, you've seen it."

Taken by surprise, he could say only, "There . . . there's grass, on the hither side of the wall, but it seems dead. Beyond that I don't know."

Tehanu looked at the king. "You walked across that land, my lord."

"I saw no beast, or bird, or growing thing."

Alder spoke again: "Lord Sparrowhawk said: dust, rock."

"I think no beings go there at death but human beings," Tehanu said. "But not all of them." Again she looked at her mother, and did not look away.

Tenar spoke. "The Kargish people are like the animals." Her voice was dry and let no feeling be heard. "They die to be reborn."

"That is superstition," Onyx said. "Forgive me, Lady Tenar, but you yourself—" He paused.

"I no longer believe," Tenar said, "that I am or was, as they told me, Arha forever reborn, a single soul reincarnated endlessly and so immortal. I do believe that when I die I will, like any mortal being, rejoin the greater being of the world. Like the grass, the trees, the animals. Men are only animals that speak, sir, as you said this morning."

"But we can speak the Language of the Making," the wizard protested. "By learning the words by which Segoy made the world, the very speech of life, we teach our souls to conquer death."

"That place where nothing is but dust and shadows, is that your conquest?" Her voice was not dry now, and her eyes flashed.

Onyx stood indignant but wordless.

The king intervened. "Lord Sparrowhawk asked a second question," he said. *"Can a dragon cross the wall of stones?"* He looked at Tehanu.

"It's answered in the first answer," she said, "if dragons are only animals that speak, and animals don't go there. Has a mage ever seen a dragon there? Or you, my lord?" She looked first at Onyx, then at Lebannen. Onyx pondered only a moment before he said, "No."

The king looked amazed. "How is it I never thought of that?" he said. "No, we saw none. I think there are no dragons there."

"My lord," Alder said, louder than he had ever said anything in the palace, "there is a dragon here." He was standing facing the window, and he pointed at it.

They all turned. In the sky above the Bay of Havnor they saw a dragon flying from the west. Its long, slow-beating, vaned wings shone red-gold. A curl of smoke drifted behind it for a moment in the hazy summer air.

"Now," the king said, "what room do I make ready for this guest?"

He spoke as if amused, bemused. But the instant he saw the dragon turn and come wheeling in towards the Tower of the Sword, he ran from the room and down the stairs, startling and outstripping the guards in the halls and at the doors, so that he came out first and alone on the terrace under the white tower.

The terrace was the roof of a banquet hall, a wide expanse of marble with a low balustrade, the Sword Tower rising directly over it and the Queen's Tower nearby. The dragon had alighted on the pavement and was furling its wings with a loud metallic rattle as the king came out. Where it came down its talons had scratched grooves in the marble.

The long, gold-mailed head swung round. The dragon looked at the king.

The king looked down and did not meet its eyes. But he stood straight and spoke clearly. "Orm Irian, welcome. I am Lebannen."

"Agni Lebannen," said the great hissing voice, greeting him as Orm Embar had greeted him long ago, in the farthest west, before he was a king.

Behind him, Onyx and Tehanu had run out onto the terrace along with several guards. One guard had his sword out, and Lebannen saw, in a window of the Queen's Tower, another with drawn bow and notched arrow aimed at the dragon's breast. "Put down your weapons!" he shouted in a voice that made the towers ring, and the guard obeyed in such haste that he nearly dropped his sword, but the archer lowered his bow reluctantly, finding it hard to leave his lord defenseless.

"Medeu," Tehanu whispered, coming up beside Lebannen, her gaze unwavering on the dragon. The great creature's head swung round again and the immense amber eye in a socket of shining, wrinkled scales gazed back, unblinking.

The dragon spoke.

Onyx, understanding, murmured to the king what it said and what Tehanu replied. "Kalessin's daughter, my sister," it said. "You do not fly."

"I cannot change, sister," Tehanu said.

"Shall I?"

"For a while, if you will."

Then those on the terrace and in the windows of the towers saw the strangest thing they might ever see however long they lived in a world of sorceries and wonders. They saw the dragon, the huge creature whose scaled belly and thorny tail dragged and stretched half across the breadth of the terrace, and whose red-horned head reared up twice the height of the king—they saw it lower that big head, and tremble so that its wings rattled like cymbals, and not smoke but a mist breathed out of its deep nostrils, clouding its shape, so that it became cloudy like thin fog or worn glass; and then it was gone. The midday sun beat down on the scored, scarred, white pavement. There was no dragon. There was a woman. She stood some ten paces from Tehanu and the king. She stood where the heart of the dragon might have been.

She was young, tall, and strongly built, dark, dark-haired, wearing a farm woman's shift and trousers, barefoot. She stood motionless, as if bewildered. She looked down at her body. She lifted up her hand and looked at it. "The little thing!" she said, in the common speech, and she laughed. She looked at Tehanu. "It's like putting on the shoes I wore when I was five," she said.

The two women moved towards each other. With a certain stateliness, like that of armed warriors saluting or ships meeting at sea, they embraced. They held each other lightly, but for some moments. They drew apart, and both turned to face the king.

"Lady Irian," he said, and bowed.

She looked a little nonplussed and made a kind of country curtsey. When she looked up he saw her eyes were the color of amber. He looked instantly away.

"I'll do you no harm in this guise," she said, with a broad, white smile. "Your majesty," she added uncomfortably, trying to be polite.

He bowed again. It was he that was nonplussed now. He looked at Tehanu, and round at Tenar, who had come out onto the terrace with Alder. Nobody said anything.

Irian's eyes went to Onyx, standing in his grey cloak just behind the king, and her face lighted up again. "Sir," she said, "are you from Roke Island? Do you know the Lord Patterner?"

Onyx bowed or nodded. He too kept his eyes from hers.

"Is he well? Does he walk among his trees?"

Again the wizard bowed.

"And the Doorkeeper, and the Herbal, and Kurremkarmerruk? They befriended me, they stood by me. If you go back there, greet them with my love and honor, if you please."

"I will," the wizard said.

"My mother is here," Tehanu said softly to Irian. "Tenar of Atuan."

"Tenar of Gont," Lebannen said, with a certain ring to his voice.

Looking with open wonder at Tenar, Irian said, "It was you that brought the Rune Ring from the land of the Hoary Men, along with the Archmage?"

"It was," Tenar said, staring with equal frankness at Irian.

Above them on the balcony that encircled the Tower of the Sword near its summit there was movement: the trumpeters had come out to sound the hour, but at the moment all four of them were gathered on the south side overlooking the terrace, peering down to see the dragon. There were faces in every window of the palace towers, and the thrum of voices down in the streets could be heard like a tide coming in.

"When they sound the first hour," Lebannen said, "the council will gather again. The councillors will have seen you come, my lady, or heard of your coming. So if it please you, I think it best that we go straight among them and let them behold you. And if you'll speak to them I promise you they'll listen."

"Very well," Irian said. For a moment there was a ponderous, reptilian impassivity in her. When she moved, that vanished, and she seemed only a tall young woman who stepped forward quite awkwardly, saying with a smile to Tehanu, "I feel as if I'll float up like a spark, there's no weight to me!"

The four trumpets up in the tower sounded to west, north, east, south in turn, one phrase of the lament a king five hundred years ago had made for the death of his friend.

For a moment the king now remembered the face of that man, Erreth-Akbe, as he stood on the beach of Selidor, dark-eyed, sorrowful, mortally wounded, among the bones of the dragon who had killed him. Lebannen felt it strange that he should think of such faraway things at such a moment; and yet it was not strange, for the living and the dead, men and dragons, all were drawing together to some event he could not see.

He paused until Irian and Tehanu came up to him. As he walked on into the palace with them he said, "Lady Irian, there are many things I would ask you, but what my people fear and what the council will desire to know is whether your people intend to make war on us, and why."

She nodded, a heavy, decisive nod. "I will tell them what I know."

When they came to the curtained doorway behind the dais, the throne room was all in confusion, an uproar of voices, so that the crash of Prince Sege's staff was barely heard at first. Then silence came suddenly on them and they all turned to see the king come in with the dragon.

Lebannen did not sit but stood before the throne, and Irian stood to his left.

"Hear the king," Sege said into that dead silence.

The king said, "Councillors! This is a day that will long be told and sung. Your sons' daughters and your daughters' sons will say, 'I am the grandchild of one who was of the Dragon Council!' So honor her whose presence honors us. Hear Orm Irian."

Some of those who were at the Dragon Council said afterwards that if they looked straight at her she seemed only a tall woman standing there, but if they looked aside what they saw in the corner of their eye was a vast shimmer of smoky gold that dwarfed king and throne. And many of them, knowing a man must not look into a dragon's eye, did look aside; but they stole glimpses too. The women looked at her, some thinking her plain, some beautiful, some pitying her for having to go barefoot in the palace. And a few councillors, not having rightly understood, wondered who the woman was, and when the dragon would be coming.

All the time she spoke, that complete silence endured. Though her voice had the lightness of most women's voices, it filled the high hall easily. She spoke slowly and formally, as if she were translating in her mind from the older speech.

"My name was Irian, of the Domain of Old Iria on Way. I am Orm Irian now. Kalessin, the Eldest, calls me daughter. I am sister to Orm Embar, whom the king knew, and grandchild of Orm, who killed the king's companion Erreth-Akbe and was killed by him. I am here because my sister Tehanu called to me.

"When Orm Embar died on Selidor, destroying the mortal body of the wizard Cob, Kalessin came from beyond the west and brought the king and the great mage to Roke. Then returning to the Dragons' Run, the Eldest called the people of the west, whose speech had been taken from them by Cob, and who were still bewildered. Kalessin said to them, 'You let evil turn you into evil. You have been mad. You are sane again, but so long as the winds blow from the east you can never be what you were, free of both good and evil.'

"Kalessin said: 'Long ago we chose. We chose freedom. Men chose the yoke. We chose fire and the wind. They chose water and the earth. We chose the west, and they the east.'

"And Kalessin said: 'But always among us some envy them their wealth, and always among them some envy us our liberty. So it was that evil came into us and will come into us again, until we choose again, and forever, to be free. Soon I am going beyond the west to fly on the other wind. I will lead you there, or wait for you, if you will come.'

"Then some of the dragons said to Kalessin, 'Men in their envy of us long ago stole half our realm beyond the west from us and made walls of spells to keep us out of it. So now let us drive them into the farthest east, and take back the islands! Men and dragons cannot share the wind.'

"Then Kalessin said, 'Once we were one people. And in sign of that, in every generation of men, one or two are born who are dragons also. And in every generation of our people, longer than the quick lives of men, one of us is born who is also human. Of these one is now living in the Inner Isles. And there is one of them living there now who is a dragon. These two are the messengers, the bringers of choice. There will be no more such born to us or to them. For the balance changes.'

"And Kalessin said to them: 'Choose. Come with me to fly on the far side of the world, on the other wind. Or stay and put on the yoke of good and evil. Or dwindle into dumb beasts.' And at the last Kalessin said: 'The last to make the choice will be Tehanu. After her there will be no choosing. There will be no way west. Only the forest will be, as it is always, at the center.'"

The people of the King's Council were still as stones, listening. Irian stood moveless, gazing as if through them, as she spoke.

"After some years had passed, Kalessin flew beyond the west. Some followed, some did not. When I came to join my people, I followed Kalessin. But I go there and come back, so long as the winds will bear me.

"The disposition of my people is jealous and irate. Those who stayed here on the winds of the world began to fly in bands or singly to the isles of men, saying again, 'They stole half our realm. Now we will take all the west of their realm, and drive them out of it, so they cannot bring their good and evil to us any more. We will not put our necks into their yoke.'

"But they did not try to kill the islanders, because they remembered being mad, when dragon killed dragon. They hate you, but they will not kill you unless you try to kill them.

"So one of these bands has come now to this island, Havnor, that we call the Cold Hill. The dragon who came before them and spoke to Tehanu is my brother Ammaud. They seek to drive you into the east, but Ammaud, like me, enacts the will of Kalessin, seeking to free my people from the yoke you wear. If he and I and the children of Kalessin can prevent harm to your people and ours, we will do so. But dragons have no king, and obey no one, and will fly where they will. For a while they will do as my brother and I ask in Kalessin's name. But not for long. And they fear nothing in the world, except your wizardries of death."

That last word rang heavily in the great hall in the silence that followed Irian's voice.

The king spoke, thanking Irian. He said, "You honor us with your truth-speaking. By my name, we will speak truth to you. I beg you to tell me, daughter of Kalessin who bore me to my kingdom, what it is you say the dragons fear? I thought they feared nothing in the world or out of it."

"We fear your spells of immortality," she said bluntly.

"Of immortality?" Lebannen hesitated. "I am no wizard. Master Onyx, speak for me, if the daughter of Kalessin will permit."

Onyx stood up. Irian looked at him with cold, impartial eyes, and nodded.

"Lady Irian," the wizard said, "we make no spells of immortality. Only the wizard Cob sought to make himself immortal, perverting our art to do so." He spoke slowly and with evident care, searching his mind as he spoke. "Our Archmage, with my lord the king, and with the aid of Orm Embar, destroyed Cob and the evil he had done. And the Archmage gave all his power up to heal the world, restoring the Equilibrium. No other wizard in our lifetime has sought to—" He stopped short.

Irian looked straight at him. He looked down.

"The wizard I destroyed," she said, "the Summoner of Roke, Thorion—what was it he sought?"

Onyx, stricken, said nothing.

"He came back from death," she said. "But not living, as the Archmage and the king did. He was dead, but he came back across the wall by his arts—by your arts—you men of Roke! How are we to trust anything you say? You have unmade the balance of the world. Can you restore it?"

Onyx looked at the king. He was openly distressed. "My lord, I cannot think that this is the place to discuss such matters—before all men—until we know what we are talking about, and what we must do . . ."

"Roke keeps its secrets," Irian said with calm scorn.

"But on Roke—" Tehanu said, not standing; her weak voice died away. Prince Sege and the king both looked at her and motioned her to speak.

She stood up. At first she kept the left side of her face to the councillors, all sitting motionless on their benches, like stones with eyes.

"On Roke is the Immanent Grove," she said. "Isn't that what Kalessin meant, sister, speaking of the forest that is at the center?" Turning to Irian, she showed the people watching her the whole ruin of her face; but she had forgotten them. "Maybe we need to go there," she said. "To the center of things."

Irian smiled. "I'll go there," she said.

They both looked at the king.

"Before I send you to Roke, or go with you," he said slowly, "I must know what is at stake. Master Onyx, I'm sorry that matters so grave and chancy force us to debate our course so openly. But I trust my councillors to support me as I find and hold the course. What the council needs to know is that our islands need not fear attack from the People of the West—that the truce, at least, holds."

"It holds," Irian said.

"Can you say how long?"

"A half year?" she offered, carelessly, as if she had said, "A day or two."

"We will hold the truce a half year, in hope of peace to follow. Am I right to say, Lady Irian, that to have peace with us, your people want to know that our wizards' meddling with the . . . laws of life and death will not endanger them?"

"Endanger all of us," Irian said. "Yes."

Lebannen considered this and then said, in his most royal, affable, urbane manner, "Then I believe I should come to Roke with you." He turned to the benches. "Councillors, with the truce declared, we must seek the peace. I'll go wherever I must on that quest, ruling as I do in the Sign of Elfarran's Ring. If you see any hindrance to this journey, speak here and now. For it may be that the balance of power within the Archipelago, as well as the Equilibrium of the whole, is in question. And if I go, I must go now. Autumn is near, and it's not a short voyage to Roke Island."

The stones with eyes sat there for a long minute, all staring, none speaking. Then Prince Sege said, "Go, my lord king, go with our hope and trust, and the magewind in your sails." There was a little murmur of assent from the councillors: Yes, yes, hear him.

Sege asked for further questions or debate; nobody spoke. He closed the session.

Leaving the throne room with him, Lebannen said, "Thank you, Sege," and the old prince said, "Between you and the dragon, Lebannen, what could the poor souls say?"

Chapter IV

Dolphin

Many matters had to be settled and arrangements made before the king could leave his capital; there was also the question of who should go with him to Roke. Irian and Tehanu, of course, and Tehanu wanted her mother with her. Onyx said that Alder should by all means go with them, and also the Pelnish wizard Seppel, for the Lore of Paln had much to do with these matters of crossing between life and death. The king chose Tosla to captain the *Dolphin,* as he had done before. Prince Sege would look after affairs of state in the king's absence, with a selected group of councillors, as he also had done before.

So it was all settled, or so Lebannen thought, until Tenar came to him two days before they were to sail and said, "You'll be talking of war and peace with the dragons, and of matters even beyond that, Irian says, matters that concern the balance of all things in Earthsea. The people of the Kargad Lands should hear these discussions and have a voice in them."

"You will be their representative."

"Not I. I am not a subject of the High King. The only person here who can represent his people is his daughter."

Lebannen took a step away from her, turned partly from her, and at last said in a voice stifled by the effort to speak without anger, "You know that she is completely unfitted for such a journey."

"I know nothing of the kind."

"She has no education."

"She's intelligent, practical, and courageous. She's aware of what her station requires of her. She hasn't been trained to rule, but then what can she learn boxed up there in the River House with her servants and some court ladies?"

"To speak the language, in the first place!"

"She's doing that. I'll interpret for her when she needs it."

After a brief pause Lebannen spoke carefully: "I understand your concern for her people. I will consider what can be done. But the princess has no place on this voyage."

"Tehanu and Irian both say she should come with us. Master Onyx says that, like Alder of Taon, her being sent here at this time cannot be an accident."

Lebannen walked farther away. His tone remained stiffly patient and polite: "I cannot permit it. Her ignorance and inexperience would make her a serious burden. And I can't put her at risk. Relationships with her father—"

"In her ignorance, as you call it, she showed us how to answer Ged's questions. You are as disrespectful of her as her father is. You speak of her as of a mindless thing." Tenar's face was pale with anger. "If you're afraid to put her at risk, ask her to take it herself."

Again there was a silence. Lebannen spoke with the same wooden calmness, not looking directly at her. "If you and Tehanu and Orm Irian believe this woman should come with us to Roke, and Onyx agrees with you, I accept your judgment, though I believe it is mistaken. Please tell her that if she wishes to come, she may do so."

"It is you who should tell her that."

He stood silent. Then he walked out of the room without a word.

He passed close by Tenar, and though he did not look at her he saw her clearly. She looked old and strained, and her hands trembled. He was sorry for her, ashamed of his rudeness to her, relieved that no one else had witnessed the scene; but these feelings were mere sparks in the huge darkness of his anger at her, at the princess, at everyone and everything that laid this false obligation, this grotesque duty on him. As he went out of the room he tugged open the collar of his shirt as if it were choking him.

His majordomo, a slow and steady man called Thoroughgood, was not expecting him to return so soon or through that door and jumped up, staring and startled. Lebannen returned his stare icily and said, "Send for the High Princess to attend me here in the afternoon."

"The High Princess?"

"Is there more than one of them? Are you unaware that the High King's daughter is our guest?"

Amazed, Thoroughgood stammered an apology, which Lebannen interrupted: "I shall go to the River House myself." And he strode on out, pursued, impeded, and gradually controlled by the majordomo's attempts to slow him down long enough for a suitable retinue to be gathered, horses to be brought from the stables, the petitioners waiting for audience in the Long Room to be put off till afternoon, and so on. All his obligations, all his duties, all the trappery and trammel, rites and hypocrisies that made him king pulled at him, sucking and tugging him down like quicksand into suffocation.

When his horse was brought across the stable yard to him, he swung up into the saddle so abruptly that the horse caught his mood and backed and reared, driving back the hostlers and attendants. To see the circle widen out around him gave Lebannen a harsh satisfaction. He set the horse straight for the gateway without waiting for the men in his retinue to mount. He led them at a sharp trot through the streets of the city, far ahead of them, aware of the dilemma of the young officer who was supposed to precede him calling, "Way for the king!" but who had been left behind him and now did not dare ride past him.

It was near noon; the streets and squares of Havnor were hot and bright and mostly deserted. Hearing the clatter of hooves, people hurried to the doorways of little dark shops to stare and recognise and salute the king. Women sitting in their windows fanning themselves and gossiping across the way looked down and waved, and one of them threw a flower down at him. His horse's hooves rang on the bricks of a broad, sunbaked square that lay empty except for a curly-tailed dog trotting away on three legs, unconcerned with royalty. Out of the square the king took a narrow passage that led to the paved way beside the Serrenen, and followed it in the shadow of the willows under the old city wall to River House.

The ride had changed his temper somewhat. The heat and silence and beauty of the city, the sense of multitudinous life behind walls and shutters, the smile of the woman who had tossed a flower, the petty satisfaction of keeping ahead of all his guardians and pomp makers, then finally the scent and coolness of the river ride and the shady courtyard of the house where he had known days and nights of peace and pleasure, all took him a little distance from his anger. He felt estranged from himself, no longer possessed but emptied.

The first riders of his retinue were just coming into the courtyard as he swung off his horse, which was glad to stand in the shade. He went into the house, dropping among dozing footmen like a stone into a glassy pond, causing quick-widening circles of dismay and panic. He said, "Tell the princess that I am here."

Lady Opal of the Old Demesne of Ilien, currently in charge of the princess's ladies-in-waiting, appeared promptly, greeted him graciously, offered him refreshment, behaved quite as if his visit were no surprise at all. This suavity half placated, half irritated him. Endless hypocrisy! But what was Lady Opal to do—gawp like a stranded fish (as a very young lady-in-waiting was doing) because the king had finally and unexpectedly come to see the princess?

"I'm so sorry Mistress Tenar isn't here at present," she said. "It's so much easier to converse with the princess with her help. But the princess is making admirable progress in the language."

Lebannen had forgotten the problem of language. He accepted the cool drink offered him and said nothing. Lady Opal made small talk with the assistance of the other ladies, getting very little from the king. He had begun to realise that he would probably be expected to speak with the princess in the company of all her ladies, as was only proper. Whatever he had intended to say to her, it had become impossible to say anything. He was just about to get up and excuse himself, when a woman whose head and shoulders were hidden by a red circular veil appeared in the doorway, fell plop on her knees, and said, "Please? King? Princess? Please?"

"The princess will receive you in her chambers, sire," Lady Opal interpreted. She waved to a footman, who escorted him upstairs, along a hall, through an anteroom, through a large, dark room that seemed to be crammed absolutely full of women in red veils, and out onto a balcony over the river. There stood the figure he remembered: the immobile cylinder of red and gold.

The breeze from the water made the veils tremble and shimmer, so that the figure did not appear solid but delicate, moving, shivering, like the willow foliage. It seemed to shrink, to shorten. She was making her courtesy to him. He bowed to her. They both straightened up and stood in silence.

"Princess," Lebannen said, with a feeling of unreality, hearing his own voice, "I am here to ask you to come with us to Roke Island."

She said nothing. He saw the fine red veils part in an oval as she spread them with her hands. Long-fingered, golden-skinned hands, held apart to reveal her face in the red shadow. He could not see her features clearly. She was nearly as tall as he, and her eyes looked straight at him.

"My friend Tenar," she said, "say: king to see king, face and face. I say: yes. I will."

Half understanding, Lebannen bowed again. "You honor me, my lady."

"Yes," she said. "I honor you."

He hesitated. This was a different ground entirely. Her ground.

She stood there straight and still, the gold edging of her veils shivering, her eyes looking at him out of the shadow.

"Tenar, and Tehanu, and Orm Irian, agree that it would be well if the Princess of the Kargad Lands were with us on Roke Island. So I ask you to come with us."

"To come."

"To Roke Island."

"On ship," she said, and suddenly made a little moaning plaintive noise. Then she said, "I will. I will to come."

He did not know what to say. He said, "Thank you, my lady."

She nodded once, equal to equal.

He bowed. He left her as he had been taught to leave the presence of his father the prince at formal occasions in the court of Enlad, not turning his back but stepping backwards.

She stood facing him, still holding her veil parted till he reached the doorway. Then she dropped her hands, and the veils closed, and he heard her gasp and breathe out hard as if in release from an act of will sustained almost past endurance.

Courageous, Tenar had called her. He did not understand, but he knew that he had been in the presence of courage. All the anger that had filled him, brought him here, was gone, vanished. He had not been sucked down and suffocated, but brought up short in front of a rock, a high place in clear air, a truth.

He went out through the room full of murmuring, perfumed, veiled women who shrank back from him into the darkness. Downstairs, he chatted a little with Lady Opal and the others, and had a kind word for the gawping twelve-year-old lady-in-waiting. He spoke pleasantly to the men of his retinue waiting for him in the courtyard. He quietly mounted his tall grey horse. He rode quietly, thoughtfully, back to the Palace of Maharion.

Alder heard with fatalistic acceptance that he was to sail back to Roke. His waking life had become so strange to him, more dreamlike than his dreams, that he had little will to question or protest. If he was fated to sail from island to island the rest of his life, so be it; he knew there was no such thing as going home for him now. At least he would be in the company of the ladies Tenar and Tehanu, who put his heart at ease. And the wizard Onyx had also shown him kindness.

Alder was a shy man and Onyx a deeply reserved one, and there was all the difference of their knowledge and status to be bridged; but Onyx had come to him several times simply to talk as one man of the art to another, showing a respect for Alder's opinion that puzzled his modesty. But Alder could not withhold his trust; and so when the time to depart was near at hand, he took to Onyx the question that had been worrying him.

"It's the little cat," he said with embarrassment. "I don't feel right about taking him. Keeping him cooped up so long. It's unnatural for a young creature. And I think, what would become of him . . ."

Onyx did not ask what he meant. He asked only, "He still helps you keep from the wall of stones?"

"Well, often he does."

Onyx pondered. "You need some protection, till we get to Roke. I have thought . . . Have you spoken with the wizard Seppel here?"

"The man from Paln," Alder said, with a slight unease in his voice.

Paln, the greatest island west of Havnor, had the reputation of being an uncanny place. The Pelnish spoke Hardic with a peculiar accent, using many words of their own. Their lords had in ancient times refused fealty to the kings of Enlad and Havnor. Their wizards did not go to Roke for their training. The Pelnish Lore, which called upon the Old Powers of the Earth, was widely believed to be dangerous if not sinister. Long ago the Grey Mage of Paln had brought ruin on his island by summoning the souls of the dead to advise him and his lords, and that tale was part of the education of every sorcerer: "The living should not take counsel of the dead." There had been more than one duel in wizardry between a man of Roke and a man of Paln; in one such combat two centuries ago a plague had been loosed on the people of Paln and Semel that had left half the towns and farmlands desolate. And fifteen years ago, when the wizard Cob had used the Pelnish Lore to cross between life and death, the Archmage Sparrowhawk had spent all his own power to defeat him and heal the evil he had done.

Alder, like almost everyone else at court and in the King's Council, had politely avoided the wizard Seppel.

"I've asked the king to bring him with us to Roke," said Onyx.

Alder blinked.

"They know more than we do about these matters," Onyx said. "Most of our art of Summoning comes from the Pelnish Lore. Thorion was a master of it . . . The Summoner of Roke now, Brand of Venway, won't use any part of his craft that draws from that lore. Misused, it has brought only harm. But it may be only our ignorance that's led us to use it wrongly. It goes back to very ancient times; there may be knowledge in it we've lost. Seppel is a wise man and mage. I think he should be with us. And I think he might help you, if you can trust him."

"If he has your trust," Alder said, "he has mine."

When Alder spoke with the silver tongue of Taon, Onyx was likely to smile a little drily. "Your judgment's as good as mine, Alder, in this business," he said. "Or better. I hope you use it. But I'll take you to him."

So they went down into the city together. Seppel's lodging was in an old part of town near the shipyards, just off Boatwright Street; there was a little colony of Pelnish folk there, brought in to work in the king's yards, for they were great shipbuilders. The houses were ancient, crowded close, with the bridges between roof and roof that gave Havnor Great Port a second, airy web of streets high above its paved ones.

Seppel's rooms, up three flights of stairs, were dark and close in the heat of this late summer. He took them up one more steep flight onto the roof. It was joined to other roofs by a bridge on each side, so that there was a regular crossroads and thoroughfare across it. Awnings were set up by the low parapets, and the breeze from the harbor cooled the shaded air. There they sat on striped canvas mats in the corner that was Seppel's bit of the roof, and he gave them a cool, slightly bitter tea to drink.

He was a short man of about fifty, round-bodied, with small hands and feet, hair that was a little curly and unruly, and what was rare among men of the Archipelago, a beard, clipped short, on his dark cheeks and jaw. His manners were pleasant. He spoke in a clipped, singing accent, softly.

He and Onyx talked, and Alder listened for a good while to them. His mind drifted when they spoke about people and matters of which he knew nothing. He looked out over the roofs and awnings, the roof gardens and the arched and carven bridges, northward to Mount Onn, a great pale-grey dome above the hazy hills of summer. He came back to himself hearing the Pelnish wizard say, "It may be that even the Archmage could not wholly heal the wound in the world."

The wound in the world, Alder thought: yes. He looked more intently at Seppel, and Seppel glanced at him. For all the soft look of the man his eyes were sharp.

"Maybe it's not only our desire to live forever that has kept the wound open," Seppel said, "but the desire of the dead to die."

Again Alder heard the strange words and felt that he recognised them without understanding them. Again Seppel glanced at him as if seeking a response.

Alder said nothing, nor did Onyx speak. Seppel said at last, "When you stand at the bourne, Master Alder, what is it they ask of you?"

"To be free," Alder replied, his voice only a whisper.

"Free," Onyx murmured.

Silence again. Two girls and a boy ran past across the roofway, laughing and calling, "Down at the next!"—playing one of the endless games of chase children made with their city's maze of streets and canals and stairs and bridges.

"Maybe it was a bad bargain from the beginning," Seppel said, and when Onyx looked a question at him he said, *"Verw nadan."*

Alder knew the words were in the Old Speech, but he did not know their meaning.

He looked at Onyx, whose face was very grave. Onyx said only, "Well, I hope we can come to the truth of these things, and soon."

"On the hill where truth is," Seppel said.

"I'm glad you'll be with us there. Meanwhile, here is Alder summoned to the bourne night after night and seeking some reprieve. I said that you might know a way to help him."

"And you would accept the touch of the wizardry of Paln?" Seppel asked Alder. His tone was softly ironic. His eyes were bright and hard as jet.

Alder's lips were dry. "Master," he said, "we say on my island, the man drowning doesn't ask what the rope cost. If you can keep me from that place even for a night, you'll have my heart's thanks, little as that is worth in return for such a gift."

Onyx looked at him with a slight, amused, unreproving smile.

Seppel did not smile at all. "Thanks are rare, in my trade," he said. "I would do a good deal for them. I think I can help you, Master Alder. But I have to tell you the rope is a costly one."

Alder bowed his head.

"You come to the bourne in dream, not by your own will, that is so?"

"So I believe."

"Wisely said." Seppel's keen glance approved him. "Who knows his own will clearly? But if it is in dream you go there, I can keep you from that dream—for a while. And at a cost, as I said."

Alder looked his question.

"Your power."

Alder did not understand him at first. Then he said, "My gift, you mean? My art?"

Seppel nodded.

"I'm only a mender," Alder said after a little time. "It's not a great power to give up."

Onyx made as if to protest, but looked at Alder's face and said nothing.

"It is your living," Seppel said.

"It was my life, once. But that's gone."

"Maybe your gift will come back to you, when what must happen has happened. I cannot promise that. I will try to restore what I can of what I take from you. But we're all walking in the night, now, on ground we don't know. When the day comes we may know where we are, or we may not. Now, if I spare you your dream, at that price, will you thank me?"

"I will," Alder said. "What's the little good of my gift, against the great evil my ignorance could do? If you spare me the fear I live in now, the fear that I may do that evil, I'll thank you till the end of my life."

Seppel drew a deep breath. "I've always heard that the harps of Taon play true," he said. He looked at Onyx. "And Roke has no objection?" he asked, with a return to his mild ironic tone.

Onyx shook his head, but he now looked very grave.

"Then we will go to the cave at Aurun. Tonight if you like."

"Why there?" Onyx asked.

"Because it's not I but the Earth that will help Alder. Aurun is a sacred place, full of power. Although the people of Havnor have forgotten that, and use it only to defile it."

Onyx managed to have a private word with Alder before they followed Seppel downstairs. "You need not go through with this, Alder," he said. "I thought I trusted Seppel, but I don't know, now."

"I'll trust him," Alder said. He understood Onyx's doubts, but he had meant what he said, that he would do anything to be free of the fear of doing some dreadful wrong. Each time he had been drawn back in dream to that wall of stones, he felt that something was trying to come into the world through him, that it would do so if he listened to the dead calling to him, and each time he heard them, he was weaker and it was harder to resist their call.

The three men went a long way through the city streets in the heat of the late afternoon. They came out into the countryside south of the city, where rough ridgy hills ran down to the bay, a poor bit of country for this rich island: swampy lowland between the ridges, a little arable land on their rocky backs. The wall of the city here was very old, built of great unmortared rocks taken from the hills, and beyond it were no suburbs and few farms.

They walked along a rough road that zigzagged up the first ridge and followed its crest eastward towards the higher hills. Up there, where they could see all the city lying in a golden haze northward, to their left, the road widened out into a maze of footpaths. Going straight forward they came suddenly to a great crack in the ground, a black gap twenty feet wide or more, right across their way.

It was as if the spine of rock had been cracked apart by a wrenching of the earth and had never healed again. The western sunlight streaming over the lips of the cave lighted the vertical rock faces a little way down, but below that was darkness.

There was a tannery in the valley under the ridge, south of it. The tanners had brought their wastes up here and dumped them into the crack, carelessly, so that all around it was a litter of rancid scraps of half-cured leather and a stink of rot and urine. There was another smell from the depths of the cave as they approached the sheer edge: a cold, sharp, earthy air that made Alder draw back.

"I grieve for this, I grieve for this!" the wizard of Paln said aloud, looking around at the rubbish and down at the roofs of the tannery with a strange expression. But he spoke to Alder after a while in his usual mild way: "This is the cave or cleft called Aurun, that we know from our most ancient maps in Paln, where it is also called the Lips of Paor. It used to speak to the people here, when they first came here from the west. A long time ago. Men have changed. But it is what it was then. Here you can lay down your burden, if that is what you want."

"What must I do?" Alder said.

Seppel led him to the south end of the great split in the ground, where it narrowed back together in fissured ridges of rock. He told him to lie facedown where he could gaze into the depth of darkness stretching down and down away from him. "Hold to the earth," he said. "That is all you must do. Even if it moves, hold to it."

Alder lay there staring down between the walls of stone. He felt rocks jabbing his chest and hip as he lay on them; he heard Seppel begin to chant in a high voice in words he knew were the Language of the Making; he felt the warmth of the sun across his shoulders, and smelled the carrion stink of the tannery. Then the breath of the cave blew up out of the depths with a hollow sharpness that took his own breath away and made his head spin. The darkness moved up towards him. The ground moved under him, rocked and shook, and he held on to it, hearing the high voice sing, breathing the breath of the earth. The darkness rose up and took him. He lost the sun.

When he came back, the sun was low in the west, a red ball in the haze over the western shores of the bay. He saw that. He saw Seppel sitting nearby on the ground, looking tired and forlorn, his black shadow long on the rocky ground among the long shadows of the rocks.

"There you are," Onyx said.

Alder realised that he was lying on his back, his head on Onyx's knees, a rock digging into his backbone. He sat up, dizzy, apologising.

They set off as soon as he could walk, for they had some miles to go and it was clear that neither he nor Seppel would be able to keep a fast pace. Full night had fallen when they came by Boatwright Street. Seppel bade them farewell, looking searchingly at Alder as they stood in the light from a tavern door nearby. "I did as you asked me," he said, with that same unhappy look.

"I thank you for it," Alder said, and put out his right hand to the wizard in the manner of the people of the Enlades. After a moment Seppel touched it with his hand; and so they parted.

Alder was so tired he could barely make his legs move. The sharp, strange taste of the air from the cave was still in his mouth and throat, making him feel light, light-headed, hollow. When at last they came to the palace, Onyx wanted to see him to his room, but Alder said he was well and only needed to rest.

He came into his room and Tug came dancing and tail-waving to greet him. "Ah, I don't need you now," Alder said, bending down to stroke the sleek grey back. Tears came into his eyes. It was only that he was very tired. He lay down on the bed, and the cat jumped up and curled up purring on his shoulder.

And he slept: black, blank sleep with no dream he could remember, no voice calling his name, no hill of dry grass, no dim wall of stones, nothing.

Walking in the gardens of the palace in the evening before they were to sail south, Tenar was heavyhearted and anxious. She did not want to be setting off to Roke, the Isle of the Wise, the Isle of the Wizards. (*Accursed-sorcerers,* a voice in her mind said in Kargish.) What had she to do there? What possible use could she be? She wanted to go home to Gont, to Ged. To her own house, her own work, her own dear man.

She had estranged Lebannen. She had lost him. He was polite, affable, and unforgiving.

How men feared women! she thought, walking among the late-flowering roses. Not as individuals, but women when they talked together, worked together, spoke up for one another—then men saw plots, cabals, constraints, traps being laid.

Of course they were right. Women were likely, as women, to take the next generation's part, not this one's; they wove the links men saw as chains, the bonds men saw as bondage. She and Seserakh were indeed in league against him and ready to betray him, if he truly was nothing unless he was independent. If he was only air and fire, no weight of earth to him, no patient water . . .

But that was not Lebannen so much as Tehanu. Unearthly, her Therru, the winged soul that had come to stay with her a while and was soon, she knew, to leave her. From fire to fire.

And Irian, with whom Tehanu would go. What had that bright, fierce creature to do with an old house that needed sweeping, an old man who needed looking after? How could Irian understand such things? What was it to her, a dragon, that a man should undertake his duty, marry, have children, wear the yoke of earth?

Seeing herself alone and useless among beings of high, inhuman destiny, Tenar gave in altogether to homesickness. Homesickness not for Gont only. Why should she not be in league with Seserakh, who might be a princess as she herself had been a priestess, but who was not going to go flying off on fiery wings, being deeply and entirely a woman of the earth? And she spoke Tenar's own language! Tenar had dutifully tutored her in Hardic, had been delighted with her quickness to learn, and realised only now that the true delight had been just to speak Kargish with her, hearing and saying words that held in them all her lost childhood.

As she came to the walk that led to the fish ponds beneath the willows, she saw Alder. With him was a small boy. They were talking quietly, soberly. She was always glad to see Alder. She pitied him for the pain and fear he was in and honored his patience in bearing it. She liked his honest, handsome face, and his silver tongue. What was the harm in adding a grace note or two to ordinary speech? Ged had trusted him.

Pausing at a distance so as not to disturb the conversation, she saw him and the child kneel down on the path, looking into the bushes. Presently Alder's little grey cat emerged from under a bush. It paid no attention to them, but set off across the grass, paw by paw, belly low and eyes alight, hunting a moth.

"You can let him stay out all night, if you like," Alder said to the child. "He can't stray or come to harm here. He has a great taste for the open air. But this is like all Havnor to him, you see, these great gardens. Or you can give him his freedom in the mornings. And then, if you like, he can sleep with you."

"I would like that," the boy said, shyly decisive.

"Then he needs his box of sand in your room, you know. And a bowl of drinking water, never to go dry."

"And food."

"Yes, indeed; once a day. Not too much of it. He's a bit greedy.

Inclined to think Segoy made the islands so that Tug could fill his belly."

"Does he catch fish in the pond?" The cat was now near one of the carp pools, sitting on the grass looking about; the moth had flown.

"He likes to watch them."

"I do too," the boy said. They got up and walked together towards the pools.

Tenar was moved to tenderness. There was an innocence to Alder, but it was a man's innocence, not childish. He should have had children of his own. He would have been a good father to them.

She thought of her own children, and of the little grandchildren—though Apple's eldest, Pippin, was it possible? was Pippin about to be twelve? She would be named this year or next! Oh, it was time to go home. It was time to visit Middle Valley, take a nameday present to her granddaughter and toys to the babies, make sure Spark in his restlessness wasn't overpruning the pear trees again, sit a while and talk with her kind daughter Apple . . . Apple's true name was Hayohe, the name Ogion had given her . . . The thought of Ogion came as always with a pang of love and longing. She saw the hearthplace of the house at Re Albi. She saw Ged sitting there at the hearth. She saw him turn his dark face to ask her a question. She answered it, aloud, in the gardens of the New Palace of Havnor hundreds of miles from that hearth: "As soon as I can!"

In the morning, the bright summer morning, they all went down from the palace to go aboard the *Dolphin.* The people of the City of Havnor made it a festival, swarming afoot in the streets and on the wharves, choking the canals with the little poled boats they called chips, dotting the great bay with sailboats and dinghies all flying bright flags; and flags and pennants flew from the towers of the great houses and the banner poles on bridges high and low. Passing among these cheerful crowds, Tenar thought of the day long ago she and Ged came sailing into Havnor, bringing home the Rune of Peace, Elfarran's Ring. That Ring had been on her arm, and she had held it up so the silver would flash in the sunlight and the people could see it, and they had cheered and held out their arms to her as if they all wanted to embrace her. It made her smile to think of that. She was smiling as she went up the gangplank and bowed to Lebannen.

He greeted her with the traditional formality of a ship's master: "Mistress Tenar, be welcome aboard." She replied, moved by she knew not what impulse, "I thank you, son of Elfarran."

He looked at her for a moment, startled by that name. But Tehanu followed close after her, and he repeated the formal greeting: "Mistress Tehanu, be welcome aboard."

Tenar went on towards the prow of the ship, remembering a corner there near a capstan where a passenger could be out of the way of the hardworking sailors and yet see all that happened on the crowded deck and outside the ship too.

There was a commotion in the main street leading to the dock: the High Princess was arriving. Tenar saw with satisfaction that Lebannen, or perhaps his majordomo, had arranged for the princess's arrival to be fittingly magnificent. Mounted escorts opened a way through the crowds, their horses snorting and clattering in fine style. Tall red plumes, such as Kargish warriors wore on their helmets, waved from the top of the closed, gilt-bedizened carriage that had brought the princess across the city and on the headstalls of the four grey horses that drew it. A band of musicians waiting on the waterside struck up with trumpet, tambour, and tambourine. And the people, discovering that they had a princess to cheer and peer at, cheered loudly, and pressed as close as the horsemen and foot guards would allow them, gaping and full of praises and somewhat random greetings. "Hail the Queen of the Kargs!" some of them shouted, and others, "She ain't," and others, "Look at 'em all in red, fine as rubies, which one is her?" and others, "Long live the Princess!"

Tenar saw Seserakh—veiled of course from hat to foot, but unmistakable by her height and bearing—descend from the carriage and sail, stately as a ship herself, towards the gangplank. Two of her shorter-veiled attendants trotted close behind her, followed by Lady Opal of Ilien. Tenar's heart sank. Lebannen had decreed that no servants or followers were to be taken on this journey. It was not a cruise or pleasure trip, he had said sternly, and those aboard must have good reason to be aboard. Had Seserakh not understood that? Or did she so cling to her silly countrywomen that she meant to defy the king? That would be a most unfortunate beginning of the voyage.

But at the foot of the gangplank the gold-rippling red cylinder stopped and turned. It put forth hands, gold-skinned hands shining with gold rings. The princess embraced her handmaidens, clearly bidding them farewell. She also embraced Lady Opal in the approved stately manner of royalty and nobility in public. Then Lady Opal herded the handmaidens back towards the carriage, while the princess turned again to the gangplank.

There was a pause. Tenar could see that featureless column of red and gold take a deep breath. It drew itself up taller.

It proceeded up the gangplank, slowly, for the tide had been rising and the angle was steep, but with an unhesitant dignity that kept the crowds ashore silent, fascinated, watching.

It attained the deck and stopped there, facing the king.

"High Princess of the Kargad Lands, be welcome aboard," Lebannen said in a ringing voice. At that the crowds burst out—"Hurrah for the Princess! Long live the Queen! Well walked, Reddy!"

Lebannen said something to the princess which the cheering made inaudible to others. The red column turned to the crowd on the waterside and bowed, stiff-backed but gracious.

Tehanu had waited for her near where the king stood, and now came forward and spoke to her and led her to the aft cabin of the ship, where the heavy, soft-flowing red and golden veils disappeared. The crowd cheered and called more wildly than ever. "Come back, Princess! Where's Reddy? Where's our lady? Where's the Queen?"

Tenar looked down the length of the ship at the king. Through her misgivings and heaviness of heart, unruly laughter welled up in her. She thought, Poor boy, what will you do now? They've fallen in love with her the first chance they got to see her, even though they can't see her . . . Oh, Lebannen, we're all in league against you!

Dolphin was a fair-sized ship, fitted out to carry a king in some state and comfort; but first and foremost she was made to sail, to fly with the wind, to take him where he needed to go as quickly as could be. Accommodations were cramped enough when it was only the crew and officers, the king and a few companions aboard. On this voyage to Roke, accommodations were jammed. The crew, to be sure, were in no more than usual discomfort, sleeping down in the three-foot-high kennel of the foreward hold; but the officers had to share one wretched black closet under the forecastle. As for the passengers, all four women were in what was normally the king's cabin, which ran the narrow width of the sterncastle of the ship, while the cabin beneath it, usually occupied by the ship's master and one or two other officers, was shared by the king, the two wizards, the sorcerer, and Tosla. The probability of misery and bad temper was, Tenar thought, limitless. The first and most urgent probability, however, was that the High Princess was going to be sick.

They were sailing down the Great Bay with the mildest following wind, the water calm, the ship gliding along like a swan on a pond; but Seserakh cowered on her bunk, crying out in despair whenever she looked out through her veils and caught sight of the sunny, peaceful vista of unexcited water, the mild white wake of the ship, through the broad stern windows. "It will go up and down," she moaned in Kargish.

"It is not going up and down at all," Tenar said. "Use your head, princess!"

"It is my stomach not my head," Seserakh whimpered.

"Nobody could possibly be seasick in this weather. You are simply afraid."

"Mother," Tehanu protested, understanding the tone if not the words. "Don't scold her. It's miserable to be sick."

"She is not sick!" Tenar said. She was absolutely convinced of the truth of what she said. "Seserakh, you are not sick. You are afraid of being sick. Get hold of yourself. Come out on deck. Fresh air will make all the difference. Fresh air and courage."

"Oh my friend," Seserakh murmured in Hardic. "Make me courage!"

Tenar was a little taken aback. "You have to make it yourself, princess," she said. Then, relenting, "Come on, just try it out on deck for a minute. Tehanu, see if you can persuade her. Think what she'll suffer if we do meet some weather!"

Between them they got Seserakh to her feet and into her cylinder of red veiling, without which she could not of course appear before the eyes of men; they coaxed and wheedled her to creep out of the cabin, onto the bit of deck to the side of it, in the shade, where they could all sit in a row on the bone-white, impeccable decking and look out at the blue and shining sea.

Seserakh parted her veils enough that she could see straight in front of her; but she mostly looked at her lap, with an occasional, brief, terrified glance at the water, after which she shut her eyes and then looked down at her lap again.

Tenar and Tehanu talked a little, pointing out ships that passed, birds, an island. "It's lovely. I forgot how I like to sail!" Tenar said.

"I like it if I can forget the water," said Tehanu. "It's like flying."

"Ah, you dragons," Tenar said.

It was spoken lightly, but it was not lightly said. It was the first time she had ever said anything of the kind to her adopted daughter. She was aware that Tehanu had turned her head to look at her with her seeing eye. Tenar's heart beat heavily. "Air and fire," she said.

Tehanu said nothing. But her hand, the brown slender hand, not the claw, reached out and took hold of Tenar's hand and held it tightly.

"I don't know what I am, mother," she whispered in her voice that was seldom more than a whisper.

"I do," Tenar said. And her heart beat heavier and harder than before.

"I'm not like Irian," Tehanu said. She was trying to comfort her mother, to reassure her, but there was longing in her voice, yearning jealousy, profound desire.

"Wait, wait and find out," her mother replied, finding it hard to speak. "You'll know what to do . . . what you are . . . when the time comes."

They were talking so softly that the princess could not hear what they said, if she could understand it. They had forgotten her. But she had caught the name Irian, and parting her veils with her long hands and turning to them, her eyes looking out bright from the warm red shadow, she asked, "Irian, she is?"

"Somewhere forward—up there—" Tenar waved at the rest of the ship.

"She makes herself courage. Ah?"

After a moment Tenar said, "She doesn't need to make it, I think. She's fearless."

"Ah," said the princess.

Her bright eyes were gazing out of shadow all the length of the ship, to the prow, where Irian stood beside Lebannen. The king was pointing ahead, gesturing, talking with animation. He laughed, and Irian, standing by him, as tall as he, laughed too.

"Barefaced," Seserakh muttered in Kargish. And then in Hardic, thoughtfully, almost inaudibly, "Fearless."

She closed her veils and sat featureless, unmoving.

The long shores of Havnor were blue behind them. Mount Onn floated faint and high in the north. The black basalt columns of the Isle of Omer towered off the ship's right side as she worked across the Ebavnor Straits towards the Inmost Sea. The sun was bright, the wind fresh, another fine day. All the women were sitting under the sailcloth awning the sailors had rigged for them beside the aftercabin. Women brought good luck to a ship, and the sailors couldn't do enough for them in the way of ingenious little comforts and amenities. Because wizards could bring good luck or, equally, bad luck to a ship, the sailors also treated the wizards very well; their awning was rigged in a corner of the quarterdeck, where they had a good view forward. The women had velvet cushions to sit on (provided by the king's forethought, or his majordomo's); the wizards had packets of sailcloth, which did very well.

Alder found himself treated as and considered to be one of the wizards. He could do nothing about it, though it embarrassed him lest Onyx and Seppel should think he was claiming equality with them, and it also troubled him because he was now not even a sorcerer. His gift was gone. He had no power at all. He knew it as surely as he would have known the loss of his sight, the paralysis of his hand. He could not have mended a broken pitcher now, unless with glue; and he would have done it badly, because he had never had to do it.

And beyond the craft he had lost was something else, something larger than the craft, that was gone. Its loss left him, as his wife's death had, in a blankness in which no joy, no new thing was or would ever be. Nothing could happen, nothing could change.

Not having known of this larger aspect of his gift till he lost it, he pondered on it, wondering about its nature. It was like knowing the way to go, he thought, like knowing the direction of home. Not a thing one could identify or even say much about, but a connection on which everything else depended. Without it he was desolate. He was useless.

But at least he did no harm. His dreams were fleeting, meaningless. They never took him to those dreary moorlands, the hill of dead grass, the wall. No voices called him to the dark.

He thought often of Sparrowhawk, wishing he could talk with him: the Archmage who had spent all his power, and having been great among the great, now lived his life out poor and disregarded. Yet the king longed to show him honor; so Sparrowhawk's poverty was by choice. Perhaps, Alder thought, riches or high estate would have been only shameful to a man who had lost his true wealth, his way.

Onyx clearly regretted having led Alder to make this trade or bargain. He had always been entirely civil to Alder, but he now treated him with regard and compunction, while his manner to the wizard of Paln had become a little distant. Alder himself felt no resentment towards Seppel and no distrust of his intentions. The Old Powers were the Old Powers. You used them at your risk. Seppel had told him what he must pay, and he had paid it. He had not understood quite how much there was to pay; but that was not Seppel's fault. It was his own, for never having valued his gift at its true worth.

So he sat with the two wizards, thinking of himself as false coin to their gold, but listening to them with all his mind; for they trusted him and spoke freely, and their talk was an education he had never dreamed of as a sorcerer.

Sitting there in the bright pale shade of the canvas awning, they talked of a bargain, a greater bargain than the one he had made to stop his dreams. Onyx said more than once the words of the Old Speech

Seppel had spoken on the rooftop: *Verw nadan.* As they talked, little by little Alder gathered that the meaning of those words was something like a choice, a division, making two things of one. Far, far back in time, before the Kings of Enlad, before the writing of Hardic, maybe before there was a Hardic tongue, when there was only the Language of the Making, it seemed that people had made some kind of choice, given up one great power or possession to gain another.

The wizards' talk of this was hard to follow, not so much because they hid anything but because they themselves were groping after things lost in the cloudy past, the time before memory. Words of the Old Speech came into their talk of necessity, and sometimes Onyx spoke entirely in that tongue. But Seppel would answer him in Hardic. Seppel was sparing with the words of the Making. Once he held up his hand to stop Onyx from going on, and at the Roke wizard's look of surprise and question, said mildly, "Spellwords act."

Alder's teacher Gannet, too, had called the words of the Old Speech spellwords. "Each is a deed of power," he had said. "True word makes truth be." Gannet had been stingy with the spellwords he knew, speaking them only at need, and when he wrote any rune but the common ones that were used to write Hardic, he erased it almost as he finished it. Most sorcerers were similarly careful, either to guard their knowledge for themselves or because they respected the power of the Language of the Making. Even Seppel, wizard as he was, with a far wider knowledge and understanding of those words, preferred not to use them in conversation, but to keep to ordinary language which, if it allowed lies and errors, also permitted uncertainty and retraction.

Perhaps that had been part of the great choice men made in ancient times: to give up the innate knowledge of the Old Speech, which they once shared with the dragons. Had they done so, Alder wondered, in order to have a language of their own, a language suited to mankind, in which they could lie, cheat, swindle, and invent wonders that never had been and would never be?

The dragons spoke no speech but the Old Speech. Yet it was always said that dragons lied. Was it so? he wondered. If spellwords were true, how could even a dragon use them to lie?

Seppel and Onyx had come to one of the long, easy, thoughtful pauses in their conversation. Seeing that Onyx was, in fact, at least half asleep, Alder asked the Pelnish wizard softly, "Is it true that dragons can tell untruth in the true words?"

The Pelnishman smiled. "That—so we say on Paln—is the very question Ath asked Orm a thousand years ago, in the ruins of Ontuego.

'Can a dragon lie?' the mage asked. And Orm replied, 'No,' and then breathed on him, burning him to ashes . . . But are we to believe the story, since it was only Orm who could have told it?"

Infinite are the arguments of mages, Alder said to himself, but not aloud.

Onyx had gone definitely to sleep, his head tilted back against the bulkhead, his grave, tense face relaxed.

Seppel spoke, his voice even quieter than usual. "Alder, I hope you do not regret what we did at Aurun. I know our friend thinks I did not warn you clearly enough."

Alder said without hesitation, "I am content."

Seppel inclined his dark head.

Alder said presently, "I know that we try to keep the Equilibrium. But the Powers of the Earth keep their own account."

"And theirs is a justice that is hard for men to understand."

"That's it. I try to see why it was just that, my craft, I mean, that I must give up to free myself from that dream. What has the one to do with the other?"

Seppel did not answer for a while, and then it was with a question. "It was not by your craft that you came to the wall of stones?"

"Never," Alder said with certainty. "I had no more power to go there if I willed it than I had to prevent myself from going."

"So how did you come there?"

"My wife called me, and my heart went to her."

A longer pause. The wizard said, "Other men have lost beloved wives."

"So I said to my Lord Sparrowhawk. And he said: that's true, and yet the bond between true lovers is as close as we come to what endures forever."

"Across the wall of stones, no bond endures."

Alder looked at the wizard, the swarthy, soft, keen-eyed face. "Why is it so?" he said.

"Death is the bond breaker."

"Then why do the dead not die?"

Seppel stared at him, taken aback.

"I'm sorry," Alder said. "I misspeak in my ignorance. What I mean is this: death breaks the bond of soul with body, and the body dies. It goes back to the earth. But the spirit must go to that dark place, and wear a semblance of the body, and endure there—for how long? Forever? In the dust and dusk there, without light, or love, or cheer at all? I cannot bear to think of Lily in that place. Why must she be there? Why can she not be—" his voice stumbled—"be free?"

"Because the wind does not blow there," Seppel said. His look was very strange, his voice harsh. "It was stopped from blowing, by the art of man."

He continued to stare at Alder but only gradually did he begin to see him. The expression in his eyes and face changed. He looked away, up the beautiful white curve of the foresail, full of the breath of the northwest wind. He glanced back at Alder. "You know as much as I do of this matter, my friend," he said with almost his usual softness. "But you know it in your body, your blood, in the pulse of your heart. And I know only words. Old words . . . So we had better get to Roke, where maybe the wise men will be able to tell us what we need to know. Or if they cannot, the dragons will, perhaps. Or maybe it will be you who shows us the way."

"That would be the blind man who led the seers to the cliff's edge, indeed!" Alder said with a laugh.

"Ah, but we're at the cliff's edge already, with our eyes shut," said the wizard of Paln.

Lebannen found the ship too small to contain the enormous restlessness that filled him. The women sat under their little awning and the wizards sat under theirs like ducks in a row, but he paced up and down, impatient with the narrow confines of the deck. He felt it was his impatience and not the wind that sent *Dolphin* running so fast to the south, but never fast enough. He wanted the journey over.

"Remember the fleet on the way to Wathort?" Tosla said, joining him while he stood near the steersman, studying the chart and the clear sea before them. "That was a grand sight. Thirty ships aline!"

"I wish it was Wathort we were bound for," Lebannen said.

"I never did like Roke," Tosla agreed. "Not an honest wind or current for twenty miles off that shore, but only wizards' brew. And the rocks north of it never in the same place twice. And the town full of cheats and shape-shifters." He spat, competently, to leeward. "I'd rather meet old Gore and his slavers again!"

Lebannen nodded, but said nothing. That was often the pleasure of Tosla's company: he said what Lebannen felt it was better that he himself not say.

"Who was the dumb man, the mute," Tosla asked, "the one that killed Falcon on the wall?"

"Egre. Pirate turned slave taker."

"That's it. He knew you, there at Sorra. Went right for you. I always wondered how."

"Because he took me as a slave once."

It was not easy to surprise Tosla, but the seaman looked at him with his mouth open, evidently not believing him but not able to say so, and so with nothing to say. Lebannen enjoyed the effect for a minute and then took pity on him.

"When the Archmage took me hunting after Cob, we went south, first. A man in Hort Town betrayed us to the slave takers. They knocked the Archmage on the head, and I ran off thinking I could lead them away from him. But it was me they were after—I was salable. I woke up chained in a galley bound for Sowl. He rescued me before the next night passed. The irons fell off us all like bits of dead leaves. And he told Egre not to speak again until he found something worth saying . . . He came to that galley like a great light over the water . . . I never knew what he was till then."

Tosla mulled this over a while. "He unchained all the slaves? Why didn't the others kill Egre?"

"Maybe they took him on to Sowl and sold him," Lebannen said.

Tosla mulled a while longer. "So that's why you were so keen to do away with the slave trade."

"One reason."

"Doesn't improve the character, as a rule," Tosla observed. He studied the chart of the Inmost Sea tacked on the board to the steersman's left. "Island of Way," he remarked. "Where the dragon woman's from."

"You keep clear of her, I notice."

Tosla pursed his lips, though he did not whistle, being aboard ship. "You know that song I mentioned, about the Lass of Belilo? Well, I never thought of it as anything but a tale. Until I saw her."

"I doubt she'd eat you, Tosla."

"It would be a glorious death," the sailor said, rather sourly.

The king laughed.

"Don't push your own luck," said Tosla.

"No fear."

"You and she were talking there so free and easy. Like making yourself easy with a volcano, to my mind . . . But I'll tell you, I wouldn't mind seeing a bit more of that present the Kargs sent you. There's a sight worth seeing in there, to judge by the feet. But how do you get it out of the tent? The feet are grand, but I'd like a bit more ankle, to begin with."

Lebannen felt his face turn grim, and turned aside to keep Tosla from seeing it.

"If anybody gave me a package like that," Tosla said, staring out over the sea, "I'd open it."

Lebannen could not restrain a slight movement of impatience. Tosla saw it; he was quick. He grinned his wry grin and said no more.

The ship's master had come out on deck, and Lebannen engaged him in talk. "Looks a bit thick ahead?" he said, and the master nodded: "Thunder squalls to the south and west there. We'll be in them tonight."

The sea grew choppier as the afternoon drew on, the benign sunlight took on a brassy tinge, and gusts of wind blew from one quarter then another. Tenar had told Lebannen that the princess was afraid of the sea and of seasickness, and he glanced back once or twice at the aftercabin, expecting to see no red-veiled form among the ducks in a row. But it was Tenar and Tehanu who had gone in; the princess was still there, and Irian was sitting beside her. They were talking earnestly. What on earth did a dragon woman from Way have to talk about with a harem woman from Hur-at-Hur? What language had they in common? The question seemed so much in need of answering to Lebannen that he walked aft.

When he got there Irian looked up at him and smiled. She had a strong, open face, a broad smile; she went barefoot by choice, was careless about her dress, let the wind tangle her hair; altogether she seemed no more than a handsome, hot-hearted, intelligent, untaught countrywoman, till you saw her eyes. They were the color of smoky amber, and when she looked straight at Lebannen, as she was doing now, he could not meet them. He looked down.

He had made it clear that there was to be no courtly ceremony on the ship, no bows and courtesies, nobody was to leap up when he came near; but the princess had got to her feet. They were, as Tosla had observed, beautiful feet, not small, but high-arched, strong, and fine. He looked at them, the two slender feet on the white wood of the deck. He looked up from them and saw that the princess was doing as she had done the last time he faced her: parting her veils so that he, though no one else, could see her face. He was a little staggered by the stern, almost tragic beauty of the face in that red shadow.

"Is—is everything all right, princess?" he asked, stammering, a thing he very seldom did.

She said, "My friend Tenar said, breathe wind."

"Yes," he said, rather at random.

"Is there anything your wizards could do for her, do you think, maybe?" said Irian, unfolding her long limbs and standing up too. She and the princess were both tall women.

Lebannen was trying to make out what color the princess's eyes were, since he was able to look at them. They were blue, he thought, but like blue opals they held other colors in them, or maybe it was the sunlight coming through the red of her veils. —"Do for her?"

"She wants very much not to be seasick. She had a terrible time of it coming from the Kargish places."

"I will not to fear," the princess said. She gazed straight at him as if challenging him to—what?

"Of course," he said, "of course. I'll ask Onyx. I'm sure there's something he can do." He made a sketchy bow to them both and went off hurriedly to find the wizard.

Onyx and Seppel conferred and then consulted Alder. A spell against seasickness was more in the province of sorcerers, menders, healers, than of learned and powerful wizards. Alder could not do anything himself at present, of course, but he might remember a charm . . . ? He did not, having never dreamed of going to sea until his troubles began. Seppel confessed that he himself always got seasick in small boats or rough weather. Onyx finally went to the aftercabin and begged the princess's pardon: he himself had no skill to help her, and nothing to offer her but—apologetically—a charm or talisman one of the sailors hearing of her plight—the sailors heard everything—had pressed upon him to give her.

The princess's long-fingered hand emerged from the red and gold veils. The wizard placed in it a queer little black-and-white object: dried seaweed braided round a bird's breastbone. "A petrel, because they ride the storm," Onyx said, shamefaced.

The princess bowed her unseen head and murmured thanks in Kargish. The fetish disappeared within her veils. She withdrew to the cabin. Onyx, meeting the king quite nearby, apologised to him. The ship was pitching energetically now in hard, erratic gusts on a choppy sea, and he said, "I could, you know, sire, say a word to the winds . . ."

Lebannen knew well that there were two schools of thought concerning weatherworking: the old-fashioned one, that of the Bagmen who ordered the winds to serve their ships as shepherds order their dogs to run here and there, and the newfangled notion—a few centuries old at most—of the Roke School, that the magewind might be raised at real need, but it was best to let the world's winds blow. He knew that Onyx was a devout upholder of the way of Roke. "Use your own judgment, Onyx," he said. "If it seems we're in for a really bad night . . . But if it's no more than a few squalls . . ."

Onyx looked up at the masthead, where already a wisp or two of fallow fire had flickered in the cloud-darkened dusk. Thunder rumbled grandly in the blackness before them, all across the south. Behind them the last of the daylight fell wan, tremulous across the waves.

"Very well," he said, rather dismally, and went below to the small and crowded cabin.

Lebannen stayed out of that cabin almost entirely, sleeping on deck when he slept at all. Tonight was not one for sleep for anybody on the *Dolphin.* It was not a single squall, but a chain of violent late-summer storms boiling up out of the southwest, and between the terrific commotion of the lightning-dazzled sea, the thunder crashes that seemed about to knock the ship apart, and the crazy storm gusts that kept her pitching and rolling and taking queer jumps, it was a long night and a loud one.

Onyx consulted Lebannen once: Should he say a word to the wind? Lebannen looked to the master, who shrugged. He and his crew were busy enough, but unconcerned. The ship was in no trouble. As for the womenfolk, they were reported to be sitting up in their cabin, gambling. Irian and the princess had come out on deck earlier, but it was hard to stay afoot at times and they had seen they were in the crew's way, so they had retired. The report that they were gambling came from the cook's boy, who had been sent to see if they wanted anything to eat. They had wanted whatever he could bring.

Lebannen found himself possessed by the same intense curiosity he had felt in the afternoon. There was no doubt the lamps were all alight in the stern cabin, for the glow of them streamed out golden on the foam and race of the ship's wake. About midnight, he went aft and knocked.

Irian opened the door. After the dazzle and blackness of the storm the lamplight in the cabin seemed warm and steady, though the swinging lamps cast swinging shadows; and he was confusedly aware of colors, the soft, various colors of the women's clothes, their skin, brown or pale or gold, their hair, black or grey or tawny, their eyes—the princess's eyes staring at him, startled, as she snatched up a scarf or some cloth to hold before her face.

"Oh! We thought it was the cook's boy!" Irian said with a laugh.

Tehanu looked at him and said in her shy, comradely way, "Is there trouble?"

He realised that he was standing in the doorway staring at them like some speechless messenger of doom.

"No— None at all— Are you getting on all right? I'm sorry it's been so rough—"

"We don't hold you answerable for the weather," Tenar said. "Nobody could sleep, so the princess and I have been teaching the others Kargish gambling."

He saw five-sided ivory dice-sticks scattered over the table, probably Tosla's.

"We've been betting islands," Irian said. "But Tehanu and I are losing. The Kargs have already won Ark and Ilien."

The princess had lowered the scarf; she sat facing Lebannen resolutely, extremely tense, as a young swordsman might face him before a fencing match. In the warmth of the cabin they were all bare-armed and barefoot, but her consciousness of her uncovered face drew his consciousness as a magnet draws a pin.

"I'm sorry it's been so rough," he said again, idiotically, and closed the door. As he turned away he heard them all laughing.

He went to stand by the steersman. Looking into the gusty, rainy darkness lit by fitful, distant lightning, he could still see everything in the stern cabin, the black fall of Tehanu's hair, Tenar's affectionate, teasing smile, the dice on the table, the princess's round arms, honey-colored like the lamplight, her throat in the shadow of her hair, though he did not remember looking at her arms and throat but only at her face, at her eyes full of defiance, despair. What was the girl afraid of? Did she think he wanted to hurt her?

A star or two was shining out high in the south. He went to his crowded cabin, slung a hammock, for the bunks were full, and slept for a few hours. He woke before dawn, restless as ever, and went up on deck.

The day came as bright and calm as if no storm had ever been. Lebannen stood at the forward rail and saw the first sunlight strike across the water, and an old song came into his mind:

O my joy!
Before bright Éa was, before Segoy
Bade the islands be,
The morning wind blew on the sea.
O my joy, be free!

It was a fragment of a ballad or lullaby from his childhood. He could remember no more of it. The tune was sweet. He sang it softly and let the wind take the words from his lips.

Tenar emerged from the cabin and, seeing him, came to him. "Good morning, my dear lord," she said, and he greeted her fondly, with some memory that he had been angry at her but not knowing why he had been or how he could have been.

"Did you Kargs win Havnor last night?" he asked.

"No, you may keep Havnor. We went to bed. All the young ones are still there, lolling. Shall we—what is it? lift Roke today?"

"Raise Roke? No, not till early tomorrow. But before noon we should be in Thwil Harbor. If they let us come to the island."

"What do you mean?"

"Roke defends itself from unwelcome visitors."

"Oh: Ged told me about that. He was on a ship trying to sail back there, and they sent the wind against him, the Roke wind he called it."

"Against *him*?"

"It was a long time ago." She smiled with pleasure at his incredulity, his unwillingness that any affront should ever have been offered to Ged. "When he was a boy who had meddled with the darkness. That's what he said."

"When he was a man he still meddled with it."

"He doesn't now," Tenar said, serene.

"No, it's we who have to." His face had grown somber. "I wish I knew what we're meddling with. I am certain that things are drawing to some great chance or change—as Ogion foretold—as Ged told Alder. And I am certain that Roke is where we need to be to meet it. But beyond that, no certainty, nothing. I don't know what it is we face. When Ged took me into the dark land, we knew our enemy. When I took the fleet to Sorra, I knew what the evil was I wanted to undo. But now— Are the dragons our enemies or our allies? What has gone wrong? What is it we must do or undo? Will the Masters of Roke be able to tell us? Or will they turn their wind against us?"

"Fearing—?"

"Fearing the dragon. The one they know. Or the one they don't know . . ."

Tenar's face was sober too, but gradually it broke into a smile. "What a ragbag you are bringing them, to be sure!" she said. "A sorcerer with nightmares, a wizard from Paln, two dragons, and two Kargs. The only respectable passengers on this ship are you and Onyx."

Lebannen could not laugh. "If only *he* were with us," he said.

Tenar put her hand on his arm. She started to speak and then did not.

He laid his hand over hers. They stood silent thus for some time, side by side, looking out at the dancing sea.

"The princess has something she wants to tell you before we come to Roke," Tenar said. "It's a story from Hur-at-Hur. Off there in their desert they remember things. I think this goes back before anything I ever heard except the story of the Woman of Kemay. It has to do with dragons . . . It would be kind of you to invite her, so that she doesn't have to ask."

Aware of the care and caution with which she spoke, he felt a moment of impatience, a flick of shame. He watched, far south across the sea, the course of a galley bound for Kamery or Way, the faint, tiny flash of the lifted sweeps. He said, "Of course. About noon?"

"Thank you."

About noon, he sent a young seaman to the stern cabin to request the princess to join the king on the foredeck. She emerged at once, and the ship being only about fifty feet long, he could observe her entire progress towards him: not a long walk, though perhaps for her it was a long one. For it was not a featureless red cylinder that approached him but a tall young woman. She wore soft white trousers, a long shirt of dull red, a gold circlet that held a very thin red veil over her face and head. The veil fluttered in the sea wind. The young sailor led her round the various obstacles and up and down the descents and ascents of the crowded, cumbered, narrow deck. She walked slowly and proudly. She was barefoot. Every eye in the ship was on her.

She arrived on the foredeck and stood still.

Lebannen bowed. "Your presence honors us, princess."

She performed a deep, straight-backed courtesy and said, "Thank you."

"You were not ill last night, I hope?"

She put her hand on the charm she wore on the cord round her neck, a small bone tied with black, showing it to him. "*Kerez akath akatharwa erevi,*" she said. He knew the word *akath* in Kargish meant sorcerer or sorcery.

There were eyes everywhere, eyes in hatchways, eyes up in the rigging, eyes that were like augurs, like gimlets.

"Come forward, if you will. We may see Roke Island soon," he said, though there was not the remotest chance of seeing a glimmer of Roke till dawn. With a hand under her elbow though not actually touching her, he guided her up the steep slant of the deck to the forepeak, where between a capstan, the slant of the bowsprit, and the port rail was a little triangle of decking that—when a sailor had scurried away with the cable he was mending—they had quite to themselves. They were as visible as ever to the rest of the ship, but they could turn their backs on it: as much privacy as royalty can hope for.

When they had gained this tiny haven, the princess turned to him and pushed back the veil from her face. He had intended to ask what he could do for her, but the question seemed both inadequate and irrelevant. He said nothing.

She said, "Lord King. In Hur-at-Hur I am *feyagat.* In Roke Island I am to be king's daughter of Kargad. To be this, I am not *feyagat.* I am bare face. If it please you."

After a moment he said, "Yes. Yes, princess. This is—this is well done."

"It please you?"

"Very much. Yes. I thank you, princess."

"*Barrezú,*" she said, a regal acceptance of his thanks. Her dignity abashed him. Her face had been flaming red when she first put back the veil; there was no color in it now. But she stood straight and still, and gathered up her forces for another speech.

"Too," she said. "Also. My friend Tenar."

"Our friend Tenar," he said with a smile.

"Our friend Tenar. She says I am to tell King Lebannen of the Vedurnan."

He repeated the word.

"Long ago long ago—Karg people, sorcery people, dragon people, hah? Yes?— All people one, all speak one—one— Oh! *Wuluah mekrevt!*"

"One language?"

"Hah! Yes! One language!" In her passionate attempt to speak Hardic, to tell him what she wanted to tell him, she was losing her self-consciousness; her face and eyes shone. "But then, dragon people say: Let go, let go all things. Fly!— But we people, we say: No, keep. Keep all things. Dwell!— So we go apart, hah? dragon people and we people? So they make the Vedurnan. These to let go—these to keep. Yes? But to keep all things, we must to let go that language. That dragon people language."

"The Old Speech?"

"Yes! So we people, we let go that Old Speech language, and keep all things. And dragon people let go all things, but keep that, keep that language. Hah? *Seyneha?* This is the Vedurnan." Her beautiful, large, long hands gestured eloquently and she watched his face with eager hope of understanding. "We go east, east, east. Dragon people go west, west. We dwell, they fly. Some dragon come east with us, but not keep the language, forget, and forget to fly. Like Karg people. Karg people speak Karg language, not dragon language. All keep the Vedurnan, east, west. *Seyneha?* But in—"

At a loss, she brought her hands together from her "east" and "west," and Lebannen said, "In the middle?"

"Hah, yes! In the middle!" She laughed with the pleasure of getting the word. "In the middle—you! Sorcery people! Hah? You, middle people, speak Hardic language but too, also, keep to speak Old Speech language. You *learn* it. Like I learn Hardic, hah? Learn to speak. Then, then—this is the bad. The bad thing. Then you say, in that sorcery language, in that Old Speech language, you say: *We will not to die.* And it is so. And the Vedurnan is broken."

Her eyes were like blue fire.

After a moment she asked, *"Seyneha?"*

"I'm not sure I understand."

"You keep life. You keep. Too long. You never to let go. But to die—" She threw her hands out in a great opening gesture as if she threw something away, into the air, across the water.

He shook his head regretfully.

"Ah," she said. She thought a minute, but no words came. Defeated, she moved her hands palms down in a graceful pantomime of relinquishment. "I must to learn more words," she said.

"Princess, the Master Patterner of Roke, the Master of the Grove—" He watched her for comprehension, and began again. "On Roke Island, there is a man, a great mage, who is a Karg. You can tell him what you have told me—in your own language."

She listened intently and nodded. She said, "The friend of Irian. I will in my heart to talk to this man." Her face was bright with the thought.

That touched Lebannen. He said, "I'm sorry you have been lonely here, princess."

She looked at him, alert and luminous, but did not reply.

"I hope, as time goes on—as you learn the language—"

"I learn quick," she said. He did not know if it was a statement or a prediction.

They were looking straight at each other.

She resumed her stately attitude and spoke formally, as she had at the beginning: "I thank you to listen, Lord King." She dipped her head and shielded her eyes in a formal sign of respect and made the deep knee-bend courtesy again, speaking some formula in Kargish.

"Please," he said, "tell me what you said."

She paused, hesitated, thought, and replied, "Your—your, ah—

small kings?—sons! Sons, your sons, let them to be dragons and kings of dragons. Hah?" She smiled radiantly, let the veil fall over her face, backed away four steps, turned and departed, lithe and sure-footed down the length of the ship. Lebannen stood as if last night's lightning had struck him at last.

Chapter V

Rejoining

THE LAST NIGHT OF THE sea voyage was calm, warm, starless. *Dolphin* moved with a long, easy rocking over the smooth swells southward. It was easy to sleep, and the people slept, and sleeping dreamed.

Alder dreamed of a little animal that came in the dark and touched his hand. He could not see what it was, and when he reached out to it, it was gone, lost. Again he felt the small, velvet muzzle touch his hand. He half roused, and the dream slipped from him, but the piercing ache of loss was in his heart.

In the bunk below him, Seppel dreamed that he was in his own house in Ferao on Paln, reading an old lore-book from the Dark Time, content with his work; but he was interrupted. Someone wanted to see him. "It will only take a minute," he told himself, and went to speak to the caller. It was a woman; her hair was dark with a glint of red in it, her face was beautiful and full of trouble. "You must send him to me," she said. "You will send him to me, won't you?" He thought: I don't know who she means, but I must pretend I do, and he said, "That will not be easy, you know." At that the woman drew her hand back and he saw that she held a stone, a heavy stone. Startled, he thought she meant to throw it at him or strike him down with it, and recoiling from her, he woke in the darkness of the cabin. He lay listening to the breathing of the other sleepers and the whisper of the sea along the ship's side.

In his bunk on the other side of the small cabin, Onyx lay on his back gazing into the dark; he thought his eyes were open, he thought he was awake, but he thought that many small, thin cords had been tied around his arms and legs and hands and head, and that all these cords ran out into the darkness, over land and sea, over the curve of the world: and the cords were drawing him, tugging him, so that he and the ship he was in and all its passengers were being pulled gently, gently to the place where the sea dried up, where the ship would go aground silently on blind sands. But he could not speak or do anything because the cords tied shut his jaws, his eyelids.

Lebannen had come down to the cabin to sleep for a while, wanting to be fresh at dawn when they might raise Roke Island. He slept quickly and deeply, and his dreams fleeted and changed: a high green hill above the sea—a woman who smiled and, lifting her hand, showed him she could make the sun rise—a claimant in his court of justice in Havnor from whom he learned to his horror and shame that half the people of the kingdom were starving to death in locked rooms beneath houses—a child who cried out to him, "Come to me!" but he could not find the child— As he slept, his right hand held the rock in the little amulet bag at his throat, clenched it tight.

In the deck cabin above these dreamers, the women dreamed. Seserakh walked up into the mountains, the beautiful dear desert mountains of her home. But she was walking on the forbidden way, the dragon path. Human feet must not walk that path, must not even cross it. The dust of it was smooth and warm under her bare soles, and though she knew she must not walk on it, she walked on, until she looked up and saw that the mountains were not those she knew, but were black, jagged precipices which she could never climb. Yet she must climb them.

Irian flew joyous on the storm wind, but the storm sent loops of lightning up over her wings, drawing her down and down towards the clouds, and as she was pulled nearer and nearer she saw they were not clouds but black rocks, a black and jagged mountain range. Her wings were tied to her sides by cords of lightning, and she fell.

Tehanu crawled through a tunnel deep underground. There was not enough air to breathe and the tunnel grew narrower as she crawled. She could not turn back. But the glimmering roots of trees, growing down through the dirt into the tunnel, gave her handholds sometimes by which she could pull herself on into the dark.

Tenar climbed up the steps of the Throne of the Nameless Ones in the sacred Place of Atuan. She was very small and the steps were very high, so that she could climb them only laboriously. But when she reached the fourth step she did not pause and turn around, as the priestesses had told her she must do. She went on. She climbed the next step, and the next, and the next, in dust so thick it had obliterated the steps and she must feel for the levels where no foot had ever trodden. She went hastily, because behind the empty throne Ged had left something or lost something, something of great importance to myriads of people, and she had to find it. Only she did not know what it was. "A stone, a stone," she told herself. But behind the throne, when she crawled there at last, was only dust, owls' droppings and dust.

In the alcove of the Old Mage's house on the Overfell of Gont, Ged dreamed that he was Archmage. He was talking with his friend Thorion as they walked the corridor of runes towards the meeting room of the Masters of the School. "I had no power at all," he told Thorion earnestly, "for years and years." The Summoner smiled and said, "That was only a dream, you know." But Ged was troubled by the long black wings that trailed behind him through the corridor; he shrugged his shoulders, trying to lift the wings, but they dragged on the floor like empty sacks. "Do you have wings?" he asked Thorion, who said, "Oh, yes," complacently, showing him how his wings were tied tight against his back and legs by many small, thin cords. "I am well yoked," he said.

Among the trees of the Immanent Grove on Roke Island, Azver the Patterner slept as he often did in summer in an open glade near the eastern edge of the wood, where he could look up and see the stars through the leaves. There his sleep was light, transparent, his mind moving from thought to dream and back, guided by the movements of the stars and leaves as they changed places in their dance. But tonight there were no stars, and the leaves hung still. He looked up into the lightless sky and saw through the clouds. In the high black sky were stars: small, bright, and still. They did not move. He knew there would be no sunrise.— He sat up then, awake, gazing into the faint, soft light that always hung in the aisles of the trees. His heart beat slow and hard.

In the Great House the young men, sleeping, turned and cried out, dreaming that they must go fight an army on a plain of dust, but the warriors they must fight were old men, old women, weak, sick people, weeping children.

The Masters of Roke dreamed that a ship was sailing towards them over the sea, heavy laden, low in the water. One dreamed that the freight of the ship was black rocks. Another dreamed she carried burning fire. Another dreamed that her cargo was dreams.

The seven masters who slept in the Great House woke, one and then another, in their stone sleeping cells, made a little werelight, and got up. They found the Doorkeeper already afoot and waiting at the door. "The king will come," he said with a smile, "at daybreak."

"Roke Knoll," Tosla said, gazing forward at the far, faint, unmoving wave in the southwest above the twilit waves. Lebannen, standing beside him, said nothing. The cloud cover had dispersed, and the sky arched its pure uncolored dome over the great circle of the waters.

The ship's master joined them. "A fair dawn," he said, whispering in the silence.

The east brightened slowly to yellow. Lebannen glanced aft. Two of the women were afoot, standing at the rail outside their cabin; tall women, barefoot, silent, gazing east.

The top of the round green hill caught the sunlight first. It was broad daylight when they sailed in between the headlands of Thwil Bay. Everyone aboard was on deck, watching. But still they spoke little and softly.

The wind died down within the harbor. It was so still the water reflected the little town that rose above the bay and the walls of the Great House that rose above the town. The ship glided on slower, still slower.

Lebannen glanced at the ship's master and at Onyx. The master nodded. The wizard moved his hands up and outward slowly in a spell and murmured a word.

The ship glided on softly, not slowing until she came alongside the longest of the docks. Then the master spoke, and the great sail was furled while men aboard tossed the lines to men on the dock, shouting, and the silence was broken.

There were people on the quay to welcome them, townsfolk gathering, and a group of young men from the School, among them a big, deep-chested, dark-skinned man who held a heavy staff that matched his own height. "Welcome to Roke, King of the Western Lands," he said, coming forward as the gangplank was run out and made fast. "And welcome to all your company."

The young men with him and all the townsfolk called out hail and greeting to the king, and Lebannen answered them merrily as he came down the gangplank. He greeted the Master Summoner, and they spoke a while.

Those watching could see that despite his words of welcome, the Master Summoner's frowning gaze went to the ship again and again, to the women who stood at the rail, and that his answers did not satisfy the king.

When Lebannen left him and came back up into the ship, Irian came forward to meet him. "Lord King," she said, "you may tell the masters that I don't want to enter their house—this time. I wouldn't enter it if they asked me."

Lebannen's face was extremely stern. "It is the Master Patterner who asks you to come to him, to the Grove," he said.

At that Irian laughed, radiant. "I knew he would," she said. "And Tehanu will come with me."

"And my mother," Tehanu whispered.

He looked at Tenar; she nodded.

"So be it," he said. "And the rest of us will be lodged in the Great House, unless any of us prefer another place."

"By your leave, my lord," Seppel said, "I too will ask the hospitality of the Master Patterner."

"Seppel, that's not necessary," Onyx said harshly. "Come with me to my house."

The Pelnish wizard made a little placating gesture. "No reflection on your friends, my friend," he said. "But I have longed all my life to walk in the Immanent Grove. And I would be easier there."

"It may be that the doors of the Great House are shut to me, as they were before," Alder said, hesitant; and now Onyx's sallow face was red with shame.

The princess's veiled head had turned from face to face as she eagerly listened, trying to understand what was said. Now she spoke: "Please, my Lord King, I will to be with my friend Tenar? My friend Tehanu? And Irian? And to speak to that Karg?"

Lebannen looked at them all, glanced back to the Master Summoner standing massively at the foot of the gangplank, and laughed. He spoke from the rail, in his clear, affable voice: "My people have been cooped up in ship's cabins, Summoner, and it would seem they long for grass underfoot and leaves above their heads. If we all beg the Patterner to take us in, and he agrees, will you forgive our seeming slight to the hospitality of the Great House for a time at least?"

After a pause the Summoner bowed stiffly.

A short, stocky man had come up beside him on the dock, and was looking up smiling at Lebannen. He lifted his staff of silvery wood.

"Sire," he said, "I took you about the Great House once, a long time ago, and told you lies about everything."

"Gamble!" said Lebannen. They met midway on the gangplank and embraced, and talking, went down onto the dock.

Onyx was the first to follow; he greeted the Summoner gravely and with ceremony, then turned to the man called Gamble. "Are you Windkey now?" he demanded, and when Gamble laughed and said yes, he also embraced him, saying, "A master well made!" Taking Gamble a little aside, he talked with him, eager and frowning.

Lebannen looked up to the ship to signal the others to come ashore, and as they came down one by one he introduced them to the two Masters of Roke, Brand the Summoner and Gamble the Windkey.

On most islands of the Archipelago people did not touch palms in greeting as was the way of Enlad, but only bowed the head or held both palms open before the heart, as if in offering. When Irian and the Summoner met, neither bowed or made any gesture. They stood stiff with their hands at their sides.

The princess made her deep, straight-backed courtesy.

Tenar made the conventional gesture, and the Summoner returned it.

"The Woman of Gont, the daughter of the Archmage, Tehanu," Lebannen said. Tehanu dipped her head and made the conventional gesture. But the Master Summoner stared at her, gasped, and stepped back as if he had been struck.

"Mistress Tehanu," said Gamble quickly, coming forward between her and the Summoner, "we welcome you to Roke—for your father's sake, and your mother's, and your own. I hope your voyage was a pleasant one?"

She looked at him in confusion, and ducked, hiding her face, rather than bowed; but she managed to whisper some kind of answer.

Lebannen, his face a bronze mask of calm composure, said, "Yes, it was a good voyage, Gamble, though the end of it is still in doubt. Shall we walk up through the town, now, Tenar—Tehanu—Princess—Orm Irian?" He looked at each as he spoke, saying the last name with particular clarity.

He set off with Tenar, and the others followed. As Seserakh came down the gangplank, she resolutely swept back the red veils from her face.

Gamble walked with Onyx, Alder with Seppel. Tosla stayed with the ship. The last to leave the quay was Brand the Summoner, walking alone and heavily.

Tenar had asked Ged about the Grove more than once, liking to hear him describe it. "It seems like any grove of trees, when you see it first. Not very large. The fields come right up to it on the north and east, and there are hills to the south and usually to the west . . . It looks like nothing much. But it draws your eye. And sometimes, from up on Roke Knoll, you can see that it's a forest, going on and on. You try to make out where it ends, but you can't. It goes off into the west . . . And when you walk in it, it seems ordinary again, though the trees are mostly a kind that grows only there. Tall, with brown trunks, something like an oak, something like a chestnut."

"What are they called?"

Ged laughed. "*Arhada,* in the Old Speech. Trees . . . The trees of the Grove, in Hardic . . . Their leaves don't all turn in autumn, but some at every season, so the foliage is always green with a gold light in it. Even on a dark day those trees seem to hold some sunlight. And in the night, it's never quite dark under them. There's a kind of glimmer in the leaves, like moonlight or starlight. Willows grow there, and oak, and fir, other kinds; but as you go deeper in, it's more and more only the trees of the Grove. And the roots of those go down deeper than the island. Some are huge trees, some slender, but you don't see many fallen, nor many saplings. They live a long, long time." His voice had grown soft, dreamy. "You can walk and walk in their shadow, in their light, and never come to the end of them."

"But is Roke so large an island?"

He looked at her peacefully, smiling. "The forests here on Gont Mountain are that forest," he said. "All forests are."

And now she saw the Grove. Following Lebannen, they had come up through the devious streets of Thwil Town, gathering a flock of townsfolk and children come out to see and greet their king. These cheerful followers dropped away little by little as the travelers left the town on a lane between hedges and farms, which petered out into a footpath past the high, round hill, Roke Knoll.

Ged had told her of the Knoll, too. There, he said, all magic is strong; there all things take their true nature. "There," he said, "our wizardry and the Old Powers of the Earth meet, and are one."

The wind blew in the high, half-dry grass on the hill. A donkey colt galloped off stiff-legged across a stubble field, flicking and flirting its tail. Cattle walked in slow procession along a fence that crossed a little stream. And there were trees ahead, dark trees, shadowy.

They followed Lebannen through a stile and over a footbridge to a sunlit meadow at the edge of the wood. A small, decrepit house stood near the stream. Irian broke from their group, ran across the grass to the house, and patted the door frame as one would pat and greet a beloved horse or dog after long absence. "Dear house!" she said. And turning to the others, smiling, "I lived here," she said, "when I was Dragonfly."

She looked round, searching the eaves of the wood, and then ran forward again. "Azver!" she called.

A man had come out of the shadow of the trees into the sunlight.

His hair shone in it like silver gilt. He stood still as Irian ran to him. He lifted his hands to her, and she caught them in hers. "I won't burn you, I won't burn you this time," she was saying, laughing and crying, though without tears. "I'm keeping my fires out!"

They drew each other close and stood face to face, and he said to her, "Daughter of Kalessin, welcome home."

"My sister is with me, Azver," she said.

He turned his face—a light-skinned, hard, Kargish face, Tenar saw—and looked straight at Tehanu. He came to her. He dropped on both his knees before her. *"Hama Gondun!"* he said, and again, "Daughter of Kalessin."

Tehanu stood motionless for a moment. Slowly she put out her hand to him—her right hand, the burnt hand, the claw. He took it, bowed his head, and kissed it.

"My honor is that I was your prophet, Woman of Gont," he said, with a kind of exulting tenderness.

Then, rising, he turned at last to Lebannen, made his bow, and said, "My king, be welcome."

"It's a joy to me to see you again, Patterner! But I bring a crowd into your solitude."

"My solitude is crowded already," said the Patterner. "A few live souls might keep the balance."

His eyes, pale grey-blue-green, glanced round among them. He suddenly smiled, a smile of great warmth, surprising on his hard face. "But here are women of my own people," he said in Kargish, and came to Tenar and Seserakh, who stood side by side.

"I am Tenar of Atuan—of Gont," she said. "With me is the High Princess of the Kargad Lands."

He made a proper bow. Seserakh made her stiff courtesy, but her words poured out, tumultuous, in Kargish—"Oh, Lord Priest, I'm glad you're here! If it weren't for my friend Tenar I would have gone mad, thinking nobody was left in the world that could talk like a human being except the idiot women they sent with me from Awabath—but I am learning to speak as they do—and I am learning courage, Tenar is my friend and teacher— But last night I broke taboo! I broke taboo! Oh, Lord Priest, please tell me what I must do to atone! I walked on the Dragons' Way!"

"But you were aboard the ship, princess," said Tenar ("I dreamed," Seserakh said, impatient), "and the Lord Patterner is not a priest but an—a sorcerer—"

"Princess," said Azver the Patterner, "I think we're all walking on the Dragons' Way. And all taboos may well be shaken or broken. Not only in dream. We'll speak of this later, under the trees. Have no fear. But let me greet my friends, if you will?"

Seserakh nodded regally, and he turned away to greet Alder and Onyx.

The princess watched him. "He is a warrior," she said to Tenar in Kargish, with satisfaction. "Not a priest. Priests have no friends."

They all moved on slowly and came under the shadow of the trees.

Tenar looked up into the arcades and ogives of branches, the layers and galleries of leaves. She saw oaks and a big hemmen tree, but most were the trees of the Grove. Their oval leaves moved easily in the air, like the leaves of aspen and poplar; some had yellowed, and there was a dapple of gold and brown on the ground at their roots, but the foliage in the morning light was the green of summer, full of shadows and deep light.

The Patterner led them along a path among the trees. As they went, Tenar thought again about Ged, remembering his voice as he told her about this place. She felt nearer him than she had been since she and Tehanu left him in the dooryard of their house in the early summer and walked down to Gont Port to take the king's ship to Havnor. She knew Ged had lived here with the Patterner of long ago, and had walked here with Azver. She knew the Grove was to him the central and sacred place, the heart of peace. She felt that she might look up and see him at the end of one of the long, sun-dappled glades. And that notion eased her heart.

For her dream of the night before had troubled her, and when Seserakh burst out with her dream of breaking taboo, Tenar had been deeply startled. She too had broken taboo in her dream, transgressed. She had climbed the last three stairs of the Empty Throne, the forbidden steps. The Place of the Tombs on Atuan was long ago and far away, and maybe the earthquake had left no throne or steps there at all in the temple where her name had been taken from her: but the Old Powers of the Earth were there, and they were here. They were not changed or moved. They were the earthquake, and the earth. Their justice was not man's justice. As she had walked by the round hill, Roke Knoll, she knew she walked where all the powers met.

She had defied them, long ago, breaking free of the Tombs, stealing the treasure, fleeing here to the West. But they were here. Under her feet. In the roots of these trees, in the roots of the hill.

So, here in the center where earth's powers met, the human powers had also met together: a king, a princess, the masters of wizardry. And the dragons.

And a priestess-thief turned farmwife, and a village sorcerer with a broken heart . . .

She looked round at Alder. He was walking beside Tehanu. They were talking quietly. Tehanu talked more readily with him than with anyone, even Irian, and looked at ease when she was with him. It cheered Tenar to see them, and she walked on under the great trees, letting her awareness slip into a half trance of green light and moving leaves. She was sorry when, after only a short way, the Patterner halted. She felt she could walk forever in the Grove.

They gathered in a grassy glade, open to the sky in the center where the branches did not reach to meet. A tributary of the Thwilburn ran across one side of it, willow and alder growing along its course. Not far from the stream was a low, lumpy house built of stone and sod, with a taller lean-to against its wall made of withies and mats of woven reed. "My winter palace, my summer palace," Azver said.

Both Onyx and Lebannen stared at these small structures in surprise, and Irian said, "I never knew you had a house at all!"

"I didn't," said the Patterner. "But bones get old."

With a little fetching and carrying from the ship, the house was soon furnished with bedding for the women, and the lean-to for the men. Boys ran back and forth to the eaves of the Grove with plentiful provisions from the kitchens of the Great House. And late in the afternoon, the Masters of Roke came at the invitation of the Patterner to meet with the king's party.

"Is this where they gather to choose the new Archmage?" Tenar asked Onyx, for Ged had told her of that secret glade.

Onyx shook his head. "I think not," he said. "The king would know, for he was there when they last met. But maybe only the Patterner could tell you. Because things change in this wood, you know. 'It is not always where it is.' Nor are the ways through it ever quite the same, I think."

"It should be frightening," she said, "but I can't seem to be afraid."

Onyx smiled. "So it is, here," he said.

She watched the masters come into the glade, led by the big, bear-like Summoner and Gamble the young weathermaster. Onyx told her who the others were: the Changer, the Chanter, the Herbal, the Hand: all grey-haired, the Changer frail with age, using his wizard's staff as a walking stick. The Doorkeeper, smooth-faced and almond-eyed, seemed neither young nor old. The Namer, who came last, looked forty or so. His face was calm and closed. He presented himself to the king, naming himself Kurremkarmerruk.

At that Irian burst out, indignant, "But you are not!"

He looked at her and said evenly, "It is the Namer's name."

"Then my Kurremkarmerruk is dead?"

He nodded.

"Oh," she cried, "that's hard news to bear! He was my friend, when I had few friends here!" She turned away and would not look at the Namer, angry and tearless in her grief. She had greeted the Master Herbal with affection, and the Doorkeeper, but she did not speak to the others.

Tenar saw that they watched Irian under their grey brows with uneasy looks.

From her they looked at Tehanu; and looked away again; and glanced back, sidelong. And Tenar began to wonder what they saw when they looked at Tehanu and Irian. For these were men who saw with wizard's eyes.

So she bade herself forgive the Summoner for his uncouth and unconcealed horror when he first saw Tehanu. Maybe it had not been horror. Maybe it had been awe.

When they were all made known to one another and were seated in a circle, with cushions and stump seats for those who needed them, the grass for carpet, and sky and leaves for ceiling, the Patterner said in his voice that still had some Kargish accent in it, "If it please him, my fellow masters, we will hear the king."

Lebannen stood up. As he spoke, Tenar watched him with irrepressible pride. He was so beautiful, so wise in his youth! She did not follow all his words at first, only the sense and passion of them.

He told the masters, briefly and clearly, all the matter that had brought him to Roke: the dragons and the dreams.

He ended, "It seemed to us that night by night all these things draw together, always more certainly, to some event, some end. It seemed to us that here, on this ground, with your knowledge and power aiding us, we might foresee and meet that event, not letting it overwhelm our understanding. The wisest of our mages have foretold: a great change is upon us. We must join together to learn what that change is, its causes, its course, and how we may hope to turn it from conflict and ruin to harmony and peace, in whose sign I rule."

Brand the Summoner stood to answer him. After some stately politenesses, with a special welcome to the High Princess, he said, "That the dreams of men, and more than their dreams, forewarn us of dire changes, all the masters and wizards of Roke agree. That there is a disturbance of the deepset boundaries between death and life—transgressions of those boundaries, and the threat of worse—we confirm.

But that these disturbances can be understood or controlled by any but the masters of the art magic, we doubt. And very deeply do we doubt that dragons, whose lives and death are wholly different from that of man, can ever be trusted to submit their wild wrath and jealousy to serve human good."

"Summoner," Lebannen said, before Irian could speak, "Orm Embar died for me on Selidor. Kalessin bore me to my throne.— Here in this circle are three peoples: the Kargish, the Hardic, and the People of the West."

"They were all one people, once," said the Namer in his level, toneless voice.

"But they are not now," said the Summoner, each word heavy and separate. "Do not misunderstand me because I speak hard truth, my Lord King! I honor the truce you have sworn with the dragons. When the danger we are in is past, Roke will aid Havnor in seeking lasting peace with them. But the dragons have nothing to do with this crisis that is upon us. Nor have the eastern peoples, who foreswore their immortal souls when they forgot the Language of the Making."

"Es eyemra," said a soft, hissing voice: Tehanu, standing.

The Summoner stared at her.

"Our language," she repeated in Hardic, staring back at him.

Irian laughed. *"Es eyemra,"* she said.

"You are not immortal," Tenar said to the Summoner. She had had no intention of speaking. She did not stand up. The words broke from her like fire from struck rock. "*We* are! We die to rejoin the undying world. It was you who foreswore immortality."

Then they were all still. The Patterner had made a small movement of his hands, a gentle movement.

His face was preoccupied, untroubled, as he studied a design of a few twigs and leaves he had made on the grass where he sat, just in front of his crossed legs. He looked up, looked round at them all. "I think we will have to go there soon," he said.

After another silence, Lebannen asked, "Go where, my lord?"

"Into the dark," said the Patterner.

As Alder sat listening to them speak, slowly the voices grew faint, fading, and the warm late sunlight of late summer dimmed into darkness. Nothing was left but the trees: tall blind presences between the blind earth and the sky. The oldest living children of the earth. *O Segoy,* he said in his heart: *made and maker, let me come to you.*

The darkness went on and on, past the trees, past everything.

Against that emptiness he saw the hill, the high hill that had been on their right as they walked up out of the town. He saw the dust of the road, the stones of the path, that led past that hill.

He turned now aside from the path, leaving the others, and walked up the slope.

The grasses were tall. The spent flower cases of sparkweed nodded among them. He came on a narrow path and followed it up the steep hillside. Now I am myself, he said in his heart. Segoy, the world is beautiful. Let me come through it to you.

I can do again what I was meant to do, he thought as he walked. I can mend what was broken. I can rejoin.

He reached the top of the hill. Standing there in the sun and wind among the nodding grasses he saw on his right the fields, the roofs of the little town and the big house, the bright bay and the sea beyond it. If he turned he would see behind him in the west the trees of the endless forest, fading on and on into blue distances. Before him the hill slope was dim and grey, going down to the wall of stones and the darkness beyond the wall, and the crowding, calling shadows at the wall. *I will come,* he said to them. *I will come!*

Warmth fell across his shoulders and his hands. Wind stirred in the leaves above his head. Voices spoke, speaking, not calling, not crying out his name. The Patterner's eyes were watching him across the circle of grass. The Summoner too was watching him. He looked down, bewildered. He tried to listen. He gathered his mind and listened.

The king was speaking, using all his skill and strength to hold these fierce, willful men and women to one purpose. "Let me try to tell you, Masters of Roke, what I learned from the High Princess as we sailed here. Princess, may I speak for you?"

Unveiled, she gazed across the circle at him, and bowed grave permission.

"This is her tale, then: long ago, the human and the dragon peoples were one kind, speaking one language. But they sought different things, and so they agreed to part—to go different ways. That agreement was called the Vedurnan."

Onyx's head went up, and Seppel's bright dark eyes widened. "*Verw nadan,*" he whispered.

"The human beings went east, the dragons west. The humans gave up their knowledge of the Language of the Making, and in exchange received all skill and craft of hand, and ownership of all that hands can make. The dragons let go all such things. But they kept the Old Speech."

"And their wings," said Irian.

"And their wings," Lebannen said. He had caught Azver's eye. "Patterner, perhaps you can continue the story better than I?"

"The villagers of Gont and Hur-at-Hur remember what the wise men of Roke and the priests of Karego forget," Azver said. "Yes, as a child I was told this tale, I think, or something like it. But the dragons had been forgotten in it. It told how the Dark Folk of the Archipelago broke their oath. We had all promised to forgo sorcery and the language of sorcery, speaking only our common tongue. We would name no names, and make no spells. We would trust to Segoy, to the powers of the Earth our mother, mother of the Warrior Gods. But the Dark Folk broke the covenant. They caught the Language of the Making in their craft, writing it in runes. They kept it, taught it, used it. They made spells with it, with the skill of their hands, with false tongues speaking the true words. So the Kargish people can never trust them. So says the tale."

Irian spoke: "Men fear death as dragons do not. Men want to own life, possess it, as if it were a jewel in a box. Those ancient mages craved everlasting life. They learned to use true names to keep men from dying. But those who cannot die can never be reborn."

"The name and the dragon are one," said Kurremkarmerruk the Namer. "We men lost our names at the *verw nadan,* but we learned how to regain them. Name is self. Why should death change that?"

He looked at the Summoner; but Brand sat heavy and grim, listening, not speaking.

"Say more of this, Namer, if you will," the king said.

"I say what I have half learned, half guessed, not from village tales but from the most ancient records in the Isolate Tower. A thousand years before the first kings of Enlad, there were men in Éa and Soléa, the first and greatest of the mages, the Rune Makers. It was they who learned to write the Language of the Making. They made the runes, which the dragons never learned. They taught us to give each soul its true name: which is its truth, its self. And with their power they granted to those who bear their true name life beyond the body's death."

"Life immortal," Seppel's soft voice took the word. He spoke smiling a little. "In a great land of rivers and mountains and beautiful cities, where there is no suffering or pain, and where the self endures, unchanged, unchanging, forever . . . That is the dream of the ancient Lore of Paln."

"Where," the Summoner said, "where is that land?"

"On the other wind," said Irian. "The west beyond the west." She looked round at them all, scornful, irate. "Do you think we dragons fly only on the winds of this world? Do you think our freedom, for which we gave up all possessions, is no greater than that of the mindless seagulls? That our realm is a few rocks at the edge of your rich islands? You own the earth, you own the sea. But we are the fire of sunlight, we fly the wind! You wanted land to own. You wanted things to make and keep. And you have that. That was the division, the *verw nadan.* But you were not content with your share. You wanted not only your cares, but our freedom. You wanted the wind! And by the spells and wizardries of those oath-breakers, you stole half our realm from us, walled it away from life and light, so that you could live there forever. Thieves, traitors!"

"Sister," Tehanu said. "These are not the men who stole from us. They are those who pay the price."

A silence followed her harsh, whispering voice.

"What was the price?" said the Namer.

Tehanu looked at Irian. Irian hesitated, and then said in a much subdued voice, "*Greed puts out the sun.* These are Kalessin's words."

Azver the Patterner spoke. As he spoke, he looked into the aisles of the trees across the clearing, as if following the slight movements of the leaves. "The ancients saw that the dragons' realm was not of the body only. That they could fly . . . outside of time, it may be . . . And envying that freedom, they followed the dragons' way into the west beyond the west. There they claimed part of that realm as their own. A timeless realm, where the self might be forever. But not in the body, as the dragons were. Only in spirit could men be there . . . So they made a wall which no living body could cross, neither man nor dragon. For they feared the anger of the dragons. And their arts of naming laid a great net of spells upon all the western lands, so that when the people of the islands die, they would come to the west beyond the west and live there in the spirit forever.

"But as the wall was built and the spell laid, the wind ceased to blow, within the wall. The sea withdrew. The springs ceased to run. The mountains of sunrise became the mountains of the night. Those that died came to a dark land, a dry land."

"I have walked in that land," Lebannen said, low and unwillingly. "I do not fear death, but I fear it."

There was a silence among them.

"Cob, and Thorion," the Summoner said in his rough, reluctant voice, "they tried to break down that wall. To bring the dead back into life."

"Not into life, master," Seppel said. "Still, like the Rune Makers, they sought the bodiless, immortal self."

"Yet their spells disturbed that place," the Summoner said, brooding. "So the dragons began to remember the ancient wrong . . . And so the souls of the dead come reaching now across the wall, yearning back to life."

Alder stood up. He said, "It is not life they yearn for. It is death. To be one with the earth again. To rejoin it."

They all looked at him, but he hardly knew it; his awareness was half with them, half in the dry land. The grass beneath his feet was green and sunlit, was dead and dim. The leaves of the trees trembled above him and the low stone wall lay only a little distance from him, down the dark hill. Of them all he saw only Tehanu; he could not see her clearly, but he knew her, standing between him and the wall. He spoke to her. "They built it, but they cannot unbuild it," he said. "Will you help me, Tehanu?"

"I will, Hara," she said.

A shadow rushed between them, a great dark bulky strength, hiding her, seizing him, holding him; he struggled, gasped for breath, could not draw breath, saw red fire in the darkness, and saw nothing more.

They met in the starlight at the edge of the glade, the king of the western lands and the Master of Roke, the two powers of Earthsea.

"Will he live?" the Summoner asked, and Lebannen answered, "The healer says he is in no danger now."

"I did wrong," said the Summoner. "I am sorry for it."

"Why did you summon him back?" the king asked, not reproving but wanting an answer.

After a long time the Summoner said, grimly, "Because I had the power to do it."

They paced along in silence down an open path among the great trees. It was very dark to either hand, but the starlight shone grey where they walked.

"I was wrong. But it is not right to want to die," the Summoner said. The burr of the East Reach was in his voice. He spoke low, almost pleadingly. "For the very old, the very ill, it may be. But life is given us. Surely it's wrong not to hold and treasure that great gift!"

"Death also is given us," said the king.

Alder lay on a pallet on the grass. He should lie out under the stars, the Patterner had said, and the old Master Herbal had agreed to that. He lay asleep, and Tehanu sat still beside him.

Tenar sat in the doorway of the low stone house and watched her.

The great stars of late summer shone above the clearing: highest of them the star called Tehanu, the Swan's Heart, the linchpin of the sky.

Seserakh came quietly out of the house and sat down on the threshold beside her. She had taken off the circlet that held her veil, leaving her mass of tawny hair unbound.

"Oh my friend," she murmured, "what will happen to us? The dead are coming here. Do you feel them? Like the tide rising. Across that wall. I think nobody can stop them. All the dead people, from the graves of all the islands of the west, all the centuries . . ."

Tenar felt the beating, the calling, in her head and in her blood. She knew now, they all knew, what Alder had known. But she held to what she trusted, even if trust had become mere hope. She said, "They are only the dead, Seserakh. We built a false wall. It must be unbuilt. But there is a true one."

Tehanu got up and came softly over to them. She sat on the doorstep below them.

"He's all right, he's sleeping," she whispered.

"Were you there with him?" Tenar asked.

Tehanu nodded. "We were at the wall."

"What did the Summoner do?"

"Summoned him—brought him back by force."

"Into life."

"Into life."

"I don't know which I should fear more," Tenar said, "death or life. I wish I could be done with fear."

Seserakh's face, the wave of her warm hair, bent down to Tenar's shoulder for a moment in a light caress. "You are brave, brave," she murmured. "But oh! I fear the sea! and I fear death!"

Tehanu sat quietly. In the faint soft light that hung among the trees, Tenar could see how her daughter's slender hand lay crossed over her burnt and twisted hand.

"I think," Tehanu said in her soft, strange voice, "that when I die, I can breathe back the breath that made me live. I can give back to the world all that I didn't do. All that I might have been and couldn't be. All the choices I didn't make. All the things I lost and spent and wasted. I can give them back to the world. To the lives that haven't been lived yet. That will be my gift back to the world that gave me the life I did live, the love I loved, the breath I breathed."

She looked up at the stars and sighed. "Not for a long time yet," she whispered. Then she looked round at Tenar.

Seserakh stroked Tenar's hair gently, rose, and went silently into the house.

"Before long, I think, mother . . ."

"I know."

"I don't want to leave you."

"You have to leave me."

"I know."

They sat on in the glimmering darkness of the Grove, silent.

"Look," Tehanu murmured. A shooting star crossed the sky, a quick, slow-fading trail of light.

Five wizards sat in starlight. "Look," one said, his hand following the trail of the shooting star.

"The soul of a dragon dying," said Azver the Patterner. "So they say in Karego-At."

"Do dragons die?" asked Onyx, musing. "Not as we do, I think."

"They don't live as we do. They move between the worlds. So says Orm Irian. From the world's wind to the other wind."

"As we sought to do," said Seppel. "And failed."

Gamble looked at him curiously. "Have you on Paln always known this tale, this lore we have learned today—of the parting of dragon and mankind, and the making of the dry land?"

"Not as we heard it today. I was taught that the *verw nadan* was the first great triumph of the art magic. And that the goal of wizardry was to triumph over time and live forever . . . Hence the evils the Pelnish Lore has done."

"At least you kept the Mother knowledge we despised," Onyx said. "As your people did, Azver."

"Well, you had the sense to build your Great House here," the Patterner said, smiling.

"But we built it wrong," Onyx said. "All we build, we build wrong."

"So we must knock it down," said Seppel.

"No," said Gamble. "We're not dragons. We do live in houses. We have to have some walls, at least."

"So long as the wind can blow through the windows," said Azver.

"And who will come in the doors?" asked the Doorkeeper in his mild voice.

There was a pause. A cricket trilled industriously somewhere across the glade, fell silent, trilled again.

"Dragons?" said Azver.

The Doorkeeper shook his head. "I think maybe the division that was begun, and then betrayed, will be completed at last," he said. "The dragons will go free, and leave us here to the choice we made."

"The knowledge of good and evil," said Onyx.

"The joy of making, shaping," said Seppel. "Our mastery."

"And our greed, our weakness, our fear," said Azver.

The cricket was answered by another, closer to the stream. The two trills pulsed, crossed, in and out of rhythm.

"What I fear," said Gamble, "so much that I fear to say it—is this: that when the dragons go, our mastery will go with them. Our art. Our magic."

The silence of the others showed that they feared what he did. But the Doorkeeper spoke at last, gently, but with some certainty. "No, I think not. They are the Making, yes. But we learned the Making. We made it ours. It can't be taken from us. To lose it we must forget it, throw it away."

"As my people did," said Azver.

"Yet your people remembered what the earth is, what life everlasting is," said Seppel. "While we forgot."

There was another long silence among them.

"I could reach my hand out to the wall," Gamble said in a very low voice, and Seppel said, "They are near, they are very near."

"How are we to know what we should do?" Onyx said.

Azver spoke into the silence that followed the question. "Once when my lord the Archmage was here with me in the Grove, he said to me he had spent his life learning how to choose to do what he had no choice but to do."

"I wish he were here now," said Onyx.

"He's done with doing," the Doorkeeper murmured, smiling.

"But we're not. We sit here talking on the edge of the precipice—we all know it." Onyx looked round at their starlit faces. "What do the dead want of us?"

"What do the dragons want of us?" said Gamble. "These women who are dragons, dragons who are women—why are they here? Can we trust them?"

"Have we a choice?" said the Doorkeeper.

"I think not," said the Patterner. An edge of hardness, a sword's edge, had come into his voice. "We can only follow."

"Follow the dragons?" Gamble asked.

Azver shook his head. "Alder."

"But he's no guide, Patterner!" said Gamble. "A village mender?"

Onyx said, "Alder has wisdom, but in his hands, not in his head. He follows his heart. Certainly he doesn't seek to lead us."

"Yet he was chosen from among us all."

"Who chose him?" Seppel asked softly.

The Patterner answered him: "The dead."

They sat silent. The crickets' trill had ceased. Two tall figures came towards them through the grass lit grey by starlight. "May Brand and I sit with you a while?" Lebannen said. "There is no sleep tonight."

On the doorstep of the house on the Overfell, Ged sat watching the stars above the sea. He had gone in to sleep an hour or more ago, but as he closed his eyes he saw the hillside and heard the voices rising like a wave. He got up at once and went outside, where he could see the stars move.

He was tired. His eyes would close, and then he would be there by the wall of stones, his heart cold with dread that he would be there forever, not knowing the way back. At last, impatient and sick of fear, he got up again, fetched a lantern from the house and lit it, and set off on the path to Moss's house. Moss might or might not be frightened; she lived pretty near the wall, these days. But Heather would be in a panic, and Moss would not be able to soothe her. And since whatever had to be done, it wasn't he who could do it this time, he could at least go comfort the poor half-wit. He could tell her it was only dreams.

It was hard going in the dark, the lantern throwing great shadows of small things across the path. He walked slower than he would have liked to walk, and stumbled sometimes.

He saw a light in the widower's house, late as it was. A child wailed, over in the village. *Mother, mother, why are the people crying? Who are the people crying, mother?* There was no sleep there, either. There was not much sleep anywhere in Earthsea, tonight, Ged thought. He grinned a little as he thought it; for he had always liked that pause, that fearful pause, the moment before things changed.

Alder woke. He lay on earth and felt its depth beneath him. Above him the bright stars burned, the stars of summer, moving between leaf and leaf with the wind's blowing, moving from east to west with the world's turning. He watched them a while before he let them go.

Tehanu was waiting for him on the hill.

"What must we do, Hara?" she asked him.

"We have to mend the world," he said. He smiled, because his heart had grown light at last. "We have to break the wall."

"Can they help us?" she asked, for the dead were gathered waiting down in the darkness as countless as grass or sand or stars, silent now, a great, dim beach of souls.

"No," he said, "but maybe others can." He walked down the hill to the wall. It was little more than waist-high here. He put his hands on one of the stones of the coping row and tried to move it. It was fixed fast, or was heavier than a stone should be; he could not lift it, could not make it move at all.

Tehanu came beside him. "Help me," he said. She put her hands on the stone, the human hand and the burnt claw, gripping it as well as she could, and gave a lifting tug as he did. The stone moved a little, then a little more. "Push it!" she said, and together they pushed it slowly out of place, grating hard on the rock beneath it, till it fell on the far side of the wall with a dull heavy thump.

The next stone was smaller; together they could lift it up out of its place. They let it drop into the dust on the near side.

A tremor ran through the ground under their feet then. Small chinking stones in the wall rattled. And with a long sigh, the multitudes of the dead came closer to the wall.

The Patterner stood up suddenly and stood listening. Leaves stormed all about the glade, the trees of the Grove bowed and trembled as if under a great wind, but there was no wind.

"Now it changes," he said, and he walked away from them, into the darkness under the trees.

The Summoner, the Doorkeeper, and Seppel rose and followed him, quick and silent. Gamble and Onyx followed more slowly after them.

Lebannen stood up; he took a few steps after the others, hesitated, and hurried across the glade to the low house of stone and sod. "Irian," he said, stooping to the dark doorway. "Irian, will you take me with you?"

She came out of the house; she was smiling, and there was a kind of fiery brightness all about her. "Come then, come quick," she said, and took his hand. Her hand burned like a coal of fire as she lifted him into the other wind.

After a little time Seserakh came out of the house into the starlight, and after her came Tenar. They stood and looked about them. Nothing moved; the trees were still again.

"They are all gone," Seserakh whispered. "On the Dragons' Way." She took a step forward, gazing into the dark.

"What are we to do, Tenar?"

"We are to keep the house," Tenar said.

"Oh!" Seserakh whispered, dropping to her knees. She had seen Lebannen lying near the doorway, stretched facedown in the grass.

"He isn't dead—I think— Oh, my dear Lord King, don't go, don't die!"

"He's with them. Stay with him. Keep him warm. Keep the house, Seserakh," Tenar said. She went to where Alder lay, his unseeing eyes turned to the stars. She sat down by him, her hand on his. She waited.

Alder could scarcely move the great stone his hands were on, but the Summoner was beside him, stooping with his shoulder against it, and said, "Now!" Together they pushed it till it overbalanced and dropped down with that same heavy, final thump on the far side of the wall.

Others were there now with him and Tehanu, wrenching at the stones, casting them down beside the wall. Alder saw his own hands cast shadows for an instant from a red gleam. Orm Irian, as he had seen her first, a great dragon shape, had let out her fiery breath as she struggled to move a boulder from the lowest rank of stones, deepset in the earth. Her talons struck sparks and her thorned back arched, and the rock rolled ponderously free, breaching the wall entirely in that place.

There was a vast, soft cry among the shadows on the other side, like the sound of the sea on a hollow shore. Their darkness surged up against the wall. But Alder looked up and saw that it was no longer dark. Light moved in that sky where the stars had never moved, quick sparks of fire far in the dark west.

"Kalessin!"

That was Tehanu's voice. He looked at her. She was gazing upward, westward. She had no eye for earth.

She reached up her arms. Fire ran along her hands, her arms, into her hair, into her face and body, flamed up into great wings above her head, and lifted her into the air, a creature all fire, blazing, beautiful.

She cried out aloud, a clear, wordless cry. She flew high, headlong, fast, up into the sky where the light was growing and a white wind had erased the unmeaning stars.

From among the hosts of the dead a few here and there, like her, rose up flickering into dragons, and mounted on the wind.

Most came forward afoot. They were not pressing, not crying out now, but walking with unhurried certainty towards the fallen places in the wall: great multitudes of men and women, who as they came to the broken wall did not hesitate but stepped across it and were gone: a wisp of dust, a breath that shone an instant in the ever-brightening light.

Alder watched them. He still held in his hands, forgotten, a chinking stone he had wrenched from the wall to loosen a larger rock. He watched the dead go free. At last he saw her among them. He tossed the stone aside then and stepped forward. "Lily," he said. She saw him and smiled and held out her hand to him. He took her hand, and they crossed together into the sunlight.

Lebannen stood by the ruined wall and watched the dawn brighten in the east. There was an east now, where there had been no direction, no way to go. There was east and west, and light and motion. The very ground moved, shook, shivering like a great animal, so that the wall of stones beyond where they had broken it shuddered and slid into rubble. Fire broke from the far, black peaks of the mountains called Pain, the fire that burns in the heart of the world, the fire that feeds dragons.

He looked into the sky over those mountains and saw, as he and Ged had seen them once above the western sea, the dragons flying on the wind of morning.

Three came wheeling towards him where he stood among the others near the crest of the hill, above the ruined wall. Two he knew, Orm Irian and Kalessin. The third had bright mail, gold, with wings of gold. That one flew highest and did not stoop down to them. Orm Irian played about her in the air and they flew together, one chasing the other higher and higher, till all at once the highest rays of the rising sun struck Tehanu and she burned like her name, a great bright star.

Kalessin circled again, flew low, and alighted hugely amid the ruins of the wall.

"Agni Lebannen," said the dragon to the king.

"Eldest," the king said to the dragon.

"Aissadan verw nadannan," said the vast, hissing voice, like a sea of cymbals.

Beside Lebannen, Brand the Summoner of Roke stood planted solidly. He repeated the dragon's words in the Speech of the Making, and then said them in Hardic: "What was divided is divided."

The Patterner stood near them, his hair bright in the brightening light. He said, "What was built is broken. What was broken is made whole."

Then he looked up yearning into the sky, at the gold dragon and the red-bronze one; but they had flown almost out of sight, wheeling now in vast gyres over the long, falling land, where empty shadow cities faded to nothing in the light of day.

"Eldest," he said, and the long head swung slowly back to him.

"Will she follow the way back through the forest, sometimes?" Azver asked in the speech of dragons.

Kalessin's long, fathomless, yellow eye regarded him. The enormous mouth seemed, like the mouths of lizards, closed upon a smile. It did not speak.

Then ponderously dragging its length along the wall so that stones still standing slid and fell grating beneath its iron belly, Kalessin writhed away from them, and with a rush and rattle of upraised wings pushed off from the hillside and flew low over the land towards the mountains, whose peaks now were bright with smoke and white steam, fire and sunlight.

"Come, friends," said Seppel in his soft voice. "It's not yet our time to go free."

Sunlight was in the sky above the crowns of the highest trees, but the glade still held the chill grey of dawn. Tenar sat with her hand on Alder's hand, her face bowed down. She looked at the cold dew beading a grass blade, how it hung in tiny, delicate drops along the blade, each drop reflecting all the world.

Someone spoke her name. She did not look up.

"He's gone," she said.

The Patterner knelt by her. He touched Alder's face with a gentle hand.

He knelt there silent a while. Then he said to Tenar in her language, "My lady, I saw Tehanu. She flies golden on the other wind."

Tenar glanced up at him. His face was white and worn, but there was a shadow of glory in his eyes.

She struggled and then said, speaking roughly and almost inaudibly, "Whole?"

He nodded.

She stroked Alder's hand, the mender's hand, fine, skillful. Tears came into her eyes.

"Let me be with him a while," she said, and she began to cry. She put her hands to her face and cried hard, bitterly, silently.

Azver went to the little group by the door of the house. Onyx and Gamble were near the Summoner, who stood, heavy and anxious, near the princess. She crouched beside Lebannen, her arms across him, protecting him, daring any wizard to touch him. Her eyes flashed. She held Lebannen's short steel dagger naked in her hand.

"I came back with him," Brand said to Azver. "I tried to stay with him. I wasn't sure of the way. She won't let me near him."

"Ganaí," Azver said, her title in Kargish, princess.

Her eyes flashed up to him. "Oh may Atwah-Wuluah be thanked and the Mother praised for ever!" she cried. "Lord Azver! Make these accursed-sorcerers go away. Kill them! They have killed my king." She held out the dagger to him by its slender steel blade.

"No, princess. He went with the dragon Irian. But this sorcerer brought him back to us. Let me see him," and he knelt and turned Lebannen's face a little to see it better, and laid his hands on his chest. "He's cold," he said. "It was a hard way back. Take him in your arms, princess. Keep him warm."

"I have tried to," she said, biting her lip. She flung down the dagger and bent to the unconscious man. "O poor king!" she said softly in Hardic, "dear king, poor king!"

Azver got up and said to the Summoner, "I think he will be all right, Brand. She is much more use than we are, now."

The Summoner put out his big hand and took hold of Azver's arm. "Steady now," he said.

"The Doorkeeper," Azver said, going whiter than before and looking around the glade.

"He came back with the Pelnishman," Brand said. "Sit down, Azver."

Azver obeyed him, sitting down on the log seat the old Changer had sat on in their circle the afternoon before. A thousand years ago it seemed. The old men had gone back to the School in the evening . . . And then the long night had begun, the night that brought the wall of stones so close that to sleep was to be there, and to be there was terror, so no one had slept. No one, maybe, in all Roke, in all the isles . . . Only Alder, who went to guide them . . . Azver found he was dozing and shivering.

Gamble tried to make him go inside the winter house, but Azver insisted that he should be near the princess to interpret for her. And near Tenar, he thought without saying it, to protect her. To let her grieve. But Alder was done with grieving. He had passed his grief to her. To them all. His joy . . .

The Herbal came from the School and fussed about Azver, put a winter cloak over his shoulders. He sat on in a weary, feverish half doze, not heeding the others, dimly irritated by the presence of so many people in his sweet silent glade, watching the sunlight creep down among the leaves. His vigil was rewarded when the princess came to him, knelt before him looking with solicitous respect into his face, and said, "Lord Azver, the king would speak with you."

She helped him stand up, as if he were an old man. He did not mind. "Thank you, *gaínha,*" he said.

"I am not queen," she said with a laugh.

"You will be," said the Patterner.

It was the strong tide of the full moon, and *Dolphin* had to wait for the slack to run between the Armed Cliffs. Tenar did not disembark in Gont Port till midmorning, and then there was the long walk uphill. It was near sunset when she came through Re Albi and took the cliff path to the house.

Ged was watering the cabbages, well grown by now.

He straightened up and looked at her coming to him, that hawk look, frowning. "Ah," he said.

"Oh my dear," she said. She hurried, the last few steps, as he came to her.

She was tired. She was very glad to sit with him with a glass of Spark's good red wine and watch the evening of early autumn flare into gold over all the western sea.

"How can I tell you everything?" she said.

"Tell it backward," he said.

"All right. I will. They wanted me to stay, but I said I wanted to go home. But there was a council meeting, the King's Council, you know, for the betrothal. There'll be a grand wedding and all, of course, but I don't think I have to go. Because that was truly when they married. With Elfarran's Ring. Our ring."

He looked at her and smiled, the broad, sweet smile that she thought, perhaps wrongly, perhaps rightly, nobody but her had ever seen on his face.

"Yes?" he said.

"Lebannen came and stood here, see, on my left, and then Seserakh came and stood here on my right. In front of Morred's throne. And I held up the Ring. The way I did when we brought it to Havnor, remember? in *Lookfar,* in the sunlight? Lebannen took it in his hands and kissed it and gave it back to me. And I put it on her arm, it just went over her hand—she's not a little woman, Seserakh— Oh, you should see her, Ged! What a beauty she is, what a lion! He's met his match. —And everybody shouted. And there were festivals and so on. And so I could get away."

"Go on."

"Backward?"

"Backward."

"Well. Before that was Roke."

"Roke's never simple."

"No."

They drank their red wine in silence.

"Tell me of the Patterner."

She smiled. "Seserakh calls him the Warrior. She says only a warrior would fall in love with a dragon."

"Who followed him to the dry land—that night?"

"He followed Alder."

"Ah," Ged said, with surprise and a certain satisfaction.

"So did others of the masters. And Lebannen, and Irian . . ."

"And Tehanu."

A silence.

"She went out of the house. When I came out she was gone." A long silence. "Azver saw her. In the sunrise. On the other wind."

A silence.

"They're all gone. There are no dragons left in Havnor or the western islands. Onyx said: as that shadow place and all the shadows in it rejoined the world of light, so they regained their true realm."

"We broke the world to make it whole," Ged said.

After a long time Tenar said in a soft, thin voice, "The Patterner believes Irian will come to the Grove if he calls to her."

Ged said nothing, till, after a while: "Look there, Tenar."

She looked where he was looking, into the dim gulf of air above the western sea.

"If she comes, she'll come from there," he said. "And if she doesn't come, she is there."

She nodded. "I know." Her eyes were full of tears. "Lebannen sang me a song, on the ship, when we were going back to Havnor." She could not sing; she whispered the words. *"O my joy, be free . . ."*

He looked away, up at the forests, at the mountain, the darkening heights.

"Tell me," she said, "tell me what you did while I was gone."

"Kept the house."

"Did you walk in the forest?"

"Not yet," he said.

EARTHSEA
Miles
25 50 100 200 300
Hogen Land
Borth
Rogmy
Osskil
Sorresk
Gut of Osskil
Norst
The Gravels
Toop
The Enlades
Ebosskil
Taon
Semel
Mt. Andanden
Bishi
Ebishi
Besu
Paln
Gmet
Losso
The Pelnish Sea
Eppaln
faliern
South Port
Hille
Derhemen
Narveduen
Onon
Selidor
Gate of Selidor
The Dragons' Run
Ully
Risk
Usidero
Ettil
Ingat
The Toringates
Ontuego
Seppish
Toming
Low Toming
Hosk
Pendor
The Inmost Sea
The Ninety Isles
Nesh
Dromgan
Roke
Thwil Town
Geath
Serd
Pody
Ensmer
The West Reach
Kaltuel
Arrins
Near Kaltuel
Simly
Faltuel
Wathort
Obb
Jessage
The Sand Isles
Lorbanery
Rood
Obehol
The South Reach
Toom
The Long Dune
Wellogy
Far Sorr